MEAN AND EVIL

MEAN AND EVIL

A BRANNIGAN'S LAND WESTERN

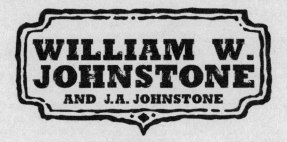

WILLIAM W. JOHNSTONE

AND J.A. JOHNSTONE

PINNACLE BOOKS
Kensington Publishing Corp.
www.kensingtonbooks.com

PINNACLE BOOKS are published by

Kensington Publishing Corp.
19 West 40th Street
New York, NY 10018

Copyright © 2022 by J.A. Johnstone

PUBLISHER'S NOTE
Following the death of William W. Johnstone, the Johnstone family is working with a carefully selected writer to organize and complete Mr. Johnstone's outlines and many unfinished manuscripts to create additional novels in all of his series like the Last Gunfighter, Mountain Man, and Eagles, among others. This novel was inspired by Mr. Johnstone's superb storytelling.

All Kensington titles, imprints, and distributed lines are available at special quantity discounts for bulk purchases for sales promotion, premiums, fund-raising, and educational or institutional use.

Special book excerpts or customized printings can also be created to fit specific needs. For details, write or phone the office of the Kensington Sales Manager: Kensington Publishing Corp., 119 West 40th Street, New York, NY 10018. Attn. Sales Department. Phone: 1-800-221-2647.

PINNACLE BOOKS, the Pinnacle logo, and the WWJ steer head logo Reg. U.S. Pat. & TM Off.

First Printing: October 2022
ISBN-13: 978-0-7860-4870-0
ISBN-13: 978-0-7860-4871-7 (eBook)

10 9 8 7 6 5 4 3 2 1

Printed in the United States of America

CHAPTER 1

"I declare it's darker'n the inside of a dead man's boot out here!" exclaimed Dad Clawson.

"It ain't dark over here by the fire," countered Dad's younger cow-punching partner, Pete Driscoll.

"No, but it sure is dark out here." Dad—a short, bandy-legged, gray-bearded man in a bullet-crowned cream Stetson that had seen far better days a good twenty years ago—stood at the edge of the firelight, holding back a pine branch as he surveyed the night-cloaked, Bear Paw Mountain rangeland beyond him.

"If you've become afraid of the dark in your old age, Dad, why don't you come on over here by the fire, take a load off, and pour a cup of coffee? I made a fresh pot. Thick as day-old cow plop, just like you like it. I'll even pour some of my who-hit-John in it if you promise to stop caterwaulin' like you're about to be set upon by wolves."

Dad stood silently scowling off into the star-capped distance. Turning his head a little to one side, he asked quietly in a raspy voice, "Did you hear that?"

"Hear what?"

"That." Dad turned his head a little more to one side. "There it was again."

Driscoll—a tall, lean man in his mid-thirties and with a

thick, dark-red mustache mantling his upper lip—stared across the steaming tin cup he held in both hands before him, pricking his ears, listening. A sharpened matchstick drooped from one corner of his mouth. "I didn't hear a thing."

Dad turned his craggy, bearded face toward the younger man, frowning. "You didn't?"

"Not a dadgum thing, Dad." Driscoll glowered at his partner from beneath the broad brim of his black Stetson.

He'd been paired with Clawson for over five years, since they'd both started working at the Stevens' Kitchen Sink Ranch on Owlhoot Creek. In that time, they'd become as close as some old married couples, which meant they fought as much as some old married couples.

"What's gotten into you? I've never known you to be afraid of the dark before."

"I don't know." Dad gave his head a quick shake. "Somethin's got my blood up."

"What is it?"

Dad glowered over his shoulder at Driscoll. "If I knew that, my blood wouldn't be up—now, would it?"

Driscoll blew ripples on his coffee and sipped. "I think you got old-timer's disease. That's what I think." He sipped again, swallowed. "Hearin' things out in the dark, gettin' your drawers in a twist."

Dad stood listening, staring out into the night. The stars shone brightly, guttering like candles in distant windows in small houses across the arching vault of the firmament. Finally, he released the pine bough; it danced back into place. He turned and, scowling and shaking his head, ambled back over to the fire. His spurs chinged softly. On a flat, pale rock near the dancing orange flames, his speckled tin coffeepot, which owned the dent of a bullet fired long ago by some cow-thieving Comanche bushwhacker in the Texas Panhandle, gurgled and steamed.

"Somethin's out there—I'm tellin' ya. Someone or some-

thing is movin' around out there." Dad grabbed his old Spencer repeating rifle from where it leaned against a tree then walked back around the fire to stand about six feet away from it, gazing out through the pines and into the night, holding the Spencer down low across his skinny thighs clad in ancient denims and brush-scarred, bull-hide chaps.

Driscoll glanced over his shoulder at where his and Dad's hobbled horses contentedly cropped grass several yards back in the pines. "Horses ain't nervy."

Dad eased his ancient, leathery frame onto a pine log, still keeping his gaze away from the fire, not wanting to compromise his night vision. "Yeah, well, this old coot is savvier than any broomtail cayuse. Been out on the range longer than both of them and you put together, workin' spreads from Old Mexico to Calvary in Alberta." He shook his head slowly. "Coldest damn country I ever visited. Still got frost bite on my tired old behind from the two winters I spent up there workin' for an ornery old widder."

"Maybe you got frostbite on the brain, too, Dad." Driscoll grinned.

"Sure, sure. Make fun. That's the problem with you, Pete. You got no respect for your elders."

"Ah, hell, Dad. Lighten up." Driscoll set his cup down and rummaged around in his saddlebags. "Come on over here an' let's plays us some two-handed—" He cut himself off abruptly, sitting up, gazing out into the night, his eyes wider than they'd been two seconds ago.

Dad shot a cockeyed grin over his shoulder. "See?"

"What was that?"

Dad cast his gaze through the pines again, to the right of where he'd been gazing before. "Hard to say."

"Hoot owl?"

"I don't think so."

The sound came again—very quiet but distinct in the

night so quiet that Dad thought he could hear the crackling flames of the stars.

"Ah, sure," Driscoll said. "A hoot owl. That's all it was!" He chuckled. "Your nerves is right catching, Dad. You're infecting my peaceable mind. Come on, now. Get your raggedy old behind over here and—" Again, a sound cut him off.

Driscoll gave an involuntary gasp then felt the rush of blood in his cheeks as they warmed with embarrassment. The sound was unlike anything Dad or Pete Driscoll had ever heard before. A screeching wail? Sort of catlike. But it hadn't been a cat. At least, like no cat Dad had ever heard before, and he'd heard a few during his allotment. Night-hunting cats could sound pure loco and fill a man's loins with dread. But this had been no cat.

An owl, possibly. But, no. It hadn't been an owl, either.

Dad's old heart thumped against his breastbone.

It thumped harder when a laugh vaulted out of the darkness. He swung his head sharply to the left, trying to peer through the branches of two tall Ponderosa pines over whose lime-green needles the dull, yellow, watery light of the fire shimmered.

"That was a woman," Driscoll said quietly, his voice low with a building fear.

The laugh came again. Very quietly. But loudly enough for Dad to make out a woman's laugh, all right. Sort of like the laugh of a frolicking employee in some house of ill repute in Cheyenne or Laramie, say. The laugh of a prostitute mildly drunk and engaged in a game of slap 'n' tickle with some drunken, frisky miner or track layer who'd paid downstairs and was swiping at the woman's bodice with one hand while holding a bottle by the neck with his other hand.

Dad rose from his log. Driscoll rose from where he'd been leaning back against his saddle, reached for his saddle ring Winchester, and slowly, quietly levered a round into the action. He followed Dad over to the north edge of the camp.

Dad pushed through the pine branches, holding his own rifle in one hand, his heart still thumping heavily against his breastbone. His tongue was dry, and he felt a knot in his throat. That was fear.

He was not a fearful man. Leastways, he'd never considered himself a fearful man. But that was fear, all right. Fear like he'd known it only once before and that was when he'd been alone in Montana, tending a small herd for an English rancher, and a grizzly had been prowling around in the darkness beyond his fire, occasionally edging close enough so that the flames glowed in the beast's eyes and reflected off its long, white, razor-edged teeth it had shown Dad as though a promise of imminent death and destruction.

The cows had been wailing fearfully, scattering themselves up and down the whole damn valley . . .

But the bear had seemed more intent on Dad himself.

That was a rare kind of fear. He'd never wanted to feel it again. But he felt it now, all right. Sure enough.

He stepped out away from the trees and cast his gaze down a long, gentle, sage-stippled slope and beyond a narrow creek that glistened like a snake's skin in the starlight. He jerked with a start when he heard a spur trill very softly behind him and glanced to his right to see Driscoll step up beside him, a good half a foot taller than the stoop-shouldered Dad.

Driscoll gave a dry chuckle, but Dad knew Pete was as unnerved as he was.

Both men stood in silence, listening, staring straight off down the slope and across the water, toward where they'd heard the woman laugh.

Then it came again, louder. Only, this time it came from Dad's left, beyond a bend in the stream.

Dad's heart pumped harder. He squeezed his rifle in both sweating hands, bringing it up higher and slipping his right finger through the trigger guard, lightly caressing the trigger. The woman's deep, throaty, hearty laugh echoed then faded. Then the echoes faded, as well.

"What the hell's goin' on?" Driscoll said. "I don't see no campfire over that way."

"Yeah, well, there's no campfire straight out away from us, neither, and that's where she was two minutes ago."

Driscoll clucked his tongue in agreement.

The men could hear the faint sucking sounds of the stream down the slope to the north, fifty yards away. That was the only sound. No breeze. No birds. Not even the rustling, scratching sounds little animals made as they burrowed.

Not even the soft thump of a pinecone falling out of a tree.

It was as though the entire night was collectively holding its breath, anticipating something bad about to occur.

The silence was shattered by a loud yowling wail issuing from behind Dad and Driscoll. It was a yapping, coyote-like yodeling, only it wasn't made by no coyote. No, no, no. Dad heard the voice of a man in that din. He heard the mocking laughter of a man in the cacophony as he and Driscoll turned quickly to stare back toward their fire and beyond it, their gazes cast with terror.

The crazy, mocking yodeling had come from the west, the opposite direction from the woman's first laugh.

Dad felt a shiver in Driscoll's right arm as it pressed up against Dad's left one.

"Lord almighty," his partner said. "They got us surrounded. Whoever they are!"

"Toyin' with us," Dad said, grimacing angrily.

Then the woman's voice came again, issuing from its original direction, straight off down the slope and across the darkly glinting stream. Both men grunted their exasperation as they whipped around again and stared off toward the east.

"Sure as hell, they're toyin' with us!" Driscoll said tightly, angrily, his chest expanding and contracting as he breathed. "What the hell do they want?" He didn't wait for Dad's response. He stepped forward and, holding his cocked Winchester up high across his chest, shouted, "What the hell do you want?"

"Come on out an' show yourselves!" Dad bellowed in a raspy voice brittle with terror.

Driscoll gave him a dubious look. "Sure we want 'em to do that?"

Dad only shrugged and continued turning his head this way and that, heart pounding as he looked for signs of movement in the deep, dark night around him.

"Hey, amigos," a man's deep, toneless voice said off Dad and Driscoll's left flanks. "Over here!"

Both men whipped around with more startled grunts, extending their rifles out before them, aiming into the darkness right of their fire, looking for a target but not seeing one.

"That one's close!" Driscoll said. "Damn close!"

Now the horses were stirring in the brush and trees beyond the fire, not far from where that cold, hollow voice had issued. They whickered and stumbled around, whipping their tails against their sides.

"That tears it!" Pete said. He moved forward, bulling through the pine boughs, angling toward the right of his and Dad's fire which had burned down considerably, offering only a dull, flickering, red radiance.

"Hold on, Pete!" Dad said. "Hold on!"

But then Pete was gone, leaving only the pine boughs jostling behind him.

"Where are you, dammit?" Pete yelled, his own voice echoing. "Where the hell are you? Why don't you come out an' show yourselves?"

...d shoved his left hand out, bending a pine branch back
.way from him. He stepped forward, seeing the fire flickering straight ahead of him, fifteen feet away. He quartered to
the right of the fire, not wanting its dull light to outline him,
to make him a target. He could hear Pete's spurs ringing, his
boots thudding and crackling in the pine needles ahead of
him, near where the horses were whickering and prancing
nervously.

"What the hell do you want?" Pete cried, his voice brittle
with exasperation and fear. "Why don't you show yourselves,
darn it?" His boot thuds dwindled in volume as he moved
farther away from the fire, spurs ringing more softly.

Dad jerked violently when Pete's voice came again:
"There you are! Stop or I'll shoot, damn you!"

A rifle barked once, twice, three times.

"Stop—" Pete's voice was drowned by another rifle blast,
this one issuing from farther away than Pete's had issued.
And off to Dad's left.

Straight out from Dad came an anguished cry.

"Pete!" Dad said, taking one quaking footstep forward,
his heart hiccupping in his chest. "*Pete!*"

Pete cried out again. Running, stumbling footsteps
sounded from the direction Pete had gone. Dad aimed the
rifle, gazing in terror toward the sound of the footsteps
growing louder and louder. A man-shaped silhouette grew
before Dad, and then, just before he was about to squeeze
the Spencer's trigger, the last rays of the dying fire played
across Pete's sweaty face.

He was running hatless and without his rifle, his hands
clamped over his belly.

"Pete!" Dad cried again, lowering the rifle.

"Dad!" Pete stopped and dropped to his knees before
him. He looked up at the older man, his hair hanging in his
eyes, his eyes creased with pain. "They're comin', Dad!"

Then he sagged onto his left shoulder and lay groaning and writhing.

"*Pete!*" Dad cried, staring down in horror at his partner.

His friend's name hadn't entirely cleared his lips before something hot punched into his right side. The punch was followed by the wicked, ripping report of a rifle. He saw the flash in the darkness out before him and to the right.

Dad wailed and stumbled sideways, giving his back to the direction the bullet had come from. Another bullet plowed into his back, just beneath his right shoulder, punching him forward. He fell and rolled, wailing and writhing.

He rolled onto his back, the pain of both bullets torturing him.

He spied movement in the darkness to his right.

He spied more movement all around him.

Grimacing with the agony of what the bullets had done to him, he pushed up onto his elbows. Straight out away from him, a dapper gent in a three-piece, butternut suit and bowler hat stepped up from the shadows and stood before him. He looked like a man you'd see on a city street, maybe wielding a fancy walking stick, or at a gambling layout in San Francisco or Kansas City. The dimming firelight glinted off what appeared a gold spike in his rear earlobe.

The man stared down at Dad, grinning. He was strangely handsome, clean-shaven, square-jawed. At first glance, his smiling eyes seemed warm and intelligent. He appeared the kind of man you'd want your daughter to marry.

Dad looked to his left and blinked his eyes, certain he wasn't seeing who he thought he saw—a beautiful flaxen-haired woman with long, impish blue eyes dressed all in black including a long, black duster. The duster was open to reveal that she wore only a black leather vest and a skirt under it. The vest highlighted more than concealed the heavy swells of her bosoms trussed up behind the tight-fitting, form-accentuating vest.

The woman smiled down at Dad, tipped her head back, and gave a catlike laugh.

If cats laughed, that was.

There was more movement to Dad's right. He turned in that direction to see a giant of a man step up out of the shadows.

A giant of a full-blooded Indian. Dressed all in buckskins and with a red bandanna tied around the top of his head, beneath his low-crowned, straw sombrero. Long, black hair hung down past his shoulders, and two big pistols jutted on his hips. He held a Yellowboy repeating rifle in both his big, red hands across his waist. He stared dully through flat, coal-black eyes down at Dad.

Dad gasped with a start when he heard crunching footsteps behind him, as well. He turned his head to peer over his shoulder at another big man, this one a white man.

He stepped out of the shadows, holding a Winchester carbine down low by his side. He was nearly as thick as he was tall, and he had a big, ruddy, fleshy face with a thick, brown beard. His hair was as long as the Indian's. On his head was a badly battered, ancient Stetson with a crown pancaked down on his head, the edges of the brim tattered in places. He grunted down at Dad then, working a wad of chaw around in his mouth, turned his head and spat to one side.

Dad turned back to the handsome man standing before him.

As he did, the handsome man lowered his head, reached up, and pulled something out from behind his neck. He held it out to show Dad.

A pearl-handled Arkansas toothpick with a six-inch, razor-edged blade.

To go along with his hammering heart, a cold stone dropped in Dad's belly.

The man smiled, his eyes darkening, the warmth and intelligence Dad had previously seen in them becoming a lie, turning dark and seedy and savage. He turned and walked over to where Pete lay writhing and groaning.

"No," Dad wheezed. "Don't you do it, you devil!"

The handsome man dropped to a knee beside Pete. He grabbed a handful of Pete's hair and jerked Pete's head back, exposing Pete's neck.

Pete screamed.

The handsome man swept the knife quickly across Pete's throat then stepped back suddenly to avoid the blood geysering out of the severed artery.

Pete choked and gurgled and flopped his arms and kicked his legs as he died.

The handsome man turned to Dad.

"Oh, God," Dad said. "Oh, God."

So this was how it was going to end. Right here. Tonight. Cut by a devil who looked like a man you'd want your daughter to marry. Aside from the eyes, that was . . .

As though reading Dad's mind, the handsome man grinned down at him. He shuttled that demon's smile to the others around him and then stepped forward and crouched down in front of Dad.

The last thing Dad felt before the dark wing of death closed over him was a terrible fire in his throat.

CHAPTER 2

"You think those rustlers are around here, Pa?" Matt Brannigan asked his father.

Just then, Tynan Brannigan drew his coyote dun to a sudden stop, and curveted the mount, sniffing the wind. "I just now do, yes."

"Why's that?" Matt asked, frowning.

Facing into the wind, which was from the southwest, Ty worked his broad nose beneath the brim of his high-crowned tan Stetson. "Smell that?"

"I don't smell nothin'."

"Face the wind, son," Ty said.

He was a big man in buckskins, at fifty-seven still lean and fit and broad through the shoulders, slender in the hips, long in the legs. His tan face with high cheekbones and a strawberry blond mustache to match the color of his wavy hair which hung down over the collar of his buckskin shirt, was craggily handsome. The eyes drawn up at the corners were expressive, rarely veiling the emotions swirling about in his hot Irish heart; they smiled often and owned the deeply etched lines extending out from their corners to prove it.

Ty wasn't smiling now, however. Earlier in the day, he and Matt had cut the sign of twelve missing beeves as well as the horse tracks of the men herding them. Of the long-looping *devils* herding them, rather. Rustling was no laughing matter.

Matt, who favored his father though at nineteen was not as tall and was much narrower of bone, held his crisp cream Stetson down on his head as he turned to sniff the wind, which was blowing the ends of his knotted green neckerchief as well as the glossy black mane of his blue roan gelding. He cut a sidelong look at his father and grinned. "Ah."

"Yeah," Ty said, jerking his chin up to indicate the narrow canyon opening before him in the heart of west-central Wyoming Territory's Bear Paw Mountains. "That way. They're up Three Maidens Gulch, probably fixin' to spend the night in that old trapper's cabin. The place has a corral so they'd have an easy time keeping an eye on their stolen beef."

"On *our* beef," Matt corrected his father.

"Good point." Ty put the spurs to the dun and galloped off the trail they'd been on and onto the canyon trail, the canyon's stony walls closing around him and Matt galloping just behind his father. The land was rocky so they'd lost the rustler's sign intermittently though it was hard to entirely lose the sign of twelve beeves on the hoof and four horseback riders.

A quarter mile into the canyon, the walls drew back and a stream curved into the canyon from a secondary canyon to the east. Glistening in the high-country sunlight and sheathed in aspens turning yellow in the mountain fall, their wind-jostled leaves winking like newly minted pennies, the stream hugged the trail as it dropped and turned hard and flinty then grassy as it bisected a broad meadow then became hidden from Ty and Matt's view by heavier pines on their right.

The forest formed the shape of an arrow as it cut down from the stream toward Ty and Matt. That arrow point crossed the trail a hundred yards ahead of them as they followed the trail through the forest fragrant with pine duff and moldering leaves.

At the edge of the trees, Ty drew the dun to a halt. Matt followed suit, the spirited roan stomping and blowing.

Ty gazed ahead at a rocky saddle rising before them a hundred yards away. Rocks and pines and stunted aspens stippled the rise and rose to the saddle's crest.

"The cabin's on the other side of that rise," he said, reaching forward with his right hand and sliding his Henry repeating rifle from its saddle sheath.

Both gun and sheath owned the marks of time and hard use. Ty had used the Henry during his town taming years in Kansas and Oklahoma, and the trusty sixteen-shot repeater had held him in good stead. So had the stag-butted Colt .44 snugged down in a black leather holster thonged on his buckskin-clad right thigh.

The thong was the mark of a man who used his hogleg often and in a hurry, but that was no longer true. Ty had been ranching and raising his family in these mountains for the past twenty years, ever since he'd met and married his four children's lovely Mexican mother, the former Beatriz Salazar, sixteen years Ty's junior.

He no longer used his weapons anywhere near as much as when he'd been the town marshal of Hayes or Abilene, Kansas or Guthrie, Oklahoma. Only at such times as now, when rustlers were trying to winnow his herd, or when old enemies came gunning for him, which had happened more times than he wanted to think about. At such times he always worried first and foremost for the safety of his family.

His family's welfare was paramount.

That's what he wanted to talk to Matt about now . . .

He turned to his son, who had just then slid his own Winchester carbine from its saddle sheath and rested it across his thighs. "Son," Ty said, "there's four of 'em."

"I know, Pa." Matt levered a round into his Winchester's

action then off-cocked the hammer. He grinned. "We can take 'em."

"If this were a year ago, I'd send you home."

Again, Matt grinned. "You'd try."

Ty laughed in spite of the gravity of the situation he found himself in—tracking four long-loopers with a son he loved more than life itself and wanted no harm to come to. "You and your sister," Ty said, ironically shaking his head. He was referring to his lovely, headstrong daughter, MacKenna, who at seventeen was two years younger than Matt but in some ways far more worldly in the ways seventeen-year-old young women can be and more worldly than boys and even men.

Especially those who were Irish mixed with Latina.

Mack, as MacKenna was known by those closest to her, was as good with a horse and a Winchester repeating rifle as Matt was, and Matt knew it. Sometimes Ty thought she was as good with the shooting irons as he himself was. Part of him almost wished she were here.

"You're nineteen now," Ty told Matt.

"Goin' on twenty," Matt quickly added.

"Out here, that makes a man." Ty jerked his head to indicate the saddle ahead of them. "They have a dozen of our cows, and they can't get away with them. They have to be taught they can't mess with Powderhorn beef. If we don't teach 'em that, if they get away with it—"

"I know, Pa. More will come. Like wolves on the blood scent."

"You got it." Ty narrowed one grave eye at his son. "I want you to be careful. Take no chances. If it comes to shootin', and we'd best assume it will because those men likely know what the penalty for rustling is out here, remember to breathe and line up your sights and don't hurry your shots or you'll pull 'em. But for God sakes when you need to pull your head down, pull it down!"

"You know what, Pa?" Matt asked, sitting up straight in

his saddle, suddenly wide-eyed, his handsome face showing his own mix of Irish and Latin, with his olive skin, light brown hair which he wore long like his father, and expressive, intelligent tan eyes.

"What?"

"A few minutes ago, I wasn't one bit scared," Matt said. "In fact, I was congratulatin' myself, pattin' myself on the back, tellin' myself how proud I was that I was out here trackin' long-ropers with the great Ty Brannigan without threat of makin' water in my drawers. But now I'm afraid I'm gonna make water in my drawers! So, if you wouldn't mind, could we do what needs doin' before I lose my nerve, pee myself, an' go runnin' home to Ma?"

He kept his mock-frightened look on his father for another three full seconds. Suddenly, he grinned and winked, trying to put the old man at ease.

Ty chuckled and nudged his hat up to scratch the back of his head. "All right, son. All right. I just had to say that."

"I know you did, Pa."

Ty sidled his mount up to Matt's handsome roan, took his rifle in his left hand and reached out and cupped the back of Matt's neck in his gloved hand, pulling him slightly toward him. "I love you, kid," he said, gritting his teeth and hardening his eyes. "If anything ever happened to you . . ."

Feeling emotion swelling in him, threatening to fog his eyes, he released Matt quickly, reined the dun around, and booted it on up the trail.

Matt smiled after his father then booted the roan into the dun's sifting dust.

Ten minutes later, father and son were hunkered down behind rocks at the crest of the saddle. Their horses stood ground-reined twenty feet down the ridge behind them.

Ty was peering through his spyglass into the valley on the saddle's other side, slowly adjusting the focus. The old trapper's cabin swam into view—a two-story, brush-roofed, age-silvered log hovel hunkered in a meadow on the far side of a creek rippling through a narrow, stony bed.

The cabin was flanked by a lean-to stable and a pole corral in which all twelve of his cows stood, a few chewing hay, others mooing nervously. Five horses milled with the cattle, also eating hay or munching grass that had grown high since the place had been abandoned many years ago. That fifth horse might mean five instead of four men in the cabin. One man, possibly whoever was buying the stolen beef, might have met the others here with the cows. Ty would have to remember that.

A half-breed named Latigo He Who Rides had lived there—an odd, quiet man whom Ty had met a few times when he'd been looking for unbranded mavericks that had avoided the previous roundup. He had never known what had happened to He Who Rides.

One year on a trek over to this side of the saddle he'd simply found the cabin abandoned. It had sat mostly abandoned ever since except when rustlers or outlaws on the run used it to overnight in. It was good and remote, and known only by folks like Ty who knew this eastern neck of the mountains well.

Rustlers had moved in again, it looked like. Ty had a pretty good idea who they were led by, too. A no-account scoundrel named Leroy Black. His brother Luther was probably here, as well. They were known to have rustled in the area from time to time, selling the stolen beef to outlaw ranchers who doctored the brands or to packers who butchered it as soon as the cows were in their hands.

Knowing the Blacks were rustling and being able to prove it, however, were two separate things.

The Black boys were slippery, mostly moved the cattle at night. They were probably working with their cousins, Derrick and Bobby Dean Barksdale. The Blacks and Barksdales made rustling in the Bear Paws and over in the nearby Wind Rivers a family affair. That they were moving beef in the light of day meant they were getting brash and would likely get brasher.

Ty grimaced, his cheeks warming with anger. Time to put them out of business once and for all.

Ty handed the spy glass to Matt hunkered beside him, staring through a separate gap between the rocks. "Have a look, son. Take a good, careful look. Get a good sense of the layout before we start down, and note the fifth horse in the corral. The odds against us likely just went up by one more man. We'll need to remember that."

"All right, Pa." Matt took the spyglass, held it to his eye, and adjusted the focus. He studied the cabin and its surroundings for a good three or four minutes then lowered the glass and turned to his father, frowning. "They don't have anyone on watch?"

Ty shook his head. "Not that I could see. They've gotten overconfident. That works in our favor."

"We gonna wait till dark? Take 'em when they're asleep?"

Ty shook his head. "Too dangerous. I like to know who I'm shooting at." He glanced at the sun. "In about an hour, the sun will be down behind the western ridges. It'll be dusk in that canyon. That's when we'll go. Knowing both the Blacks and Barksdales like I do, they'll likely be good and drunk by then."

Matt nodded.

Ty dropped to his butt and rested back against one of the large rocks peppering the ridge crest. He doffed his hat, ran a big, gloved hand brusquely through his sweat-damp hair. "Here's the hard part."

"The hard part?"

"Waiting. Everyone thinks lawdogging is an exciting profession. Truth to tell, a good three-quarters of it is sitting around waiting for something to happen."

"Good to know," Matt said. "In case I ever start thinkin' about followin' in my old man's footsteps."

"Forget it," Ty said, smiling. "You're needed at the Powderhorn. That's where you're gonna get married and raise a whole passel of kids. We'll add another floor to the house." Suddenly, he frowned, pondering on what he'd just said. "That is what you'd like to do—isn't it, Matt?"

A thoughtful cast came to Matt's eyes as he seemed to do some pondering of his own. Finally, he shrugged, quirked a wry half-smile, and said, "Sure. Why not?"

Ty studied his oldest boy. He'd always just assumed, since Matt had been a pink-faced little baby, that the boy would follow in Ty's footsteps. His ranching footsteps. Not his lawdogging footsteps.

Now he wondered if he'd made the wrong assumption. His own father had assumed that Ty would follow in Killian Brannigan's own footsteps as a mountain fur trapper and hide hunter. That they'd continue to work together in the Rockies, living in the little cabin they shared with Ty's hardworking mother halfway up the Cache la Poudre Canyon near La Port in Colorado. Killian Brannigan had been hurt when Ty had decided to go off to the frontier army and fight the Indians and then, once he'd mustered out, pin a badge to his chest. One badge after another in wide-open towns up and down the great cattle trails back when Texas beef was still being herded to the railroad hubs in Kansas and Oklahoma.

Those years had been the heyday of the Old Western gunfighter, so Ty, too, had had to become good with a gun.

Despite what Ty had said to Matt about lawdogging being three-quarters boredom, it had been an exciting time in his life. While he'd visited his parents often, he'd never regretted the choice he'd made. Being a mountain man and working in tandem with his mountain woman, Ciara Brannigan, pronounced "Kee-ra," had been his father's choice. Killian and Ciara had both been loners by nature and had preferred the company of the forests and rivers to that of people. While Ty had loved his parents and enjoyed his childhood hunting and trapping and hide-tanning alongside his mother and father, he'd been ready to leave the summer he'd turned seventeen.

And leave he had.

Now he realized he should have known better than to assume that his own son would want to follow in his own ranching footsteps. It wasn't a fair assumption to make. And now Ty wondered, a little skeptically as he continued to study his son, if he'd been wrong. He hoped he wasn't, but he might be. If so, like his own father before him, he'd have to live with the choice his son made. That time was right around the corner, too, he realized with a little dread feeling like sour milk in his belly.

He just hoped Matt didn't make Ty's own first choice. He didn't want his son to be a lawman. He wanted him to stay home and ranch with Ty and the boy's mother, Beatriz.

Time passed slowly there on the top of that saddle.

The sun angled westward. Deep purple shadows angled out from the western ridges. Birdsong grew somnolent.

Ty kept watch on the cabin. While he did, two of the four men came outside, separately and at different times, to make water just off the dilapidated front stoop. Another came out to empty a wash pan. That man came out the cabin's back door a few minutes later to walk over to the corral and check on the cattle that were still mooing and grazing uneasily. That was one of the Barksdale brothers clad in a ragged broadcloth coat and floppy-brimmed felt hat. He wore two pistols on his hips and held a Winchester in his hands.

On the way back to the cabin, he took a good, long, cautious look around. Then he reentered the cabin through the back door.

While Ty kept watch, Matt rested his head back against a rock, tipped his hat down over his face, and dozed.

Finally, Ty put his spyglass away and touched his son's arm. "Time to go, son," he said. "Sun's down."

He picked up his rifle and looked at Matt, who yawned, blinking his eyes, coming awake. He wanted to tell the kid to stay here, out of harm's way, but he couldn't do it. Matt wouldn't have listened, and he shouldn't have. He wasn't a kid anymore. He was almost twenty and he was part of a ranching family. That meant he, like Ty, had to protect what was his.

Ty hoped like hell they got through this all right. If anything happened to that kid, his mother would never forgive Ty and Ty would never forgive himself.

CHAPTER 3

Using the spyglass earlier, Ty had chosen his and Matt's route down the ridge. He followed it, crouching low, holding the rifle even lower so that any stray last rays of sunlight wouldn't glisten off the breech.

He and Matt weaved their way around rocks, boulders, clumps of brush, occasional aspens, pines, and wind-gnarled cedars. As they moved, Ty kept a close watch on the cabin. A single window was in the wall facing him but it was shuttered. He thought he could see the flicker of a lamp between the cracks in the shutter.

As he and Matt gained the bottom of the canyon, Ty started to hear men's voices from inside the cabin. It was dusk, and the cows had settled down. The two sets of cousins—and likely an extra man to go with the extra horse in the corral—were likely gambling, smoking, drinking.

Good. The more distracted and drunk they were, the better.

Ty and Matt continued to weave around cover until they approached the creek, its brown water glinting dully in the last green light showing in the sky. With Ty again leading the way, he and Matt followed a game trail down into the creek's deep cut. Ty found a shallow ford and was halfway across it when he stopped suddenly.

A man's voice yelled, "Halloo the camp!"

The voice was followed by the growing clatter of what sounded like a buggy's wheels. The sound was coming from Ty's right and on the other side of the stream.

"Royce!" came a voice from the cabin. "Royce, is that you? About time you're gettin' here. Me an' the boys—we's needin' some um, um, *socializin'*!"

A girl's ribald laughter joined the clatter of the buggy wheels.

Ty swung his head around to share an incredulous look with his son.

He continued on across the stream then removed his hat and climbed partway up the bank on the opposite side. A few feet from the top, he dropped to his hands and knees. Matt removed his own hat and came up to lie belly down to Ty's right. Both men edged cautious looks over the lip of the cut, swiveling their heads to the right to gaze at the front of the cabin and its sagging front porch on which all four of the rustlers now stood, some easier to see than others because of the angle.

Ty winced as he watched a small, black surrey pull up to the front of the cabin. Two men and two women were inside, a man and a woman on each of the buggy's two quilted leather seats. The men were duded out in cheap suits and bowler hats. The women looked like brightly colored birds in their gaudy, very low-cut and sleeveless dresses. One wore a yellow dress with black lace and twirled a matching yellow parasol above her head. The other girl wore a red dress with white lace and held a matching red parasol.

The girl in the red dress was a redhead. The girl in the yellow dress was a blonde.

Both were comely figures, by anyone's standards—even by the standards of a fifty-seven-year-old, happily married family man.

The two men were laughing and passing a bottle back and

forth as the man sitting up front with the blond stopped the mouse brown dun in the buggy's traces. He set the brake and drew the blond to him, planting a long, hungry kiss on her brightly painted red lips.

Matt turned to his father, his eyes cast with disbelief. "Parlor girls?" he asked very softly, just above his breath.

"Looks like," Ty said, also very softly. "I recognize one of the men—the one in the front. Used to be a deputy sheriff out of Wendigo. Tony Miller. A drunkard and lout. Don't recognize the other gent. Both must be friends or, hell, maybe even relatives of the Blacks and Barksdales. Lord knows those people breed like rabbits."

"So, what?" Matt said. "They're gonna have a *party* out here?"

"Looks like." Ty cast his gaze toward the cabin again as the two men stepped down from the buggy then extended their hands to help the two women down.

The four men on the porch were talking and laughing, obviously anticipating the pleasures of the flesh that would soon be theirs. When the jovially conversing men and tittering girls had disappeared into the cabin, Ty ran his thumb along his jaw in frustration.

"That right there is not good," he said. "Now there's maybe seven men and two girls."

"What're we gonna do, Pa?"

Ty shook his head. "Damned if I know. I sure don't want those girls getting hurt."

"Maybe we'd best wait till they leave. They didn't unhitch the buggy, so it's likely they're not gonna stay all night."

"Yeah," Ty said. "They probably just paid for a couple of hours or so."

"We gonna wait 'em out?"

"Have to," Ty said, thoroughly disgusted by the unexpected turn of events. "I'm not losing that beef."

Matt groaned and shook his head. "Another long wait."

"See? That's what lawdoggin's like." Ty winked. "Best stick to ranching."

Matt chuckled and shook his head.

They both lay patiently, belly down, watching the cabin, hearing the sounds of male and female revelry issuing from inside. Ty found his cheeks warming with embarrassment. He wasn't sure how much Matt knew about the pleasures of the flesh. He'd never asked and Matt had never told him. Whatever the young man's experience had been, he was sure getting an earful of it now.

After an hour or so, someone started scraping away on a fiddle.

There were the shuffling thumps of dancing accompanied by sometimes raucous laughter.

Then the fiddle died and there were more love sounds accompanied by the more sedate sounds of men playing cards. Coins clinked together. The men were starting to slur their words.

Suddenly, a man's truculent shout issued from the cabin. "Ouch! What the hell did you do that for?"

A girl screeched, "I told you I don't like that. Now *stop*!"

"I paid good money for you, little Miss Ida," the man yelled. "I'll do any damn thing I please!"

The other men laughed.

The other girl said, "Show some manners, Lou! If Ida doesn't like it, then you don't do it!"

For a time nothing but a low conversational hum and the clinking of coins as the bulk of the men continued their card game was heard.

The silence was broken by another female cry. "That's enough. I've had it. I wanna go back to town! Royce, take us back to town!"

There was a sharp crack as though of a hand striking flesh.

The girl screamed. A slapping sound as she struck the floor.

Ty and Matt shared a quick, exasperated look then returned their enervated gazes back to the cabin in which a man laughed.

"I'm gonna shoot that little lady!"

The girl screamed a half-second before a revolver barked loudly.

Both girls screamed, and there was much scrambling around inside the cabin until the front door opened. In the light shed by the open door, Ty watched the blonde run naked out onto the porch and into the night straight out and away from the cabin, quickly disappearing in the nearly pitch-black darkness that had settled down over the cabin since the four visitors had arrived.

A man just as naked as the girl and whom Ty assumed was Lou—probably an outlaw cattle buyer—staggered out onto the sagging front stoop. There was the ratcheting click of a gun being cocked. The man raised the pistol, yelling, "I'm gonna take me some target practice on that soiled dove!"

Matt made a quick movement to Ty's right.

Ty turned to see his son raise his Winchester over the lip of the bank and click the hammer back.

"Matt, wait!" Ty rasped out.

Too late. The carbine roared, flames lapping from the barrel.

The naked man screamed and stumbled sideways, firing his pistol into the porch floor and his bare foot. He howled again and then fell out of sight with a resolute thud.

"Ah, hell!" Ty yelled. He grabbed his hat and rifle and leaped up onto the bank. "Matt, you stay here. All hell's gonna break loose and I don't want you in on these odds!" He turned and ran toward the cabin in which men were scrambling around and yelling, no doubt grabbing pistols and rifles. The girl still inside the cabin was sobbing.

"I *am* in on these odds, Pa!" Matt yelled behind Ty.

"Matt—dammit, go back!"

But Ty heard the stubborn thuds of his son's running feet behind him. He merely cursed and shook his head, intent on killing as many of the rustlers as he could before they could kill him and his son. That there would be more shooting could be no doubt.

Ty ran toward the front corner of the cabin but stopped when a half-dressed man appeared, stepping out from a corner of the cabin and holding a Winchester. Ty recognized the stocky Bobby Dean Barksdale with a bullet-shaped, egg-bald, hatless head. Barksdale grimaced, showing his teeth, and leveled his carbine on Ty. Ty got his shot off first, punching Barksdale straight back onto the stoop behind him and nudging Barksdale's own shot wide.

Ty took off running again and as he rounded the cabin's front corner, Matt hot on his heels, Ty shot Barksdale's brother, Derrick, just as that Barksdale ran out the front door. Ty's bullet punched through the dead center of Derrick's chest, throwing him back into one of the suited gents, the drunkard and loutish Tony Miller.

Miller screamed as he went stumbling back into the cabin.

The man Matt had shot was cursing and trying to gain his feet on the other side of the stoop. He was reaching for the carbine he'd dropped, whipping a pain-racked, enraged look at Ty. Ty was about to shoot him but held the shot when Matt, standing beside Ty, shot the man twice with his own Winchester then racked another round into his rifle's action.

"Not bad, kid," Ty said, a little discomfited at the ease with which his son had dispatched ol' Lou but impressed just the same.

He leaped up onto the stoop and peered through the cabin's wide-open door. Derrick Barksdale lay on the floor just inside. Beyond him, the cursing and grunting Tony

Miller was gaining his feet after being knocked down by Barksdale's lifeless body that was shaped very much like his brother's.

Ty pumped another round into the Henry's breech, aimed quickly, and fired, blowing a forty-four caliber hole through Miller's right cheek and out the back of his head, casting a nasty stream of blood, brain, and bone matter onto the table littered with bottles, cards, scrip, and specie behind him.

"Holy crap—it's Brannigan!" shouted Luther Black, crouching behind the potbelly stove right of the table.

He raised his head and shoved a fistful of a nickeled, top-break Schofield over the top of the stove. The Schofield bucked and roared, the bullet slamming into the wall to Ty's left but not before kissing the nap of Ty's left shirtsleeve. Ty racked another round in the Henry, aimed quickly, and fired. He aimed too quickly. His bullet spanged off a cast-iron skillet hanging from a ceiling support post just left of where Luther Black was cocking his Schofield again.

"I got him, Pa!" Matt said, stepping into the cabin beside Ty, raising his smoking carbine, aiming quickly but coolly, and turning Black's left eye to cherry jelly.

Black merely said, "Uh!" then, head bobbing wildly, sagged down out of sight behind the stove.

"Good shootin', son," Ty said, again discomfited as well as impressed, racking another round into the Henry's breech.

"Thanks, Pa."

Ty turned to the right, where the other man in the suit, likely Royce, was aiming a pistol over an overturned chair, yelling, "You go to Hell, Brannigan!"

"You first, Royce!" Ty yelled. He recognized him now as Royce Tipple, a card sharp who must be dabbling in stolen cattle these days.

Ty and Matt both fired two shots through the chair, breaking it apart, and into the suited Royce, who was even still wearing his bowler hat. Royce rose, screaming and triggering his six-shooter into the air then flying backward with a crash through the window behind him, which, oddly still had some glass in its frame. That made the girl sprawled belly down on the old, dilapidated fainting couch against the same wall as the window scream all the louder, although her screams were muffled by the worn velour of the couch.

Cursing and triggering the pistol in his fist, Leroy Black suddenly rose up from behind a cupboard sitting near the bottom of the stairs that led to the cabin's second, half story. Fortunately, Leroy was so drunk and nervous, both rounds flew out the open door between Ty and Matt. Cursing and wailing, Black swung around and ran up the stairs.

Ty started running toward the stairs but stopped when Matt said, "I got him, Pa!"

Pumping another round into his Winchester, Matt ran across the cluttered, filthy cabin, hurdling obstacles, then up the stairs, taking the steps two at a time. Hearing running feet in the ceiling and seeing dust sift down through the cracks between the logs, Ty stood frozen in place, incredulous. There was a shrill scream and then a loud rifle report.

"*Ohhh!*" he heard Leroy cry.

More stumbling caused more dust to sift down between the cracks in the ceiling then Leroy reappeared at the top of the stairs. This time he was rolling butt-over-tea-kettle down the steps, grunting with each turn, making the rickety stairs wobble precariously.

He piled up at the bottom on his back, groaning. He dug his elbows and heels into the floor and arched his back up off the floor then dropped with a grunt. Clad only in a filthy balbriggan top, he lay still with a blood-oozing hole in his brisket.

Boots thudded slowly on the stairs.

Matt appeared, coming down one step at a time, resting the still-smoking rifle on his shoulder. At the bottom of the stairs, he stepped over the dead Leroy Black and turned to Ty with a faint, self-satisfied smile on his lips.

Ty wagged his head, caressed his chin between thumb and index finger. "Son," he said, scowling his incredulity, "I do believe you and that rifle have been spending some time alone together." More and more, he was coming to know less and less about his oldest.

"Dang near as good as Mack—wouldn't you say?"

Ty smiled. It was a stiff smile.

CHAPTER 4

MacKenna Brannigan reined in her sleek Appaloosa she'd named Cervantes after her mother's favorite Spanish author at the lip of the canyon and stared down at the cool, black water gathered in a broad pool at the bottom of the falls. She pinched her plump bottom lip between her gloved thumb and index finger and wrinkled her brows that were the same black as the straight black hair hanging down to the small of her back, pondering.

Her skin crawled luxuriously at the prospect of that cold water caressing every inch of her tired, sore, sweaty body. She'd been brush-popping strays all day in anticipation of the autumn gather, and the last cow and calf had taken her nearly an hour to free from the hawthorn thicket they'd gotten themselves entangled in. Buggy work in there, too. The horseflies had been as thick as thieves.

Hot, dusty, sweaty work. The calf had given Mack a nice kick in the knee for her trouble, ungrateful little cuss.

MacKenna looked at the falls where Lone Squaw Creek dropped down the bone-smooth granite wall into the canyon thirty feet below her. There wasn't much of a flow this time of the year, late-summer, but the round, granite-edged pool was full. The black water, lolling in its bed like coffee in a cup, glinted in the sunshine.

. Mack glanced up at the west-angling sun. It was likely around three-thirty. She was a good hour-and-a-half ride from the Powderhorn, her family's ranch. She should get back and grain and rub down Cervantes and help her mother start supper. On the other hand, wasn't she due a quick, refreshing swim after a long day that had started at the first blush of dawn?

Besides, her mother, Beatriz, had the help of Mack's twelve-year-old sister, Caroline. Her father and brother probably wouldn't be back to the headquarters anytime soon, anyway, as they'd ridden farther west on the open range, tracking the herds that had scattered in that direction over the summer. Ma would probably wait supper for them.

So, Mack had time for a quick swim.

The pretty, outdoorsy girl's almond-skinned, hazel-eyed face blossomed in a sudden, delighted smile beneath the brim of her low-crowned, flat-brimmed, black Stetson trimmed with a band of hammered silver conchos. She swung down from the Appaloosa's back, dropped the reins, ground-tying the horse, and quickly kicked out of her boots and pulled off her gloves. She dropped her hat on the ground, crown down, and in less than a minute her brush-scarred, black leather chaps, denim jeans, cream work shirt, red neckerchief, camisole, pantalettes, and socks lay in a loose pile beside it.

"Stay fella."

Cervantes swung his head around and gave the seventeen-year-old girl's left ear an affectionate nuzzling.

Mack chuckled at the tickling sensation of the horse's leathery muzzle against her ear, patted the wither once more, and said, "I'll be right back." She swung around and stood at the lip of the canyon, stretching her arms high above her head, enjoying the luxurious feeling of being naked, not wearing anything but the smile on her face, in the clean mountain air, no one around for miles, giving her total privacy, something not easy to find at the Powderhorn with her two brothers and annoying kid sister and parents always around.

She ran her hands across her chest that had all the boys and even many men staring when she rode into town for supplies. The ogling devils. Mack gave a caustic grunt as she leaned back to shake out her long hair, feeling the silky ends caress her backside.

But then, she supposed she should be glad that men found her attractive. They had ever since she'd turned fourteen and had started growing tall, slim, and curvy in all the right womanly places. She supposed she was glad, mostly. But she had to admit being a little repelled by those stares that often seemed a little too bold, too goatish, too lingering through eyes that seemed fawning but also threatening.

Maybe that's why she liked being alone so much. She'd been riding alone out here to the falls every chance she found since she'd stumbled upon this remote place a couple of years ago when, like today, she and her father and brother had been out scouting their herds and hazing some of the cattle closer to home in anticipation of roundup.

Again, Mack raised her arms high above her head, rose up and down on her toes, then lunged up and forward and over the lip of the ridge, her supple, long-legged, almond-colored body arcing out over the dark water, her black hair, which she'd inherited from her Mexican mother, lifting high like the wing of a raven taking flight. She straightened out her body and submitted to gravity that pulled her straight down over the water—down . . . down . . . down. The black pool off which the sun winked growing larger and blacker and more sun-kissed before her . . . until first her hands and then her head and shoulders impaled the surface.

She angled deep, body cleaving the cool water, chicken flesh rising in delight across every inch of her. She pushed off the pool's sandy bottom with her hands and, gently kicking her feet, swam back toward where the sun lay like a shimmering golden gown on the pool's surface straight above her. Her waving hands and then her head impaled the gown, and the refreshingly cool water ran down her face and she drew in deep draughts of the winy mountain air that smelled like wet rock and mushrooms.

Leaning forward, she swam across the pool one way then back the other way, silently rejoicing at the cold water scouring away the hours and layers of trail sweat and grime. She kicked off the canyon's stone wall once more and started swimming toward the other side, near where the water overflowed through a natural stone trough and into the creek snaking away to the south at the base of the canyon wall.

On the ridge crest above her, Cervantes whinnied shrilly.

Mack gasped with a start and stopped swimming. She stared up the thirty-foot canyon wall to where the appy stood, facing away from the canyon, nervously switching its tail.

Another horse's answering whinny rose in the distance beyond Cervantes.

"Oh, damn," Mack said, teeth chattering a little against the cold. "Someone's coming!" Her mind flashed on her Winchester carbine snugged down in the sheath strapped to her saddle. Fear tightened the little muscles running up and down along her spine as she hovered there in the pool, treading water.

Maybe it was only Pa and Matt. She doubted it, though. She doubted they knew about this falls or this short stretch of canyon, as it was very remote, pretty well hidden, and no cows ever ventured down that steep, pine-studded ridge to the east. That was the only way down to the canyon. Mack doubted many folks knew about this stretch of the aptly named Lone Squaw Creek. Maybe the Indians who'd lived there long ago and whose bright, spidery pictures she occasionally spied on the canyon walls.

She'd happened upon it herself by riding up the creek

alone one day, adventuring farther from home than she should have been. She'd never mentioned anything about it to anybody. She'd always thought of it as her own secret place where she could wander now and then to be alone with her own naked body and her own private thoughts.

Her heart quickening, she considered scrambling up the ridge—an easy climb downstream a few dozen yards, just beyond where the pool overflowed into the creek—and arming herself with her rifle. On the other hand, whoever was coming would likely see her long before she could reach the rifle, and she was butt naked.

She treaded water in the pool, waiting, heart thudding. She couldn't hear much above the plopping sounds of the falls to her left.

But she assumed the riders were approaching the canyon when the appy whickered, arched its tail, and sidestepped nervously along the lip of the canyon, so close to the edge Mack was afraid Cervantes would tumble over the side. Fearing that as well as whomever was approaching, Mack stared tensely up the ridge.

Cervantes sidled farther down canyon along the lip of the ridge, making quick, startled movements, arching its tail, knocking gravel into the canyon.

Stop, Cervantes! Mack silently willed the horse.

Finally, a horse and rider appeared at the top of the ridge, near where the Appaloosa had been standing a minute ago. Another horse and rider appeared, pulling up to the right of the first man, who appeared dressed in a suit and was wearing a bowler hat. The second rider was a woman, Mack was surprised to see. Not just any woman, either. A woman with long, straight, flaxen hair flowing down her bare shoulders. Her shoulders were bare because she wore only a leather vest held together with leather ties; the tight leather vest accentuated more than concealed her ample bosoms.

Two more riders pulled their own mounts up beside the

blonde—a big, raw-boned, severely-featured Indian with long black hair hanging down past his shoulders from beneath a low-crowned straw sombrero. He wore a buckskin tunic open to halfway down his dark-red chest, the garment's leather laces untied.

The man sitting his horse beside the Indian was a big white man. He was as tall as the Indian but broader, fleshier, his bearded face owning an air of crudeness and mindless brutality. He could have been a miner or a track layer or a gandy dancer. Mack had seen his like in Warknife. The big Indian studied her with his stony black eyes. The big, bearded white man sat his horse, looking down at Mack, grinning darkly through small eyes set beneath steeply ridged, thick, brown eyebrows.

"Well, well, well. What do we have here?" Mack heard the blonde say above the prattling and plopping of the slow-running falls. She had a strangely high-pitched voice, a girlish voice.

"Touché, my dear, touché." This from the man on the far left of the four-person group—the dandified looking man in the suit and bowler hat. He was clean-shaven, handsome.

Still, Mack did not like the way he was gazing down over the side of the ridge at her. She didn't know how much of her they could see from their position, but she slid one arm over her bosoms, treading water awkwardly with just her legs and one arm.

"Hot diggity ding-dong *damn*!" said the big, crude-looking white man, grinning and slapping his thigh. "Imagine comin' upon something like *that* way out here!"

Mack's heart beat faster.

She'd never seen these men or that woman before. She'd have known if she had. They were a memorable lot, she'd give them that. There was a bizarre air about them. A dangerous air. A menacing air. That they were riding on the wrong side of the law there could be little doubt.

And here they were, sitting their horses on the ridge above where Mack was treading water one-handed, as naked as the day she was born but in the full bloom of young womanhood.

Fear ran wild in MacKenna's heart. Her throat constricted. Her tongue felt swollen.

The handsome white man in the suit smiled as he turned his head to his left and said, "You like what you see down there, big fella?"

"I like what I see down there just fine!"

The handsome man threw his head back and laughed, showing a complete set of even, white teeth. He stopped laughing suddenly and glanced at the Indian. "Bear?"

The Indian slid a rifle from his saddle boot and cocked it.

Mack's heart shriveled as it leaped and rolled in her chest.

She prepared to take a deep breath and drop down into the pool but forestalled the action when the blonde leaned over and tapped the Indian's shoulder. "Sheath it."

The Indian turned to her, scowling. "She's seen us," he said, tonelessly but louder.

The other two men turned to the woman, as well, frowning.

"Sheath it," the woman said again, gazing down at Mack, her expression impossible to read. She had the bluest eyes Mack thought she'd ever seen. But they were cold, cold eyes. They seemed to gaze right through MacKenna. She smiled suddenly. "You're no threat to us—are you, young lady?"

Mack swallowed, shook her head.

"I said *are* you, young lady?" the woman yelled louder in her strange, girlish voice.

Again, Mack shook her head. "No!" she returned. "I'm no threat!"

"That's good," the woman said, an off-putting smile on her rich, full lips. She had a doll-like face but a menacing air. Her voice was high-pitched, girlish, though she had to be somewhere in her late twenties. "You mention us to anyone, we'll ride back and kill you and kill your whole family—understand? You, I'll leave to those two over there to figure out what to do with." She canted her head to indicate the Indian scowling over his Winchester at Mack and the thuggish, goatishly grinning white man.

She turned back to MacKenna and the smile left her lips though it had never touched her cold, blue, blue eyes. "Understand?"

Mack nodded. She felt so shriveled up and terrified it was hard to keep treading water and felt herself sinking lower and lower.

"All right, then," said the woman. "We're gonna consider that a promise."

The handsome man and the Indian continued to scowl skeptically at the woman though the big white man's lusty eyes remained on Mack.

"What's so special about her?" the Indian wanted to know.

The blonde kept her cold gaze on Mack. "Sheath it," was all she said.

Glowering angrily, the Indian sheathed his Winchester.

The handsome white man gave a wry chuckle, shaking his head at the woman. He turned to Mack and said, "You remember the warning, pretty girl. We're *bad*. Bad as there's ever been." He winked deviously then reined his horse around and booted it into a trot along the edge of the canyon.

The blonde was slow to take her eyes off of Mack. She finally did, throwing her head back and laughing with delight and derision, then turned her horse and trotted off after the handsome white man.

The Indian spat disgustedly over the side of the ridge then turned his horse as well, and rode off after the other two. As he did, Mack could see that he was trailing a pack horse—one with a pair of bulging saddlebags draped over the saddle and a large burlap sack hanging from the saddle horn.

The big, ugly white man followed the Indian. He, too,

was trailing a pack horse with a similar pair of bulging saddlebags draped over the saddle as well as a burlap sack, likely a trail supply bag. As he rode along the lip of the ridge, heading upstream, he turned to Mack, rose up in his saddle, grinned, and made a lewd gesture, then turned his head forward and was gone.

A long sigh of immense relief fairly exploded out of Mack.

She hadn't realized it until now, but she'd been holding her breath for the past several minutes.

CHAPTER 5

It was good and dark when Ty and Matt Brannigan rode through the portal of the Powderhorn Ranch headquarters, through the open gate and into the yard.

It was good and dark without any lilac remaining in the west, but a three-quarter moon cast a wedge-shaped pearl sheen across the yard, and dark where the light was blocked by trees, buildings, and corrals. The two and a half-story main lodge constructed of stout logs and boasting a broad front porch lay to the right, on the opposite side of the yard from the barn, the stable, the corrals, blacksmith shop, and small bunkhouse.

Most of the lodge's windows shown with guttering lamp-light. A lamp hung from a roof support post on the porch, showing a silhouetted figure sitting on the top porch step—either Beatriz or MacKenna, Ty opined. The figure was too tall for twelve-year-old Caroline. The Brannigan's black and white collie dog, Rollie, had been sitting beside the figure on the steps but as Ty and Matt trotted their horses over to the main corral, Rollie ran down the porch steps and across the yard, barking, tail wagging delightedly.

"Pa!" came Mack's eager voice from the porch.

Ty glanced over his shoulder at his daughter jogging toward him and her brother, long hair bouncing on her shoulders. "Hope Ma didn't throw our supper out, Mack. I know we're gettin' home well after the coons are headin' out but—*whoa!*"

Ty had just dismounted his coyote dun and MacKenna literally hurled herself into his arms, wrapped her arms around his waist, squeezing him tightly, burying her face in his chest, sniffing as though taking comfort in his odor— foul as it must be at the end of a long day on the range, consolidating scattered herds.

"Good Lord, honey," Ty said, chuckling and returning his daughter's hug. He hadn't had one like that from his maturing and independent seventeen-year-old daughter, had thought he might never again, in fact, so by God he was going to enjoy it. He rocked her from side to side. "I declare you're as happy as Rollie to see the likes of your ol' pa an' brother!"

Mack pulled away, smiled up at her father. "Just glad to have you home, that's all."

Ty frowned suddenly. "Say, you're not in trouble, are you?"

"What?"

"You know—buttering me up before your mother tells me—"

Mack placed a fist on her hip and scowled up at him. "Can't a girl be glad to have her pa and big brother home without incurring suspicion?" She walked over to Matt, snapped his hat brim with her index finger, then wrapped her arms around him, as well. "Hi, big brother."

"Hi, sis," Matt said, chuckling and returning his sister's hug while casting his father a curious look. "You musta either got bucked off a horse and hit your head, or you musta been real *worried* about us!"

"Neither, really. I knew you could both handle yourselves. Just . . . you know"—Mack hiked a shoulder and turned to her father gazing down at her incredulously—"just glad to have everybody home, is all. I know I'm growin' up, but I reserve the right to enjoy us all being together at home once in a while. I can still do that for a few more years, can't I?"

Truth was, Mack had been so frightened by the four hard-cases earlier—*little girl* frightened—that on the ride home she could feel little else but the need to see her father again, to have his big, muscular arms wrapped around her. That embarrassing little-girl fear had ridden along inside her ever since she'd climbed up out of the pool, dressed, mounted her horse, and ridden back to the Powderhorn.

It was still inside her though she'd decided not to tell her father about her encounter. It had been almost too frightening to admit to, and she was afraid that her father and brother might ride out after those four obvious cutthroats. She deeply did not want them to do that.

Ty Brannigan, a former lawman, was as capable a man as Mack had ever known, and she was proud to call him her father. Still, she didn't want him and Matt on those curly wolves' trail. There had been something deeply sinister, almost maniacal, about that bunch. She just wanted to forget about them as fast as she could, if forgetting such an encounter were possible.

"For a few more years, honey," Ty said, nudging his daughter's chin with his thumb.

"You are awful late, though," Mack said, frowning up at him. "*Did* you run into trouble out there?" In fact, she had been worried that Ty and Matt might have encountered the same four hardcases that she had.

"I reckon you could say that," Matt said, uncinching his saddle then pulling the saddle off his horse's back with a grunt.

"What does that mean?" Mack asked quickly, worriedly, as Matt slung his saddle over the corral's top slat.

"Rustlers," Ty said, also removing his saddle from his horse's back.

"Oh, just rustlers," MacKenna said, hugging herself as though against a chill. "That's good." She looked down and toed a pebble.

"That's *good*?" Matt said, chuckling incredulously.

Ty set his own saddle atop the corral and turned to Mack again. "It's all taken care of, though, honey. No word to Ma, all right?"

Mack cocked one boot out and gave her father a slant-eyed, admonishing look. "More secrets from Ma, eh?" She shook back her thick black hair and smiled snootily. "I thought you weren't going to keep secrets anymore."

"Shhh!" Ty said, holding a finger to his lips and casting a quick, cautious glance toward the well-lit lodge house. "Just this one more. We ran into a kind of bad situation, and she'd only lose sleep over it."

Indeed, it had been a nasty situation though neither of the percentage girls had been harmed. At least, not physically. To say that they'd been traumatized by all the blood and violence would be an understatement.

It had turned out the girls were from a road ranch not far from where they'd ended up in the cabin with the Blacks and the Barksdales. After hastily burying the dead men together in a temporary single grave where'd they'd remain until Ty could get word to the marshal in Warknife, he and Matt had escorted the girls back home to Ma Doyle's place. A big, cheery, full-hipped and bountiful bosomed woman in her fifties, Ma Doyle promptly ushered the sobbing pair inside to warm baths and much coddling from her and the other girls.

Then Ty and Matt had lit out for home. They'd return for the cattle at first light.

Ty heard the lodge door open and turned to see his wife, Beatriz, and his youngest son, Gregory, step out onto the porch.

"Tynan!" Beatriz called. She turned her head and said

something to Gregory, who at fifteen stood as tall as his mother. The boy hurried down the porch steps and into the yard.

At least, it was hurrying for Gregory, a big kid for his age, with large hands and feet he tended to get mixed up a lot, and a little on the lazy, dreamy, awkward side. Mostly dreamy, Ty wanted to believe. Gregory strode in his heavy-footed way, dragging his boot heels with every step, toward where Ty, MacKenna, and Matt stood in front of the corral.

"I'll tend the hosses for you, Pa, Matt," he said as he approached. He hooked a thumb over his shoulder. "Ma's got supper on the range for you. She says you'd best eat it before she gives it to Rollie."

Ty grabbed the thick-set, rawboned kid's leather-billed immigrant hat off his head and brusquely ran his hand over Gregory's thick mop of wavy sandy hair. "Thanks, son. You been mindin' your p's an' q's?"

"Don't I usually?" Gregory said with a tolerant sigh, grabbing the reins of his father's dun and then Matt's blue roan.

"Thanks, sprout!" Matt gave his younger brother a kick in the seat with the side of his boot.

"Ouch!" Gregory complained but maintained his world-weary air, which he shared with his younger sister, Caroline. Leading the horses toward the corral gate, he said, "Knock it off! I'm doin' you a favor and you're interruptin' my wood carving!"

Gregory's favorite hobby aside from fishing every chance he got was carving animals from ash wood. He'd stay up late into the night, carving by lamplight at the desk in his room, then take till nearly mid-morning to fully awaken. He was not a natural horseman, so Ty mostly kept him at the headquarters, tending the stock, barn, and stable and often sending him on supply runs to town in the ranch's old buckboard that boasted the Powderhorn's brand, a Circle P, burned into the outside of each side panel as well as the tailgate.

Gregory was also becoming a fair to middling blacksmith and farrier.

"Did you get that black mare shod, Gregory?" Ty called as his youngest son lifted the wire latching loop from over the corral's gate post.

"Yep."

"Did she give you any trouble?"

"Nah." Gregory turned a grin to his father and cut his mocking eyes at his brother. "Maggie likes me. She don't like Matt. She tries to kick him every chance she gets!"

"Yeah, well," Matt said, batting his hat against his chap-clad thighs, making dust billow in the moonlight angling over him. "She's the only woman I ever known who wasn't sweet on me." He hooked his arm around MacKenna's neck and lightly, playfully raked his knuckles across the back of her head. "Ain't that right, Miss Cutie-pie?"

MacKenna gave a laughing cry as she bent forward, reaching up to fight off her brother's assault. "This one isn't sweet on you, either, and if you keep that up, I'm gonna kick you as hard as Maggie does—and it won't be in the leg, neither!"

"Ouch!" Matt yowled. "You would, too!"

Ty laughed and started for the house. "Come on, children. I'm so hungry my belly thinks my throat's been cut!"

"Comin', Pa. Come on, sis." Matt wrapped his arm around Mack's shoulders and started striding toward the house. "I'll be your escort this evening, Miss Brannigan."

Mack laughed then wrapped her arm around her brother's waist, rose up to peck his cheek, and leaned into a long, exaggerated, playful stride beside him.

Chuckling, Matt lunged forward to match his sister's stride.

"Tynan," Beatriz said. His tall, lovely, Mexican wife, at

forty her black hair threaded with only a few rare strands of gray piled into a neat bun atop her head, frowned down at him with concern as he stepped up to the bottom of the porch steps. "Why so late?"

"I've been worried sick, Pa!" This was from twelve-year-old Caroline, standing just outside the open lodge door, holding yarn and knitting needles in her hands. She was in her nightgown and her hair shone with a recent brushing. "I thought bad men had come for you again!"

As high-strung as her mother often was, Caroline was the worry wart in the family. Ty supposed she had reason, though. After all, three men holding a grudge had come gunning for Ty only a few short months ago, and both Matt and MacKenna had gotten caught in the whipsaw though thank God no harm had come to either one.

"Not to worry, ladies," Ty said, doffing his hat and feeling his ears burn a little at the lie he was about to tell against his previous resolve to hold nothing back from his wife. "The herd just strayed a little farther west than we figured. Just took a little extra runnin' down is all. Nothin' to worry your pretty heads about."

"I hope that's all," Beatriz said, giving him a skeptical look with her wide, black eyes as Ty climbed the steps and wrapped his arms around her, hugging her close. He held his right arm out to Caroline, who stepped forward to join the hug.

"He's lying, Ma," the girl said, scowling up at her father, eyes cast with skepticism. She'd learned that from her mother, Ty thought. "I can always tell when he's lying."

"You can?" Ty said, chuckling and trying to hide his chagrin as he kissed his wife's cheek. "How can you tell?"

"Your ears turn red."

At twelve, Caroline was too smart for her own good. Or maybe for the rest of the family's own good. She wasn't as pretty as her older sister. She was still a little too skinny and mousy and her light brown hair, which she wore neck-length, was a little too thin and stringy. Her tan eyes, a compromise between Ty's hazel and Beatriz's coffee black, were always serious and often scolding.

Bookish rather than outdoorsy like her sister, Ty thought that one day Caroline might make a good schoolteacher. Those eyes alone would keep the entire class on its best behavior.

She was also smarter than he'd realized, and observant, Ty now realized more than ever. He'd be damned if he didn't feel his ears warming and likely turning brick red just like she'd said!

"Pshaw!" Ty leaned down to peck Caroline's cheek. "You're always thinkin' someone's stackin' the deck—ain't you, my little wildflower?"

"Don't patronize me," Caroline scolded him. "I'm going back to the parlor. One of us is busy." She swung around and headed for the door with the knitting in her hands.

"'One of us is busy,'" MacKenna mocked her younger sister snottily.

"Say, what you're knitting there, half-pint?" Ty called after her.

Caroline stopped just inside the door and turned, holding up the knitting and needles. "Socks for Ivy's baby."

The answer took Ty aback. He cast his surprised gaze to Beatriz, who gave a knowing smile.

"You don't say," he said, shutting his gaze to MacKenna, who'd come up to stand with Matt beside Ty and Beatriz.

MacKenna's cheeks colored in the flickering glow of the lantern light. She turned to her father and said, "I told her she should. I would myself but Caroline's the knitter in the family. I'm all thumbs."

Both daughters' responses had caught Ty off-guard. The "Ivy" Caroline had mentioned was Ivy Battles, the daughter of a neighboring rancher, Jake Battles, who'd been murdered by his son Cass back around the time that the last batch of hardcases, the Parmelee brothers, had ridden into the country to exact revenge on Ty for having sent one of them, Shep Parmelee, to prison for twenty-five years back during Ty's lawdogging days.

But the real reason Ty was surprised by the girls' responses was because Ivy Battles was the young lady who'd lured away from Mack the young horse gentler whom MacKenna had fallen in love with. In fact, young Brandon Waycross, whose real name had turned out to be Brandon Talbot, had gotten Ivy in the family way not long after he'd started romancing MacKenna when he'd been gentling horses for Ty at the Powderhorn compound and living in the bunkhouse.

MacKenna and Ivy had never been friends. Naturally, Ty had figured that Brandon's and Ivy's betrayal of his oldest daughter would have driven an even larger wedge between them. He was impressed, however, that MacKenna had allowed bygones to be bygones and had even considered the needs of the couple's as-yet unborn child.

"Yes," MacKenna said as though reading her father's mind. "I've buried the hatchet. Ivy's alone now without her father and brother."

(In fact, MacKenna had been the one to have killed Cass Battles in self-defense after she and Ty had learned that he had been his father's actual murderer after having tried to pin the blame on Brandon.)

"Of course, she has Brandon, but her family's gone." Mack shrugged a shoulder. "I see no reason not to be neighborly and help her out with the baby if she needs it. And I think she's gonna need it. I know I would."

Matt turned to his sister with a fawning grin. "You know what, sis? You ain't only cuter 'n a speckled pup—you're sweet!" Loudly, he pecked his sister's cheek.

MacKenna snorted and rolled her eyes. And with a mock air of revulsion she used her sleeve to wipe away the kiss.

"Inside, inside!" Beatriz said, hazing her brood toward the door. "Your father and brother must eat and go to bed!"

"No truer words, my dear," Ty said, keeping his arm around Beatriz as they started together toward the door.

The growing thunder of approaching horses stopped him.

He turned back toward the yard striped with pearl moonlight. "Who could that be that this time of night?"

"Probably more hardtails after my pa!" Caroline cried.

CHAPTER 6

"I left my carbine in my saddle boot, Pa," Matt said.

"So did I," Ty said, turning away from the house to walk up to the edge of the porch, gazing off beyond the ranch portal and open main gate. "I left the gate open, too."

Not that trouble couldn't climb through a gate.

"I'll fetch my Winchester," MacKenna said.

She stepped through the house's front door but stopped when a familiar voice yelled, "Hello the Brannigan Ranch!" above the growing rataplan of the thudding hooves.

The muscles that had tightened in Ty's back eased their grip. He glanced over his shoulder at Beatriz standing with an arm drawing the frightened Caroline close against her. "That's Chris," he said.

"*Sí*," Beatriz said, casting her gaze into the darkness just beyond the entrance portal, where the jostling shadows of three horseback riders were beginning to take shape and definition. She recognized Warknife Town Marshal Chris Southern's voice as well as Ty did.

The old lawman was Ty's best friend, but Beatriz had doctored the lawman back to health after Southern had been shot by one of the Paramelee brothers who'd been gunning for Ty. Southern had gotten off relatively easily, all things considered. The same three brothers had murdered

Warknife's only doctor, old Doc Hinkenlooper, when they'd forced the man to ride out to their hideout to dig a bullet out of Shep Parmelee's shoulder.

A bullet that MacKenna had given Shep as a reward for terrorizing her when she'd been riding home one day from Warknife.

Chris Southern had spent a week in bed at the Powderhorn. His wife, Molly, had joined him from their little house in town, for the pair, who'd never had children, were inseparable and still deeply in love despite having been married nearly forty years.

Now the old lawman galloped his steel dust gelding through the ranch portal and into the yard, the moonlight and lamplight from the porch clarifying his lean, grayheaded features set beneath his crisp, gray Stetson. Two men followed him single-file through the portal and then checked their mounts down as they followed Southern up to the porch on which the entire Brannigan family stood in a clump, gazing at the newcomers.

"Chris, you old reprobate," Ty said, "I hope Molly knows you're ridin' around in the country again way after your bedtime!"

When Southern had followed the doctor and the two tough-nut Parmelee brothers who'd kidnapped the sawbones out of his house in Warknife late one night, Molly had not known where her husband had gone. She'd been asleep, and he hadn't wanted to awaken her. When Chris didn't return home because he'd taken that bullet from the Parmelees, after they'd killed Hinkenlooper, the poor woman had been worried sick until Ty had sent Matt and MacKenna to fetch her from town.

"Not to worry, Ty," Chris said, holding up a gloved hand palm out. "My lovely bride knows all about this night's shenanigans." He glanced around at Ty's own wife and brood gathered around him, Beatriz having moved up to stand beside her man, Ty's arm wrapped around her shoulders, her arm curved around his waist.

"What's this—the entire Brannigan family out here on the porch this lovely, moonlit, early fall evening? Where's the fiddle?"

Beatriz smiled. "No fiddle tonight, Marshal Chris. We all gathered here to find out what kept my husband and Matt out on the range so late. They just rode in." She glanced skeptically up at Ty. "I'm not sure I got the entire story. But then, I rarely do." She gave Ty's side a playful pinch.

Southern chuckled then glanced at the two men flanking him—both men decked out in three-piece suits and wearing deputy U.S. marshal's badges pinned to wool vests. One was beefy, gray-mustached and older, probably somewhere in his late fifties, early sixties. The other was lean, clean-shaven, darkly handsome, and much younger than his partner. "Ty, I'd like to introduce you to Deputy U.S. Marshals Tom Calhoun and Adam Parker out of Cheyenne."

Calhoun was the older man. Parker, the younger. Both men rode up even with Southern, one to each side of the town marshal, and nodded and pinched their hat brims.

"Evening, Mister Brannigan," Calhoun said. "Heard a lot about you over the years. I must say I was a little surprised to hear you were ranching out this way. On the other hand, I reckon I stopped hearing about your town taming exploits a good, oh, ten, fifteen years ago."

"Make it twenty," Ty said, "though it does pain me a little to say that. My Lord—where has the time gone? On the other hand, I have a pretty good little brood to show for it." He glanced at his family gathered around and behind him.

"You sure do," Deputy Marshal Adam Parker said. His admiring eyes were on MacKenna, who stood to Ty's left.

In the light of the porch light, Ty glanced at his daughter to see her cheeks color with a blush. Not usually a shrinking violet, she lowered her gaze to the toes of her boots. Ty thought he could hear her heart thudding in her chest, feel her body temperature rise.

"Why, thank you, Marshal Parker." Ty wrapped his free arm around Mack. "This here's my lovely daughter, MacKenna."

Parker quickly doffed his hat and dipped his chin. "A pleasure it is to meet you, Miss Brannigan."

"The pleasure is all mine, Marshal," MacKenna said with one of her trademark winning smiles.

The older marshal, Calhoun, glanced at his younger partner then cast Ty a knowing smile and a wink. Gregory, apparently having seen the way Mack and the young deputy were looking at each other, nudged Mack playfully from behind. MacKenna took one stumbling step forward then turned her head quickly, hair flying, and cast her brother a hard-eyed glare over her shoulder.

Ty introduced the rest of his clan, but Parker's shiny, smitten gaze kept returning to MacKenna. Ty wasn't surprised. MacKenna usually hogged the male attention.

"To what do we owe the honor of the visit?" Ty asked Southern.

"And with that," Beatriz broke in, "the rest of us will retire indoors. Children, let's leave your father and his guests to their business."

"Ah, Ma!" Gregory complained. "Just when it was startin' to get interestin'!"

All three lawmen laughed, as did Ty.

When Beatriz got the bunch ushered inside, Ty said, "Light an' sit a spell, gentlemen. Plenty of chairs up here on the porch."

As Ty went over and arranged four wicker chairs in a circle around a small whicker table on which he and Gregory often played a few games of checkers before retiring to their upstairs bedrooms, the lawmen dismounted, loosened their saddle cinches, and wrapped their reins around the hitch rails fronting the porch. The three dusted the trail dust from their coats and pants and came up and took seats.

When his three guests were seated, Ty sat down, as well, beside Southern, his and Chris's backs to the lodge's front wall. He'd arranged the chairs near the lamp so they wouldn't be conversing in the darkness. He had a feeling something was pressing on the three men's minds.

All three politely doffed and held their hats.

Southern hooked his hat on his bony right knee, grunted around in his chair, and said, "The federals here, Ty, are tracking four killers who robbed an army payroll between Fort Collins and Cheyenne around the middle of last week."

"They killed all six men in the contingent," Calhoun added. "Including the paymaster. Those who the bullets didn't kill, got their throats slit. They died choking on their own blood."

"A really bad bunch, Mr. Brannigan," said Adam Parker.

"Sounds like it," Ty said. "But what do they have to do with me?"

"We tracked 'em into the Bear Paws," Parker said. "Tracked 'em into the camp of two men they killed not far from your range."

"Oh?" Ty said, arching his brows with somber interest.

Southern turned to Ty again, his expression serious, his voice low. "Dad Clawson and Pete Driscoll."

"Oh, hell!" Ty said. "I just saw those boys two days ago working a herd over by Lone Squaw Creek. I stopped and had a cup of coffee with 'em. Good men, both."

"They were killed near the creek last night," Calhoun said. "Shot. Throats slit. Horses and grub sacks stolen. Bodies left to the crows and turkey buzzards," the older lawman added distastefully.

Adam Parker turned his hat in his hands before him, worrying the brim. "That throat slitting is the trademark of

Smilin' Doc Ford, a cold-blooded, knife-wielding pistolero from these very mountains."

"I've heard his story," Ty said. "Very bad sort."

"He runs with three others just as bad as him. One's a woman," Parker added.

"Zenobia Sparrow," Calhoun said. "'Zena' for short. She has paper on her. They all do. The other two men in the bunch are a big full-blooded Arapaho named Bear and a white man called Hungry Jack Mercer. Ford, Bear, and Hungry Jack met in prison."

"The men they killed last night were not—" Parker cut himself abruptly off when the lodge door scraped open.

Ty turned to see MacKenna step out onto the porch carrying a wooden tray on which sat a speckled black coffee pot and four white mugs.

"Oh, Miss Brannigan!" Parker rose so quickly from his chair that he nearly fell back into it.

"Oh, don't get up," MacKenna said. "We Brannigans don't hold with formalities out here, Marshal Parker." She smiled at the young marshal beaming down at her from a good height—maybe six-one or so, Ty thought—then glanced at her father. "Do we, Pa?"

When Parker had gained his feet, the bigger, older man, Calhoun, pushed his considerable bulk up out of his own chair, glancing from Parker to MacKenna then back again, a knowing smile growing on his gray-mustached mouth. Ty vaguely noted the man was breathing heavily from the effort of heaving himself out of his chair.

"No, we certainly do not."

"Well, if they're gonna stand, I'm gonna stand," said Marshal Southern, also gaining his feet, chuckling dryly, his old knees creaking with the effort.

"Please don't, Marshal!" MacKenna scolded him, setting the tray down on the whicker table ringed by the four chairs.

Ty smiled at his lovely daughter, whose lustrous hair

shone with a brushing she must have just given it. Steel hoops dangled from her ears. She'd made quite an impression on young Parker. The deputy U.S. marshal couldn't take his eyes off her. He looked as though he wanted to say something but couldn't find the words. MacKenna had that effect on men, Ty had noticed before. It was happening more and more lately. Like her mother at that age, she was a raving beauty: it was hard for a man to pull his gaze from her.

Ty felt conflicting emotions on the subject. Both proud and protective.

Straightening and glancing from Parker to Calhoun, MacKenna said, "Does anyone take cream or sugar?"

"Coal . . . coal-black for me, Miss Brannigan," Parker said, having a little trouble finding his voice. His mouth looked a little stiff, making it hard for him to speak.

"Me, too," Calhoun said.

"Please, Deputy Parker, it's MacKenna. Like I said, we Brannigans don't hold with formalities out here."

Parker smiled and nodded once, slowly. "Only if you'll call me Adam."

"All right," Mack said, turning toward the door then glancing over her shoulder at the young man, her dark eyes glinting in the lantern light. Huskily, she said, "Adam it is. If you need anything else, let me know."

She winked then strode to the door, opened it, cast the gaping deputy another ravishing smile, and flounced through the door and into the lodge, drawing the door closed behind her.

That little coquette, Ty thought. *She's gonna make that boy want to cut his own arm off with a rusty saw!* He chuckled to himself at the notion.

Southern and Calhoun sagged back down into their chairs.

Calhoun glanced up at his younger partner, who was still standing, staring at the door. "Uh . . . you can sit down now,

Marshal Parker. The lady's gone." He gave Parker's arm a playful swat with his hat.

Marshal Southern slapped his thigh, wheezing out a delighted laugh.

Young Parker flushed and sat down. He cleared his throat and said, "You have a right pretty daughter, there, Mister Brannigan."

"I've been told," Ty said.

"You must be very proud."

"As well as armed," Ty said, patting the gun and holster still thonged on his right thigh.

Again, Southern laughed. Calhoun snorted.

Again, Parker blushed.

Quickly composing himself and picking up his coffee cup, Parker said, "Now . . . um . . . what was I saying before . . . ?"

"We were so rudely interrupted?" Southern said with another bright-eyed, jeering look at the younger lawman.

Having none of the razzing, Parker sipped his steaming mud then said, "Ah, yes, I remember. I was saying that the two men this Smilin' Doc Ford's bunch killed near here were not the first men they killed since murdering the soldiers and stealing the payroll money."

Calhoun blew ripples on his own coffee. "They killed a couple of jaspers not far from Cheyenne and butchered a cow. They stayed the night at the couples' farm before moving on in the morning, leaving most of what was left of the cow on the spit they'd cooked it on."

"Shot them both, slit their throats," Parker added. "We lost their trail along Lone Squaw Creek. For the life of us, we tried to pick it back up and just couldn't find it. We're thinking they must have ridden *up* the creek, through the water, thus throwing off anyone who might be on their trail."

Calhoun said, "So we rode to town to visit with Marshal Southern about possibly finding a good tracker, one who knows the area and might be able to pick up those killers' trail again or at least help us find a way through the peaks to the north that they might have taken. As I said, Ford is from here, so he knows the country well."

"We think they're headed for Montana," Parker said. "That's where they usually hole up after a robbery, cooling their heels and planning the next one."

"I think I can help." Mack's voice startled Ty.

He turned quickly to see his daughter standing in the open lodge door, gazing gravely at the four men over whom the lantern shunted light and shadows.

"Earlier . . . I saw them," Mack added thinly. "I saw the route they took to the northwest." She turned to her father.

Ty would be damned if Mack didn't have a pale, wide-eyed, haunted look. He couldn't remember her with such an expression before. Not even when she was younger and had been awakened by a nightmare.

She turned to Adam Parker and said in that same thin, low voice, "They're really bad, aren't they?" She narrowed her eyes. "I mean, really, really *bad*."

CHAPTER 7

"You *saw* those killers, Mack?" Ty asked.

"I think I did, Pa." MacKenna gave an involuntary shudder, remembering the four riders ogling her from the ridge. She glanced from Calhoun to Parker. "Three men and a woman? A flaxen-haired woman? One of the men looked like an Indian. Full blood."

Parker and Calhoun shared an interested look.

"That's them," Calhoun said.

"Where'd you see them, Mack?" Marshal Southern asked.

"Along Lone Squaw Creek," Mack said. "Near the falls."

Ty frowned. "What falls?"

Mack shrugged. "I don't know its name. Or if it even has a name. I found it a few years ago by following the creek upstream. It's not an easy place to get to if you don't follow the stream starting at Dutchman's Gulch, but when I explored a little more, I found a way."

Marshal Southern smiled. "Young lady, you know that country better than I do, and I ranched out there for dang near twenty years!"

"She knows it better than I do," Ty said, also smiling at his daughter wistfully. "I didn't know there was a falls on Lone Squaw Creek." He frowned suddenly, concerned.

"How good a look did you get at those killers, Mack? Or, more important, how good a look did they get of you?"

MacKenna felt heat rise in her cheeks. She shook her head, hating herself for lying but not wanting to tell these men that she'd been swimming naked in the pool. Not wanting to tell her father how close she had come to death. It was hard for her to even think about that part, much less talk about it.

"Not sure they saw me," she said quickly, thinly, feeling as silly as a fibbing schoolgirl. "I don't think so, anyway. I got a pretty good look at them, though, when they rode past the canyon." She looked from Parker to Calhoun. "They had the look of killers about them. I saw that right away. And they were leading two packhorses."

"Likely the cowpunchers' mounts," Deputy Parker said. "Using them to haul the loot. They played out a couple of other stolen mounts south of here, before they entered the Bear Paws."

"Could you direct these men to that canyon, Mack?" Marshal Southern asked. "Where you saw those four killers."

MacKenna frowned, pondering the question. Finally, she shook her head. "I don't think so. It's very broken country. I sort of had to feel my way through it to the canyon the first several times I rode in there from the west. I don't think I could give directions. I'd have to show you."

She glanced at her father.

Ty turned to Calhoun. "Once I pick up their trail, I'll likely have a good idea which trail they're taking through the northern ridges and can direct you from there."

"We'd appreciate that, Mister Brannigan," Parker said. He looked at MacKenna and nodded. "Appreciate your help, as well, Miss Brannigan."

MacKenna shook her head. "Uh-uh. Nope. What'd I tell

you? It's MacKenna. If I decide I like you well enough, I might even let you call me Mack."

Parker grinned.

The other men including Ty smiled. He reflected how much MacKenna was like her mother had been when Ty had first met the beautiful Beatriz in her father's bank in Warknife. The young Mexican woman had been only nineteen years old and working as an accountant after several years of schooling in Mexico City. Beatriz had had her daughter's expressive eyes, ravishing smile, and subtle, playful coquetry that had made a man want to chew his knuckles.

The old saw had it right. The apple didn't fall far from the tree.

Ty turned to Parker and Calhoun. "You gentlemen are welcome to spend the night. I have that little bunkhouse over there. It's outfitted for hands though I hired on very rarely, as needed. Mack and her brother have grown up and proven to be all the help I need. So far, I've kept my holdings small enough to be manageable." He turned to Mack. "I'm just hoping one of my kids will stick around and run the place after I'm gone."

He was reflecting on his earlier reflection regarding the unspoken plans of his oldest boy. Now he found himself wondering, however briefly and vaguely, about what Mack would do once she was married. He'd always hoped she'd marry the son of a neighboring rancher or maybe a businessman's son in town, and that she'd stick around. Maybe live here at the Powderhorn with her family, in which case he'd add another lodge to the place, one in which his grandchildren would grow up.

Now, however, Ty was beginning to doubt his earlier assumptions. Mack might very well marry a man like young Parker here, not a stockman at all, and live away. Ty wondered with a building uneasiness what would become of the Powderhorn in a few years.

Would it continue after he was six feet under?

Anyway, he was glad he had the bunkhouse. It might just come in handy someday, as it would tonight.

"I second that, Mister Brannigan. MacKenna. We'd appreciate your help." Calhoun sat back in his chair, covering his mouth and yawning. "Been a long day. I reckon Adam and I'd best accept your hospitality and turn in. We'd best get an early start in the morning."

"We'll outfit you with Powderhorn mounts," Ty said. "They'll get you farther than those livery nags you rode in on."

"We'd appreciate that, too," said Marshal Parker.

"With that," Chris Southern said, placing both arthritic hands on his chair arms and hoisting his lean frame up out of the chair, "I'll bid you all adieu. Molly will be worried if I dally." He looked at Ty and then at MacKenna. "I, too, appreciate your help. Both of you." He narrowed his eyes at Ty. "Stay safe out there. Don't take any chances."

"I don't intend to." Ty smiled. "My lawdogging days are over. As soon as I know I have these men on the right route through the northern peaks, Mack and I will turn tail and head for home."

"I wouldn't have it any other way," Calhoun said, and heaved his own considerable bulk up out of the chair with effort, his cheeks turning red. "When it comes to tangling with killers—that's what Adam and I get paid to do."

He glanced at his younger partner and gave a self-assured smile.

Parker returned the expression in kind.

"I'll trail your livery mounts back to town, Gentleman," Marshal Southern said. "Good night."

* * *

The men and MacKenna said good night, and Mack's father went into the kitchen and sat down to his supper at long last. Matt had eaten his meal and gone to bed.

Mack headed to bed, too, but instead of sleeping she tossed and turned.

Turned and tossed . . .

Tossed and turned.

Finally, with a disgusted sigh, she punched her pillow, rolled onto her back, and stared up at the heavy-beamed ceiling. Why on earth couldn't she sleep? Just an hour ago she'd been dead-dog-tired.

But she knew why she couldn't sleep.

An hour ago, she hadn't yet met the handsome young deputy U.S. marshal, Adam Parker. She dug her upper teeth into her lower lip and smiled up at the ceiling, not seeing the ceiling but the face of the blue-eyed, darkly handsome young lawman.

That's what . . . or who . . . was making her restless and sleepless.

He'd looked so handsome and official in his three-piece suit with the gold-washed chain of his timepiece sagging over his chocolate brown leather vest between the lapels of his brown, broadcloth jacket. He wore a big, bone-gripped Colt in the cross-draw position on his left hip. Like the man himself, the Colt looked big and official. Mack wondered how good he was at wielding it.

She smiled and let out a devilish, delighted schoolgirl snicker then quickly covered her mouth with her hand, cheeks warming with shame.

She reflected on the fact that the reason she couldn't sleep was because she was happy. Excited. Separately or together, those had been foreign emotions to her for the past year and a half. Ever since the bewitching young horse gentler, Brandon Waycross who had turned out to be Brandon Talbot, had broken her heart.

Brandon had used the Waycross alias because he'd been the youngest boy in a bank-robbing family, and he'd been wanted by the law though he'd since convinced Mack's father, Marshal Southern, and the local prosecuting attorney that he'd only held the horses for his father and older brothers. Beyond that, he hadn't participated in any of his family's bank robberies. The charges against him had been dropped, and now he was living out at the neighboring Anchor Ranch with the young woman he'd married recently—Ivy Battles.

The young woman he'd betrayed MacKenna with after having professed his love to her.

MacKenna had tumbled for young Brandon, who'd had such an easy smile and such a mysteriously gentle and affective way with horses that whatever horse he was currently working with would follow him around the corral and even the ranch yard as though unwilling to break the connection. That had been how MacKenna had felt, too.

Even after he'd betrayed her with Ivy. Had made a baby with Ivy.

Mack had hated herself for feeling that way. Her heart still ached for a young man who'd gotten another girl in the family way.

That's why she'd felt neither happy nor excited in a long time. Too long of a time for a young woman her age, at the cusp of turning eighteen.

Now she felt both of those things together, and they were keeping her from sleeping. Her body felt warm. Her nerves seemed to be writhing around just beneath her skin.

Oh, well. No use fighting it.

She threw back her covers and dropped her feet over the side of the bed, poked each into a soft, wool-lined, elk skin slipper she'd sewn herself over the previous long, Bear Paw Mountain winter. It was when the Brannigans made most of their own clothes—over the winter, using skins and furs from cattle or game they'd killed the previous summer.

Mack did not bother changing out of her nightgown. She grabbed her homemade bearskin coat, which she'd made from the skin of a bear her father had shot two winters ago and shrugged into it. The coat hung down to just below her knees. She'd likely need the heavy garment because it was getting late in the year and she'd felt a knife edge to the breeze earlier, when she'd been out on the porch with the lawmen and her father.

With Adam Parker.

She snickered again, dug her hair out from beneath the coat's collar, and tossed it down her back. She plucked her Stetson off a wall peg and set it on her head. Like most cow punchers, she never went anywhere without her hat. She strode to the door, and a few seconds later she was dropping quietly down the night-dark stairs that creaked softly beneath her tread, and then she quietly opened the lodge's front door, stepped out, and drew the door closed behind her.

The night was very dark but the burnt-orange moon, illuminating the scalloped edges of clouds around it as it sank in the west, cast enough light that she could see her way down the porch steps, and crossed the yard to the horse corral.

She leaned forward against the top rail of the corral, casting her gaze to her family's beloved remuda. Several of the horses were standing, asleep on their feet, while others lay on their sides or with their legs tucked beneath them, snoots on the ground before them, like dogs. MacKenna's presence hardly made them stir. One switched its tail in friendly greeting, but they were all so accustomed to the girl—even felt a kinship with her, she wanted to believe—that they remained as they'd been, asleep or maybe one-quarter awake, mostly under the sandman's influence.

At peace in their worlds.

Mack sighed, reached up to run her hands through her hair, glanced at the sky awash with glittering stars. She glanced at the small, low, shake-shingled bunkhouse sitting to the right of the corral. She glanced away quickly, feeling a little embarrassed about wondering what the young marshal looked like when he slept. She smiled. She kept thinking of him as young, but she guessed he was a good seven or eight years older than she. Still, she did think of him as young.

Good Lord—she'd just met the man!

She frowned suddenly, peering into the shadows beyond the bunkhouse. She'd heard something. Pricking her ears, she listened intently. The sounds grew gradually until she recognized them as footsteps. Someone was walking toward her from the far side of the ranch yard.

MacKenna stared toward the loudening footsteps. She did not feel afraid. Not even after what had happened earlier at the falls. The footsteps had a casualness about them—a man simply out taking a leisurely stroll.

A man who couldn't sleep, perhaps?

MacKenna's heart quickened a little as, gazing into the shadows, she watched a man-shaped figure gradually take definition, parts of him—a cheek, his neck, a bending knee—limned by stray strands of star- and moonlight. The man was tall and lean, and he wore a high-crowned Stetson not unlike the hat her father always wore.

Mack's heart quickened a little more.

It was Deputy Parker.

She knew it even before he approached from a hundred feet away and she could see him more clearly. He was clad in only red longhandles, broadcloth coat, boots, and hat. As he began angling toward the bunkhouse, he lifted his hand to his mouth. The coal of a cigarette glowed as he drew on it. Pale smoke billowed out in the darkness around his head.

He tossed away the quirley. It sparked as it struck the

ground with a soft thud and rolled. When he'd thrown the cigarette, he'd turned his head toward the corral. He stopped abruptly.

Good, she thought.

He'd seen her. She wasn't sure he would in the near darkness, and she did not want to call out. Not only might his partner in the bunkhouse or her slumbering family in the lodge house overhear, but she did not want to seem bold.

Or maybe she didn't want to seem so careless with her heart. After all, it had been so recently broken.

The young lawman stood gazing toward her for another couple of seconds then started walking toward the corral in the slow, easy way he'd been walking a minute ago. He walked up along the front of the corral, running his hand along the top rail, bouncing it playfully. He stopped fifty feet away from MacKenna, canted his head to one side—the shadow of his hat brim hid his face—and said softly, "Miss Brannigan? That you?"

"Nope." Shaking her head, MacKenna stepped back away from the corral and turned to face the young deputy, crossing her arms on her chest.

He stepped forward into a strand of moonlight and she saw the white line of his teeth as he grinned. "MacKenna."

"That wasn't so hard, now, was it?"

She waited until he was closer then said, "What're you doing up so late? Didn't you hear your partner? We'll be pulling out bright and early."

"What about you?"

"What about me?"

"Didn't you hear my partner? We'll be pullin' out bright an' early."

MacKenna shrugged. "The sandman was bein' right stingy with his sand tonight."

"Yeah," Deputy Parker said with a sigh. "Me, too. Funny, I usually sleep like a log."

"Maybe it's the unfamiliar bed."

"Could be. Don't think so."

"Oh?"

"What about you? Don't you usually sleep like a log, MacKenna?"

"Do I seem like a girl who usually sleeps like a log?"

"You do," Deputy Parker said, crooking a half-smile and canting his head to the other side.

"Oh? How so?"

"No bags under the eyes."

"Oh."

"Usually, girls who don't sleep got bags under their eyes, and grouchy dispositions." The deputy paused, dropped his voice and made it softer. "They're not half as beautiful as you."

She flushed at the compliment, tried to ignore it. "Sounds like you've had plenty of experience with girls with bags under their eyes and grouchy dispositions, Deputy."

"Oh, I have."

"I'm sorry."

"Don't be. Having met you makes up for all of them."

MacKenna narrowed one eye and wagged an admonishing finger at him. "You, sir, are a charmer."

"I'm not usually. I can't believe I just said what I did. I'm usually kinda shy and tongue-tied around women. Especially beautiful women. See? There I go again. I'm not usually that bold."

"Hmm. I'm beginning to wonder."

The young deputy took one step forward, pitched his voice even lower. "I'm glad you'll be riding with us tomorrow."

"Me, too." MacKenna stepped back up to the corral, folded her arms on the top slat, and glanced over her shoulder at the handsome young man. "Pretty country out that way."

"Prettier with you in it."

"There you go again."

He stepped up to the corral beside her, only a few inches away, and crossed his own arms on the top rail. "Tell me . . . is there a young man in your life?"

"Not anymore there's not."

"Recently?"

"Sort of."

"What happened?"

MacKenna shook her head. "I don't want to talk about him. I haven't thought about him at all tonight, and that's a record for me."

"He broke your heart."

Again, Mack shook her head. "Not gonna talk about it."

"Can I steal a kiss?"

"Already?" MacKenna gave a husky chuckle. "No." She turned her head forward then turned back to him, grabbed his longhandle top by the front, pulled him toward her, and kissed him smack on the mouth.

Chapter 8

Ty had far too keen a sense of hearing not to have heard MacKenna leave the house earlier. He hadn't considered intervening. Mack had too good a head on her shoulders to be up to mischief. At least, any mischief that might get her in trouble or compromise her honor.

He'd also heard her return and had noted a little more spring in her step than in the steps she'd taken leaving the house and walking down the stairs. Ty smiled. So, the girl was smitten. She was nearly eighteen. She had a right to be smitten.

Ty was glad for her, especially after her rude awakening to male betrayal after Brandon Talbot had stepped out on her with Ivy Battles. It was time she be distracted by another young man, and Adam Parker seemed like a good sort to Ty, whose eye had gotten especially critical after Mack had started becoming a woman.

Besides, she was no longer the innocent girl she'd been when she'd been following the handsome young horse gentler around the breaking corral, when Brandon had been living in the bunkhouse and gentling a string of raw horses for Ty.

She was stronger now. Wiser. She'd watch her step with young Marshal Parker.

When he'd heard her return to her room, easing her door shut with a soft click, Ty fell asleep. But it was an uneasy sleep. He woke every half hour or so, rolled over, fell into another light sleep only to be awakened again by his own mind a half hour to forty-five minutes later. He rolled over once more . . . and then again . . . until, during another such uneasy awakening, he glanced out the window and saw the gray smudge of early dawn in the east.

Outside, the birds were singing.

Must be four-thirty or so. He'd get up and start the coffee. He threw his covers back and started to rise but stopped when Beatriz placed her hand on his arm.

"Tynan?" she said, her voice throaty from sleep.

He lay back down, rolled toward her, spooned his big body against hers, and nuzzled her warm, smooth neck. "*Sí*, my darling one. Did I wake you?"

She squeezed his arm. "Why couldn't you sleep?"

"Ah, hell," Ty said. "I kept you awake, didn't I?"

"Answer the question, *mi amore*." Beatriz rolled to face him. "If it's the baby, I have decided I have enough children. It was a whim."

Ty frowned. "The bab—oh!"

He'd almost forgotten that several months back Beatriz had told him that she'd wanted another child. It was during the previous trouble with the Parmelee brothers and Jake Battles' murder, and Ty had been wounded in the arm. That had made Beatriz more aware of his mortality. Her own mortality, just having turned forty, had been weighing heavy on her, too. She'd been feeling old, and she'd thought that having another baby inside her might make her feel young again.

Now her frown deepened, and her Mexican dark eyes grew darker with Latin anger. "You forgot my request, mi amore?"

"No, no, no, I didn't really forget it," Ty said, accustomed to moving quickly into reconciliatory territory. He'd been married to this fiery Latina for over twenty years, after all. He was accustomed to it. "I just hadn't thought about it in a while, is all. Too many other things on my mind. You've decided you don't want another child, love?"

"*Sí.* I thought maybe that was what was making you feel restless." Beatriz sat up, adjusting her pillows then resting back against them, against the large, ornate, Mexican-style headboard Ty had carved right after they'd been married. "It was not?"

Ty shook his head, sitting back against his own pillows. "No."

"Was it MacKenna?"

Ty glanced at her, curious.

"She went out last night. When I went downstairs for water, I heard her talking with that young marshal." Beatriz placed her hand on his shoulder. "Don't worry—they only talked. Mostly," she added with a wry half smile and a wink.

"Oh, hell—I know they only talked. Mostly." Ty snorted. "She's fiery like her momma but, not unlike her momma, she's not quick to give up her heart."

"She was with Brandon."

"She was a different girl with Brandon. Younger. She's wiser now."

"In some ways, it's a pity."

"That's men for you," Ty said.

Again, Beatriz placed her hand on his shoulder and rolled to face him once more. "It wasn't you. You never betrayed me. You would never betray me." She gave a wan smile. "You only kept a former lover of yours from me."

She meant Devon Hayes, a woman Ty had loved and had even planned to marry back in Kansas until she'd abandoned him only days before they would have been hitched. Devon had turned up in Warknife recently, taking part ownership in a locally famous watering hole, the Longhorn Saloon. Partly, she'd come because she knew Ty ranched in the area and part of her had wanted to refire that old flame again.

Ty had quickly changed her mind, however. Ty and his family, that was, after Devon had come to know them all and see what a happy bunch they all were.

"Now, dearest," Ty said, "you know exactly why—"

Suddenly, Beatriz smiled. She'd only been trying to get his goat. He'd convinced her months ago there'd been nothing duplicitous in his not having told her about Devon. When Ty had come to Wyoming soon after Devon had abandoned him for a life on the stage, he'd wanted to wipe the slate clean. Start fresh. He'd thought little of Devon after she'd so abruptly left, and that was why he'd never even considered telling Beatriz about her.

That was Beatriz, though. She liked to get his goat once in a while. To keep him in line. That was all right with him. He'd been a hard-nosed town tamer for many years, and the town marshal of Warknife for a few years before he'd married Beatriz. After he had married, however, he'd realized that even hard-nosed town tamers needed to be kept in line.

His lovely Beatriz was just the woman to do it. He was grateful to her. He'd once been hard and rough, too swaggering and cocky. She'd smoothed down most of those hard plains, had made him a better husband and father. A better man.

"Tell me now," Beatriz prodded him once more. "Why couldn't you sleep?"

Ty stared off across the room, which was mostly brown mist and uncertain shapes at this early hour. He frowned, pondering. He gave a dry chuckle, wagged his head. "I'm not sure I can even quite put my finger on it. I guess it's Matt . . . and MacKenna, too. After I saw her so charmed with the young lawman, and being so charming—"

"I told you not to worry about her."

Ty turned to Beatriz, placed his hand on her leg. "I'm not

worried about her. I'm not worried about Matt, either. He'll make a helluva man. Already has, in fact."

He had no intention of telling Beatriz about the dustup earlier in which Matt had more than proved his worth in a fight, something that made Ty proud while at the same time scaring the heck out of him. Partly, the fear came from having realized his son was not whom he'd thought he was and might not match the future Ty had mapped out for him—at least, the one he'd mapped out in his own mind.

Keeping his befuddled gaze on his wife's chocolate eyes that were beginning to reflect a little of the wan gray light filtering through the two east-facing windows, Ty said, "I feel like I'm losing my hold on them."

It was Beatriz's turn to frown. She cut it with an ironic half smile. "Your hold on them? What hold did you think you have on either of them? They are *our* children, after all, mi amore." She leaned over to kiss his cheek. "Yours and mine. What hold do you think anyone can have on *them*? Did you not leave your father's mountains to fight the Indians and to be a lawman? Did I not stray from my father's wishes to marry a rich businessman? Instead, I wedded a roughhewn gringo lawman who carried a big gun and a rakish smile. *Dios mio!*"

"That's the problem with you," Ty said, hooking his own smile. "You're smarter than me. I should have figured that one out myself."

"In what way do you think you are losing your so-called *hold* on Matt and MacKenna?"

"I just realized today that Matt might not be as in love with ranching as I thought he was."

"No, you are correct, mi amore." Again, Beatriz smiled, this time ironically. "He is too enamored of his father's legendary past. He wants a little taste of the man you were before you married and settled down. You see, he, like you, has a wild streak. I have long thought he might have to leave here some day to go out and make his own way in the world and then possibly return later—after he's proven himself to be the man his father once was. A *legend*."

Ty winced. "Most legends die young. I almost died young. Several times. And now I've got men comin' after me from time to time, endangering my family."

"That is what is so hard about being a parent—is it not, Tynan?"

"What is?"

"Living under the illusion at least while your children are young that you have control of their lives. And then learning, once they've grown older and have become men and women of their own, how little control you *really* have." Beatriz reached up to place a gentle hand on his cheek. "Don't lose sleep over it, my love. It is the way of the world."

Ty sighed. "And MacKenna . . ."

"*Sí*, what about MacKenna?"

"She might be gone someday, too."

"*Sí*." Beatriz smiled and nodded again sagely. "I told you she is like me." Again, Beatriz kissed his cheek, rubbed it in with her finger. "We have to let them go, you and me. It is the struggle."

"Struggle," Ty said. "Good word for it."

She patted his shoulder. "You'd best get up now, my love. It's getting late. Your tracking skills are required."

"Right." Again, Ty tossed the covers back. He dropped his feet to the floor.

Beatriz grabbed his arm and scuttled forward against his back to whisper into his ear, "You bring her home safely to me, Tynan. You bring yourself home safely to me, too. I understand your and MacKenna's need to help the lawmen. But you do as I say." She kissed his ear then tugged on the lobe a little, enough to make it hurt.

Ty smiled over his shoulder at her. "See there? You're guilty of it, too."

Beatriz frowned. "*¿Qué es que?*" What's that?

"The illusion of control." He winked, kissed her lips. "Don't worry. I'll do my best."

Feeling easier about the situation than he had before, he rose. He knew his beloved was right—he had to let go sooner or later.

Sooner or later.

Let's make it later.

Dressing, he smiled to himself.

CHAPTER 9

"You and the old man took down all seven men, eh?" Warknife Town Marshal Chris Southern asked Matt the next morning around nine a.m. in Southern's little Warknife office and jailhouse.

"Mmm," Matt said as he sat at the marshal's desk, writing out an affidavit attesting to what had occurred at the old trapper's cabin the previous evening.

Just after his father and MacKenna had ridden out with the deputy U.S. marshals, Matt had, as his father had instructed, ridden back to the trapper's cabin to fetch their stolen beeves. After Ty and Matt had returned the two frightened doves to the road ranch the night before, it had been too late to fetch the stolen cattle. Never a good idea to herd cattle, especially frightened cattle, in the dark.

After hearing all that gunfire, the cattle were indeed frightened.

So, early this morning Matt had hazed the herd back onto Powderhorn graze then following his father's further instructions, rode to Warknife to do what he was doing—writing out the affidavit explaining the dustup out at the trapper's cabin. His father had taken Chris Southern aside the previous night and briefly told him what had happened, so Matt's appearance in town this morning, to tie up all loose legal ends, had been expected.

"You threw down on them long-ropers, too, eh, Matt?" Sitting on the other side of the desk from Matt, Southern leaned forward suddenly and slammed a folded newspaper down loudly, then yowled a curse when the fly he'd targeted buzzed off into the shadows around the four jail cages at the back of the room, all empty and with doors standing open. Southern rarely held prisoners during the week. He might have been old, but he and his two capable deputies did a good job of keeping the town's proverbial wolf on its leash.

He'd asked the question regarding the demise of the rustlers in a skeptical tone.

Matt was trying to concentrate on what he was writing with the ink pen, so he responded with only another "Mmm."

Again, the unadorned reply did not seem to satisfy the marshal.

Matt felt the old man's scowling gaze on him as, chewing his bottom lip, he focused on the last sentence he was writing.

"*Both* of you? *You*, too? You accounted for turning a couple of those scoundrels toe down, as well? Not just your father?"

With a sigh of relief to be done with the narrative he'd written out in blue-black ink—he was far more comfortable in a saddle wielding a lariat than he was sitting at a desk with a pen in his hand—Matt signed his name at the bottom of the paper then returned the pen to its tray with its accompanying scrolled silver ink bottle. He glanced across the desk at the old marshal and said, "I wouldn't say it if it wasn't true, Marshal Southern. Pa told me to tell it just like it happened, and I did."

Southern grimaced and waved a hand in front of his face as though to dismiss his own skepticism like one of the late-summer bluebottle flies flitting about the room. "Oh, I know, I know. I'm not sayin' you'd lie about such a thing. I didn't mean that. It's just that—boy, oh boy, you must be darn near as good as your pa with your shootin' irons! Let me see that." Southern reached across the desk with one knobby, arthritic, red hand, and slid the affidavit toward him and onto his coffee-stained blotter. He quickly read the three-quarter-page report, clucked, shook his head, and then signed his own name below where Matt had signed his and labeled himself a "witness."

"Surely impressive," Southern said, setting the paper back down on the blotter. "I'll send this over to the county prosecutor. He'll likely need to seat a coroner's jury, and you and your pa will have to come to town to testify. Just to make it all legal, you understand. Ty knows that part like the back of his hand."

Matt ran a hand through his longish hair then picked up his Stetson off the marshal's desk and set it on his head and adjusted it for the angle he liked. "That's pretty much how Pa explained it. These days everything's gotta be all official." He snorted a laugh. "If old Mister Battles, God rest his colicky soul, was still alive and had run those men down, they'd be low-hanging fruit on the nearest cottonwood."

"Yes, they would," Southern said. "Nothin' legal about it but it was a lot simpler for me!" He slapped his hand down on his desk and crowed a laugh. He studied Matt with a funny little smile on his face, suddenly pensive. "The apple don't fall far from the tree—does it, boy?"

Matt rose, frowning. "What's that, Marshal?"

"You must've picked up your pa's talents with firearms. Ty told me he'd been teaching you and MacKenna how to defend yourselves with carbines and pistols. But you must have some natural talent, as well." Southern eyed the Colt .44 Matt wore tied down on his right thigh. "Don't let it go to your head."

"Oh, I won't, Marshal Southern."

"What do you wear that thing for, anyways? Why don't

you leave it at home? The carbine's good enough for rustlers and coyotes."

Matt patted his holster. "I don't know. Pa always wears his, so I always wear mine. No tellin' who you're gonna run into."

"Your pa wears his because, as having been a lawman of more than a little renown, he occasionally attracts trouble." Southern squinted up at the tall, lean, handsome young man gravely. He slowly shook his head. "You don't have that history. You don't *want* that history. The only thing about you that could attract trouble is wearing that gun to town."

Matt frowned down at the gun, closed his hand over the grips once more, and slipped the piece from the leather. He twirled it twice on his finger then dropped it smoothly back down into the holster. "The way I see it, this hogleg keeps folks from messin' with me." He grinned. "I haven't been messed with lately, is all I'm sayin'."

Southern shook his head again as he gazed darkly up at the young man. "Don't romanticize it, boy."

"Don't romanticize what?"

"Killin'. Gun work."

"Oh, I don't, Marshal Southern," Matt said, meaning it. At least, he thought he'd meant it. "Really."

Or did he romanticize it? He wasn't sure. All he really knew was that he liked how he felt walking and riding around with the pistol on his leg. He liked how he'd taught himself to twirl it and toss it. He supposed he felt tougher, more confident with the gun than without it, though his father had told him back when Ty had first been teaching Matt and MacKenna how to shoot, that guns did not make you tougher, and they shouldn't make you more confident.

They were just tools, like any other tool. You used them only when you needed them. Otherwise, you did everything you could to avoid having to use them. Until you absolutely had to use them, you ignored the fact that you were carrying them in the same way you ignored carrying a hammer or a saw.

Matt supposed wearing the impressive-looking hogleg made him look older than his nineteen-going-on-twenty years. That was important to him, though he'd rarely reflected on it consciously. Also, the hogleg as well as the carbine in his saddle boot made him feel more like his pa, a man who he also, mostly unconsciously or maybe half-consciously, idolized for his storied, town-taming past.

For the colorful life he'd lived before he'd turned to ranching.

"Well, if you'll excuse me, Marshal," Matt said. "I reckon I'd best get back to the ranch. Double the work to do now that Pa and MacKenna are off chasing those payroll thieves."

"Good day to you, Matt. Thanks for comin' in. Say hi to your mother for me." Southern leaned back in his chair and patted his lower chest. "I can't thank her enough—well, her and Devon Hayes, I should say—for diggin' that bullet out of my ornery old hide. They sure did a good job. I was only laid up for a month or so. Feel good as new, now." He grinned. "Molly an' me even started dancin' again at the old dance hall down by the river!" Again, he slapped his desk and wheezed a laugh.

"Good to hear, Marshal," Matt said, chuckling as he headed for the door. "Good to hear." He opened the door. "I'll tell ma you said hey." With that, he went out and drew the door closed behind him.

Matt looked up and down the busy main street, squinting against the dust that a mule team pulling a lumber dray had just kicked up. He didn't get to town alone very often. Gregory usually drove the supply wagon to town. Matt was pretty much confined to either the headquarters or the range around it. Truth be told, life could get pretty dull on a ranch. He enjoyed being in town, could feel the electricity of the hubbub in the air.

He wished he could stay longer.

Reluctantly, feeling the pang of having to return to the same ol' ranch work he'd been doing since he'd been old enough to poke a stirrup, he unwrapped his reins from the hitch rack fronting the marshal's office, grabbed the apple, and pulled himself into the leather. As he swung out into the street, he could hear the tinny pattering of a piano in a saloon somewhere to the west behind him as he turned his roan toward the east, the direction of the trail back to the Powderhorn that followed the cut of Whiskey Creek.

The din of the street wrapped around him like a comfortable glove. The clomping of hooves. Squeaking of wheels. Men howling and laughing.

Like brightly painted birds, pretty girls gathered on second-floor brothel balconies, yelling good-natured obscenities down at the passing men. One of those pretty girls even yelled at Matt as he passed the Pink Lady bawdy house on his right. Matt flushed with embarrassment but smiled up at the girl, pinching his hat brim to her.

"You're gonna just ride on by, cowboy?" the girl said, drawing her pretty, painted mouth corners down in a pout. "Oh, fooey on you!"

"Yeah," Matt said under his breath. "Fooey on me."

The Longhorn slid up on his left. He looked at it through a veil of tan dust that had been kicked up by the local stagecoach that had just trundled past him, accompanied by the hooraw-ing of the driver and the popping of the jehu's blacksnake over the team's backs.

In the corner of his left eye, he'd glimpsed a pretty girl in a picture hat trimmed with ostrich feathers wink at him through the stagecoach's rear window. He craned his head to follow the stagecoach with his gaze, but the girl, of course, was gone, lost somewhere behind all that roiling dust.

Just as Matt often felt his own young life was dashing past him in a roiling dust cloud while he toiled endlessly out at the Powderhorn, all the pretty girls getting taken by men who either lived in town or came to town more often than Matt did.

"That tears it," he said aloud, and jerked his reins hard left, drawing the pinto up to one of the three hitch racks fronting the tony Longhorn Saloon partly run by his father's old flame, Devon Hayes. He could at least stop for a single beer, "for cryin' in the Queen's ale," an expression his old grandfather, Killian Brannigan, used to annunciate in his rolling Irish brogue. Every once in a while, his father bought him a beer in town.

Ty had bought Matt his first beer when Matt had turned sixteen. Matt liked beer. He just never got much of an opportunity to have a glass. Well, he'd have one now and then he'd ride back to the Powderhorn and work an extra-long day to make up for the lost time. That was fair, wasn't it?

Sure it was.

He swung down from the saddle, tied the reins, mounted the big, three-story, clapboard building's broad front porch, and pushed through the batwings. Just as his father always entered and stepped to one side, habitually not wanting to outline himself against the light, Matt did the same thing. He took a quick study of the room, inhaling the malty smell of beer, the molasses-like smell of whiskey, of the old wood and varnish, man sweat, and ladies perfume.

He liked those smells. To him, a young man who didn't get to town very often, they were as intoxicating as anything he could drink.

The bar had only a few customers at the early hour, some seated at tables, three local businessmen standing at the bar, which ran along the wall to his left. One of those businessmen was conversing with the big, blond-mustached bartender while cracking an egg open on the edge of his beer schooner then letting the egg roll out of the shell and into the glass, sunlight angling through a window flashing brightly off the yolk.

Matt saw Devon Hayes standing at a table to his far right at the rear of the room, conversing with the three men seated there. She was leaning forward against the table, appearing to be having a serious conversation with one of the three men in particular, her thick, curly red hair spilling down her back and around her shoulders.

Matt had found himself liking Miss Hayes during the several days she'd spent at the Powderhorn headquarters waiting for her ankle to heal. She'd broken the ankle in a fall from her horse not far from the Powderhorn headquarters, so Matt's father, who'd found her, had taken her to Matt's mother for doctoring.

Of course, that had been a little awkward at first for Miss Hayes and the entire Brannigan family. But they'd all warmed to each other, and even Matt's mother now considered Miss Hayes a friend, as did Matt himself. He liked it that she'd known his father when Ty Brannigan was wild and free, his big pistol sliding easily and quickly into his hand and roaring.

Matt turned his gaze away from Devon Hayes and the three men she was conversing with, and sauntered over toward the bar, admiring the beer with the egg lolling on the bottom.

"For corn's sake, woman," a man suddenly yelled behind him, "I told you she was no good, an' I want my money back or I'm gonna tear this damn place *apart*!"

CHAPTER 10

Matt stopped and turned around, frowning.

"I told you, Mister Hardin," Miss Hayes said to one of the three men seated at the table before her. "You are not going to get your money back. You spent the entire night with her, and I heard no complaints until this morning. Not only that but you cut her lip!"

Matt said, "Everything all right, Miss Hayes?" before he'd even realized he was going to say it.

She swung her head around to look at him over her shoulder, and arched her brows in surprise. "Matt . . ." Straightening, she glanced around as though looking for another person—Matt's father, most likely.

They usually came to town together, sometimes even had a beer in the Longhorn. Now that Miss Hayes had straightened, Matt could better see the man she'd been addressing—a stocky, droopy-eyed bulldog in a snazzy three-piece suit and with thick auburn hair that appeared still mussed from a restless night's sleep.

He had long, auburn side whiskers and a thick, dragoon-style mustache. His little round, heavy-lidded eyes were hard and flat and mean as he slid his gaze from the woman to Matt.

He gave Matt the quick up-and-down, flaring one nostril

distastefully. Mockingly, through a sneer that revealed two large front teeth beneath the mustache, he said, "Everything all right, Miss Hayes?"

Miss Hayes glanced at him quickly then returned her gaze to Matt. She held up one hand and smiled stiffly. "Everything's fine, Matt. Thank you. I'll be right with you."

"If you say so," Matt said, returning the hard look of the man who'd mocked him. He turned, resumed walking toward the bar, and could hear Miss Hayes and the man she'd been conversing with—quarreling with, rather—resume their conversation.

She was saying, "That's my final word on the matter, Mister Hardin. Now, I'll buy that drink for you, and when you're finished, you will leave. Once you've left, you will no longer be welcome at the Longhorn."

The man gave a caustic chuff and slapped the table. In the back bar mirror, Matt watched him sag back in his chair, lower jaw hanging with wordless exasperation. The other two men, whom he'd been playing poker with, gave wry snorts.

Matt turned his head forward as he bellied up to the bar. Hearing footsteps behind him, he glanced in the back bar mirror again to see Miss Hayes striding toward him, the pleats of her burnt-orange, lace-edged gown billowing around her long legs. She wore a white shirtwaist with a ruffled front and a gold necklace which danced and glinted in the sunlight as she walked.

Even in her forties, she was a beautiful woman. Even Matt, only nineteen, could appreciate that. She really must have looked like something twenty-some-odd years ago, when she and her father had been together.

But then ol' Ty Brannigan had probably cut a nice figure, too. Matt didn't doubt that a bit. His father was still a big, handsome man. Matt was proud of him, proud to be Ty Brannigan's son.

"Matt, where's your father?" she asked, stepping up to the bar beside him, laying one freckled, beringed hand flat atop the mahogany.

"He's out chasing owlhoots, just like the old days," Matt said with a smile. "A couple of deputy U.S. marshals came calling at the Powderhorn last night, asked him for tracking help. So, he and Mack rode out with them early this morning."

Miss Hayes frowned. "Mack, too?"

Matt grinned. "Long story."

"I see. So, you rode to town alone and I'll just bet you need a beer to cut the trail dust before getting back to work." Miss Hayes slapped the bar and turned to the barman who was pulling a beer for one of the businessmen standing to the right of Matt and herself. "Arnold, one of those new ales for the Brannigan lad. On the house!"

"Oh, that's not necessary, Miss Hayes," Matt said, digging into a front jeans pocket. "I got—"

"Nonsen—"

She didn't finish the word before she was interrupted by a gruff voice saying, "Brannigan lad, eh?"

Matt and the woman both turned to see the man she'd been arguing with standing just in front of the batwings, facing her and Matt, a belligerent, slant-eyed glare on the man's face, an evil leer on his mouth all but hidden by the thick mustache. A black bowler sat on his head. His thick hair curled back behind his ears.

He wore two pistols—handsome, ivory-gripped .45s—tied down on his broadcloth-clad thighs and held both flaps of his black, broadcloth jacket back behind the pretty hoglegs. "So, you're Ty Brannigan's kid."

"What's that to you?" Matt said.

Miss Hayes placed a hand on Matt's shoulder. "No, Matt. Please." She hardened her voice and glared at the man she'd been arguing with. "Hardin, get out of here! Get out of here now before I call for the marshal!"

Keeping his eyes on Matt, the man called Hardin said, "What's the matter—Ty Brannigan's kid can't fight his own battles?"

Matt was about to respond, anger rising inside him, but Miss Hayes cut him off. "There will be no fight." She thrust her right arm and pointing finger toward the door. "Get out of here now, Hardin!"

"You heard the lady!" bellowed the barman behind Matt.

In the periphery of his vision, Matt could see the big apron jerking his head around as though looking for something—likely a shotgun or some other weapon.

Hardin kept his eyes on Matt. "Kind of uppity, ain't ya, boy? Kinda full of yourself. Just cause your Ty Brannigan's son. That don't mean squat to me!"

Matt didn't respond. He knew the man wasn't expecting a response. Matt just stood returning Hardin's glare with a hard one of his own. His heart had quickened, but he took deep, even breaths, calming himself, remembering that his father had often said that when it came to gun work, staying calm and keeping your head was more important than speed. He was vaguely surprised to feel little fear.

The man before him, a good ten years older than Matt, appeared a practiced gunman. Matt had never faced down a man like this before.

But he was not scared. He felt something, but he wasn't sure what it was.

A thrill?

He was maybe going to die here this morning, but the thought didn't seem to bother him overmuch. It seemed to excite him.

Could that be possible?

To his left, Devon Hayes said sharply, "Matt, take your hand away from your gun. He's trying to bait you into a—"

On the heels of a devilish smile twisting Hardin's mouth beneath his thick, auburn mustache, the man's right hand jerked toward the ivory handle of his right-side hogleg.

Boom!

The thundering report made the entire room pitch.

To Matt's left, Miss Hayes gasped and closed her hand over her mouth.

Matt stared in mute shock at the Colt in his hand. Smoke curled from the barrel.

Beyond the outstretched gun, Hardin stood staring at Matt, the man's eyes wide, bulging, glossy with confusion. His own pretty Colt was only halfway out of its holster. He turned to look at the weapon and then at the blood oozing from the hole in the dead center of his chest.

He lifted his head to stare again at Matt. His hand holding the Colt opened. The Colt slid down over the side of the holster and struck the floor with a resolute thud.

Hardin opened his mouth to speak, moved his lips several times before the words issued. "I'll . . . be . . . damned."

He staggered backward, got his feet entangled, twisted around, fell forward onto a table, and then slid down the table to the floor where he rolled onto his back and gave a loud exhalation as he died.

CHAPTER 11

As his coyote dun lunged up yet another in a series of steep rises and followed MacKenna and her handsome Appaloosa into cool pines, Ty said, "Good Lord, daughter— where on God's green earth are you leading us, anyway?"

Mack hipped around in her saddle and cast her father a foxy smile from beneath the brim of her black Stetson. "You'll see in due time, Pa." She slid her smiling countenance to the young deputy U.S. marshal riding a copper bay gelding from the Powderhorn remuda directly behind her. "In due time." She winked at young Parker.

As his horse climbed behind MacKenna's Appaloosa, Adam Parker glanced over his shoulder at Ty and said, "You know, Mister Brannigan, if I didn't know better, I might suspect your lovely daughter had thrown in with those owlhoots and was tryin' to get us good and lost!" He turned his head forward to face MacKenna again.

The girl cast that winning smile back over her shoulder and said, "All in good time, Deputy Parker," her hazel eyes flashing devilishly. She turned her head forward and put the Appy up onto the crest of the ridge they'd been climbing for the past twenty minutes.

Ty chuckled.

Riding behind him on a mouse brown dun also from the Powderhorn remuda, Deputy U.S. Marshal Tom Calhoun chuckled, too. "Good Lord, Brannigan—I do believe that girl of yours is going to kill my partner. I'm not sure his young heart can take her."

"No," Ty said with an ironic chuff, "not many can."

They were riding far enough behind the youngest two riders in their group that the older men's conversation wasn't likely to be overheard. Ty glanced behind him again and said, "But you know, Calhoun, I got a sneaking suspicion he doesn't mind!"

They both laughed.

Keeping his gaze hooked over his shoulder at Tom Calhoun, Ty suddenly frowned. The older of the two federal lawmen didn't seem to be feeling well. His face was bloated and red though there were some pale streaks running through his sweat-slick cheeks, as well. His blue eyes were rheumy, and his wheezing breath sounded like sandpaper run across a slab of coarse wood.

"You all right, there, Marshal?"

The lawman looked at Ty as they crested the breezy ridge and followed Mack and Adam Parker straight south through a broad stretch of relatively flat terrain carpeted in wheat and brome grass and mountain sage. "Me?" Calhoun said. He gave a quick, offhand wave with his left, gloved hand then used that hand to cover his mouth as he coughed.

When he was done coughing, he spat a gob of what Ty thought might be blood-laced phlegm onto a pale rock. The older lawman gave another wave and said, "The altitude is getting to me a little. I'll be fine once I'm used to it."

"The farther we go, it's gonna get higher. Those northern saddles are higher than this—some of the highest spots in the Bear Paws."

Calhoun shook his head as he coughed once more and again spat to the side. "I'll be fine."

As he turned back forward, Ty gave his own head a fateful shake. The lawman didn't look good. Ty had known plenty of men plagued with the affliction of consumption. The way Calhoun was coughing told him he might have met one more.

High climbs were hard on weak, consumptive lungs. He wasn't so sure Calhoun was the best man to run to ground the four killers he and Parker were following. On the other hand, Ty well knew that U.S. marshals were nearly always spread mighty thin, there being far more criminals on the still wild-and-wooly frontier than federal badge toters to run them down.

He hoped young Parker could make up for any skills Calhoun might have been lacking due to age and illness—if he were actually ill, that was. He sure looked ill.

Ahead, MacKenna hipped around in her saddle again to announce, "One more short, steep climb, gentlemen!"

"Oh, God," Ty thought he heard Calhoun grunt behind him.

Ty winced. No, the man didn't look good and he didn't sound good, either.

Ahead lay a pine-studded ridge up which MacKenna disappeared, Cervantes lunging smoothly upward, tail arched. Parker booted his horse into a lope then horse and rider lunged up the ridge behind MacKenna, also quickly disappearing into the pines.

When Ty reached the ridge's base, he stopped the dun and turned to Calhoun riding up behind him. "You go ahead," Ty said, canting his head to indicate the ridge.

The older marshal, whom Ty judged was right around his own age, maybe a little older, gave a grim smile. "Afraid I'll fall out of my saddle?"

"You don't look too good."

Putting some angry steel in his voice, Calhoun dipped his chin and flared a nostril. "You're starting to beat that same kettle a little hard, Brannigan. If I say I'm fine, I'm fine. I just need to get used to this thin air's all."

"All right." Ty threw up a placating hand then booted the dun on up the ridge.

The dun took the incline easily, fluidly, and Ty steered him around low-hanging pine boughs. A hundred and fifty feet ahead, he could see the blue sunlit sky where the ridge crested out. He could also see the silhouettes of his daughter and the young deputy marshal sitting side by side, facing away from the slope. Stirrups flapping, keeping his head low, and leaning forward, Ty rode the dun in a meandering pattern, finally cresting out on the ridge to the right of young Parker.

"It's just through those pines, now, Pa," MacKenna said, leaning forward to see around Deputy Parker.

Ty nodded, glanced behind him at Calhoun making his way up the ridge on the mouse brown dun. Ty could hear the man coughing and blowing even more loudly than his horse. He could hear the labored breathing above the horse's thudding hooves crunching pine needles, cones, and brush.

Ty turned to Parker. "What's the matter with him?"

Parker winced. "Not looking good?"

"Not one bit."

Both Parker and MacKenna glanced over their shoulders at the older marshal who'd just then checked down his horse, curveting it sideways to the slope, apparently taking a badly needed breather.

Turning back to Ty, Parker said, "He doesn't want anyone to know. He's afraid the chief marshal will retire him." He tapped his chest. "Lungs."

"Consumption?"

Parker nodded.

"You should tell someone. You and him are on the trail of some very desperate desperadoes."

Again, Parker winced. He glanced down the steep grade at his partner then turned back to Ty and placed two fingers to his lips. "This job is all he has. He lost his wife five years ago. They didn't have any kids. He's desperately afraid of retirement." He glanced over at MacKenna regarding him with concern in her eyes beneath beetled brows. "In his situation, I can't say as I blame him."

Keeping his voice low, Ty said, "I can sympathize. But he's not gonna be much of a help to you if and when you catch up to those four killers."

"Yeah, Adam," MacKenna said. "Pa's right. If he's not in good health . . ."

Parker looked at her, shook his head, and smiled reassuringly. "You'd be surprised after seein' how he is now, but when the chips are down, Tom Calhoun is as good as any two other *healthy* lawmen I know. I really wouldn't want to be out here with anybody else."

Having heard hoof thuds, Ty glanced back down the ridge and saw Calhoun and the bay lunging on up the ridge, the older lawman nearly losing his hat to a pine bough. He grabbed it just before it would have tumbled off his shoulder and held it down over his saddle horn.

Ty sighed as he turned back to Parker. "If you say so."

"What's all the palverin' about up here?" Calhoun said as his dun took the last lunging leap up onto the crest of the ridge, pulling up between Ty and his partner. He was sweating badly, his broad chest rising and falling heavily. His coat sleeve was torn where a branch had grabbed it. A spot of blood stained his lower lip. He glanced at his younger partner. "You know what I always say—if you got time to chin, you got time to do almost anything more useful."

He cast his gaze across Parker to MacKenna. "How much farther, young lady?"

"Two minutes straight through those trees, Marshal Calhoun."

"Let's get her done, then!" Calhoun raised his elbows, leaning forward, and put the steel to his horse's flanks.

The dun leaped forward into a rocking lope.

Parker turned to Ty. "See?" Then, he, too, put the steel to his own mount, and loped after his partner.

Ty and MacKenna shared a darkly fateful glance.

Ty shook his head and touched spurs to his dun's flanks. "Shall we, baby girl?"

"Right behind you, Pa."

Ty and the coyote dun rode up out of the trees, and Ty drew rein as he stared wide-eyed into the stone-walled canyon yawning before him.

As he and MacKenna had ridden through the last stretch of trees, Ty had heard the loudening clatter of falling water. He'd felt the humidity rising, and a coolness in the air cutting the midmorning, early-autumn heat. He saw the falls fifty or so yards to his right, the white water dropping slowly, idyllically into the saucer-like black pool below that overflowed itself nearly directly below Ty and continued as a creek to Ty's left.

"Beautiful!" Deputy Parker intoned where he sat to Ty's right.

MacKenna rode Cervantes up from behind Ty and drew rein between the two men. "This is . . . or was . . . my own secret place," she said, making a mock sour expression as she glanced between her father and the young man on her right.

"Sorry you had to betray it, baby girl," Ty said. "I tell you what I'll do. Just as soon as we're sure we have these two federals on the killers' trail, I will scour my mind of this place." He turned back to stare into the dark, narrow canyon that was all rock and water. "As lovely as it is."

"Me, too," Parker said, casting Mack a dimple-cheeked smile.

"Don't worry," Mack said with a smile of her own. "There are other such places . . . just a little farther out, is all."

Parker leaned forward to look around Mack at Ty and said, "Give a precocious and beautiful young lady a horse, and the mountains are hers."

"I don't know what beauty has to do with it," Mack told him, arching a skeptical brow.

The young marshal blushed and shrugged. "Just wanted to get that in."

"If it's all the same to everyone else," Calhoun said, sitting to the right of Parker and mopping his face with a red handkerchief, "I'd like to get down to brass tacks." He looked at Mack. "This is where you first saw those killers, Miss MacKenna?"

"Yes, sir. Just up the canyon a ways, right above the pool. You should be able to pick up their trail over there. They must have taken a different route up here because I didn't see any sign on the route I always take. But you should be able to cut theirs just a few feet yonder." She raised her chin to indicate Calhoun's far right.

Calhoun turned his puffy, rheumy-eyed face to Parker. "All right, then, Junior—let's get after it."

"You got it, partner." Parker shot Ty a proud smile as though to again say, "See? The old man still has it." He neck-reined the bay to the right and booted him on up canyon after Calhoun.

Chapter 12

Ty and MacKenna rode up along the edge of the canyon, nearing where the upper creek dropped over the ridge to become the falls on their left. Ahead of them the two federal lawmen stopped their mounts and looked down.

The older man said something to his partner then glanced over his shoulder at Ty and MacKenna. "Prints and a pile of horse apples here."

Calhoun stepped down from his saddle and dropped to a knee. He poked a finger into the manure, sniffed it, and turned to Ty as the rancher and MacKenna stopped their horses twenty feet away from the lawmen. "Sure enough, roughly a day old." Still on one knee, Calhoun looked at MacKenna. "Which direction did you say they were heading, little lady?"

When MacKenna didn't say anything, Ty turned to her, frowning curiously. She'd suddenly gone pale and appeared lost in thought.

"Mack . . . ?" he said.

MacKenna gave a little start then flushed and shook her head quickly. "Oh, I'm sorry. They followed the canyon to the northwest."

Marshal Parker swung down from his own mount and dropped to a knee beside Calhoun. The two men conversed, glancing up to where the canyon angled north and west roughly a quarter mile beyond them. While the two lawmen talked, likely laying out their plans for tracking the four desperadoes, Ty turned to MacKenna, who still looked a little pale, her eyes pensive beneath stitched brows.

"You all right, honey?"

MacKenna turned to him, gave a fake half smile. "Sure, Pa." She fingered a stray lock of black hair from her cheek then cast her troubled gaze down into the canyon where the black pool of water lolled in its stony bed.

"They saw you, didn't they?"

Mack turned back to her father again, frowning. "What's that, Pa?"

"They saw you. You were swimming, weren't you?"

MacKenna stared at him without saying anything for a full thirty seconds. Then she nodded but remained silent.

Ty reached over to slide her long hair back behind her shoulder, brushing his fingers gently across the back of her neck. "They were up here . . . watching you . . . weren't they?"

A rare sheen of emotion touched Mack's eyes. She drew a breath, nodded once more.

"They didn't—?"

"No, Pa." She shook her head again quickly. "Nothing like that. One of them threatened me with a rifle. He didn't like that I'd seen them. But the woman riding with them made him stand down. Then . . . they just rode off." She studied her father with that troubled expression again, wanting to say more but having trouble finding the words.

"What is it, honey?" Ty prodded her gently.

"Pa, they warned me that if I mentioned that I'd seen them, they'd"—Mack drew a deep breath, steeling herself against her fear—"they'd come back and kill my family." Tears welled in her eyes.

Ty sidled his dun up close to the appy, leaned over, and

wrapped his arms around MacKenna's shoulders, drawing her close against him, rubbing her back. "There, there, baby girl. That's not gonna happen. You know that."

Mack nodded and said in a voice pinched with emotion, "I know. It was just . . . I'd never been so afraid. Me down there in that water . . . them up here. My rifle was up here on Cervantes." She drew her head back and looked gravely up at her father. "I didn't have a stitch on. They just"—she shook her head, her mouth twisting a revolted expression—"ogled me like I wasn't even a person. Just some piece of meat for them to feast their eyes on . . . and to threaten."

She shook her head and brushed tears from her cheeks with the backs of her hands. "Sorry, Pa. I wasn't going to tell you. I didn't want to worry you with it. I just had to share it, is all."

A searing rage burned in Ty's chest, flaring up from behind his heart. No man . . . or woman . . . ogled his daughter . . . threatened his daughter and got away with it. He suddenly felt a nearly overwhelming compulsion to track those four vermin down himself and lay waste to each and every one of them. Even the woman. She might have kept the men off MacKenna for her own reasons, but since she was riding with those killers, she was a killer, too, and deserved to die as bloody as they did.

"You all right, Tom?"

Parker's voice nudged Ty out of his angry reverie. He turned his head to see Calhoun down on all fours where he'd been kneeling by the horse apples. Parker knelt beside the older man, one hand on the man's shoulder, gazing down at him with concern.

"I'm all right, I'm all right," Calhoun said, giving a dry chuckle then lifting a placating hand. He turned over to sit on his butt and leaned back against a large rock. His bloated face was paler now. Sweat glistened on it. "Just got a little dizzy there for a minute." He gave a sheepish laugh.

Ty and MacKenna shared another worried look then Ty swung down from his saddle. "Tell you what. Let's take us a little break. We've ridden good and hard. Time for some coffee, maybe a little jerky."

"Good idea," MacKenna said, swinging down from Cervantes's back. "I'll build a fire."

"Why don't you and Marshal Parker take a little walk, honey?" Ty shuttled his glance from Mack to Parker and back again. "Give us older fellas a little time to chin like older fellas like to do." He glanced quickly at Calhoun and added with a wry smile, "Though of course if there's time to chin, there's time to do almost anything more useful."

Calhoun gave a sardonic snort.

Ty looked at MacKenna again. She nodded her understanding then, loosening her saddle cinch, turned to where Parker was still on one knee beside his partner. "Shall we, Marshal?"

Parker glanced once more at Calhoun, then at Ty, his face serious, eyes worried. Rising, he nodded and walked over to loosen his own saddle cinch and to give his dun room to breathe and to more freely graze the brome grass growing between the canyon and the forested slope.

Ty not only wanted to have a private word with Calhoun, he wanted a diversion for MacKenna. He knew a walk with the handsome young marshal would get her mind off her harrowing, demeaning experience of yesterday. No woman should have to experience something like that.

Ty just hoped those three men and that woman hadn't ruined the canyon for her. A girl needed a quiet, magical place to call her own. Especially one who worked as hard as MacKenna did. Who was as good and deserving of such a place, as Mack was.

As MacKenna and Adam Parker walked off along the canyon rim together, Ty gathered an armload of blowdown branches. When he returned to where Calhoun sat leaning back against the rock, the lawman pulled down the handkerchief he was again mopping his face with.

"I know what you're gonna say, Brannigan." Calhoun gave a grim smile and shook his head. "It's not gonna happen."

"Sometimes a man has to know when to call it quits," Ty said, setting down the wood to start looking for rocks with which to build a fire ring.

Calhoun grimaced then gazed off into the canyon. "This is all I have."

Ty laid out the rocks then broke up the branches he'd gathered and, using pinecones and twigs for tinder, he built a fire and then erected a steel tripod over the fledgling flames. He filled his coffee pot with water from his canteen then hung the pot from the tripod.

He sat down on a log by the fire, facing the lawman leaning back against the rock and continuing to gaze pensively, wearily into the canyon. The breeze nipped at the brim of Calhoun's cream Stetson, jostled the gray hair hanging down over the back of his shirt collar, nibbled at the curled ends of his mustache.

Ty drew his makings sack from under his shirt where it hung against his chest from a leather thong and began building a quirley.

Calhoun looked at him. "How long you been married?"

"Twenty years," Ty said, dribbling chopped Durham onto the wheat paper troughed between the first two fingers of his right hand.

"Do you miss it?"

Ty glanced over at the man, brows arched curiously.

Calhoun gave a wolfish smile. "Being a lawdog of some repute."

Ty shook his head then let the hide pouch hang down

against his shirt. "Not a bit." He began to slowly shift the tobacco around on the paper and to roll the paper closed, bits of tobacco dripping from both ends of the cylinder, the thin paper crackling softly in his large, brown fingers. He glanced over at the lawman again. "No family?"

Staring into the canyon again, Calhoun shook his head. "I had a wife." He turned to Ty. "Dead."

"I'm sorry to hear that."

"I'd quit for her, but since she's not here . . ."

"I understand," Ty said, firing a lucifer to life on his thumbnail then touching the match to the cigarette, puffing smoke. "We need something to keep us going."

"I may look like hell right now, but once I get my second wind, I'll be fine as frog hair split four ways. And when the chips are down, Brannigan, there's no better man to have in a fight but—" Calhoun thumbed himself in the chest.

You may have a proud grin on your lips, Ty thought, regarding the man over his smoldering quirley. *But I've rarely seen such a bald fear of death in a man's eyes.*

The look in Calhoun's eyes—terror, desperation, fear that if he stopped moving the abyss would reach up and claim him—caused a chill to ripple up and down Ty's own back. He'd never thought he'd feared death. But maybe he did. With each year that passed, leaving one less to live . . . to enjoy the ranch and his family . . . maybe he feared it more and more . . .

Way down deep in his soul where he dared not peer too often.

Vaguely, absently, he studied his smoldering cigarette and thought, *Maybe we should have that extra child, after all, Beatriz and I.*

But would a child hold off the Reaper?

When the water boiled, Ty added a heaping handful of Arbuckles from the pouch in his saddlebags. He returned the coffee to boil and when it boiled again he used a leather swatch to remove the pot from the fire. He added a little cool water from his canteen to settle the grounds then filled two cups and took one over to Calhoun.

"Ah," the man said, looking better, the fear of death no longer so stark in his gaze.

Ty was glad. That look had made him uncomfortable.

"Good, black mud," the lawman said. "You like it strong, too, I see."

"Strong enough to float a plow blade," Ty said, sitting back down on his log. He blew on the coffee, sipped, took another sip of the bracing brew, then looked over the steaming cup at Calhoun. "Can I make a suggestion?"

Calhoun sipped his own brew then looked over his cup at Ty, cautiously curious.

"Let me ride along with you fellas."

Calhoun pursed his lips, shook his head. "No. We have their trail now. We can track 'em ourselves. Besides, you're not in the business anymore."

"Who knows—maybe I do miss it?" Ty said with a shrug. He didn't want to tell them what the four outlaws had done to MacKenna, terrifying her. He wanted to run the savages down himself. He wanted to make sure they *were* rundown. Because of Calhoun's health, he didn't have much confidence in the man. Because of his youth, Parker would need the help of an older, more experienced man.

"That's a load of crap, and you know it, Brannigan." The color had returned to Calhoun's cheeks. His ire was up, his eyes hard and angry. "You're a happy family man. Leave the lawdogging to those of us still wearing the badge."

"You couldn't use a third hand? An experienced third hand?"

Calhoun studied him, the antipathy growing in his eyes. "You don't think I can do it."

"That's not it," Ty lied.

"You don't think I can do it. That's why you want to help."

Calhoun shook his head, anger turning his ears red beneath his Stetson. "Forget it. I can do my job. You go on home with your daughter and do yours."

"What's going on?" came MacKenna's voice from behind Ty.

He glanced over his shoulder to see her and young Parker approaching along the canyon rim, concern showing on both their faces.

"What's going on is we're pulling our picket pins and forking trails," Calhoun said loudly. "Adam, tighten your saddle cinch. Time to ride." Calhoun climbed heavily to his feet, tossed the dregs of his coffee into the fire. "Thanks for the java," he told Ty then dropped the cup into the grass beside him. He walked over to his horse and tightened the cinch.

A minute later, he and Parker were mounted up. Parker cast Ty a questioning look then turned to MacKenna, doffed his hat, and held it over his chest. "Sure was nice meeting you, Mack. Thanks for the help."

"The pleasure was all mine, Adam," MacKenna said, smiling up at him.

"Thanks for the horses, Mister Brannigan," Parker said. "We'll get them back to you soon."

"Take your time and be careful," Ty said.

When young Parker and the ailing Calhoun had galloped off, Mack turned her own incredulous gaze to her father. "What was that all about?"

Ty stared after the two quickly diminishing lawmen. "Darlin'," Ty said with a darkly wistful air. "That was about the fear of gettin' old . . . of dyin'. Never seen a man have it so bad."

He turned to Mack and grimaced. "It's downright catching!"

CHAPTER 13

Danny Campbell swung the splitting maul down over the chopping block, smoothly cleaving the stove-sized pine log down its middle. Two similarly sized pieces of the log flew out away from the block and clattered onto the ground, adding to the growing pile of split stove wood growing up around the block.

Danny looked down at his bare right arm. He'd taken his shirt off to work in the heat and now he inspected his bicep, flexing it, smiling at the growing bulge. He was strong for a twelve-year-old. Not particularly tall but he was strong, by God. And he had a thick mop of copper-red hair, just like his father. Splitting wood two or three times a day, and wielding a pick and shovel with his father, had made Danny strong and thick in the shoulders. He was proud of that fact.

He was proud, too, that he, like his pa, who was over there by the creek butchering a deer he'd shot the evening before, could put in a full day's work and hardly even be tired, and be just as ready to go again the next morning as he'd been ready to go the previous one.

Danny glanced at his tall, red-headed father, who was also working bare-chested, butchering the doe, and smiled. Danny liked working with his pa. He'd liked working with both his ma and his pa, but now that Ma was gone, he had only Pa to work with out here in Preacher's Coulee, where he and his pa hunted game for a grocer in Warknife and prospected for gold.

Danny especially liked having work to do, the harder the better, since Ma had died giving birth to Danny's sister, Evelyn, who had also died and was buried with Ma behind the cabin. Like Pa had said, it was best to keep busy. Your problems didn't weight so heavy when you were busy.

Pa had been right.

Danny lowered the maul, holding the hickory handle down low near the iron head. He glanced at his bicep again, smiled to himself, then picked up another log from the pile that abutted the cabin's front wall behind him, to the right of the door he'd left propped open with a rock to let the heat out after his and his father's noon meal. He set the log on the chopping block and, taking the maul in both hands, raised it high above his head, sucking in a deep breath and hardening his jaws.

The breeze picked up suddenly. There was a chill in it.

A knife-edge coldness.

Danny frowned and lowered the maul, looking around at the aspen leaves that were just starting to turn at this altitude and time of the year, early autumn. They flashed silver as the breeze jostled them. He looked down at his chest, broad for a twelve-year-old, and was surprised to see chicken flesh rising behind the sweat. He looked up, half-expecting to see swollen purple storm clouds closing in over the valley, but no. They sky was a vast arch of lake-blue, not a cloud or a scrap of cloud in sight.

Again, the breeze blew, rattling the leaves and making a pine bough give a ratcheting scratch across the cabin's shake shingled roof behind Danny. A woodpecker had been fool-ishly tapping its beak against the tin chimney pipe just a minute ago, but when the breeze had turned chill, the big, awkward-looking, red-headed bird had wheeled off, giving its crow-like cry of alarm.

Danny looked at his father. "Hey, Pa," he called, "you feel that?"

Galvin Campbell had been working with his back to Danny as he'd been carving roasts and steaks from the deer hanging upside down from a branch of the big aspen before him, its rear legs spread wide. The tarpaulin-covered wheelbarrow beside the tall, red-headed man, who still spoke with a thick Irish brogue, was mounded with meat he and Danny would later jerk or salt to preserve it.

Campbell turned toward Danny, his hands and forearms slick with blood as was the skinning knife he held in his left hand. "Feel wha—" He cut himself off when a cackling cry sounded from the aspen copse fifty yards or so to Danny's left and through which Preacher's Creek weaved, flashing brightly in the afternoon sunshine.

Danny frowned in that direction, feeling that knife-edge chill again though the air had suddenly turned still.

Oddly still.

Danny's father turned to Danny, frowning, and Danny and his father said at the same time, "What was that?"

Again, came the crackling cry. It was a little louder this time and it had shifted position slightly. The cry came from behind Danny's left shoulder as he faced his father and the creek that wended its way through the aspens beyond Galvin Campbell.

Campbell turned quickly to Danny and said, "Wildcat."

He tossed his knife into the wheelbarrow with the meat, quickly toweled off his hands and arms (though he mostly just smeared the blood around, Danny saw) then strode quickly toward the cabin. Danny stood frozen, still holding the splitting maul down low before him, still feeling that knife-edge chill though the breeze had died as he cast his wary gaze into the aspens.

His father brushed past him and stepped into the cabin to emerge a few seconds later wearing his floppy-brimmed black hat and wielding two old Spencer repeating rifles. "Here."

Danny turned to his father and dropped the maul just in time to catch the rifle his father tossed him. Galvin Campbell worked his own Spencer's heavy trigger guard cocking mechanism, jacking a round into the action, then walked around Danny, saying, "You stay with the deer. It's likely after the deer!"

Campbell bounced into a jog, the long ears of his mule eared boots dancing as he ran, holding his hat onto his head with one hand, the Spencer repeater in his left hand. Like Danny, Galvin Campbell was left-handed. That had been another thing Danny had been proud to share with his father but at the moment he wasn't feeling proud of anything.

Only scared.

Yeah, he was scared. A little ashamed to admit it to himself, he usually prided himself on his bravery. But he was shaking down deep in his knees.

Why?

He'd heard wildcats before. Even seen them. Usually at night. Not during the day. They hadn't made him fearful. At least, not like this. His feet felt so heavy in his own mule-eared boots he wasn't sure he could move them though he needed to walk out farther away from the cabin to go stand by the deer.

He watched as his father slowed to a walk and raised his rifle just before entering the aspens, the trees closing around him, swallowing him, removing him from view.

For some reason, his father's disappearance intensified Danny's trepidation.

He looked at the deer. He had to get over there in case the wildcat somehow worked around the cabin and came up on it from the creek. If it was a big cat, it could swoop in, rip the deer out of the tree—or rip a good part of it out of the tree—and be gone in the blink of an eye.

That thought made Danny shudder. If it could do that to the deer . . .

He glanced over at the aspen copse again, where his father had disappeared. Strangely silent over there. He looked at the deer again, willed his right foot into motion, bringing it forward, setting it down.

There . . . there. Good. Just keep going, Danny . . .

He willed the left foot into motion.

The right one.

The left.

Again . . . again . . .

And then, heart thudding, he stood near the deer, holding the rifle in both hands, looking around warily.

Suddenly, the cat wailed again. Louder, closer this time.

It was followed by what sounded to Danny's ears like a woman's shrieking laugh.

A gun thundered. Danny nearly leaped out of his boots.

The gun thundered again. Again.

Again, rose a woman's crazy, malevolent laugh.

A man shouted in an oddly flat, guttural voice, "You're gonna die, brother!"

Another gun blast, making Danny nearly leap out of his boots again.

He stood trembling, staring toward the aspens. He wanted to call out for his father, but he couldn't seem to get any air across his vocal cords. His throat was dry. His tongue felt heavy and as dry as the leather on his boots.

"Danny!"

Again, the boy jerked with a start. It was his father's voice.

"Danny!" The cry was accompanied by the thuds of running feet growing louder.

"P-Pa . . . ?" Danny said, shuffling forward, staring into the trees around where his father's cries had issued.

"Danny!" came his father's voice again just as Galvin Campbell emerged running from the trees, scissoring his arms, lifting his knees.

He'd lost his rifle. As he ran toward Danny the wind blew his hat off his head. He kept on running, yelling, "Danny—get into the cabin! Get into the cabin!" He swung his arm to indicate the cabin to Danny's left. "Get into the cabin! *They're after the mules!*"

Heart racing, Danny turned but again he had trouble getting his feet to move.

Another gun barked.

Danny's father grunted and stumbled forward as he ran, throwing his arms out to both sides, like wings. Danny saw red on his father's chest just below his left shoulder.

The gun barked again, again.

More red shown on Danny's father's chest as Galvin Campbell weaved sharply to the left and then to the right, looking as though he were about to fall but somehow managing to keep his feet beneath him, arms spread wide as though they really were wings and he was desperately trying to take flight.

The gun barked again.

Galvin Campbell's head jerked up and back and he took two more long, floppy-footed strides forward before he collapsed, struck the ground, and rolled, kicking up dirt, pine needles, and old leaves.

"Pa!" Danny screamed and, dropping his rifle, ran forward.

He ran hard toward his father, sobbing, his heart a frightened little bird flopping around in his chest, looking for a way out.

"Pa!" he screamed again.

Something plunked into the ground behind him with a spanging whine. He'd felt the heated curl of air just off his left ear. The plunking sound was followed by the rifle's report. Danny stopped dead in his tracks and stared ahead, lower jaw hanging. Pale powder smoke wafted between two aspens.

He also saw the black-hatted head of a blond-headed woman. She had a pretty, oval face with eyes as blue as a mountain lake and a devilish glint in them. Her wide, full mouth was set in a devilish grin. She was holding a rifle in her black-gloved hands and laughed as she lowered the weapon.

Danny heard the rasp of a fresh shell being racked into the rifle's firing chamber.

An unseen man whooped and hollered. "Shoot that little devil, Zee!"

Danny gasped, wheeled, and ran, surprised that he could run when only a few minutes ago his feet had felt like lead. But run he did—pumping his arms and legs, sucking air into his lungs.

Devils. That's what were in those woods. It wasn't no cat, but devils led by a flaxen-haired, blue-eyed devil woman . . .

The woman laughed and pumped several more rounds into the ground around Danny, who yelped and leaped, nearly falling with every spanging whine and dust plume. He'd run into the canyon beyond the woods. He'd hide in there. They wouldn't find him in there.

He didn't want to die.

Oh, please, God, don't let me die!

The cabin was coming up close on his right. He ran past the front door, leaping several unsplit logs. Funny to think just a few short minutes ago he'd been so peacefully splitting wood, getting ready to start the fire in the smoke house so he and Pa could jerk and smoke the venison.

Now he was running from a pack of devils led by a flaxen-headed devil woman. . .

He'd just cleared the cabin when a man stepped out from the cabin's front corner and into Danny's path.

Danny gasped as he stopped, stared up at a handsome man in a three-piece butterscotch suit.

Hope lifted in Danny. Surely this man wasn't a devil. He looked too nice to be a devil. Maybe he'd heard the shooting and come to render aid.

"Help!" Danny cried, bringing his hands to the side of his head. He dropped to his knees, sobbing. "They killed my pa!"

He gazed through teary eyes at the man standing over him.

The man smiled gently down at Danny. Then the smile broadened and darkened, becoming a weird corruption of a smile, as the man swung his right hand back behind his left shoulder. The handsome man's blue eyes became a devil's eyes—flat and evil. When the hand came forward, sunlight winked off the knife in the man's hand just before the blade carved a burning line across Danny's throat.

CHAPTER 14

Matt stared down at the smoking Colt in his hand.

He looked down at Delvyn Hardin lying dead on the floor.

Hardin—a pistolero of some repute. Matt had heard the name. And he'd beat him at the draw and killed him.

A pale, freckled hand closed over the Colt and shoved it down, and it was only then Matt remembered Devon Hayes was standing beside him. He turned to her.

She stared up at him, shock in her eyes. "My God," she whispered.

The two men who'd been sitting with Hardin were on their feet, shuttling their shocked gazes between Matt and the man he'd killed. Matt knew them both. They were townsmen who'd been playing poker with Hardin. They looked at each other, stunned, gathered up their coins and greenbacks, donned their bowler hats, and hurried to the door.

They cast their stunned glances over their shoulders at Matt once more just before they pushed through the batwings and were gone.

The batwings hadn't finished clattering back into place before they opened once more, and Town Marshal Chris Southern stepped into the saloon, one hand over the grips of the Remington revolver he wore high on his right hip. He looked down at Delvyn Hardin lying dead on the floor in a pool of his own blood.

"What in God's name . . . ?" He let his voice trail off when his gaze found Matt. "Nooo," he said slowly, shaking his head. He walked into the room, angling toward Matt and Devon Hayes standing with their backs to the bar.

Matt holstered the Colt and met Southern's gaze. He'd been calm a minute ago, before he'd shot Hardin. But his heart was tattooing a fervent rhythm against his breastbone. He couldn't believe what he'd just done. He was both appalled and—what?

Excited?

He drew a deep, calming breath and said, "He drew first, Marshal." He raised a placating hand, palm out. "I only came in here to have a beer and talk to Miss Hayes."

"The boy's right, Marshal," Miss Hayes said quietly, glancing again at Matt. "Hardin drew first."

Southern stepped back and looked down at the dead man again. He pointed down at the body as if it were possible to mistake who he was referring to when he said, "You mean—that's Delvyn Hardin? The regulator from Colorado?" He was looking at Devon Hayes.

She nodded slowly. "I don't know what he was doing here, but he's been in town several days. Him and several others of his ilk. Probably working for some big cattleman. I've served Hardin before in Cheyenne, and he always made sure I knew exactly who he was. He was very proud of his reputation. He usually starts trouble sooner or later, but he didn't start any trouble until this morning when he wanted his money back after a night with one of my top girls— whose lip he busted, I might add."

She glanced at Matt again, the shocked, haunted look returning to her gaze. "Matt shot him, all right. Only after Hardin drew first." She kept her eyes on Matt as though she were seeing him for the first time, and he was no longer

Matthew Brannigan, son of her old beau, but someone else she wasn't sure she knew as well as she'd thought she did.

Matt found himself liking that. He knew he shouldn't. But he'd be damned if he didn't. He also knew he shouldn't be as impressed with his handiwork in Delvyn Hardin, a noted regulatory and gunslinger, lying dead on the floor before him.

Miss Hayes kept staring at him. Was she looking for his father in his eyes?

"What caused the confrontation in the first place?" Marshal Southern was staring hard at Matt, his gray eyes crinkled at the corners with deep concern and suspicion.

Miss Hayes started to speak but Marshal Southern said quickly, "Let him tell it."

Matt said, "When I entered the saloon, I saw Miss Hayes having a serious conversation with Mister Hardin. I just asked her if everything was all right. Apparently, Hardin didn't like that. When he found out I was Ty Brannigan's son, he came over to rawhide me. Well, I don't rawhide," he announced with some pride.

Miss Hayes rolled her eyes and gave a little chuff of indignation.

"You don't rawhide, eh?" Southern said through a crooked smile. "Well, ain't you proud of yourself? Now you've killed a man. Proved how much you've been practicin' with that hogleg of yours. Now you've killed a gunslinger . . . at only nineteen years old."

"To be honest with you, Sheriff," Matt said, removing his hat and deftly shaping the crown, "that fast draw of mine was as much of a surprise to me as it was to Hardin." He set the hat back on his head and glanced in the mirror to make sure he had the angle right. "Must be some natural ability. Pa, he said he was never all that fast, but Pa never was one to crow about himself."

"And neither are you," Miss Hayes said, scowling at him angrily. "At least, I've not known you to crow . . . until now."

"I wasn't crowin'," Matt said, suddenly indignant. "Marshal Southern asked me what happened, and I told him."

Southern and Miss Hayes shared a glance and a fateful sigh.

Southern turned back to Matt, his eyes hard and commanding beneath the brim of his gray Stetson. "Get out of town, Junior. Go home and stay there, and don't forget to tell your pa about your milestone here today. The one you're so dadgummed proud of."

"I'm not proud of it," Matt said. It was a lie but he was only half-conscious of the lie. It wasn't like him to feel proud about killing a man; he wasn't accustomed to it. "It just happened!"

Southern hooked his thumb over his shoulder. "Git!"

"I haven't had my beer yet. Besides, don't you need me to fill out another one of those affidavit things?"

"I'll write up the report and have you and Miss Hayes and Arnold back there sign it later." Arnold Winton was the bartender still standing down at the far end of the bar where he'd retreated after Hardin had braced young Matt. He grimaced and shook his head.

"No beer," Southern said. He looked up at the younger man who stood a couple of inches taller than him. "Get home. And the next time you come to town, don't wear the hogleg. If you do, I'll lock you up."

"You can't do that!"

"Watch me!"

Matt glanced at Miss Hayes then looked back at Southern again, gave an angry chuff and headed for the batwings. He stepped through the doors as a pretty girl ran toward him from across the street. She was nearly runover by Norman Kellogg, foreman of the Two Bar Over Eight Ranch west of town.

"Arlis Jessup, good Lord, girl—watch where you're *goin'*!" Kellogg said, shaking a gloved finger at the girl as he and the wagon continued trundling and rumbling down the street.

Arlis ran up to Matt, holding the hem of her dress above her low-heeled, black patten shoes, her brown sausage curls hanging in a mess around her pretty, heart-shaped, blue-eyed face. She wore a crisp, cream and brown patterned gingham dress which now, after her dash across the street, was streaked here and there with clay-colored dust. The matching brown ribbon in her hair hung askew.

"Matt, I just heard!" Arlis cried. She grabbed his arm and stepped up to gaze with concern into his eyes. "Are you all right?"

"Boy," Matt said, "word sure carries fast around this town!"

"It's not really true—is it?"

"Is what not true?"

"That you killed that gunfighter and human snake, Delvyn Hardin? He's said to be the one who killed Mr. Nordstrom for Mr. Fettig last year in that little land war they had brewing over by the Avalanche River. I read all about it in one of the *National Police Gazettes* we sell in the mercantile."

"I killed him, all right," Matt said, glancing around and noting more than a few dubious looks being cast his way by passersby in the street and on the boardwalks. "He didn't leave me much choice. He braced me an' drew first, so I—" He threw his arms out and shrugged.

Again, Arlis grabbed his arm. "Matt, you didn't!"

"Arlis, if you'll forgive me, but Marshal Southern's drawers are all in a twist over the situation, and I've been ordered out of town." Matt walked over and untied his reins from the hitchrack. "You'd swear I was the one who braced *Hardin* and reached first!"

Arlis followed him over to the hitch rack. "Matt, you don't want that kind of trouble."

"What kind of trouble?"

"Being the boy who killed Hardin."

Matt gave Arlis an ironic, sidelong glance. His pride was bubbling up again; he just couldn't seem to keep it in check. But then again, it wasn't everyday a nineteen-year-old *boy* shot a seasoned gunfighter in a one-on-one shooting match. "I don't think you can call me no boy no more, Arlis. I don't mean to preen, but that was a man's shootin' in there." He walked over to the side of his horse. "I didn't realize I'd gotten that fast, but I'm glad I have or that'd been me lyin' in there in a pool of my own blood and not Hardin."

"Matt!"

Matt had been about to reach for his saddle horn and to toe a stirrup. He turned around sharply and said, "Oh, what is it now, Arlis? I gotta get on back to the Powderhorn." The girl, who was three years younger than he, a year younger than MacKenna, was starting to annoy him.

But then Arlis Jessup, who worked in Jessup's Mercantile right alongside her father and mother, had been annoying him for the past several years, fawning all over him whenever he and his father visited the mercantile or the little coffee and donut shop Mrs. Jessup ran in a side shed attached to the main building.

Arlis would follow Matt around spilling rumors about townfolks—no girl was more of a busybody than Arlis—and telling him about the stories she read, especially the stories she read in the *Police Gazette*. Matt considered the girl too young and flighty to be taken seriously as a romantic interest though he had sat with her at last year's Fourth of July rodeo and hadn't minded the conversation all that much. She hadn't seemed as nervous and girlish as she did most of the time when he and his father visited the mercantile.

But she was back being just as nervous and flighty as she usually was.

MacKenna loved to tease Matt about Arlis, sometimes even sliding fake love notes from "Arlis" under his bedroom door at night. Arlis had slipped a couple of such notes in the packages she'd wrapped up for him and his father. They'd been the gooiest things Matt had ever read, and they'd embarrassed him, especially because his nosy family always seemed to find them in the packages and read them before he did!

In one note she'd written, "You don't know what you do to me. Your eyes are just Heavenly," so MacKenna often muttered those exact words to him with sisterly jeering.

That didn't do much for making Arlis any less annoying as she eyed the revolver thonged low on Matt's right thigh, and said, "I knew as soon as you started wearing that thing there was going to be trouble."

Matt frowned and slapped the gun, caressed the staghorn grips. "You did?"

"Follow me." Arlis swung around and looked over her shoulder at him.

Again, Matt frowned. "What?"

"Follow me, Matt. There's something I have to show you."

"Arlis, I don't have time for your foolishness. I have to get back—"

"Follow me, young man, or I'll never speak to you again!"

She fairly screamed the order and the threat. Matt glanced around, cheeks burning. More than a few people had overheard and were staring skeptically, muttering speculatively among themselves.

As far as the threat went, Matt wasn't at all averse to the notion of Arlis never speaking to him again. On the other hand, he didn't want her to continue to make a spectacle of both of them out on the street. So instead of toeing a stirrup, he turned his horse around and looked at Arlis glaring at him over her shoulder, her cornflower blue eyes bright with emotion.

He frowned skeptically and sighed. "Where we goin'?"

She turned her head forward. "This way."

"Listen, I don't have much time."

"Just follow me," Arlis said, marching stiffly, chin down, fists bunched at her sides, out into the street. She was heading for a cross street.

Again, she seemed oblivious of passing traffic, and one wagon coming from one way and two sun-seasoned horseback riders coming from another way had to rein in abruptly or they'd have run her down.

"Good grief, Arlis!" Matt said, then hurried after the determined girl, leading his horse by its reins. He waved apologetically at the two horsemen, both ranch hands, one a Mexican named Gutierrez, one a Scot unimaginatively called Scotty, he'd known for years in the way he knew a lot of hands from neighboring ranches due to the yearly fall gathers.

Both men regarded him with—what? New admiration?—which told him they, too, had heard the news of his having killed Delvyn Hardin. That made him throw his shoulders back a little.

When Matt and Arlis were safely across the main avenue and heading along the cross street which was considerably less busy and shaded on both sides by large cottonwood trees, Matt again said, "Arlis, where on earth are we goin'?"

She kept up a determined stride straight down the middle of the cross street.

"Keep your pants on. You'll see in a minute," she said, head aimed forward, chin down.

They approached a large house on the right side of the street, set back behind more cottonwoods which striped the house with cool, blue shade. The house was a two-story, white, clapboard affair with green shake shingles and green shutters and a front porch that ran the length of the house. The house was fronted by a well-trimmed yard in which healthy trees, including several apple and pear trees, and shrubs grew behind a white picket fence.

"Arlis," Matt said, approaching the wrought-iron hitch rack that stood before the gate in the picket fence, "now, I know this is your family's house. If this is some trick to get me inside—"

"We're not going inside," Arlis said without looking at him, tripping the latch and pulling open the gate. "We're walking around behind it."

Matt sighed in exasperation and tossed his mount's reins over the hitch rail. He'd come this far without really knowing why except that the girl was simply so determined that he had to admit being curious about where she was leading him. He followed her through the gate, up the cobbled path to the front porch, turned right along another cobblestone path that ran along the front of the porch then around the side of the house to the back where there were more fruit trees and shrubs.

Arlis led him down yet another cobblestone path deep into the backyard. They climbed a low rise upon which another sprawling cottonwood stood. Beneath the cottonwood was a marble gravestone standing inside a low, black iron fence. The grave fronting the stone was paved with small, pale rocks. The grass around the grave was neatly trimmed.

On the stone had been inscribed:

ANDREW PAUL JESSUP
Born
August 1, 1855
Died
September 3, 1875
Forever loved . . .
Forever mourned.

Matt turned to Arlis who stood staring down at the marker. "Your brother?"

He had a distant recollection of hearing rumors about Arlis's brother, several years older than she, having left home and dying under mysterious circumstances. Matt had never heard the full story. He doubted anyone around Warknife had heard it; it had seemed something the Jessups had wanted to keep secret, which of course had made the folks of Warknife all the more curious and the untold story all the more mysterious and alluring.

"My brother, Andy." Arlis turned to Matt, her eyes somber. "He took to wearing a gun like yours. He fancied himself right handy with it. He liked the way he looked with it hanging off his leg, liked the way the young ladies admired him for his pretty pistol and the way he could twirl it on his finger.

"He practiced with it all the time when he wasn't working at the mercantile"—she turned to gaze straight out beyond the grave at another rise—"right up there on that hill. The shooting frayed our mother's nerves and Pa tried to take the gun away from him but Andy wouldn't have it. Instead, he left home with it. Two months later he came back home—in a pine box with a bullet in him."

The girl held a finger to her left temple. "Right here. Turned out Andy was right fast with his gun. That made other men want to see if they were faster. One turned out to be faster, and that's why my brother is buried right here instead of working at the mercantile and being my brother and Pa's son."

Arlis paused, glanced back at the tree-shaded house. "Broke Mama's heart. She couldn't bear to live here anymore, so she went back East. That's where she is now, living with my grandparents. It's only Pa and me living here now . . . working at the mercantile." She looked up at Matt. "You ever notice how Pa always looks sorta sad and lonely, and never says much?"

Before Matt could respond, Arlis slowly shook her head. "He wasn't always like that, I'm told, though I don't remember much about what he was like before Andy left home." She stared up at Matt sadly.

Matt looked down at the grave again. "I'm sorry, Arlis." He gave his shoulder a slight shrug. "Maybe for Andy it was worth it. Living a short, exciting life rather than living a longer life at the mercantile."

"Would it be worth it to you, Matt?" Arlis stared up at him, canting her head to one side. "I reckon that's what you got to figure out—isn't it?"

CHAPTER 15

"What happened here, MacKenna?" Deputy U.S. Marshal Adam Parker had asked her as they'd walked back along the edge of the canyon together, leaving her father and the older lawman, Tom Calhoun, to talk privately.

MacKenna pulled a wheat grass stem, held it up and down in her fingers, twisting it, staring at it contemplatively. "What's that?"

"I wasn't trying to eavesdrop, but I overheard you and your father talking. Something happened here. Between you and the four killers we're tracking."

MacKenna glanced into the canyon. The pool lay behind them as they followed the runoff-fed creek. Still, her gaze went back to the previous day.

"I'm afraid I wasn't being honest when I said they hadn't seen me." MacKenna turned to the young deputy walking beside her. "They did. They saw me. I"—she looked down at the wheat straw in her fingers—"I was in the pool."

"I had a feeling. As soon as I saw the pool, I had a feeling I knew what you'd been doing here." Adam smiled at her.

She liked his smile. It was warm, kind, understanding, and comforting all at the same time.

"Swimming. What else would a girl being doing alone in such an inviting place?"

MacKenna looked at the weed in her fingers again. "I shouldn't tell you this . . . not very ladylike . . . but I left my clothes up here. My Winchester, too."

"Ah."

"Don't go pondering on it too hard, Deputy!" Mack nudged him playfully with her elbow.

Adam chuckled. "Hard not to, but I understand." He looked at her seriously. "You were in the water and vulnerable. And they were up here."

"Yes."

He stopped, placed his hands on her shoulders, and turned her to face him. "Anything else you want to tell me, Mack?" His voice was gentle, again comforting.

"Nothing happened like what you might think. But they . . . were up here . . . and I was down there. That's all I'll say on the subject except that the dark one—who might be Indian, I suspect—drew a rifle and would have shot me to prevent me from doing just what I'm doing—siccing the law on them."

"That must have been terrifying, MacKenna."

She gave an involuntary shudder, remembering how large and black the maw of the Winchester had been as it bore down on her in the pool. "It was."

"Obviously, he didn't shoot you."

"The woman, the blonde . . . she stopped him."

"Ah." Adam nodded slowly, meaningfully, letting his pensive gaze light off over the canyon for a moment.

"Does that make sense to you?"

"Miss Zenobia Sparrow was in prison. A woman's prison. That changes some people."

"Ah. Well, she saved my life though I don't feel particularly beholden to her." Mack dropped the weed and raised her hands to her neck, crossing her arms on her chest. "The way she looked at me chilled me as bad as the way the men looked at me."

"I'm sorry you had to endure that," Adam said. "It makes what you're doing here and now, with me and Tom, all the more impressive. You're very brave, MacKenna."

"Funny, I don't feel all that brave. Just determined they be run down. Have you ever had the feeling you were confronting raw evil? I'm mean, pure evil? Like someone had opened Hell's doors and let the demons out and you were staring right at them?"

"I've been doing this work only a couple of years, but, yes." He shook his head quickly. "But not like those four. They're different. They enjoy killing . . . and terrorizing. They get pleasure from instilling fear in their prey."

"I'm no wilting wallflower, Adam. I don't frighten easily." With an ironic smile, she added, "I've *never* fainted," then continued. "But remembering those four ghouls gives me a chill all across my body and makes my heart race."

"I'm so sorry, MacKenna." He drew her to him, wrapped his arms around her and hugged her gently.

His arms felt good. She placed her cheek against his chest and enjoyed the comforting strength she felt in his body.

She lifted her head, narrowed one eye, and smiled up at him. "You know what? I think I'm ready for you to call me Mack. If you want."

It was the deputy's turn to smile. "Oh, I want."

"You don't think me too forward?"

He frowned. "Not at all."

"Even after last night?" she said, broadening her smile and slitting both eyes.

He smiled again. "Not at all."

"I just want you to know I never initiated a kiss with a man before last night. You were my first."

He raised both hands placatingly. "I assure you I cast no judgment. I simply enjoyed it. Now, then . . ." He glanced back to where MacKenna's father and Marshal Calhoun were sitting by the fire, far enough away, a good hundred yards, that they couldn't have seen Mack and Adam clearly even if they'd been looking this way, which neither was. "Maybe it's time I did some initiating of my own."

"Maybe so," Mack said, reaching over to give his necktie a squeeze.

His eyes warmly passionate, Adam slid his head toward hers, bent her slightly backward and to one side, and closed his mouth over hers. Passion rose in her, warming her down deep in her bones, all the way to her soul. She wasn't ready for the kiss to end when he ended it and found herself keeping her lips pressed against his with an involuntary, frustrated groan as he straightened.

She pulled her mouth from his and felt a blush warm her cheeks.

He smiled endearingly at that, and kissed her once more, quickly, and ran the first two fingers of his right hand lightly across her cheek. "Ah, Mack . . ."

"Yes?" She brushed her own fingers across his cheek.

"I wish so many things."

"Me, too. One day at a time, I reckon—eh, Adam?"

He nodded. "I reckon." He glanced back over to where her father and Calhoun sat by the fire. "I hear raised voices. We'd best get back. Tom can really get his dander up when the topic of his health is broached."

"Right," Mack said.

Adam smiled at her, gave her hand an affectionate squeeze.

Together, they turned and started walking back in the direction of her father, the ailing lawman, and the small coffee fire her father had built.

"Go with God, Adam," Mack said as she watched the young marshal ride off with the older one. She turned to her father. "What're we gonna do, Pa?"

Ty rubbed his jaw. "I don't know."

"Do you think Calhoun will make it?"

"Don't know the answer to that one, either."

"If he doesn't, Adam is going to be going against those four devils alone. Even two is steep odds. But one . . ." MacKenna looked up at her father, worry in her eyes.

Ty gazed off toward where the two lawmen had disappeared around a bend in the canyon, heading northwest. He chewed his mustache, pensive, then drew a deep breath and let it out slowly. "I'm gonna lay back a ways. But I'm gonna follow 'em."

"I'm going with you!" MacKenna said, turning to face him, cocking one booted foot forward, and planting a decisive fist on her hip. "You can't send me home, Pa. I know I haven't known Adam more than a few hours, but he's a good man and he means a lot to me. I simply will not be sent home!" She lifted one foot and set it down sharply, resolutely, narrowing her eyes stubbornly as she gazed up at her father.

"All right."

MacKenna frowned, taken aback. "What?"

"I know there's no sending you home. I've tried that before, and you defied me. Saved my bacon once or twice because of it." Ty chuckled wryly. "Besides, I'd only have to keep an eye on my back trail for you. Keeping an eye on you will be a whole lot easier if you're riding beside me."

MacKenna lowered her fist from her hip, her expression a little stunned. "Thank you, Pa."

"Besides," Ty said, turning to face his daughter, leaning forward, and placing his hands on her shoulders. "After what they did to you, ogling you like a piece of meat in that pool, threatening you, I reckon you deserve a shot at them. *If* it comes to us having to take a shot at them, *if* the federals can't do it alone. If it comes to that, we're going to do it my way, understand?" He thumped himself in the chest. "No carelessness or recklessness, Mack."

MacKenna nodded, smiled. "I wouldn't have it any other way, Pa."

"All right." Ty kissed her cheek. "Why don't you join me for a cup of coffee? We'll let Parker and Calhoun get a good distance ahead before we start shadowing them. If Calhoun even suspects we might be on his back trail, he'll be madder than an old wet hen."

"I feel sorry for him," Mack said, reaching into a saddle-bag pouch for a coffee cup. "I could see the fear in his eyes."

"Yeah," Ty said, removing the coffeepot from the tripod. "He doesn't want to believe he's on the way out." He filled MacKenna's cup with the piping hot brew. "What's worse, he's a man saddled with a hard job, and he knows if he gives it up, he'd only be giving the nod to the man with the scythe." He shook his head. "Darn tough business—life. Sometimes."

Ty refilled his own cup then returned the pot to the tripod, dropped the leather swatch near where Calhoun had dropped his cup in the grass, and returned to his perch on the log.

MacKenna sat down on a rock near her father, facing him on the same side of the fire, and blew on her coffee. "You ever think about that, Pa?"

"What? The reaper?"

Mack hiked a shoulder and nodded.

Ty sipped his coffee and gave his own shoulder a shrug. "You can't get to be my age, pushin' sixty, and not think about it, I reckon." He smiled across his steaming cup at his daughter. "Don't worry. I got a few years left. I intend to see you married and with a Brannigan-wild little papoose or two."

Mack chuckled and sipped her coffee. She swallowed and made a face, her cheeks coloring. "Dang, you make it strong!"

"That's why your hair's black!"

"You've been telling me that since the first time you let me sip from your cup."

"And that it would put hair on your chest."

"And I've been telling you since then I don't want hair on my chest!" MacKenna laughed. "Matt always used to peek under his shirt to see if he had any coming up."

They both laughed at that and drank their coffee.

Ty suddenly had a lonesome feeling. He wasn't sure where it had come from until he pondered on it briefly. Then he knew. He took another sip of his steaming mud and glanced over his cup at his daughter. "The way you look at that young man, I'd swear you thought he was the one."

"I don't know, Pa. Maybe he is." Mack glanced at him speculatively. "How would you feel about that?"

"Old."

"I reckon I can't hang around here forever."

"Sure, you could," Ty said.

"If I were to hitch my star to Adam's wagon—just hypothetically speaking, mind you, since I only just met the man last night—I reckon I'd have to leave the Powderhorn."

Ty sipped his coffee and rested his cup on his knee. "I reckon you would. I'd hate to see you go. Both your ma and I would."

"Funny," Mack said, shaking her head and gazing pensively into the fire that had burned down to only two small flames. "I spent my entire childhood wanting it to pass. Wanting to grow up and for my life to begin. I didn't realize *that* was my life, too." She looked at her father. "Now I suddenly feel frightened. As exposed as I felt in that pool yesterday, with those savages' eyes on me."

"That's the way of it, baby girl."

"I don't know if I want to fall in love and get married and move away."

"When it happens, you'll be ready. Rest assured, Mack."

"Will you be ready, Pa?"

Ty smiled. "No. But like I said, that's the way of it."

Mack gazed into the fire again. "What about Matt?"

"What about him?"

She turned to her father again, her eyes grave. "I got a feeling he's ready, Pa. That he's been ready to test his wings . . . elsewhere. Don't get me wrong. He loves the Powderhorn. But I think he might be wondering what it might be like . . . away from it."

Ty winced. "I just started to get that notion myself. He's too damn good with his guns. I'm worried about him."

"Don't be, Pa. He has a good head on his shoulders, Matt does. He'll make the right decision."

Ty drew a deep breath as he lifted the coffee cup from his knee, stretched his legs out before him, and crossed his ankles. "Sometimes being young and making the right decisions do not go hand in hand. Even when you have a good head on your shoulders. Sometimes you need to make your own mistakes. That's how you learn." He lifted the cup to his lips, his eyes grim, fearful. "That can be the way of it, too. I hope not in Matt's case. Could get him killed. I reckon we'll see."

"I reckon we should stop putting the cart in front of the horse—eh, Pa?" Mack gave her father a gentle smile.

Ty winked at her. "Good idea. Come on." He rose, tossed the last of his coffee into the fire, then kicked out the flames. "Let's tighten our cinches and get a move on."

"We're burnin' daylight, Pa!"

"We're burnin' daylight, Mack!"

Chapter 16

"I don't know, Tom—maybe we'd better stop for the night," Deputy U.S. Marshal Adam Parker said.

He'd just drawn his horse up beside his partner, Deputy U.S. Marshal Tom Calhoun, who'd reined in for a drink from his canteen and to mop sweat from his forehead. He'd been doing that all day—stopping, sipping from the canteen he filled at the creeks they came to, and mopping sweat from his face.

Calhoun lowered the handkerchief, glanced over at his partner, a good thirty years his junior, and cocked an eye at the sky. Scowling incredulously, he said, "What're you talking about, Junior? We have several hours of good light left."

Parker shrugged. "Might be best."

"Might be best for who? *Me?*"

Parker sighed. "Look, Tom, you've been fighting the altitude all day. Your breathing sounds like a smithy's bellows. What you need is a good long—"

"Keep it movin', Junior," Calhoun said, stuffing his handkerchief back into a pocket of his broadcloth jacket. "When we can no longer make out those killers' trail, then we'll stop." He gave his younger partner a hard, commanding look and nudged his dun ahead with his spurs.

Parker studied the man's back. Stubborn old soul. Calhoun

wouldn't give an inch. The way he looked—all washed out and royally beaten from the inside out—Parker had a strange, sinking feeling the man might very well die tonight and leave him alone to run down those four savages all by himself.

If Parker had to do that, he would, but he didn't like the idea of it. He'd seen the four savages' handiwork, and it was some of the worst he'd seen. Cold-blooded killers who actually enjoyed killing. And terrorizing, too. He remembered what MacKenna had told him about her encounter in that otherwise storybook canyon, and he remembered the looks of bald-faced terror that had remained on the faces of the two drovers they'd killed near the Brannigans' Powderhorn Ranch.

On the other hand, Calhoun seemed so sick even if he did live to run down the four human savages, Parker doubted he'd be much help. True, in the past when the chips were down, Calhoun had always shaken off his suffering and had fulfilled his obligations as a federal badge-toter. But Parker had never seen him in as bad a shape. He was practically on death's doorstep.

Nudging forward the tough copper bay gelding MacKenna had picked out for him back at the Powderhorn headquarters, Adam felt a smile tug at his mouth corners.

MacKenna.

Thinking of the beautiful, black-haired, hazel-eyed Mexican-Irish beauty buoyed him against his dread of his partner's demise. He was glad he and Calhoun had acquired a pair of Powderhorn mounts. It meant they had a very good reason to stop at the Powderhorn headquarters again once their job was complete.

Parker had to admit, if only to himself, to being completely and thoroughly smitten by the girl.

He kept his eyes on the canyon trail he and Calhoun were following, noting the occasional horse apples and shoe prints that confirmed to him and his partner they were still on the killers' trail though there were few other trails in this remote neck of the Bear Paws. The lawmen were quartering generally to the northwest, though the various watersheds they'd traversed over the course of the day had hopscotched around quite a bit, switching directions. While he tried to keep his mind on the trail, in the back of the young deputy's mind, he remembered the sensation of young Miss Branni-gan's silky lips on his—

He'd never been quite so taken with a girl so quickly.

Then again, he'd never before met anyone quite like MacKenna Brannigan, as beautiful and frank and intelligent as she was earthy and, despite her having made the first move the previous night, even shy.

Yeah, she was shy and tender and playful and sweet and—

"All right. Gettin' mighty dark out here." Tom Calhoun broke into his partner's thoughts just after they'd climbed up and over another rocky pass. "Now, I reckon we'd best set up camp and build a fire."

Parker turned to the older man. The two sat together in yet another narrow canyon, a creek chuckling in the pines off the trail's left side, above the peeping of chickadees and the screeching of a blue jay.

Calhoun frowned. "What is it?"

Parker just realized he must have been wearing a sur-prised expression.

He glanced around, feeling his cheeks warm with embar-rassment, suddenly realizing that sure enough, while they'd been riding for the past couple of hours he'd been so deep in romantic thoughts and notions he hadn't even noticed the sun had gone down and the canyon was all purple shadows and black tree stems. The sky was dark green. A single star shimmered in the branches of a sprawling spruce, like a lone Christmas tree decoration.

Calhoun chuckled. "Must be nice bein' young. Being able to fill up your head with a young and beautiful lady!" He chuckled again then grew serious. He reached over and placed a fatherly hand on Parker's left shoulder. "Listen, Junior, she's cuter'n a speckled pup. But don't fill your head so full of her that she gets you killed, understand? Keep your wits about yourself."

Again, Adam's cheeks warmed with chagrin. His partner was right. The four devils they were on the trail of were nothing to trifle with. Adam had to keep on his toes. Fortunately, Calhoun had been riding ahead of him and watching for the killers' sign. If he himself had been in the lead, he might have lost the spoor by now and gotten them both hopelessly lost.

"Good advice, Tom. I've filed it. Thank you."

"Come on, kid," Calhoun said, reining his roan off the trail and into the pines, heading toward a crease between two rocky buttes. "I spotted a good place to camp up yonder while you were pondering that good-bye kiss earlier."

Adam's lower jaw dropped and his eyes widened. "You saw?"

Calhoun wheezed a laugh. He glanced over his shoulder at the younger man. "I might have one foot in the grave, but I still got eyes, don't I? Good ones, too." He turned his head forward and wagged it. "Just wish I could say the same for my lungs." He stopped his horse inside the crease between the buttes.

The crease was a wash, dry this time of the year, carved down between two low cutbanks sheathed in berry shrubs and wild mahogany. Calhoun glanced over at Adam. "How's this look?"

Parker looked around, nodding. He glanced up the ridges surrounding them, nodded again. "Good cover here."

When Calhoun didn't say anything, Adam looked at him.

Tom was looking around at the ridges, chin raised, frowning, his ragged breaths rumbling up from deep in his chest.

"What is it?" Adam asked.

Calhoun's frown turned more severe. "I don't know." He glanced at Adam. "Just had a strange feelin's all." He chuckled. "Must be old-timer's disease to go along with these lousy lungs." He leaned to his left and climbed heavily down from his saddle. When he was on the ground, he looked around again, scowling up at the ridges, then shook his head as though to clear it and set to work loosening his saddle cinch.

Adam cast his own cautious gaze at both ridges. Nothing up there but rocks and pines and birds flitting around, the late light flashing gold off their wings. He eyed the older lawman warily, wondering if Calhoun's bad lungs paired with the thin air at these climes was messing with his head. All Adam needed was for Calhoun to start jumping at shadows.

Despite Adam telling Calhoun that he'd set up camp and do the cooking, Calhoun insisted on doing his part.

As the light continued to bleed out of the sky and the air grew more and more chill, Calhoun's breathing grew raspier. Still, because Parker had gathered wood and started the fire, Calhoun insisted on cooking. He whipped up a stew with beans, fat back, and a potato, and handed a steaming plate to his partner. His gaze suddenly cold and hard beneath the brim of his Stetson he said quietly, "There's something on the ridge yonder." He canted his head to his left, indicating the ridge rising on the north side of the wash.

Adam started to turn his head in that direction.

"No, don't look!" Calhoun wheezed, and spat a gob of blood and phlegm.

"How do you know?" Adam asked him.

"Spied movement near the top not two minutes ago."

Adam frowned skeptically. "You sure?"

"Certain-sure."

Adam stepped back away from the fire with his plate, sat down on a log, facing north, and took up his fork as though he were about to start chowing down on his supper. With the hand holding the fork, he poked his hat brim back off his forehead and took a quick look up the ridge.

It was too dark to see anything up there.

Ladling up a plate of the stew for himself, Calhoun took another quick look toward the top of the northern ridge, then grabbed a fork and came over and sat down beside Adam.

"You sure there's somethin' on that ridge, Tom?" Adam asked him.

Calhoun forked a bite of meat and potatoes into his mouth. Chewing, he said, "Yep."

"Pretty dark."

"I saw somethin' move."

"Tree branch?"

"No wind."

Adam glanced at his partner again, his heart quickening slightly. "You think it might be one of them we're after?"

"Only one way to find out." Calhoun forked another bite of food into his mouth, keeping his head down, feigning nonchalance. "On the count of four," he said, chewing and keeping his gaze on his plate, "set your plate down on the ground, grab your rifle, and slip down the wash to the west. I'll go east."

"We're gonna climb up there?"

"Best we go to them than sit here waiting for lead, Junior."

Again, Adam glanced at him skeptically. He couldn't see his partner making a steep climb like that. "You sure?"

"Certain-sure." Calhoun forked another bite into his mouth and, staring down at his plate, chewing, he said, "One . . . two . . . three . . . *four.*"

They each quickly set their plates down, reached for their

rifles leaning up against the same tree, and stepped out away from the fire. Adam moved west along the wash, crouching and levering a round into his Winchester's action. Calhoun moved east, quickly disappearing into the darkness beyond the fire.

Adam was skeptical, but he'd make the climb. Calhoun had seemed so certain he'd seen something on the ridge. On the other hand, his brain might be foggy from lack of oxygen. He looked better now since they'd stopped riding, but Adam had still been able to hear the man's deep, rumbling breaths, and Calhoun continued to spit blood from time to time.

When Adam had walked fifty yards or so west of the fire and the fire was merely a small, flickering glow in the darkness behind him, he followed a game path up out of the wash and through the shrubs lining it. Just beyond the shrubs, he dropped to a knee and studied the rise before him.

It would be a steep climb even for him at twenty-six years old. He didn't see how Calhoun was going to make it in his condition and pushing sixty.

With a quick, fateful sigh and a head shake, nervously opening and closing his hands around his rifle, Adam rose and started moving up the ridge. He wended his way around pines and rocks of all sizes including wagon-sized boulders. He moved slowly, taking his time, keeping his eyes and ears skinned for the slightest movement.

He had Calhoun to thank for his stealth and keenness of mind. It had been Tom who'd taught him to take his time, to slow his mind down and to keep it in the moment, to be aware of everything around him, the slightest movement. He'd been paired with Tom when he'd first started in the Service, because Tom was older, wiser, and more experienced. Adam was glad to have learned from him despite the older man's cantankerousness.

He knew from Tom that even the flicker of a single leaf

might reveal a rifle being aimed his way. Yeah, he had Tom to thank for that.

Poor Tom. He wasn't the man he used to be. The climb was likely a wild goose chase.

About all Adam was liable to get out of it was one dead partner. As he climbed, feeling his heart pumping and his lungs working in the thin air, feeling the strain in his thighs and knees—in his *young* thighs and knees—he couldn't imagine Tom making a similar ascent of the ridge.

There'd been no way Adam could have talked him out of it, though. Once Calhoun had made his mind up about something, there was no changing it. Since his affliction had started coming on strong around a year ago, he was more easily insulted, to boot.

Hope you're makin' it, Tom.

Adam stopped near a wind-gnarled cedar and dropped to a knee. He looked back down the ridge then up toward the crest. He was roughly halfway to the top, maybe sixty or so yards left. So far, the night had been as quiet as a held breath. Not even the slightest stirring of a breeze. No movement whatever.

If something were up here, he would already know it. *Damned wild goose chase.*

He continued forward, crossed a talus slide, wincing as the rocks slipped and slid and ground together audibly beneath his boots. When he was across the slide, the climb grew steeper as he neared the craggy crest, moving through a natural corridor between lumps of dark granite. Twice he had to hoist himself with his elbows up an especially steep rise to the next ledge of rock.

He gained the crest. Staying low, he looked around.

Nothing. Only stars flickering above him, more rock jutting darkly around him. He had a clear view across the bullet-shaped crest and the steep slopes to his right and left. If one of those killers was up here, he'd surely have known it.

With a weary sigh, he continued forward. He intended to descend the bluff the way Calhoun was climbing it . . . if the man was still climbing and hadn't fallen over dead, his heart having exploded from the strain.

Adam crossed the butt's crest and started down through large thumbs of rock jutting to each side.

As he emerged from the corridor, a raspy voice yelled to his right, "Adam, run!"

Adam heard the clatter of gravel to his left. It was dribbling down the side of one of the boulders forming the corridor he'd just emerged from. He looked up to see two eyes glowing red in the darkness, boring down on him from atop the rock. As the wildcat's mouth opened and long, savagely curved teeth shone white in the darkness, a loud, snarling roar filled Adam's head, making his eardrums rattle.

Ancestral dread nearly made his own heart explode.

The cat was crouched low, butt in the air—almost a playful pose. But there was nothing playful about the puma's intentions. It whipped its tail up against its side then lunged off the boulder with its back feet, the long, large-pawed body growing enormous as the big cat flung itself down toward its prey.

Adam yelped and tried to run but got his feet entangled.

A rifle thundered, chasing the echoes of the big cat's savage scream across the star-capped night.

A brief, savage wail sounded in the darkness just above the young deputy marshal as he fell belly down, smashing his chin hard against the ground. As he groaned, the cat slammed onto his legs—a hot, heavy, writhing burden. Adam closed his eyes against certain death—which did not come.

The cat, sprawled across the back of Parker's lower body from his butt to his feet, lay unmoving except for the hammering of the heavy heart against his backside. The heartbeat slowed then it stopped, and the cat's large, heavy body, which filled the young marshal's nose with the sweet, gamey smell of something wild, lay slack against him.

Adam pushed up on his hands and cast a wide-eyed, terrified look over his right shoulder. Sure enough, the cat lay on the backs of his legs, its head snugged up against the small of his back, pinning him down. It might have been an oversized lover curled up against him, sound asleep. In the darkness, blood shone where the bullet had gone into one side of its head, just below the ear, and exited the opposite side, blowing out a fist-sized chunk of bone, brains, blood, and fur, which streaked the ground beyond the cat for several feet.

Crunching footsteps sounded to Adam's right.

He heard Calhoun's wheezing, raking breaths before the man's hatted silhouette took shape in the darkness, stepping out from between two rocks. Tom held his rifle up across his chest. He walked slowly over to where Adam lay pinned down by the cat.

Calhoun stopped, pinched his broadcloth trousers up at the thighs, and squatted down with a grunt. He set his rifle butt down beside him and leaned on it. He looked at young Adam and grinned, the sweat on his face glistening in the starlight.

"I still got it, Junior." Calhoun winked.

CHAPTER 17

The screeching rifle report echoed across the night.

Sitting with his legs crossed Indian style by the fire he'd let burn down to glowing coals, Ty looked up with a start as he cleaned his rifle. Where she lay on the other side of the fire from her father, resting back against the wooly underside of her saddle, MacKenna gasped.

She sat up, eyes wide and round. "Rifle shot."

Ty nodded, frowning off in the direction from which the report had come—straight west. MacKenna turned to stare that way, as well.

"Only one," Ty said after several seconds had passed.

"Only one so far," Mack said, her voice quiet, toneless.

Ty let a minute pass, then another. Tied to picket pins in the darkness behind him, the horses were whickering quietly. The report had put them on edge.

"Just the one," Ty said. "Could've been anybody."

"Calhoun and Adam are west of us," Mack said, still staring in that direction. She turned to her father again, frowning. "I heard what sounded like a roar just ahead of the shot. A cat?"

Ty nodded. "I heard it, too." He kept his ears pricked for a time then resumed running an oily rag down the barrel of

his Henry repeater. "We'll check it out in the morning. Too
dark out there now."

Mack drew a deep breath, let it out slowly, then lay back
down against her saddle.

Ty knew she was worried. She'd put a lot of stock in
Adam Parker.

At the first wash of dawn, Mack was up ahead of her
father the next morning.

Ty heard her stirring. He poked his hat up onto his forehead and opened his eyes. She was folding her soogan. She
looked at him, gave a shrug and a guilty smile.

She rolled and tied the bedroll. "Burnin', daylight, Pa."

Ty sighed, threw back his blankets, and reached for his
boots. "The older a man gets, the earlier mornin' seems to
come." But he knew morning couldn't have come early
enough for Mack.

Aside from a few sips of coffee and bites of jerky, they
skipped breakfast and were on the trail ten minutes later,
following the same trail the lawmen had followed to the
west. Judging by the tracks the men had left yesterday, Ty
figured they were only a couple of miles ahead of him and
Mack, following the spoor of the four killers.

The sun was poking its shimmering lemon head above
the horizon between silhouetted mountain peaks behind
them when they climbed a saddle and started down the other
side.

"Whoa," Ty said, drawing back on his dun's reins.

"What is it?" Mack said from behind him.

She drew her Appaloosa up alongside him, and they both
stared at the furry beast hanging from its hind feet from a
pine along the right side of the trail. Frowning curiously, Ty
put his horse forward and stared up at the beast gazing down

at him through glassy, brown, heavy-lidded eyes. Dried blood stained both sides of the animal's head.

"Painter," Ty said. "Puma."

"Look there, Pa."

Ty followed his daughter's pointing finger to something on the trail at the bottom of the pass. Two neat collections of rocks. Together, he and Mack walked their horses down to level ground and sat staring at the two words the rocks formed, one above the other.

"Go back," Mack read, turning to Ty.

He gave a dry chuckle then glanced at the cat again and then at the two words formed by the rocks. "The old scudder knows we've been shadowing him."

"How did he know?" Mack said, planting an indignant, gloved fist on her hip and turning her exasperated gaze to her father again.

Ty shrugged. "I thought we were staying back far enough, but I reckon Marshal Calhoun is savvier and more on his game than I gave him credit for. Wouldn't doubt if it was him who shot that cat."

"What're we gonna do? We're not going to go back, are we?"

Again, Ty shrugged. "The jig is up, baby girl. Calhoun knows we're shadowing him and he's made it clear enough how he feels about it."

"We're not turning around?"

Ty nodded and looked at the words written in stone once more. "We've insulted the man, Mack. Doubted his abilities. Yes, we're going back."

Ty reined the dun around and started back up the pass.

"But, Pa . . ."

"Come on, Mack."

"They're two against four savages!"

"They're the law, Mack. They have the authority to say

who rides with them and who doesn't. Calhoun has made it plain enough he doesn't want our help."

Ty stopped the dun at the top of the pass and gazed back down at Mack still sitting her appy, Cervantes, at the bottom, gazing up at her father with taut-jawed, bright-eyed defiance.

"I bet Adam does," she said.

"Wouldn't doubt it a bit." Ty grinned down at his pretty daughter. "But he has ulterior motives." He reined the dun around and started back down the pass.

Silence reigned behind him for three long seconds before he heard her pitch her voice with deep frustration and punching her chap-and-denim-clad thigh. "*Oh, hell!*"

The appy's hooves clomped behind Ty, growing louder as she approached the top of the pass.

Ty chuckled at his gamesome girl.

Since they had an early start and their horses were fresh, they managed to make it back to Powderhorn graze late in the afternoon of that same day.

They were only about a couple of miles from head-quarters when Ty heard the crackle of distant gunfire from straight ahead. He and Mack shared a curious look then nudged their horses into ground-chewing gallops. They rode through an aspen copse and as they approached the far end, Ty slid his Henry from his saddle sheath. The gunfire was getting loud enough he knew he was within a hundred yards or so of the shooters.

MacKenna followed suit, single-handedly levering a round into her carbine's breech.

Ty checked the dun down just inside the grove and curveted the mount as MacKenna reined in her own mount to his right. They stared out at a broad bowl of prime, autumn-cured, tawny graze ringed by more aspens.

Three men were hunkered down behind two boulders

roughly a hundred yards nearly straight out beyond Ty and Mack's positions at the edge of the aspens. The three men were throwing lead up a low rise to Ty's left, at another man lying belly flat behind what appeared a dead horse. The fourth man was firing his own Winchester over the dead horse, using the horse's saddle as a prop, at the three men below him.

The head of the man behind the dead horse was bare, his cream Stetson lying crown down on the ground behind him. Right away, Ty recognized the lanky frame and the longish brown hair hanging over the collar of the fourth man's red plaid shirt. Ty's heart hiccupped in his chest.

"Matt!" he and MacKenna yelled at nearly the same time, exchanging a quick, fervent glance.

Keeping his head low behind the dead horse, Matt whipped a look toward his father and sister. The young man's face was taut with pain. Ty understood then the source of that pain mainly because of the way Matt was returning fire with only one hand, his left hand and arm hanging slack at his side.

He'd been hit.

"You wait here, Mack!" Ty said as he rammed spurs against the dun's sides.

MacKenna watched her father gallop off down the bowl, heading for the three rifle-wielding shooters throwing lead at Matt. Pa was quartering around them to the south, intending to flank them, yelling, "*Hyah! Hyah!*" to his horse, shooting the Henry one-handed, cocking it one-handed.

Mack arched her brows in appreciation of her father's talents. "Not bad for an old guy," she heard herself mutter.

Two of the shooters directed their fire at her father, but the third one . . . and yet a fourth one Mack hadn't seen until now as he was hunkered down behind a low knoll a good distance from the others . . . continued to throw lead at Matt, keeping him pinned down behind his dead horse, a cream gelding Caroline had dubbed Frisky.

Mack glanced at her father's retreating back. Chewing her lip in consternation, she looked at Matt returning fire with his Winchester one-handed from over the top of the dead cream. Rifles continued to chatter down in the bowl where Mack saw her father rein back sharply on the dun's reins and swing down from the leather, hunkering down behind the broad bole of a lightning-topped pine.

Mack turned to Matt again to see more bullets hammer the dead body of the poor cream and tear up the blond grass around it and her brother, who winced sharply and pulled his head back as he must have taken a graze across his cheek.

"That tears it!" the girl raked out finally and booted Cervantes out of the trees. She wasn't going to sit there while the shooters kept her brother pinned down. She neck-reined the appy left and spurred it into a hard gallop, heading up the rise toward her brother.

Matt turned his head to face her then dropped the carbine and waved his arm at her violently, "Mack, go back! Go back!"

"Like hell!" When Mack was ten feet from her brother, she dropped down the running appy's left side, hit the ground, and rolled, losing her hat but loosening her joints to ease the strain of the fall and the roll. She rolled three times, clinging to her carbine. When she came to a stop, her hair flying wildly around her head and shoulders, she saw the appy glance back at her.

"Keep going, Cervantes! Keep going!" she yelled, not wanting another dead horse—especially the beautiful Appaloosa, which was her favorite of the entire Powderhorn remuda.

Shaking his head in consternation and trailing his reins,

Cervantes continued on up the rise and into the fir forest beyond.

As lead curled the air around her head, MacKenna crawled quickly up to the dead cream and lay belly down to the right of her brother, raising her Winchester and resting it atop the saddle, narrowing one eye as she looked for a target among the scattered large rocks in the bowl beneath her.

"Mack, darn it, I told you to—"

"Oh, hush!" she said, squeezing the carbine's trigger and grimacing when the man she'd targeted pulled his hatted head and rifle back behind his covering boulder and her round merely plumed dirt and tore up weeds behind him. "Looks to me like you're in a bit of a fix here, big brother!" Gritting her teeth, Mack racked another round into her Winchester's chamber.

She winced as a bullet whined past her to spang off a rock behind her. She lined up her sights on the man who'd just poked his head out from behind his rock to fire the round at her.

Mack drew a breath, held it, squeezed the trigger.

The man was pulling his head and rifle back behind his rock again, but Mack's bullet clipped the crown of the man's high-crowned black hat, blowing it off his head. The man jerked his head down behind the rock quickly with a surprised yowl.

"Whoo-hooo!" Mack cried, pulling her head down and racking another round into the carbine's chamber.

"Look at my little sis shoot!" Matt intoned, hunkered low behind the dead horse. An eyelash streak of blood on the nub of his right cheek was visible where the bullet had grazed him.

Mack pulled her head and rifle back up again to see smoke puffing from behind two rocks, the orange flames of the rifles lapping to her right, toward her father down on one knee behind the lightning-topped cedar roughly fifty yards from the nearest two shooters throwing lead at him.

Ty slid his head and rifle out from behind the tree and returned fire, evoking a guttural curse. One of the two men who'd just fired at him rose from behind his covering rock, stumbling backward and twisting to his right. He yelled again, angrily, and just as Ty fired at him, MacKenna squeezed her carbine's trigger.

Ty's round plunked into the man's upper right chest, turning him toward MacKenna, whose own round punched into the man's chest a little lower down. The man gave another yell and stumbled backward, losing his cream hat, throwing his arms out, the wings of his black duster rising like enormous wings. He dropped his rifle then fell backward, rolled onto his side, and lay still.

To MacKenna's left, staring over the top of the horse, Matt pumped his fist in the air and gave a wild rebel yell.

Meanwhile, the other three shooters were running off across the clearing toward where Mack could see two horses standing at the edge of another pine woods, reins dangling, switching their tails anxiously at the gunfire. She held fire because she was too far away from the retreating shooters to do anything but waste bullets. Ty, however, stepped out from behind the cedar, dropped to a knee, and triggered four rounds, angrily pumping the Henry's lever.

His bullets spit up dirt and grass around the three men just before one high-tailed it into the trees while the other two did the same but not before grabbing the reins of the two mounts and jerking the horses along behind them.

Ty turned toward MacKenna and Matt, raised his rifle above his head, and waved it, giving the all-clear signal. MacKenna returned the signal with her carbine. Ty shouldered his rifle and walked over to where his horse stood at the edge of the trees behind him.

MacKenna turned to her brother. "How bad you hit?"

CHAPTER 18

"How bad you hit?" Ty echoed his daughter's query as he trotted his dun up to where MacKenna and Matt were kneeling together near the dead cream that had been fairly riddled with bullets during the lead exchange.

Ty hated losing a horse, but he hated seeing his son wounded even worse. He'd never had to experience that before, and the notion scared the holy heck out of him.

MacKenna was knotting the neckerchief she'd wrapped around the bloody wound in her brother's upper left arm. "Not bad at all, Pa," she said. "I cleaned it out with water from Matt's canteen. Now I've wrapped it. I reckon we'd best leave the rest for Ma."

"Really just a scratch, Pa." Matt winced and scowled up at his father. "Sure hurts like blazes, though."

"Even grazes usually do." Ty swung down from the dun's back, dropped the reins, and walked over to stand over his two oldest children. Fear remained heavy inside him. When he'd first realized it was Matt down behind the dead horse and that the four shooters were shooting at him, his heart had kicked like a mule.

It still was.

"What happened?" he asked.

"I was riding out to make sure we'd cleared out all of

those steers from the graze beneath Sandoval Ridge, and they bushwhacked me. Hit the cream just after I heard them galloping after me and I swung around to face them."

Ty glared down at MacKenna. "I thought I told you to stay in those trees."

MacKenna finished knotting the neckerchief then placed her hands on her thighs and gave her father an admonishing look. "Pa, you didn't really think I wasn't going to help my brother, did you?"

Ty gave a frustrated chuff then turned his attention to his son. "How in holy blazes did you get crossways with Joe Walsh?"

Still on his knees with his sister, one hand clamped over the knotted handkerchief, Matt scowled up at Ty. "Who's Joe Walsh?"

"A snake-eyed, poison-mean regulator out of New Mexico. Probably works for one of the big cattle syndicates that's been pushing into the Wind Rivers and Bear Paws the past couple of years. Likely here to kill nesters because that's how those big syndicates usually handle them. But you're no nester, Matt. What's goin' on?"

Matt turned a little pale as he swiveled his head to gaze down at the man Ty and Mack had shot and who lay on his side where he'd fallen. In the black duster coppered by the late sunshine angling down over the spruce-green forest, he looked like an enormous dead bird. "Regulator, eh?"

"They were likely all regulators riding together. Out with it, son. How'd you get crossways?"

Looking stricken, Matt said, "Uh . . ."

MacKenna took out a flowered handkerchief, moistened it with her tongue, and dabbed at the bullet graze on her brother's cheek. "What is it, Matt?" She looked up at her father, her eyes cast with concern and curiosity, then returned her attention to her brother.

Matt lifted his gaze to his father. He looked like he'd just chugged a quart of buttermilk that had sat outside in the sun too long. "I'm, uh . . . I'm afraid I have a confession to make."

"Spill it," Ty said, crossing his big arms and leaning on one hip.

"Remember, you sent me to town yesterday? To tell Marshal Southern about the dead rustlers?"

"I do."

"Well, I shot a man, Pa."

"Who?" Ty and Mack said at the same time.

"I wrote out that affidavit thing for Marshal Southern and I thought I'd have a beer before I headed back to the Powderhorn."

"Keep goin'," Ty prodded his son, dread settling like a too-heavy meal inside him.

"I went into the Longhorn. That's where"—Matt paused, ran his tongue across his bottom lip—"where I shot"—he switched his gaze to his sister for some reason—"Delvyn Hardin."

Ty could feel his heart beating in his right temple. "You shot Del Hardin?"

MacKenna looked up at Ty, frowning. "Who's Del Hardin?"

"Regulator," Ty and Matt said at the same time.

Ty cast his dreadful gaze down at the dead man lying in the copper sunshine in the black duster. "Likely ran with Walsh and those other shooters." He returned his gaze to Matt. "That's likely why Walsh and the others came after you. They rode with Hardin, took it personally that you shot one of their own."

"He gave me no choice, Pa," Matt said. "He was hoorawing Miss Hayes and I called him on it. He came up to the bar to shake me down. He drew first." Matt switched his gaze to his sister again. "I had to shoot him." He shook his head slowly from side to side. "I had no choice. Ask Miss Hayes. She saw the whole thing."

"Del Hardin is supposed to be fast," Ty said, deeply incredulous. "Greased lightning fast!"

Matt shrugged. "Yesterday, I was faster."

"You were?" Mack asked in surprise.

Ty stared down at his son. Matt stared up at his father. What Ty saw in his son's eyes made that too-heavy meal settle even heavier inside him. He saw chagrin in those eyes, but behind the chagrin lay pride.

Matt had been riding high after killing the known gunslinger and regulator. Maybe feeling a little ashamed of feeling so good about killing a man, but still, he was proud of himself in the way only a nineteen-year-old could feel proud about killing a man who should have been faster with a hogleg than he was.

Ty felt a deep disgust for his oldest son. He'd never felt that way before about any of his children. It hurt him even more than finding out Matt had gotten himself tangled up in a one-on-one showdown in a Warknife watering hole. That's what he'd done, all right. He'd gotten himself tangled up in that fight.

Maybe he hadn't started it, but he'd helped bring it on. Maybe he hadn't set out to get into that fight when he'd set out for Warknife that morning, but he'd been wearing that pretty hogleg on his thigh for a while now, in the same fashion Ty wore his. In fact, Matt's gun was very much like Ty's own, a .44 with staghorn grips—and either consciously or unconsciously, Matt had been wanting to use it.

In public.

Ranch work wasn't enough for him. The boy was good at it, and he worked doggedly from sunup to sunset. But it wasn't enough for him. Whether because of his father's example or because of his father's formerly wild Irish blood running through his veins, Matt had set his hat for adventure—maybe a little of the adventure Ty himself had wanted at Matt's age—and had gone against his parents' wishes to find it.

Ty stared down at his son without saying anything for so long Matt finally flinched and turned away. MacKenna frowned up at Ty uneasily.

To Matt, Ty said, "We'll talk about this later. Did you tell your ma?"

Matt shook his head.

"I'll leave it to you to tell her," Ty said. "About this, she deserves to know. It's going to hurt her. She doesn't want that life for you anymore than I do. But, unlike me, she's sensed you might be headed in that direction. Unlike me, she sees things for what they are and not just what she wants them to be. She should know she had it right and what she might be in for."

Ty wagged his gloved right index finger sternly down at his son, who was still on his knees though MacKenna had climbed uneasily to her feet and stood off to one side. "But later, you and me are gonna have us a sit down chat about this. I've been through it. I know what happens. The kind of thing that happened here today. You kill a man, his friends or family come after you. You should have learned that from the Parmelees." Ty turned away and drew a ragged breath, filling up his broad chest and gazing off into the eastern distance, dimming as the sun quartered down in the west. "Fetch your horses," he said, his tone weary. "We're heading home so your ma can tend that wound."

He felt the uneasy gazes of both of his children burning into him.

No one said anything for over a minute.

Then Matt climbed to his feet, walked over to Ty, placed his hand on his father's shoulder. "Pa—"

"Fetch your horses!" Ty said sharply.

"Honey," he called to MacKenna, "you and Matt will be riding double!"

"Matt's been shot! Matt's been shot!" Caroline cried as Ty, Matt, riding with Mack, and MacKenna reined their horses up to the hitch rack fronting the Powderhorn lodge's big front porch. Sitting on the front porch steps, churning butter, she had seen the bloody bandanna tied around her brother's arm.

"Now, now, darlin'," Ty said, "don't be getting your bloomers in a twist. Why, I've cut myself worse shavin'!"

But that didn't deter the high-strung young Caroline one bit. She turned to yell at the house behind her, "Ma, come quick. Matt's been shot!" She whipped around to her father, her wide eyes lit with anxiety, threw her arms in the air, and said, "I just knew this was gonna happen again!"

"Oh, hush, squirrel," MacKenna said, swinging down from her Appaloosa's back. "You're gonna wake ol' Gramps up on cemetery hill with your caterwauling!"

"Maybe he needs to be woken up and talk a little sense to this family!" Caroline intoned. "Do we all have to dodge bullets *all* the *time*?" She ran up the porch steps, skirting the butter churn, and ran to the lodge door, opened it, and poked her head inside. "Ma! Come quick—" She stopped abruptly and stepped back as Beatriz appeared in the doorway.

Stepping out onto the porch wearing an apron over a simple gingham day frock, she dried her hands on a towel. "What's this about Matthew being shot?" she asked, her dark eyes cast with concern as she strode quickly up to the edge of the steps and stopped.

"I took a graze, Ma, but it's nothin' as serious as the squirrel is makin' it out to be. Not even as bad as the graze

Pa took during the previous trouble with the Parmelee brothers."

"What's this about Matt bein' shot?" Gregory asked as he strode in his lumbering way from the direction of the black-smith shop where the Powderhorn supply wagon sat with one wheel off its hub and leaning against the side panel. The fifteen-year-old doffed his leather billed immigrant hat and brushed a soot-stained wool shirtsleeve across his sweaty forehead.

"It's a scratch, Gregory," MacKenna said. Turning her gaze to her older brother, she added more quietly and darkly, "But it could've been much worse."

"I'll say it could have," Ty couldn't help adding as he tossed his reins over the hitch rack. To the overall-clad Gregory, he said, "Tend these horses, will you, son?" To Matt, who had just dismounted MacKenna's horse, he said, "Come on, boy. Let's get you inside and have your ma tend that burn for you."

"What happened?" Beatriz asked as Ty and Matt started up the porch steps with MacKenna close behind them.

When Ty and Matt reached the top of the steps, Ty stopped beside Beatriz and said, "I'm gonna let him tell it." He glanced at his oldest son who continued on to where Caroline was holding open the lodge's stout oak door, re-garding her big brother somberly and with anxiousness still flaring in her light brown eyes.

Beatriz clucked her disapproval and swung around to her youngest daughter. "Caroline—"

"I know," Caroline said in a haughty tone, turning to follow Matt into the house. "Fetch your medical kit! That's all I'm here for—to fetch things!"

A beautiful painter's palette sunset silhouetted between western ridges when Ty came back out onto the porch. He didn't look to the west. He hadn't come outside to appreciate the sunset though he did that often before he and Gregory started a game of cribbage or checkers, as was their tradition before bed. Before bed for Ty, anyway. He knew Gregory usually carved for an hour or so after he'd gone to his room, for Ty had often seen the lamplight beneath the boy's closed bedroom door and heard the *snick-snick-snicks* of Gregory's knife fashioning a horse or some wild animal like a mountain lion or a snarling grizzly bear standing on its rear legs.

Ty wasn't thinking about the sunset and he wasn't thinking about Gregory, though. He sat down heavily in one of the wicker chairs, putting his back to the lit kitchen window behind him and beyond where Beatriz, MacKenna, and Caroline washed dishes and straightened up the kitchen on the heels of supper.

Ty sat back in the chair and ran his hands through his still-thick, strawberry blond hair stitched with more than a few strands of gray at this late date in his life. At least, it felt late tonight. He felt old. Weary and old and out of sorts. He smoothed his long hair back from the temples, fingered his mustache pensively for a time, then reached inside his buckskin shirt for his makings sack. He dragged it out, opened it up, removed the rolling papers, and began to fashion a quirley.

He was halfway done when the lodge door opened and boots thudded on the porch to his left. He knew it was Matt without having to look. The young man said nothing. He walked up to the top of the steps and stopped, looking out over the darkening barnyard striped with the soft coppers and salmons of the sunset angling into the yard from the west.

Still, he said nothing. He just stood there with his left arm in a sling before him, wearing a clean shirt and with his hair freshly combed and still damp from his pre-supper grooming, which was a tradition at the Powderhorn. Everyone sat up to the table freshly scrubbed and groomed.

Ty rolled the cigarette closed, sealed it, twisted it, dug a lucifer out of his shirt pocket, and snapped it to life on his thumbnail, which was nearly as thick as a seashell and much the same color. He'd lost the nail a few times over the years though he felt himself lucky to have come this far with both thumbs, as losing thumbs to the too-slow dally of a lariat around a saddle horn was a common malady on the range.

He inhaled deeply on the quirley, blew the smoke out into the darkening yard beyond the porch, scratched the back of his head with a sigh, and said, "Come on over here and sit down."

Matt glanced over his shoulder at him then swung around and walked over to sit down in the chair positioned to his father's left. Matt leaned forward, rested his elbows on his thighs, and entwined his hands together. They were big hands, Ty noticed. Large and muscular and rope-burned from range work, which the boy was good at.

Which the man was good at, rather. For Matt was a man now . . . though he was still plagued with boyish notions.

Just like Ty had been himself at Matt's age.

"All right, Pa," Matt said, drawing a deep breath and staring out over the porch rail. "I'm here now."

"That's what I wanted to talk to you about."

Matt turned to regard him, light brown brows ridged curiously.

"About being here . . . or leaving." Ty drew on the quirley again, blew the smoke plume out over the porch rail, and turned to his oldest. "Have you made up your mind?"

Matt grimaced, shook his head. "Honestly, Pa, I don't know."

"Figure it out. Soon. If you're going to go, go. I don't want you bringing more trouble out here. As long as you're here, you won't be wearing that hogleg to town anymore."

Matt looked away pensively for a time and then nodded slowly. He turned to his father again and nodded. "I understand." He turned his head forward to stare into the ranch yard for a time.

When Ty said nothing more but just sat smoking and thinking, Matt turned back to him. "Is that all, Pa?"

Ty nodded, said softly. "That's all, boy."

"Think I'll turn in, then. The arm's mighty sore." Matt rose from the chair and clomped slowly, wearily over to the door.

As he drew it open, Ty said, "Sleep well, Matt."

Matt turned to him, nodded. "You, too, Pa." He went inside and closed the door behind him.

Ty took another long drag of the cigarette and blew the smoke out into the thickening night around him.

CHAPTER 19

"What's on your mind, Junior?" Deputy U.S. Marshal Tom Calhoun said from where he sat on the opposite side of the campfire from his partner, Adam Parker.

Adam looked up from the tin coffee cup he just now realized he'd been staring into, tapping his index finger on the rim. "The boy. The little red-headed boy. The older man—likely the boy's father." He shook his head, still feeling sick and stricken after having followed the killer's trail into the yard of the cabin outside of which they'd found the two bodies. "Why?"

"You know as well as I do—they kill for pleasure," Calhoun said matter-of-factly. He coughed, wiped blood from his lip with his blood-stained handkerchief which he'd wrung out in creeks and springs several times over the past two days. "I've seen it a few times before." He swallowed, shook his head. "But never like that."

"They could have robbed that man and his boy, taken their horses or mules or whatever they found in the corral behind the place. Taken whatever grub they'd wanted. They hadn't had to kill them. It makes no sense. They're obviously taking a remote, rugged route through these mountains because there's less chance of them being followed. Yet with this senseless killing, they're carving a wide swath."

"They don't think they're being followed," Calhoun said, brushing a speck of white ash from the rim of his cup. "They think they can do whatever they want, to whoever they want. They can take their pleasure in killing free of retribution."

"They left MacKenna alive," Adam pointed out.

"That one's hard to figure. But, then again, maybe not," Calhoun said, regarding his partner with a knowing air. "You've heard the woman's reputation."

"They could have taken her. MacKenna, I mean."

"Probably would've slowed them down. I'm sure Zee Sparrow was the reason they left MacKenna alive and in that pool. Too pretty to kill. Zena runs things, I've heard. Smilin' Doc might think he does, but I got a feelin' they all pretty much dance to the woman's fiddle." Calhoun sipped his coffee, coughed throatily again, and added, "Besides, with the kind of money they're carryin', they can all buy any woman they want. Take any woman they want once they're clear of the mountains and are on their way to Montana."

Adam picked up a stick from the pile he'd gathered earlier, before night had closed over the canyon they'd made camp in, and dropped it on the fire, building up the flames against the increasing mountain chill. "Can't get that boy's eyes out of my mind." He winced, blinked as though to clear the horrific vision from his own eyes. He glanced across the fire at his older, more experienced partner. "Why'd he have to kill him like that?"

"The knife across the throat?" Calhoun gazed darkly back at his partner and tapped a finger to the side of his head, just beneath his hat brim. "Because Smilin' Doc ain't right in the head. He was probably smilin' when he did it—when he looked into that poor boy's frightened eyes and ran his knife across the poor kid's throat." He nodded slowly, pursing his lips. "Sure, I bet he was smilin', all right."

Adam gave a shudder. "I just hope I get the opportunity to drill a bullet through his head."

"Not if I get to him first," Calhoun said with a crooked smile. He chuckled.

The chuckle quickly turned into a violent coughing fit at the end of which Calhoun spat out another gob of blood-laced phlegm. Breathing heavily, raggedly, he wiped his mouth once more then took a pull from the small, flat brown bottle he tugged on from time to time and which seemed to quell the worst of his attacks.

He corked the bottle and sagged back against his saddle, his face pale and swollen. He appeared thoroughly spent.

Adam stared at his partner with a concern he was growing weary of. "Tom . . . ?"

Calhoun opened his eyes and smiled. "Don't worry. I'm not gonna die. Might look like it." Still smiling, he shook his head, blinked slowly. "I looked like I had one foot in the grave last night, too, didn't I?" He narrowed a shrewd eye at his partner. "Hell, Junior, if it weren't for me and that eagle eye of mine, you'd be painter bait."

Adam smiled at that but then gave another shudder, remembering the big, hot, furry bulk of the puma lying on top of him. He'd been a second, maybe a second and a half away from certain, bloody death . . . if not for his partner, who'd somehow made the climb without his lungs blowing out and had managed to plant a killing bullet in the painter's head.

"Believe me, partner, I'll remember that shot on my deathbed," Adam said.

"You musta been thinkin' about her, eh? When you let that cat sneak up on you. Your swim-happy friend, Miss MacKenna Brannigan." Calhoun gave a wink.

Cheeks warming with embarrassment, Adam lifted his cup to his lips once more. When he'd taken a drink, he sighed and said, "I wish I had that excuse. No, I just got careless. Took my mind off the danger, put it on you." He frowned, still amazed but pleased that his old, sick partner had spied the cat up there on that bluff from clear down in their camp.

"Nah," Calhoun said, shaking his head again, his broad chest rising and falling slowly but heavily, making a low rumbling sound Adam could hear beneath the fire's crackling and popping and a distant coyote's yodeling. "I ain't gonna die tonight, Junior. I'm a stubborn son of Satan. I'm not gonna die without runnin' those four devils to ground. They're the worst I've ever seen, judging by their workmanship. No way I'm givin' up the ghost until those four are either in shackles or turned toe down."

"All right," Adam said, taking the last sip of his coffee and tossing the dregs on the fire, which crackled and steamed. "I'm gonna hold you to that."

Calhoun tugged his hat brim down over his eyes and snuggled back against his saddle, settling low and crossing his arms on his chest. "Good night, Junior."

"'Night, Tom."

Adam set his cup aside. He sat up, removed his six-gun and cartridge belt, and wrapped the belt around the holster. He placed the rig on the ground to his right, within an easy reach if he needed it. His Winchester rifle leaned against a near tree.

Over the course of the day, the trail of the killers he and Calhoun were after was growing warmer, as though they were slowing down for some reason. Calhoun had opined aloud that maybe one of the horses or mules they'd stolen out of the corral of the man and boy they'd killed—tracks had clearly indicated there'd been two more mounts in the corral in addition to the single mule they'd left behind— might be slowing them down. Or maybe the terrain, which was getting more and more rugged as they drew nearer the Bear Paws' western-most pass, was making them slow their progress to save their mounts.

Whatever the reason, it appeared the gap between the two federal lawmen and their quarry was narrowing. Calhoun had told Adam if they pushed their horses and didn't lose a shoe or one of their mounts didn't go lame, they might be able to catch up to the four killers by the end of the next day. The notion pleased Adam. After seeing what the killers had done to the two drovers and then to the man and the boy, the man shot in the back, the boy's throat cut, he couldn't wait to confront those killers face-to-face.

Fear rose in him at the notion, but that was only natural. He'd faced down killers before. For a brief time, he'd been a Pinkerton before joining the Marshal's Service on the recommendation of one of his supervisors, who'd had federal connections. He hadn't faced down the lowly grade of desperate vermin these killers were, but he'd face them down, too. And he and Calhoun would be hauling their dead carcasses back to the Powderhorn sprawled belly down across their saddles.

Then Adam would see MacKenna again.

The notion made him smile.

Snores rose on the other side of the dimming fire. Snores mixed with low, rumbling coughs. Calhoun was asleep.

Old Tom would make it, Adam thought. By God, he'd make it. Stubborn old fella. He wouldn't go down until their quarry was run to ground. Adam believed that now himself, and the thought gave him comfort. Not only because he didn't want to have to take the four killers down single-handedly—what man would?—but because old Tom was like a father to Adam, the father he had lost when very young on his family's small New Mexico horse ranch. He was not looking forward to parting ways with the older man.

That would be a sad day.

He drew up his soogan blankets against the growing cold then reached over to toss another stick on the fire. He'd keep the fire built up. In his condition, Tom needed to be kept warm. The killers were far enough ahead Adam could risk keeping the fire built up tonight.

He shivered. Besides, he was cold, too.

He removed his hat, set it down beside him, snuggled down in his blankets, and rolled onto his side. He indulged in a quick memory of the kiss he'd shared with young MacKenna back at the canyon, smiled, then let the day's hard ride pull him down into the warm, dark, soothing depths of a good night's sleep.

Something woke him.

He opened his eyes, surprised to see a good bit of gray light washing into the canyon. He'd slept so deeply he'd lost all sense of time. He hadn't woken even once to tend nature, like he usually did. He'd slept straight through.

Blinking sleepily, he rolled onto his back and looked around. Fog hung heavy in the canyon, almost like wet, gray blankets hung from pine and aspen boughs. It was so heavy, in fact, that it obscured old Tom still lying on his back against his saddle. The man was still snoring, mouth opening and closing . . . opening and closing . . . gray-mustached upper lip fluttering. His hat had fallen off during the night and lay on the ground to his left.

The snores were so raking and grinding Adam winced at what must be the emaciated condition of the poor man's lungs.

But the snores were not what had awakened Adam.

They once had. In fact, when he and Tom had started riding together, Adam had had to stuff cartridge casings in his ears to drown the noise. After a year or so, however, he'd become so inured to the old man's infernal sawing that he hardly ever even noticed it anymore.

Something else had drawn him up out of the deep sleep he'd indulged in.

His right hand sliding over to his .45 resting in its holster, he slowly sat up, looking around, still blinking sleep from his eyes. He glanced over his shoulder toward where he and Calhoun had picketed their horses.

A cold stone dropped in the lawman's belly.

Neither horse was where they'd left them.

CHAPTER 20

Heart thudding, Adam turned to Calhoun and said softly but stridently, "Hey, Tom!"

Calhoun stopped snoring, grunted, then resumed sawing logs again.

"Tom!" Adam said, louder, rising quickly and lifting his gun and holster up off the ground.

He wrapped the belt around his waist, cinched it, then stooped to retrieve his hat. He glanced at his partner again. He was about to call to him again but then it occurred to him that the horses might have simply pulled their picket pins and wandered off. It had happened before. Maybe that was what he'd heard. He'd let Tom sleep. The poor man hadn't gotten much sleep the past several nights; his own coughing had kept him up. Finally, he was getting some good sleep.

Adam grabbed his rifle and walked into the trees where he and Calhoun had picketed the horses, moving slowly, looking around, able to see little but the fog that rose and fell, swirling like heavy smoke in a closed room. He continued walking away from the camp, squeezing his rifle in his hands. The mounts had probably drifted off for better graze.

He stopped suddenly.

The sound came again. It sounded like the soft, forlorn cry of a girl.

What would a girl be doing out here?

The cry had come from ahead and to his left, so he angled in that direction, glancing over his shoulder toward the camp. Calhoun was still snoring but far enough away that Adam could barely hear him.

"Help!" came the girl's cry again, clearer this time. Anguished.

It had come from the smoke-like clouds of swirling fog straight ahead of him now.

He continued forward, squinting, straining his eyes to see into the fog but able to see only a few feet ahead of him. The fog was disorienting, dizzying. Several times he stumbled over his own feet.

"Help me!" came the girl's cry again. "I'm hurt!" A sob followed the plaintive wail.

Adam moved slowly forward, looking around but keeping a close eye on the ground so he didn't trip and fall. As the fog slithered around him, sometimes opening briefly then closing again, he had the sense of wading through water. "Where are you?" he called.

"Here! I'm over here!"

Frowning, Adam adjusted his course slightly then continued walking. The fog opened and closed, revealing pines and gold-leafed aspens before obscuring them again. He found himself crossing a clearing in which the fog was thicker than before. His boots crunched the lightly frosted grass. He tripped over a rock, stumbled forward, and nearly fell.

"Here!" the girl cried, closer now, somewhere not far ahead. "I'm here! I'm injured!" Another sob. "Oh, it hurts!"

"I'm coming!" Adam returned then stumbled forward and dropped to his knees when he found himself climbing a rise that he hadn't seen. He grunted, cursed, pushed to his feet, continued climbing.

Warmth touched the back of his neck. Gold light shone through the fog to dapple the ground around him. He glanced behind him. Through the mistlike fog he could see the buttery orb of the sun lifting its head between two eastern ridges. Around him, the fog was thinning, already burning off as the ground warmed.

He seemed to be climbing with the sun. With every step he took, the air warmed around him, and the fog thinned. Birds chirped. Squirrels chittered. The forest was coming alive with the sun and the dissipating fog.

"Hurry!" the girl cried. "Oh, why can't you hurry? I'm *hurt*!"

"What happened?" Adam called, a little breathless from the climb, squeezing the rifle in his hands where he held it up high across his chest.

His heart was thudding. But not from the climb.

Fear?

But the girl sounded like a child.

He broke through the last wisps of the fog and into pure, golden, warm sunlight as he stepped up onto the bald crest of the ridge.

He stopped suddenly. Another cold stone dropped into his belly.

A cold, wet stone that weighed as much as a gold ingot.

"Adam!" Tom shouted behind him, his phlegmy voice distant but echoing. "It's a damn *trap*!"

Adam stood frozen, unblinking, staring straight ahead.

A woman and two men stood before him, twenty feet away. The woman stood between the two men—a big, rawboned, severely featured Indian on her right, a bearded, pot-bellied white man as tall as the Indian standing on her left. The Indian wore a low-crowned straw sombrero and a bear fur coat over buckskins. The white man wore an age-coppered broadcloth jacket under a dusty, ragged, spruce green duster, the duster flaps pulled back behind two six-shooters holstered high on his broad hips.

The three stood six feet apart, the woman with her feet widely spread, grinning.

The woman was tawny-haired, beautiful, tall for a woman though her head came up only to the men's shoulders. She wore a long, black leather duster over a black leather vest tightly tied with leather thongs across her ample breasts. Her flaxen hair hung straight down past her shoulders. Her face was oval-shaped, freckled, blue-eyed. It was a china doll's face.

The woman's and the white man's cunning smiles broadened as they stared like two hungry wolves at Adam, jeering in their coldly cunning eyes.

The Indian stared stonily at Adam, holding a Yellowboy rifle casually on his shoulder, rolling a long stem of grass between his thick lips. His black eyes were set deep in copper sockets above the severely chiseled plains of his face. The eyes were like two hard, black rocks seen through shallow water. They were cold, soulless. There was something inhuman about them.

"Adam!" Tom's voice called, louder, from behind him. "*Stop! It's a trap!*"

In Adam's right ear a man's soft, almost gentle voice said, "Your partner's right, Adam."

Adam whipped around, heart jerking, racing. He'd just started to thrust the Winchester out before him when he saw the suited, handsome man standing in front of him and a little to his left, drawing his right hand back low behind him then thrusting it forward with a smile and a soft grunt.

"Oh!" Adam said, feeling the knife blade burn into his belly, low on his right side.

Instantly, he dropped the rifle and fell to his knees.

He closed his hands over the blood oozing out of him

and looked up at who could be only Smilin' Doc Ford, as handsome and nattily dressed and bowler hatted as he was poison mean.

Doc winked down at Adam, the evil man's smile dimpling his cheeks. "Don't worry—I'm not gonna kill you till your partner gets here."

His smile broadened to show a full set of very white teeth. The sun glinted in his killer's eyes.

"Oh, Adam," Calhoun wheezed as he stumbled through the fog, heading in the direction he'd heard the girl's cries. "That's what they do first," he muttered to himself. "They confound and terrorize." He remembered the looks of horror that had remained on the two drover's faces as well as on the faces of the man and the boy lying dead outside their cabin.

"Take pleasure in it—*oaff!*" he grunted as he tripped over a deadfall unseen in the fog. He struck the ground hard on his belly, lost his hat and his rifle. Cursing, heart fluttering, his disease-wasted lungs felt like two raisins in his chest. The climb up the steep ridge after the cat had cost him.

He winced, shook his head, drew a couple of ragged breaths then pushed up onto hands and knees. He lifted his head, gazing through the thinning fog straight ahead of him. Eerie silence now. No more calls from the girl. Woman, rather. She had to be Zenobia Sparrow. Former stage actress, former prison inmate, Calhoun remembered from the file he'd read on her. A couple of years ago, after she'd gotten out of a woman's prison in Oklahoma, she'd tumbled for the handsome gambler, gunman, and cold-blooded killer, Smilin' Doc Ford. He had also been a guest of a territorial prison—one in which he'd met the other two killers riding with him, the Indian known only as Bear and the other known as Hungry Jack Mercer.

Cold-blooded killers, all. They'd killed for fun before they'd taken to robbing army payrolls, stagecoaches, even trains, to fund their frequent killing sprees. Wherever they went, they left a trail of bodies behind them though no one had ever been able to pin specific murders on them. But slashed bodies showing up in mining camps and cow towns they'd been known to have visited was just too much of a coincidence.

The funereal silence despite the piping birds and chattering squirrels wrapped around Calhoun's ragged lungs and weak ticker, squeezing. Dread filled him, made his heart chug.

Adam . . .

There's been no gun shots, no more noise whatsoever.

They had him.

Calhoun grabbed his hat, set it on his head. He grabbed his rifle, set it butt down, and used it to help hoist himself to his feet. Grunting against the burn in his lungs, he started forward.

"Tom!" Adam's voice rose from somewhere in the dispersing fog ahead of Calhoun, beyond the clearing he found himself in, following Adam's trail of bent grass and crushed pinecones. "Don't come! Get out of here!"

Calhoun stopped, hardened his jaws, squeezed his rifle in his gloved hands. They had him, all right.

Dread weighing heavy in him, Calhoun continued forward, slanting shafts of the rising sun burning through the fog around him, thinning it, burning it off, melting the frost.

"Tom!" Adam's voice cut through the birdsong again, pitched with anguish. "Please don't come! MacKenna had it right—they're *devils*!"

"Oh, I know," Calhoun said, quickening his pace, swinging his head from left to right and back again, knowing he was probably walking into a trap. But he'd be damned if he'd turn tail. He had to help Adam. He had to confront those devils even though it would likely be on their own terms. Maybe he could kill one of them. That would be something, anyway.

He left the clearing, started up a rise.

His heart hammered and his lungs blazed as he climbed. Hacking up blood, spitting it out, sucking some back in felt as though he might drown on the stuff. He shifted his rifle to one hand, used the other hand to push off his left knee, back-and-bellying his weak carcass up the rise the same way he'd managed to climb the ridge the previous night. He'd made it then; he'd make it now.

Make it, he did, slowly. Crouching low, knowing the four killers might very well be up there, he looked around.

Nothing. No one.

Only short brown grass, a few small pines, and rocks. Slowly, he moved forward across the ridge crest, which stretched away for maybe fifty yards before it appeared to drop away again into another canyon or valley. He saw boot prints, a splash of dark red blood. Scuff marks where a man might have been dragged ahead across the crest of the ridge.

Calhoun stopped, looked around a bit more, his throat dry, a vein throbbing in his temple. He continued forward, crouching over, holding the rifle in both hands, ready to bring it to bear at any second. Sweat dripped down his cheeks. He was breathing as though he were still climbing.

He approached the ridge's far edge, watching the pine forest reveal itself. More of the valley nearer the ridge spread out before him as he continued closing on the edge. He stopped suddenly, looking down, blood searing through his veins.

At the bottom of the ridge, maybe fifty feet out and away from the base, Adam sat his copper bay beneath a stout pine. A bough arched over him. A noose had been tied around

Adam's neck. The other end had been thrown up over the pine bough and was tied off near the bottom of the tree.

He sat straight-backed in the saddle, hatless, blood glistening on his brown wool vest down low on his left side. His hands were tied behind him. His face was pale, eyes cast with agony and terror.

The copper roan's reins were tied around the horn.

Staring up at Calhoun, he glowered and shook his head. The movement caused the horse to flinch, shift its weight from one hoof to another.

"Adam . . ." Calhoun said, heart kicking like an angry mule in his chest.

Again, the younger man shook his head. "No," he said, tightly and just loudly enough Calhoun could hear him. "Get outta here, Tom! They're all around! They'll kill us both!"

Again, the roan shifted, side-stepped so that the slack was taken out of the rope above Adam's head, which was bent to one side, a dreadful grimace on his face.

"No!" Calhoun thrust one hand out, palm forward. "Don't talk!"

He looked around as blood and phlegm bubbled up out of his throat. He spat it onto the ground, looked around at the trees to each side and behind Adam and the roan. He could see no sign of the killers. Of course, they were back in the trees. They wanted him to move on down the ridge to save his friend before the horse stepped out from under the pine.

No doubt they were enjoying the show, the pain and havoc they wrought.

Rage burned in Calhoun. Rage and terror. In the next second, that horse might step out from under the tree. Calhoun chewed his lip. He had to do something or Adam would die for sure.

Before he'd thought about it further, he stepped down off the crest of the ridge, cocking the Winchester and aiming it straight out before him. His heart felt as though it were turning somersaults in his chest. His chest expanded and contracted with each labored, rumbling breath. He returned his gaze to Adam.

As before, he sat taut, head angled to one side, wincing, shaking his head slowly, mouthing the plea, "No! No! No!" over and over again. Tears dribbled down his cheeks.

Calhoun took another step, another, his gaze going to the horse, meeting the animal's eyes and silently beseeching it to remain still.

He took another step, another . . . another.

His right boot clipped a rock and he stumbled forward, his knee buckling. He dropped to that knee with a grunt and shot another quick look at the horse just as it whickered, shook its head, and stepped forward.

"No!" he couldn't prevent himself from yelling. "Stay! *Stay!*"

He heaved himself to his feet just as the horse lunged forward off its hind legs, swerved to Calhoun's left and broke into a full-out gallop, leaving Adam hanging from the pine bough.

"No!" Calhoun shouted as he broke into a run.

Horror seared him as he watched Adam twist and turn beneath the pine bough, kicking furiously so that he turned two quick circles, making sickening gurgling sounds as he strangled.

"Curse you sons of the Devil!" Calhoun bellowed as he ran down the slope, within a hundred feet of Adam now and closing in his shambling, heavy-footed way.

He could hear Adam strangling, see his face swelling and turning red, hear the rope creaking, see the bark from the bough dropping around him, some of it landing on his shoulders.

When he was fifty feet from the tree, a bayonet of red-hot agony seared Calhoun's heart. His knees turned to water and he dropped and rolled, his right arm going numb, an unseen hand clamping itself around his neck and squeezing. He dropped the rifle and, making strangling sounds himself as the seizure gripped him, heaved himself back to his knees in desperation.

His right hand was suddenly a claw, so he left the rifle where he'd dropped it.

Having to drag his right arm because he could no longer feel it, he crawled on one hand and his knees toward the tree, keeping his terror- and desperation-bright gaze on where the rope was tied off on a spike branch near the bottom of the bole.

"Ah, God! Ah, God!" he cried, seeing in the corner of his left eye his partner's spasms slowing, the strangling sounds dying, as well.

Calhoun's legs gave out a few feet from the base of the tree. Lying belly down, he flung his left arm forward, grappling with the rope with his fingers. His folding knife was in his pocket, but he didn't think in his decrepit state he'd be able to reach it in time.

"Oh, Adam!" he wailed, fumbling with the knot. His fingers had little feeling.

A shadow slid along the ground to his left. Another to his right.

He froze, let his hand drop to the ground, and turned his head over his right shoulder to see Smilin' Doc Ford in his natty suit and bowler hat standing over him, a warm smile on the handsome devil's dimple-cheeked face.

Calhoun could see the flaxen-haired Zenobia Sparrow standing with the two others, the full-blood Indian and the big, thuggish, bearded white man, Hungry Jack Mercer. The two big, brutish men flanked her. She stood with one high-topped black boot cocked forward, one nicely rounded hip jutting to one side, her bare arms crossed on the tight leather vest that did little to conceal her ample wares.

"Who put you on our trail, Marshal?" she wanted to know. "No way two federals, one on his deathbed, could've tracked us all this way."

"We covered our trail good when we left them drovers," the Indian said in his guttural fashion, close-set black eyes drilling into the woman, angrily.

"Had to be the girl," said Hungry Jack.

A boot was rammed into Calhoun's left side. He looked over that shoulder at Smilin' Doc Ford grinning down at him again. "Was it the girl? Come on, lawman. You can tell us. Those two horses you and your partner were riding wear the Powderhorn brand. Ty Brannigan owns the Powderhorn, doesn't he?"

"He sure enough does," said the big, ugly man called Hungry Jack.

Calhoun's gaze drifted past Ford to his young partner hanging from the pine bough. Nearly still in death, Adam's eyes were wide and bright in terror. His face was long and pale. He'd kicked out of one boot, and it lay on the ground below him. The sock on that foot was halfway off.

His enflamed heart lurching, Calhoun turned to the handsome devil, Ford. He tried to speak but no longer had the breath. He just glared, thinking of MacKenna, pleading silently with these killers, *No . . . no . . . no. Leave the Brannigans alone.*

Doc squatted beside Calhoun. "The pretty, black-haired, swimming princess is from the Powderhorn, isn't she? She's one of Ty Brannigan's kids."

"No . . . no . . . no," Calhoun managed to wheeze out, that unseen hand squeezing his neck even harder, twisting the last life out of him.

"What're you thinkin', Doc?" the woman asked, smiling devilishly. "Thinkin' you might wanna go back and make good on your threat?"

"Wouldn't have to if you'd let me shoot her," said the Indian.

The woman gave him a saucy look. "Let it go, amigo."

Doc smiled down at Calhoun and shrugged. "Somethin' to think about." He winked down at Calhoun, who just gaped up at him, his fire burning out fast. "Get revenge on the Brannigan family."

The last thing the old lawman saw was Smilin' Doc reach into his boot for a short, sharp-bladed knife.

He didn't feel the blade slide across his throat. He was already dead. But just before his spirit lifted from his body, the last thing he thought was *At least I didn't give the soulless demon dog the satisfaction of killing me.*

CHAPTER 21

Something pulled Ty up out of the warm arms of sleep. He opened his eyes, instantly frowning.

He'd been dreaming he was back in the Never Summer Mountains with his parents, outside their tight little log cabin, tanning hides with his mother while his father sat on a chair outside the cabin's front door, sawing on his fiddle— a slow, melodic ballad that Killian Brannigan had learned as a child in Ireland. It was a cool autumn day with dander-like snowflakes slanting down from a leaden sky.

A large bonfire snapping and crackling in the yard kept father, mother, and son warm.

It had been a good dream. Ty had been back in the soothing, secure sheath of boyhood, protected by and provided for by his parents. It was before he'd been assaulted by the dull but persistent pokes of the wanderlust stick. He'd been enjoying the dream and was annoyed when it had suddenly faded, like the sun obliterated by a heavy cloud, and that warm, secure feeling was replaced by a feeling of . . . what?

Unease.

A vague apprehension firing his nerve endings just beneath his skin.

Pretty sure that apprehension had been initiated by a

sound, he lifted his head from his pillow, propped himself up on his elbows, and pricked his ears, listening.

Beside him, Beatriz's slow, deep breaths stopped. She stirred with a groan, turned to him with a soft rustling sound in the darkness. "What is it, mi amore?"

"Not sure."

Ty tossed the covers back, rose, and walked over to one of the room's two windows. He slid the lace curtains back, lifted the window slowly, wincing against the wooden scraping sound, not wanting to wake the children. He crouched to poke his head out of the opening, the cool, early autumn air touching him, causing goose flesh to rise at the back of his neck.

The night was very quiet, only the faint rustling of a breeze.

That silence was broken by the single yip of a coyote from somewhere up the ridge behind the barn.

Ty kept listening.

The yip came again from a little closer than before.

Ty shrugged, shook his head. Just a coyote. He heard them almost every night at the ranch. They rarely troubled him unless he had young calves on the place. Besides, Rollie usually ran them off when he wasn't out chasing raccoons or hunting rabbits in the woods after dark. The coyote couldn't have been what had pulled Ty out of his dream.

The yip sounded again. It was followed by three more in quick succession, nearly a yodeling sound but not quite. It had come from lower on the ridge, possibly directly behind the barn.

Ty frowned.

Coyote?

Skepticism touched him. Those last yodels hadn't quite sounded coyote-like. Back during the Indian Wars, Indians made sounds like that, communicating with each other and/or trying to confuse and frighten their quarry. Ty knew that from personal experience. More than a few nights he lay

awake in some sandy arroyo in *Apacheria*, listening to those
eerie, coyote-like yodels made by men and half expecting a
poison-tipped arrow to come screeching in from the darkness to perforate his young hide.

"Just a coyote, Ty," Beatriz said from the bed. "Rollie will
keep it out of the yard."

Ty gazed across the yard at the horses. A few were stirring more than they usually did when only one or two coyotes howled. Sometimes an entire coyote chorus would raise
a racket from one of the near ridges, and the horses wouldn't
pay much attention to that unless the coyotes were close.
They weren't afraid of coyotes unless a whole pack was
close. At least, the older ones weren't. Cats and bears, sure. .

One or two coyotes, no.

From the window, Ty could hear a few nervous wickers,
see one of his stallions, a handsome roan that had been
gentled by Brandon Talbot when he'd still been known as
Brandon Waycross, lift its fine head and jutted its long
snout forward to sniff the northern breeze. It gave its tail a
swift, nervous switch.

Ty lowered the window. "Maybe."

"You don't think so?"

"Not sure the horses do. I'm going to take a walk around.
Make me feel better."

"You had a nightmare?"

Ty grabbed his hat off a wall peg. "I had a dream. A good
one."

"Then why are you tense? No handsome young men on
the place to trouble your oldest daughter's sleep." That last
she'd said with a smile; he'd heard it in her voice.

Ty chuckled and stepped into his boots by the door. "Go
back to sleep, my love. I'll be back in a minute. Just restless,
I reckon."

Ty grabbed the Henry which had been leaning against the
wall by the door.

Seeing this, Beatriz said, "Be careful."

"It's nothing, I'm sure. Like I said, just restless."

"A restless man with maturing children and too much on his mind."

Ty chuckled. He hoped that's all it was though he'd discovered of late that having maturing children was no laughing matter.

He opened the door, stepped quietly into the hall, and drew the door closed behind him. Hearing Gregory laughing softly in his sleep, Ty walked down the hall on the balls of his feet and descended the stairs to the foyer. Ignoring the painting his father had done of his mother lounging in a Poudre Canyon meadow on a striped trade blanket with a picnic basket, Ty pulled his buckskin coat off a wall peg, shrugged into it, and went out.

He stepped up to the edge of the porch, staring into the darkness of the ridge rising behind the barn, listening.

Again, came the yodeling howl.

Apprehension grew in Ty. "That was no coyote," he muttered.

It was a man trying to sound like a coyote. Only, there was no answering wail. So what was he doing if not signaling?

Indians were no longer on the prod in this country.

Ty moved quietly down the porch steps and into the yard. He angled toward the barn. Halfway across the yard and moving around the stone tank at the base of the windmill, he stopped suddenly, again pricking his ears.

A catlike cry rose in the darkness to his left.

"What was that?" he muttered.

Cat?

The cry came again, longer and rising and falling several times in pitch.

The coyote's howl rose from the ridge behind the barn.

Only, the howl belonged to no coyote. Just like that

catlike cry had come from no cat. Someone was toying with him.

Who? Why? More cutthroats with chips on their shoulders, like the Parmelee brothers of a few months back?

An owl hooted from higher up on the ridge. It hooted three, then four times.

Only, it had been no owl.

Blood quickening, Ty moved toward the west front corner of the barn and peered down the side toward the rear. Something flashed back there. A brief flicker of starlight off something metallic.

A rifle?

Footsteps rose, boots crunching dry grass and gravel.

Ty jacked a cartridge into the Henry's breech and aimed the rifle straight down the side of the barn toward the back. "Who's there?"

The footsteps continued, dwindling.

Keeping the rifle aimed straight out from his shoulder, Ty strode along the side of the barn, heading in the direction of the footsteps that grew fainter with each soft, crunching thud. He quickened his pace, heart thudding, resting his right index finger against the Henry's eyelash trigger, ready to draw it back at a moment's notice.

He stopped at the barn's rear corner. The footsteps sounded from ahead and slightly right. The man was climbing the ridge; Ty could hear faint, labored breathing but he could see nothing in the darkness.

"Who are you and what the hell do you want?" Ty called, hearing the consternation and anger in his voice. Damn his past, anyway.

If this indeed was his past come calling again.

What . . . *who* . . . else?

He'd just stepped out away from the barn, intending to head up the ridge to follow the lurker when a voice called behind him, "Pa, what's goin' on?"

Ty stopped, glanced back over his shoulder to see his son's tall, lean silhouette in the darkness up near the barn's front corner. "Matt, stay there!"

"Pa?" That was MacKenna's voice.

Ty saw her silhouette in the darkness behind her brother. They were both holding carbines.

"You, too, Mack. Stay there. Someone's out here. I'm gonna find out who. I think there's more than one, so stay there and stay on your toes. Make sure nobody gets inside the house!" With that, he turned his head forward and broke into a jog, following a path through the brush at the base of the ridge and began climbing.

Again, the catlike cry rose from the darkness to his left.

The coyote howled straight ahead and above him, from maybe two hundred feet away.

Beyond where the howl had come from, that owl hooted again—three quick times, in brash mockery.

Up the ridge to Ty's right, a man laughed—a high-pitched guffaw, which echoed around the bowl in which the ranch headquarters lay behind and below Ty, the home of his family.

That home was being threatened once more.

Anger burned hot inside of Ty. He quickened his pace, running hard, breathing hard, wincing at the aches in his aging knees but increasing his pace just the same.

Something shrieked out of the darkness to Ty's right. The bullet spanged off a rock behind him and to his left an eye wink before the rifle that had fired the bullet barked and flashed. Ty dropped to a knee, aimed the Henry up the ridge to his right, in the direction he'd spied the flash, and triggered three quick rounds, the Henry leaping in his hands and thrusting back against his shoulder, peppering his nose with the smell of cordite.

His own shots hadn't stopped echoing when a man's

voice came out of the darkness straight ahead and above him. "Stop shootin', Brannigan, or you'll shoot your horses!"

Another laugh cut through the darkness from the same direction as the bullet. A sharp crack sounded, as though of a hand against flesh.

A horse whickered and thuds sounded, growing louder. So did the sound of squawking tack and the jangle of bit chains. Jostling, silhouetted figures appeared in the darkness fifty feet up the bluff from Ty. Starlight flashed off two pairs of eyes and then, as the horses thundered toward him, their shapes quickly clarified.

Ty stepped to one side as both horses, the copper roan young Adam Parker had been riding running a little behind the mouse brown dun Marshal Calhoun had been riding, galloped past him, heading on down the ridge. Nearly side by side the horses separated only to avoid trees and brush clumps.

Ty gazed after them, a dark dread pooling like warm water in his belly.

As the horses had passed, he'd seen the two figures lashed across the horse's backs. A boot had brushed across Ty's right thigh before the dun had galloped on down the ridge where both it and the copper bay were swallowed by the darkness.

Sick to his guts as well as buoyant with rage, Ty swung around, raised the Henry, and fired shot after shot into the darkness straight above him and to the right. Gritting his teeth against the rush of fury coursing through his veins like acid, he fired until he'd emptied the sixteen-shot repeater and the hammer dropped benignly with a ping.

The echoes of his furious shots chased each other skyward until silence fell over the butte.

Silence . . . save for the distant thudding of galloping horses across the belly of the bluff to Ty's left. Even if he'd had more .44 cartridges, there'd have been no point in capping them. The riders were out of range and quickly putting even more space between them and Ty.

Ty lowered the smoking Henry and spat an enraged curse. He turned slowly to gaze down the slope, hearing his horses as they entered the ranch yard with their grisly cargoes. A cold thought touched him.

MacKenna.

Breaking into a run down the slope, Ty shouted, "Matt, get your sister into the house!"

"Matt!" he called again as he ran. "Get her into the house!"

He didn't want her to see what those two horses were carrying. Especially what one of them was carrying.

But just as he rounded the corner of the barn, he stopped abruptly. The two horses stood out front of the corral. Matt and MacKenna stood beside one of them. MacKenna was on her knees, slumped forward against the side of the horse, one hand resting on the head of the man who'd been tied belly down over the blowing horse's saddle.

Clad in only his longhandles, boots, and hat, Matt stood behind her, gazing down at her and holding his Winchester.

Ty sighed and strode slowly forward. His heart thudded from the run, from all that had occurred at the Powderhorn headquarters on the previously benign night. He hadn't yet wrapped his mind around the fact that the four killers had been here. They'd come toting the bodies of the two dead lawmen.

"Didn't you hear me?" Ty asked Matt as he walked up to where Matt stood gazing sadly down at his sister.

Matt turned to him, said softly, "I tried, Pa."

Ty gazed down at MacKenna. He had no words. She hadn't known the young lawman long. But she knew he certainly hadn't deserved this.

MacKenna knelt with her head down, one hand on the back of Adam Parker's head, digging her fingers into the soft, brown, curly hair. Slowly, she turned to gaze up at her father from over her right shoulder. She didn't say anything. She just gazed up at him. There were no tears in her eyes. Only a wild fury.

"Ty?" Beatriz called from the lodge on the opposite side of the yard.

Ty turned toward her, saw that she'd lit a hurricane lamp and was holding it aloft by its bale. Clad in a nightgown and a powder blue robe, she stood atop the porch steps, staring toward Ty, Matt, MacKenna, and the horses. Gregory just then came out to stand on the porch behind her, yawning, stretching, wearing only his longhandles, his hair spiked up around his head from sleep.

"Yes, honey?" Ty said.

"Is Caroline out there?"

Ty looked around quickly. Not seeing his youngest, he turned to Matt. "Did Caroline come out here?"

"No," Matt said, shaking his head, frowning. "Leastways, I haven't seen her."

Ty turned back to Beatriz. "She's not in her room?"

"No."

Blood turning to ice in his veins, Ty broke into a hard run to the house, yelling, *"Caroline!"*

CHAPTER 22

"Caroline!" Ty yelled again as he ran up the stairs two steps at a time.

When he gained the top of the staircase, dread filled him. At the hall's far end was an open window. Wide open. Open wide enough for a man . . . or a woman . . . to crawl through.

A sturdy outside trellis would have made the climb an easy one.

Ty took two running strides down the hall. Caroline's room was the third one on the right and nearest the window. Her door was open. Ty ran into the room and froze, staring down in horror at the empty, rumpled bed, the covers tossed carelessly back.

A bracket lamp had been lit in the hall as well as in Ty and Beatriz's bedroom. As the watery light angled through the open doorway, Ty saw a single, red hair ribbon laid out atop Caroline's pillow. He walked closer to the bed, stared down at the pillow. The red ribbon had been shaped into a heart.

Running footsteps thundered on the stairs. Ty could feel the reverberations through his boots. He turned just as MacKenna ran into the open doorway and stared down at the empty bed. She gasped and clamped a hand over her wide-open mouth, her eyes large and round and bright with horror.

Matt came up behind MacKenna, gentled his sister aside, and stepped into the room. "I don't get it," he said, frowning at his father. "Where's the squirrel?"

Ty was in such shock he couldn't speak.

MacKenna walked slowly over to the bed and plucked the hair ribbon up off the pillow. She looked at her father. "They've taken her."

"What's this all about?" Beatriz had just stepped into the room, placing her fists on her hips and casting her incredulous gaze at her husband. "Who has taken Caroline?" Her throaty voice quavered with barely checked emotion.

"The men they—Parker and Calhoun—were after," Ty heard himself say tonelessly, his heart turning somersaults in his chest.

"The men and the woman," MacKenna said, staring down at the ribbon she was fingering.

"Ty!" Beatriz said, a sheen of tears glazing her eyes as she, too, clamped a hand over her mouth as though to stifle a wail.

Matt turned to her, wrapped his mother in his arms.

"You two stay with her," Ty said, sidling past Matt and Beatriz, heading into the hall and then into his and Beatriz's room.

MacKenna followed him. She was dressed as her mother in a nightgown and robe, her black hair hanging messily down over her shoulders. "Pa, what are you going to do?"

"I'm going after them." Ty kicked out of his boots. "You and Matt stay here with your mother. I'm going to chase them down before they get too far."

"Pa, it's dark," MacKenna countered, her own voice quavering with emotion.

What had happened was unthinkable. She was as stunned as her father.

Caroline . . . taken.

Grabbing his buckskin trousers off a wall peg, Ty squeezed

his eyes closed against Beatriz's crying and wailing issuing from Caroline's room. He kept his voice low, but he could hear it, like MacKenna's, quivering with raw emotion—worry, horror, and unbridled fury. "There's only one trail out of this valley."

"If you're going, I'm coming with you."

Ty whipped a hard look at her, raising his voice like he hardly ever had with his children, jutting a commanding figure at her, his hazel eyes blazing with Celtic fury. "You're going to do what I say for once in your life, MacKenna! You are going to stay here with Matt and your mother! She needs your help worse than I do! That's final!"

His fury had been so raw and untethered MacKenna blanched against it, shaking her head once, hair flying. She took a step backward, resting her hands against the edge of her parent's dresser abutting the wall behind her.

Ty dressed quickly, stepped back into his boots, and grabbed a box of .44/40 cartridges from a bureau drawer. MacKenna still stood by the dresser, scowling at him. Ignoring her, Ty left the room and turned to where Matt was holding his bawling mother in his arms down the hall to Ty's left. "Take care of her, son. I'll be back soon with your sister."

"Tynan!" Beatriz's voice wailed after him as he descended the stairs. *"You bring her back to me—do you hear, Tynan?"*

Without responding—his heart had turned cold with deadly purpose—he continued down the stairs. Gregory stood in the open doorway, one hand on the head of Rollie, who must have heard the commotion and come running back into the yard. Standing beside Gregory crying softly, the dog sensed something was deeply wrong in the Brannigan household. Gregory didn't say anything as Ty gained the bottom of the stairs. Appearing to be in shock, the fifteen-year-old absently patted the head of his beloved dog.

When Ty met his gaze, Gregory averted his eyes. The

thought of his little sister having been kidnapped was too much for him to wrap his mind around.

Ty felt the same.

He stepped past the boy and the dog, giving Gregory's shoulder a single, reassuring pat—at least, he attempted to make it reassuring—and dropped down the porch steps. Stiff-backed and tense with tension, he strode quickly to the corral.

Ten minutes later, he'd roped and saddled his blue roan, led it out of the corral, and swung up into the leather. He glanced at the horses over which the two dead lawmen had been tied. In his horror over Caroline, he'd forgotten about them. Likely, MacKenna and Matt would tend to the bodies.

He reined the horse around to the west and gave it the steel. Horse and rider lunged into a hard gallop across the yard and through the portal and into the rangeland beyond. Enough starlight provided light and Ty could see the pale ribbon of trail relatively well. At the moment that was good enough for him. When the trail began threading steep butte country beyond the Whiskey Creek Trail he would lose the light.

Deep down, he knew MacKenna had been right. But only a vague rationality lingered in his brain. Mostly that organ was a father's brain incensed by the notion that four cutthroats who'd wiped out an entire army payroll contingent and had cut the throats of two innocent drovers had taken his youngest daughter. That the innocent Caroline was right now in the company of those four, cold-blooded killing machines.

Seeing that empty bed had stopped him cold, had instantly bled away his good sense. Right now, he was not a cool-headed former lawman but merely a father charging after the brutes who'd taken his daughter. He didn't care how dark it was and how impossible it would be to track them if they left the main trail, which they would no doubt do.

He didn't care, either, about the danger he was putting himself and his horse in. The horse could throw a shoe or stumble into a chuckhole and kill them both, but Ty kept it lunging ahead at a dead run. Hat pulled down low on his forehead, he crouched low over the roan's poll, desperation pounding hard inside him.

Several times he reined up to look around and listen. He heard nothing but the rustles of burrowing night creatures and the screech of a distant night bird.

Finally, when it was apparent the roan could not continue at the hard-charging pace, Ty reined up atop a low saddle and looked around as though he would be able to see anything in the deep darkness of rugged country. Cursing, he shucked the Henry from its sheath, levered a round into the action, brought the butt plate to his right shoulder, and aimed at the sky, picking out a single, flickering star as though it was the fate that had brought the tragedy of the horrific night.

He fired three quick rounds, lowered the rifle, and bellowed, "*Where are you?*"

The echoes of the wail dwindled to silence.

Then he was answered by Caroline's small, terrified voice muffled by distance. "*Pa!*"

"*Caroline!*"

"Here, Pa!"

But where?

Ty gazed into the murky darkness right of the trail. She was somewhere to the northwest. As he'd vaguely suspected they'd left the trail. Probably a half mile to a mile away from him.

A woman's laughter cut through the silence that had followed Caroline's second wail. The lunacy in that laugh stabbed Ty like a dull, rusty knife.

A man's voice rose in the night from the same direction

as Caroline's yell and the woman's laugh. "Want her back, Brannigan?"

Again, the woman laughed.

Ty clamped the Henry under his arm and cupped his hands around his mouth. "Of course, I want her back! Take me instead! I'm the one you want!"

Again came the woman's demented, mocking laugh.

"No, no!" came the man's voice again. "We'll give you the sprout in exchange for Bathing Beauty!"

"Bathing Beauty?" Ty muttered to himself, brows ridged with befuddlement. Then he understood. *MacKenna.*

They'd put it together that Mack had told him and the lawmen about having seen the killers at the waterfall. They'd killed the lawmen then turned around and came back to get revenge.

They could have been halfway to Montana if they'd just kept riding. But, no, they'd turned around and come back to wreak bloody havoc. Ford knew the Bear Paws well enough to know the Powderhorn was the ranch closest to the waterfall on Lone Squaw Creek. They'd seen the Powderhorn brand blazed into the two horses Ty had given Calhoun and Parker. That's what had told them where to find MacKenna.

Ty's blood ran cold in his veins. Demented devils was what they were. Four sick, sadistic human devils had Caroline.

As if to confirm his estimation, Caroline screamed as though in agony. "*Pa!*" she yelled. "*I wanna come home, Pa!*"

Ty slammed the end of his left fist down hard against his saddle horn. He swallowed a hard knot of emotion in his throat and yelled, his voice quavering with bereavement and terror, "You'll be home soon, honey! I promise!" He shook his head as though to clear the nerves entangled in his brain then hardened his jaws in fury and shouted, "*Ford, if you hurt that girl, there will be nowhere you can run, nowhere you can hide that I won't find you and kill you—hard.*

Long and hard! Each one of you!" He rose in his saddle and shouted even louder, *"Do you understand me, you cold blooded devils?"*

The woman's infuriating laugh rose again.

Then came the voice that was likely that of Smilin' Doc Ford. "See you on down the trail, Brannigan! Bring Bathing Beauty! We'll make the exchange! One Brannigan daughter for another!"

An owl hooted in mockery.

A coyote yodeled.

Neither were from an actual owl or coyote.

Beneath Ty, the roan was still blowing. He had run it hard. Too hard to continue. Even if it could continue, there was no way he'd be able to follow the killers' trail. He had to return to the Powderhorn, wait for first light two or three hours away, saddle a fresh horse—*two* fresh horses—and start again.

He gave a ragged sigh, doffed his hat, and ran his hand through his hair in frustration. Setting the hat back on his head, he slid the Henry into its sheath then reined the roan around and started back in the direction of the Powderhorn. His heart beat miserably, that organ feeling swollen and sore.

Never before had he felt so wretched.

"Oh, Adam." MacKenna sunk her fingers into the young man's curly hair as she slid her knife under the barrel of the mouse brown dun. Carefully, she sawed through the rope tying Adam's bound wrists to his feet.

The head lowered as the body, stiff in death, dropped down the side of the saddle.

"Got him?" Mack asked her brother.

"Got him," Matt said.

MacKenna rose quickly and helped her brother ease the body down to the ground. They were fully dressed now.

Earlier, they'd tucked their terrified mother into bed with a glass of brandy though she rarely ever drank anything stronger than coffee and frowned on anyone who did. Beatriz made an exception for the brandy, which she considered medicinal. MacKenna and Matt had been going to stay with her until she slept but she'd wanted to be alone.

MacKenna rolled Adam onto his back and winced. She ran her fingers across the ugly rope burn encircling his neck and turned to Matt, scowling. "What'd they—What'd they *do* to him?"

"Hung him, looks like," Matt said, grimacing and shaking his head.

MacKenna stared down at the dead young man in horror. His half-open eyes were cast in terror. His face was pale in the darkness. MacKenna ran her fingers down the lids but they were too stiff to close. He continued to gaze up at her as though silently pleading for help that would never come.

MacKenna lowered her head, brought her hands to her face, and sobbed.

"Here, here," Matt said, drawing his sister to him and wrapping his arms around her shoulders. "I'm so sorry, sis."

MacKenna wrapped her arms around Matt's waist and turned the sobbing loose but briefly. They still had more work to do. They'd already cut Deputy Marshal Calhoun down from the copper bay but they needed to carry the bodies into the barn and cover them with blankets. Then they'd tend to the horses.

It was good to have work to do on such a night. It was good to have a distraction from their worry over Caroline. But not this kind of work.

Mack pulled back away from her brother, scrubbed tears from her cheeks with her hands, sniffed, choked out one more sob. "Let's get them into the barn."

"Mack, I can do that. Why don't you go inside?"

MacKenna shook her head. "I want to help take care of

them." She looked at her brother gravely. "You see, Matt—this is my fault. I got them both killed."

"No, no. You did not, sis."

"Sure, I did. Those four horrible people told me not to tell anyone I'd seen them. But I told the lawmen."

"You had to, Mack!"

"I know!" MacKenna shook her head. "Still, if I hadn't these two men would likely still be alive"—her lips trembled—"and we'd still have Caroline right here where she belongs!" MacKenna crossed her arms on her chest, turned her head to one side, and sobbed.

Matt placed a comforting hand on his sister's arm. "Mack!"

MacKenna shook her head, scrubbed tears from her cheeks once more, then crouched over Deputy Parker's ankles. "Let's get Adam into the barn."

She and her brother carried the two dead lawmen into the barn, laying them out on tables in the tack room where predators wouldn't likely get at them before they could be tended to more properly. What that would entail, Mack had no idea. She supposed she and/or Matt would haul the bodies to town in the buckboard wagon though she couldn't imagine doing anything except riding out at first light to help her father retrieve Caroline.

He'd strictly forbidden her to do so, though. And he'd really meant it. Mack didn't see how she could cross him. Not this time. Even if the death of the lawmen and Caroline's kidnapping had been her fault.

She didn't know how she would do it, but she would remain at the Powderhorn with Matt and let her father bring her sister back to them. He could do it. If anyone could, Tynan Brannigan could. Even going up against a quartet of devils like those she'd seen on the ridge above the falls.

* * *

MacKenna and Matt had returned to the house but went back out again when they heard the weary clomps of a horse entering the yard. Each holding a rifle on the off chance the rider might have been one of the killers returning, they watched their father ride up to the porch. In his buckskin coat, craggy face beneath the broad brim of his high-crowned Stetson and his tired eyes bright with frustration, he looked worn out and ragged in his grief and desperation.

MacKenna began to wonder if he could run the killers down, after all. Ty Brannigan appeared to have aged a good ten years in the past couple of hours.

Ty looked at Matt. "We ride at first light. Going to put your shooting skills to good use."

Hope rose in MacKenna as she stepped forward, placing a hand on her chest. "Me, too, Pa!"

Ty reined the roan around and started for the corral. "Absolutely not."

CHAPTER 23

Caroline felt the burn of a hard yank on her ear and screamed against the agony.

The blond woman who'd taken her out of her room and clamped a hand across Caroline's mouth and nose so hard she'd passed out halfway down the second-floor hall of her family's house turned to see the big, bearded brute lean toward her.

He snarled. "I told you to quit your infernal bawling, you little brat! Anymore, and I'll pull your damn ear right off and eat it!"

Rage boiling over inside her, momentarily tempering her terror, Caroline flung up her left arm and slammed her elbow against the bearded man's mouth. The man grunted and jerked his head back, eyes wide and round, bright with disbelief.

Caroline herself couldn't believe what she'd done.

"Why, you—!"

Caroline screamed as the back of the bearded man's left hand slammed against her mouth, throwing her off the woman's walking horse. Caroline hit the ground with another scream, rolled twice, and lay in the dust beside the trail, terror washing over her once more, her lips burning from the man's savage slap.

"Jack, what the hell are you doing?" the woman shouted.

"If she don't quit her infernal bawlin', I'm gonna kill her!" Jack spat out.

Caroline, who lay belly down beside the trail, glanced up to see that all four riders had stopped their horses and turned them to stare down at her. Even in the darkness, she could see how stony their eyes were. The handsome man in the suit sat with a funny smile on his mouth, regarding her as though she amused him. Though he was sort of smiling, his eyes were hard as rocks.

Caroline stopped crying.

She wasn't sure what had suddenly come over her but staring up at the four savage people who'd taken her from her family, she suddenly managed to push down her terror. She was surprised to have found a strange resolve inside her to no longer give them the satisfaction of witnessing her fear.

Pa had once told her most animals sensed fear in people. Fear encouraged predators. They'd been out picking choke-cherries one day along a creek a mile from the house and Caroline had suddenly spied a wolf watching them from the berry-laden branches. The wolf's ears had been pricked, head lifted, working its black nostrils at the end of its long, gray snout.

Caroline had dropped her bucket of chokecherries and given a frightened cry.

He had closed his reassuring hand around her arm and said quietly into her ear, "Push back the fear. Then the old Brannigan courage will rise up and make you feel better. What's more, it will discourage the wolf."

She'd done that and realized he had been right. She'd felt better. And the wolf had pulled its head back into the bushes and disappeared.

Wolves.

That's what these four were.

They were wolves feeding off her fear. Enjoying it. They were enjoying terrifying Ty Brannigan's young daughter.

Still on the ground Caroline continued to press down her fear deep inside her. As she did, she felt an angry courage rise to take its place. Or at least to help hold it down. And she realized she had suddenly stopped quivering as she'd been doing since regaining consciousness on the back of the woman's horse as they climbed up the ridge behind the house, taking Caroline farther and farther from her family.

The old Brannigan courage calming her, Caroline sat up, brushed her fist across her bloody mouth, and stared coldly, defiantly back at the four wolves eyeing her in the darkness. Starlight glinted in their eyes.

The handsome man in the suit and bowler hat suddenly stopped smiling and glanced at the woman sitting a cream horse beside his claybank. He frowned curiously, incredulously. The woman returned the look then swung down from her horse and glanced at the ugly bearded man sitting beside the big, brutally featured, dark-skinned man. Both men also stared curiously down at Caroline.

Having quelled her fear puzzled them. Maybe even disappointed them though they'd been tired of hearing her sobs. But then she realized she'd gotten tired of hearing her sobs, as well.

"You kill her, and then where we gonna be?" the woman said to the bearded men, rolling her eyes and wagging her head in disgust.

The bearded man brushed his gloved hand against his mouth and looked at it.

Caroline felt a strange satisfaction that blood glistened in the starlight on the man's lower lip. She'd given him as good as she'd gotten. That was the Brannigan way.

"Brannigan ain't gonna make no trade, anyways," the man called Jack said, flaring a nostril of his broad nose above his tangled beard.

"That's not the point," said the handsome man, smiling again in satisfaction as he looked at Jack. "We have her. That's enough. We'll kill her father when he comes after her . . . after we've given him a good, long scare."

The woman squatted in front of Caroline. "Did he hurt you bad, little one?"

Caroline could tell the concern in the woman's squeaky, childlike voice was fake. Caroline could tell. She shook her head and glared at the bearded man. "I'm just fine."

The bearded man snarled and ran his fat tongue across his bloody lower lip.

The woman smiled and extended her hand to Caroline. "Give you a hand up?"

"Don't need it." Caroline pushed herself up off the ground. She glared up at the woman whom she'd heard called Zena or something like that. Hardening her jaws, she said, "Best let me go. My pa is going to make you pay big for taking me. He is Ty Brannigan, and he was one of the best lawmen in the West at one time!"

That brought a chuckle from the handsome man, who leaned forward against his saddle horn and said, "Oh, we know who Ty Brannigan is, little one. We'll just see how many cartridges he has left in his old gun. Yessir, we'll see about that." He looked at Zena and said, "Get her back on your horse. We got more ground to cover before we take a break."

"Why are you doing this?" Caroline asked. "Why did you take me from my family?" She felt fear climb back into her mind, making her lower lip flutter but, clenching her fists at her sides, she suppressed it and hardened her jaws and her eyes.

"Your sister double-crossed us," the woman said. "After I kept Bear from feeding her a pill she couldn't digest. That's how she repays me—makin' me look the fool!"

The bearded man chuckled, and Zena shot him a hard look and told him to shut up, squinting her blue eyes at him.

The bearded man turned away from the crazy woman's glare.

"So, you're going to"—again, Caroline had to press back the raw emotion threatening to swamp her once more—"kill our pa?"

The handsome man smiled.

The crazy woman winked at Caroline, who flinched under the woman's lunatic gaze.

Wolves. Lunatic wolves . . .

All at once Caroline realized it wasn't going to be enough for her just to be brave. No, she had to *do* something. She had to get away from these four killers. Pa would still hunt them down and kill them, but something told Caroline that *she* needed to do what she could to save herself. She needed to escape these four wolves, or she might very well die before Pa could save her.

The realization amazed her, as did her sudden determination. She'd always seen herself as not only the smallest of the Brannigan family, but also the weakest. Like Ma, she was nervous. MacKenna was the strongest of the Brannigan daughters. MacKenna was beautiful. She was as brave as any man, and she'd been shooting guns and riding horses as well as any boy her age since she'd been younger than Caroline, who'd never thought she would ever, *could* ever, measure up to her older sister.

But she was beginning to think she'd been wrong.

The proof would be in the pudding, however. She'd have to see if she really could measure up to her sister. At her first opportunity, she'd make her escape.

"Come on, little girl," Zena said, "you heard the man. Get mounted." She moved around behind Caroline, grabbed her under her arms, and brusquely hoisted her up onto the cream's back. The woman climbed into the saddle ahead of

Caroline and Caroline reluctantly grabbed the woman's duster for purchase.

They set out again, Zena and Caroline following the handsome man Caroline had heard called Doc, the bearded man, and then the big, dark man Zena had called Bear.

A right fitting name, Caroline thought as she and Zena brought up the rear.

Swaying with the cream's movements, Caroline looked at her hands clutching the woman's duster. *Her hands were free. They hadn't tied her. They didn't see her as a threat.* Inwardly, Caroline smiled, buoyed by the thought. But the smile faded when she looked at the twin bulges in the sides of the woman's duster, a few inches below where Caroline clutched the leather.

Caroline had never fired a gun before.

She didn't know how. Even if she could reach inside the woman's duster and pull one of those big guns, she wouldn't know how to fire it. She wished again that she'd been more like MacKenna and had insisted Pa teach her to shoot a gun the same as he'd taught Matt. If she made it out of this nasty business, Caroline would have Pa teach her how to shoot, so if she ever found herself in another pinch like this one . . .

As it was, if she was going to make her escape, she'd have to do it without a gun.

A half hour after the bearded man had so brutally assaulted Caroline, which probably made him feel like a real big man, indeed, they stopped to rest the horses and build a fire for coffee.

The woman and the men sat around drinking coffee and nibbling jerky and biscuits. No one offered Caroline anything to eat or drink. That was all right. She wasn't hungry. While the horses grazed with their belly straps dangling, Caroline sat where they'd ordered her to sit—on a rock near them—and thought and thought about a way she might be able to slip out of the wolves' savage clutches.

Her heart beat frantically, and her palms grew slick. She knew MacKenna would find a way to get away from these four, but now that it was almost light, they could clearly see Caroline slip away. Besides, they were in open ground in a broad valley along a twisting little creek on the banks of which no trees grew. No way could she escape without them easily running her down and likely making her pay in the worst way, which might very well entail more than just a slap across the mouth.

She touched her tongue to the jelly-like blood on her lip then clutched her hands together anxiously. *No.* She shook her head and unclenched her hands. *No fear. You have to be brave. You have to be calm and think your way out of this. That's the Brannigan way.*

You can't escape now, but you will later. Look at them. They're not even looking at you. The handsome man is bragging to the others about how well he knows these mountains. He'd grown up here, Caroline thought he'd mentioned. *He knows all the routes to anywhere, the best routes to keep from being easily tracked. And he's telling how he'll have Pa riding in circles.*

Hah! Riding in circles. Tynan Brannigan? They'd see.

Later, you'll find a way to escape them, make them feel the fool for thinking you were no threat. You're a Brannigan, after all!

After the Indian's horse threw a shoe in the early afternoon, and they had to stop and let him and the bearded man reset it, Caroline came up with a way to make her escape.

Her heart beat fast. But not with anxiety.

With the expectation of soon being free to outwit her captors and return to her family.

CHAPTER 24

"Miss Zena?" Caroline said.

The woman looked up from where she sat back against a tree. She'd been waiting for the bearded man and the Indian to reset the shoe on the bearded man's horse's right rear hoof. To kill time, she been cleaning one of the two fancy-looking silver pistols she wore in pretty, black holsters and appeared most proud of. She rolled a sharpened matchstick between her lips. It looked strange—a pretty woman rolling a matchstick between her lips. But then, she wasn't like most pretty women.

This woman was a wolf. A pretty wolf. But a wolf, just the same.

"What is it?" Zena said with an impatient air. She narrowed an eye at Caroline and pointed the pistol at her, wagging it like an admonishing finger. "Do yourself a favor, little miss, and don't make yourself a bother. I don't like kids in the first place, and you are not that valuable to me. Your father's going to come after us whether you're alive or not."

She cast a snide look at the handsome man, Doc, who sat in the shade of a rock overhang. It was warm, and he'd removed his coat and was fanning himself with his bowler hat.

The handsome man smiled at Zena with one half of his mouth.

Caroline watched. Funny how when he smiled his eyes became a snake's eyes.

That's because he has the soul of a snake, she thought, suppressing another shudder of fear and revulsion, keeping up her determination to be tough and clear-headed.

The soul of a diamondback rattlesnake.

But then, the woman did, too. The heart of a wolf, the soul of a snake.

Caroline rose from the rock she'd been sitting on and crooked her finger at the woman. "Can I have a private word?"

The woman scowled at her, incredulous. "What?"

"I have a private matter I need to discuss with you."

The woman continued to frown at her. Then, understanding, she smiled and glanced at Doc, who chuckled.

"I do believe the little woman needs to pay nature a call, Zee." He canted his head toward Caroline. "Don't let her out of your sight."

"Oh, she's not gonna run off," Zee said. "Where would she go?" She looked at Caroline again. "She'd be wildcat bait before nightfall though there's not much to eat on her spindly little frame," she added with a disdainful nostril flare.

Caroline couldn't help but shudder at that. Not the insult. She knew she was skinny and mousey, nothing like MacKenna. She'd shuddered at the wildcat remark. That was something she hadn't considered. In fact, the only thing she *had* considered was getting away from these four wolves. She hadn't thought about what she'd do after that. She was likely a good many miles from the Powderhorn.

How would she find her way home? She'd never been in this part of the Bear Paws before.

Still, after a few moments' reconsideration, she decided she'd rather take her chances with the mountains and the wildcats than with these four. Even considering she didn't know where she was, or what predators haunted these mountains, she was better off on her own. Besides, Pa, Matt, and MacKenna were likely on her trail. Somehow, they'd find her.

"Keep an eye on her," Doc insisted.

The woman holstered her pistol then heaved herself to her feet with an angry groan. "All right, all right. Come on, little Brannigan girl!"

She grabbed Caroline's wrist and walked off in the direction Caroline had hoped she'd be taken, into thick brush and shrubs beyond which rose a forested ridge. To keep her from whining about her bare feet, the woman had given her a pair of soft deerskin moccasins, so she no longer had to endure the pricking of grass and pebbles.

When they'd walked into the brush far enough that the men could not see them, the woman stopped.

The woman turned around, giving her back to Caroline. "All right. Get to work."

"I'm nervous, so it might take me a minute," Caroline said, slowly backing away from the woman, scouring the ground with her gaze. "Best get comfortable."

Giving an exasperated groan, the woman walked over to a large rock and sat down on it. She glanced over her shoulder and said, "Hurry up. We don't have all day!"

"If you rush me it's just gonna take me longer," Caroline warned, her eyes suddenly landing on what she'd been looking for.

The woman sighed and shook her head. "Why did you have to be the only Brannigan girl in the house? I'd been hoping to snatch Bathing Beauty!"

Caroline walked very slowly and quietly to her right, crouched, and, keeping one eye skinned on the woman, who kept her head turned forward, picked up a stout branch that must have tumbled from a near pine tree. Hefting the branch in both hands, her heart thudding, Caroline walked very slowly toward the woman who just then removed the glove from her right hand to nibble a fingernail.

Fortunately, a light breeze rustled the grass and the branches around them, covering the slight crunching sound Caroline could not help making with her feet.

She came to within six feet of the woman . . . then four. She raised the branch and swung it back behind her right shoulder . . . and stopped—

—just as the woman glanced over her own shoulder and said, "You done ye—" She didn't finish the question.

With a fierce grunt, Caroline had swung the branch forward and smashed it against the woman's left temple, creating a loud, crunching thud and breaking it in two.

"*Oh!*" and, losing her hat, the woman tumbled sideways from the rock.

Caroline dropped the half still in her hand, swung around, and ran as fast as she could, her heart fluttering. She ran through the brush toward the ridge.

Behind her, she heard the woman curse and yell, "*That little . . . that little—!*"

"Zee, what's goin on?" Doc yelled.

"That little— She *hit* me!"

Caroline did not look behind her but kept running as fast as she could, leaping obstacles, pushing through brush and shrubs and then began climbing the ridge, weaving around the columnar pines.

Behind her, the woman cursed louder, shriller, and the men's voices rose.

"Where is she?" Doc said amidst the thuds of running feet and crunching brush.

"She smacked me on the head. That little catamount!"

"Where did she go?" Doc asked, louder.

"That way, I think. She brained me good. She can't weigh much more than that branch she hit me with!"

Footsteps grew louder behind Caroline, who grunted in panic as she climbed the ridge, pulling at bushes and tree limbs, tugging herself up the steep incline. She cast a quick glance over her shoulder, was glad that the four wolves were shielded from her view by the trees and heavy brush that carpeted the ridge. That meant she was shielded from their view, as well.

But their running footsteps grew louder until Caroline could also hear breaths being raked in and out of straining lungs. They were gaining on her. Dang her short legs, anyway!

She was nearly to the top of the ridge when she saw a large, dead tree trunk lying on the ground just ahead of her. She crouched to peer inside.

It was hollow.

She moved back down the ridge a few feet, shoved a fir branch aside to take a peek at her pursuers, and felt a hitch in her heart when she saw the big Indian, the bearded man, and the man called Doc running toward her—closer than she'd thought and spread out in a nearly even line across the belly of the slope. The woman was running in a heavy, shamble-footed way behind them, holding one hand against her left temple, where Caroline had brained her.

Caroline had to raise a little smile at that. She hadn't thought she'd had it in her to brain a full-grown woman. Or anyone else, for that matter. But the chips were down, so she'd done it, all right. Pa would have been proud!

The smile faded when she realized Doc ran with his bowler hat in one hand and held one of his pretty silver pistols in his other hand. The expression on his face was sort of a frozen snarl. That look told Caroline that if he caught her, she'd be a goner for sure.

She stepped back, eased the branch back into place then ran over to the log. She crouched to peer inside again. Seeing the nasty dark-brown gunk, mushrooms, and even some animal fur inside, she gave a little shudder of revulsion. When second thoughts started to assault her, she said under her breath, "The chips are down, Caroline!"

Judging by the loudness of the men's footsteps, they'd be on her in less than a minute. She drew a breath, steeling herself against the repulsive thing she was about to do, then dropped to her butt, stuck her feet and then her legs into the log and wriggled her way inside. Since it was a little larger than she was, she'd thought she could fit, but it was a little tighter than she'd expected. Completely not thinking about the soft stuff she was lying in, she pulled her head and shoulders inside several inches.

The only way the wolves would see her was if they thought to check the log.

That thought had no sooner drifted over her brain than thuds assaulted the ground nearby—close enough that she could feel the reverberations in the ground beneath her. A man grunted to her left, on the slope's decline, and then there was a heavy thud and another grunt to her right, on the slope's incline. Through a hollow knot in the log, she saw the big Indian leap the log and, pulling down his arms, which he'd raised like wings as he'd made the leap, ran straight up the slope from her, for a moment close enough she could easily have hit him with a rock!

Her heart gave an especially painful lurch.

She could see Doc running up the slope to the left of the big Indian. She couldn't see the bearded man, but he was likely running up the slope on the other side of Doc.

Caroline waited, ears pricked, listening.

More footsteps sounded on the slope's decline. It was a shuffling sound accompanied by groans. As the sounds grew louder, Caroline began to hear the woman's labored breathing. Then a louder groan. The footsteps and the breathing continued to grow louder until the woman came into Caroline's view nearly straight out away from the log. Caroline wasn't a good judge of distance, but she thought the woman, clad in her long black duster, flaxen hair hanging messily about her shoulders, was probably about as far as the Powderhorn house was from the barn.

The woman stopped and, breathing hard, lowered her head, groaned, and used a finger to probe her bloody temple. She shook her head sharply, making a face, and cursed.

Caroline heard her say tightly, "Darn little catamount!"

Scrunched low in the hollow log, Caroline winced anxiously. If the woman turned her head to her right, there was a good chance she'd see Caroline hunkered down in the log. As though the woman had read the anxious thought, she turned her head toward Caroline.

Caroline sucked a quiet breath through gritted teeth, her blood turning chill in her veins. She couldn't see the woman's eyes clearly, but she appeared to be looking right at Caroline.

Caroline's heart banged . . . banged . . . banged . . .

Then the woman turned her head forward and continue walking up the slope.

Caroline followed the woman with her gaze.

Keep going . . . keep going . . .

The woman's black-clad figure dwindled, slowly becoming consumed by the shadows of the trees before she gained the top of the slope, the sunlight bathing her as she continued shambling forward and then disappeared from Caroline's view.

Caroline tried to wriggle toward the log's opening.

Panic gripped her when she couldn't slide her shoulders forward.

Stuck!

Violently, she waggled her shoulders this way and that, loosening them then wriggling forward until her head then her shoulders and then the rest of her was climbing out of the log.

Whew!

She stared toward the top of the ridge.

"Come out, come out, wherever you are, little Brannigan girl!" she heard Doc's distant, muffled, jeering voice rise from the other side of the ridge.

He seemed to be a good distance away. *Good.* Caroline thought over quickly what she'd do.

She'd run back down the ridge and find a better hiding place. Eventually, they'd give up trying to find her and mosey on up the trail.

Wouldn't they?

She'd overheard them discussing stolen money they'd stashed up the trail somewhere before they'd ridden back apparently to kill Pa and terrorize his family.

Wolves. Worse than wolves. Worse than snakes, even.

They'd eventually move on without her and retrieve their money. Caroline had proven to be a thorn in their sides. Sooner or later, they would have realized she wasn't nearly as valuable a captive as they'd thought she was. By slipping away from them she was saving them a bullet.

She heard herself give a little snicker at that but no sooner had the snicker escaped her lips than her shoulders jerked with a shudder, as well. She still couldn't wrap her mind around all that had happened to her in less than a day. Her mind felt numb, and she had the sense that she was living a dream.

A nightmare.

Had she really been kidnapped out of her bed and hauled off by four crazy killers?

Somehow, so far . . . she'd managed to survive.

That seemed the most amazing thing about the whole thing. Yeah, she'd survived. If you'd have told her what was going to happen to her last night, she'd have thought she'd die of fright. But the fear hadn't killed her. She'd turned the tables on her fear. Turning it to anger and determination, she'd used it. She brained the woman and had them practically running in circles.

She ran to the bottom of the hill. Then, breathless, stopped and looked around. Where to now?

To her left was a little crease between ridges. To her right were the horses.

Hmm. Caroline chewed her bottom lip.

The horses . . .

CHAPTER 25

"I don't understand this," Ty said around the smoldering cigarette dangling from between his lips as he adjusted the focus on his field glasses. "The gang's tracks lead northwest but I just saw four riders round a bend in the trail down yonder, heading northeast."

"You sure, Pa?" Matt asked, lying belly down beside his father at the lip of the canyon, which was called Petticoat as it had been carved by what no doubt some humorous young surveyor had dubbed Petticoat Creek.

"Certain-sure." Ty kept staring through the glasses though the riders had disappeared around a bend in the canyon wall.

"Tryin' to trick us?"

"Maybe they think they can work around us, flank us." Ty lowered the glasses, sucked on the quirley and blew smoke out his nose, saying, "Backshoot us."

"Did you see Caroline?"

Ty shook his head. "Can't be sure. Thought I saw one of the riders riding double but they were too far away and moving too fast. I can't be sure."

"I don't understand, Pa. Why take Caroline?"

"Tormenting us. Me. MacKenna. When I was Warknife Town Marshal, I had a few run-ins with Smilin' Doc. He likely blames Mack for the deputy marshals." Ty looked at his son and tapped his temple with his right index finger. "Insane. Lunacy. For the pure pleasure of instilling terror. Some folks are wired that way. Doc Ford grew up in these mountains, raised by a sadistic alcoholic miner and shotgun farmer who killed his wife right in front of Ford when he was maybe ten years old. Does somethin' to a boy, seein' somethin' like that."

"Didn't he kill his father?" Matt asked.

"That's the story. A neighbor found Homer Ford dead in his cabin with his throat cut, the boy gone. Ford would have been around only sixteen at the time."

"I've heard that story," Matt said, gazing somberly down into the broad, deep canyon carved between two steep sandstone ridges.

"How he was raised was bad. Hard bad. But it's no excuse for what he became." Ty stretched his lips back from his teeth in barely bridled rage. "I'm gonna kill him like the rabid cur he is. He'd just better not harm Caroline before I get the chance."

Slowly, Matt shook his head and turned his grave gaze to his father. "The squirrel must be so frightened. Probably paralyzed with fear."

"No doubt. She's the nervous one in the family. Come on." Ty stowed the binoculars in their baize-lined leather case and rose. "Let's get her back."

He took a last drag off the quirley then dropped it and toed it out. It was only around noon, and he didn't normally smoke much, but that was his fourth cigarette of the morning. His nerves were shot. Those savages had his little girl. He was not a fearful man, but he was frightened now.

Chilled right down to his core.

Of course, it didn't help that he kept imagining the worst.

He and Matt had saddled two horses each so they could push harder and faster than the gang that had Caroline. Ty hoped to catch up to them before they made Peacock Ridge at the edge of the Bear Paws though their sudden course switch had him wondering why they headed that way. It was the only northern outlet.

He and Matt switched horses and mounted up then rode northwest along the lip of the canyon, looking for a way down. Judging by the tracks of the four horses he'd been following, Ford must have entered the canyon farther west along the rim. Ty knew this neck of the Bear Paws well enough to know a route to the canyon floor not far ahead.

He wanted to get into the canyon faster and get the jump on his quarry. As the crow flies, they were probably only about a mile ahead. Though she didn't weigh very much, Caroline must be slowing them down.

Good. Ty just hoped it didn't get her killed.

But no. If Ford was going to kill her, he'd likely do it in front of her father. He'd derive much more pleasure from killing Ty Brannigan's daughter in front of Ty. That's the kind of devil Ty had always heard he was and now knew it first-hand.

Ty winced at the horror of the notion, scrubbed a gloved fist across his mouth then found the nearest route down to the canyon floor, the start of which was only a slight gap between two boulders well concealed but marked by animal tracks and deer beans. He and Matt and the two horses they trailed by lead lines rode through cottonwood saplings and then they were heading down the steep slope via the switchbacking game trail.

Though it was a tough, precarious trek along a trail little wider than the span of a large man's hand, they'd chosen the most sure-footed mounts in their remuda. After a twenty-minute descent, they gained the canyon floor without so much as a stumble.

Fifteen minutes later, they were on the trail winding around the bend in the canyon wall at the point where Ty had spied Ford's bunch. Ty's heart quickened. They were making better time than he'd expected. If all went well, and he and Matt could catch up to the kidnappers and surprise them, they might have Caroline back by good dark.

He and Matt pushed hard. They did not stop for lunch or coffee, but only to water their horses at infrequent creeks and runout springs. They ran into a time-wasting problem, however, when they lost their quarry's trail in rocky terrain and found themselves having to turn around and backtrack. Ty scouted the ground closely, sometimes dismounting and leading his two horses, scrutinizing the terrain until he picked up the kidnapper's trail once more.

Then he switched his saddle to his second horse, as did Matt, mounted up, and resumed his hard push.

The backtracking had cost them good time, however, and by the time they smelled a cookfire, it was late in the afternoon. Shadows stretched long from the pines looming over the trail they were following. They drew rein just below the crest of a low, rocky saddle, dismounted, then, each shucking his rifle from his saddle boot, they stole up to the crest of the ridge and hunkered low behind rocks and cedars.

Ty removed his hat and peered through a gap in the rocks and small pines.

Below, in a narrow, pine-choked valley, lay an old stage relay station halfway along the route between Somerset and Empire, both towns as abandoned as the relay station. Or at least as abandoned as the old relay station *had* been. Four horses milled in the corral behind the place, which was shaded by tall pines and firs.

The main station building—a long, low, shake-shingled log cabin—fronted the corral and the log barn that abutted the corral. It had a small front porch whose unpeeled pole rail had rotted out and lay mostly buried in the brush that had grown up around the cabin. The shakes on the roof wore a heavy coat of green moss, pinecones, and needles from the pines standing tall around the station.

What had captured the brunt of Ty's attention was the smoke lifting from the rusty tin chimney pipe angling up out of the ceiling.

"Cooking supper," he muttered, fingering his mustache.

"How we gonna play this one, Pa?"

Continuing to finger his mustache, Ty studied the chimney pipe. He turned to Matt lying belly down beside him. "See that stove pipe?"

"Sure do."

"We're gonna smoke 'em out. If they run out the front, shoot 'em. But only if you have a clear shot at them. When I see Caroline, I'm gonna leap down from the roof, grab her, and start blasting away myself."

"How're you gonna get up on the roof?"

"I'll find a way. I always did." Ty winked.

"What if they have her tied up inside?"

"At least she'll be out of the line of fire. When they're all toe-down, I'll run in and get her out. She'll have bloodshot eyes for a while, but she'll be back with us again."

Matt studied the cabin, wide-eyed and serious. Slowly, he nodded. "You got it, Pa."

"All right." Ty crabbed back down the slope toward the waiting horses. "I'm gonna work around behind 'em." He rose, dusted off his buckskin pants. "Give me a good, twenty or thirty minutes or so. I'll wave from the roof."

Matt twisted a nervous smile. "You, uh . . . you've done this sort of thing before, eh, Pa?"

Ty slid his rifle into his saddle boot. He glanced at his son, smiling shrewdly. "A pretty effective maneuver if I do say so myself." He swung up onto his chestnut's back. "They'll be right surprised. I'm sure—no, I know—they're not expecting us this soon."

"Go with God, Pa," Matt said, returning his father's confident smile. "Go with God."

Ty winked. "Thanks, son."

He reined the chestnut into the pines right of the trail and rode through the pines across the belly of the saddle until he figured he was roughly a quarter mile east of the stage relay station. Then he rode up to the ridge crest, peered down the other side and back to his left.

He could see the old stage road curving along the base of the saddle before him, but the station itself was out of sight around a bend in the ridge.

Good.

He put the chestnut up and over the ridge, angling it down the other side. When he bottomed out on the next valley, he crossed the stage road that hadn't seen any stage traffic in a good five years, since the gold had played out of this neck of the mountains and the towns of Somerset and Empire had become ghosts, and entered the pine forest beyond.

He rode roughly a hundred yards north, trotting the chestnut that fleetly leaped deadfalls and blowdowns, then swung west, in the direction of the cabin. He slowed the horse to a walk, peering straight ahead through the trees, watching for the station, mindful of the fact the four horses in the corral behind the main building might very well whinny out a warning the four kidnappers had company.

As he neared the station, he cast his gaze to the orange orb of the sun dropping westward. He had to get atop that cabin while there was still enough light for Matt to pick out his targets. If it got too dark, the operation would prove too dangerous, and they would have to wait till morning.

Ty desperately did not want to wait. Every minute Caroline was in the clutches of those four savages was another minute she could very well end up dead.

As the chestnut kept moving forward, a privy and a couple of moldering, outlying sheds—maybe a woodshed, maybe a springhouse, maybe a keeper shed— appeared in the trees at the edge of the forest. The barn and the corral with the four horses appeared to the left of the falling down buildings.

After a few more soft footfalls, Ty could see the back of the cabin beyond the barn and the corral. His heart quickened. He had to be careful the horses didn't alert the gang in the cabin to his presence. He stopped the chestnut, swung down from the saddle, tied the reins to a pine branch, and shucked his Henry from the boot.

Walking slowly but purposefully forward, and holding the Henry up high across his chest, he kept a hand over the brass breech so a stray salmon ray of the setting sun didn't reflect off of it and possibly give him away. He'd seen two windows in the cabin's rear wall. He hadn't been able to tell if there was a back door, but he'd seen what he'd thought was a rain barrel between the windows. If it wasn't too rotten to hold his weight, he'd use it to climb up onto the roof.

However, the windows in addition to the four horses in the corral made his plan a tricky one.

If he was spotted approaching the place, Caroline might very well die.

The thought was a dry knot in his throat.

Very slowly, very quietly, his chest rising and falling slowly, deeply with each anxious breath, Ty approached one of the moldering outbuildings, walked up the right side of it till he was near the front corner, then dropped to a knee behind a wild berry shrub and cast his gaze through the branches toward the cabin.

He saw the two windows and, sure enough, a rear door, which he had anticipated. The rain barrel stood to the left of the door.

The door meant the gang and Caroline, if she wasn't bound, could run out either the front or the back so Ty would have to take care of the back from the roof. If they all ran out the front door, which was likely, he and Matt would throw down on them as long as they had clear shots.

Both rear windows had flour sack curtains drawn over them. The trouble was the curtains were so tattered and thin they could be seen through from inside . . . and from outside. Ty could see occasional figures moving past the windows. However, the brush and shrubs had grown up so tall around the cabin Ty thought he could probably crawl through them without being seen.

That buoyed him.

He just had to worry about the horses.

He poked his head forward, around the corner of the shed, and peered toward the corral on his left. He couldn't see much of the corral beyond the barn, but the horses were in there, all right. Not much he could do about that. He just had to move slowly and quietly and hope and pray the mounts did not give him away.

Ty dropped low, crawled around the right side of the shrub then continued crabbing forward through the summer-cured wheat grass, brome, sage, and wild shrubs, including a few wild raspberry shrubs. He moved slowly, chewing his cheek, peering up through the brush toward the cabin, watching it grow larger and larger as he approached. He also cast several looks toward his left flank. He could see the horses in the corral. All four stood still as statues, three facing away from Ty.

One, however, a tall grulla, stood watching him, twitching one curious ear.

Ty winced at that. "Quiet, hoss," he muttered under his breath. "Quiet, hoss . . ."

As though in defiance of his plea, the horse lifted its head and loosed a ripping whinny.

CHAPTER 26

Ty cursed and dropped flat in the grass, heart thudding against the ground.

"What the hell was that?" said a muffled voice from inside the cabin.

Another man said something not loudly enough for Ty to hear clearly through the log wall.

"I *know* it was one of the horses," said the first man impatiently. "Check it out."

Ty stiffened against the tension inside of him; he lay as flat as he could. If he was seen, he'd have to run into the cabin shooting. He did not want to have to do that. He did not want to have all that lead flying around his daughter.

Foot thuds rose from inside the shack.

A latch clicked.

Hinges squawked.

Another foot thudded as a man stepped out onto the rotting plank-board stoop fronting the door. Then silence. Ty slowly removed his hat, set it down beside him, lifted his head about six inches, and glanced up through the grass to his left. It was bending in the slight breeze. He continued lifting his head until the man standing on the stoop came into view. But just as Ty got a brief look at the man, a murky figure in the fading light who appeared to be in longhandles and was holding a rifle, he turned and stepped back inside the cabin.

He closed the door with another hinge groan and latch click.

"Nothin' out there. Crap, no one rides out this way anymore."

A few more boot thuds then the scrape of a chair across floor puncheons.

Relief washed through Ty. From inside he could hear the clinking of coins as the devils resumed their poker game.

It was the time to make his move.

He donned his hat, rose quickly to his knees and cast another glance toward the corral. The grulla was still watching him. One of the others, turned away from him, had craned its neck to look at the stranger, as well. Silently praying the mounts wouldn't raise another fuss, Ty moved quickly but as quietly as possible to the cabin's rear wall.

He glanced again at the horses, wincing, holding two fingers to his lips despite recognizing how nonsensical the gesture was, then ducked beneath the window, and moved past the door.

Another whicker rose from the corral.

"There it goes again!" yelled a man inside the cabin.

Damn!

Ty dropped down behind the rain barrel, kneeling and doffing his hat, pressing his left shoulder up taut against the cabin, trying to make himself as small as possible.

"That's just Demon," said another man inside the cabin. "He's wanting more oats. You know how he is about his oats!"

"I'm gonna check it out this time myself," said the loud talker. "Could be them bounty hunters."

Hmm, Ty thought. So, the gang has bounty hunters trailing them, too.

He was glad he'd caught up to them before the bounty hunters had. Bounty hunters wouldn't be as careful about extracting Caroline from the killers' clutches before throwing down on them even if they knew the killers had her.

Ty cast his enervated gaze toward the corral and cursed. All four horses had moved up to the front of the corral and were staring at him, the grulla switching its tail edgily.

Silently, Ty cursed over and over again. Even for a man who loved his horses almost as much as his family, horses could sure be a pain in the rump sometimes. He remembered similar situations from his lawdogging days. Horses and dogs and sometimes women could really throw a wrench into the spokes of a lawman's attempt to throw down on holed-up owlhoots.

Boots thudded loudly, angrily. The door clicked and groaned.

Ty stretched his lips back from his teeth and closed his left hand around the Henry's cocking lever, preparing for the worst—going in shooting before any of the killers could kill Caroline.

He kept his gaze on the horses and was glad to see they were no longer staring at him. They were staring at the man in the doorway. Or whom Ty assumed was in the doorway, looking around.

Again, the grulla switched its tail.

"Oh, hell," the man in the doorway said just before the door slammed shut with a bang. "You're right—it's that damn devil of a grulla of yours wantin' more food!"

"It's wantin' sugar," said another man, chuckling. "J.T.'s always givin' him sugar. Demon'll eat it right out of his coat pocket!"

More chuckles.

Ty frowned at that. He didn't remember the two, now-deceased lawmen mentioning anyone named J.T. then shrugged. Maybe J.T. was the horse's previous owner. Ty returned his attention to the plan and looked at the rain barrel. About half full of water, it appeared relatively sturdy.

He leaned his rifle against it, placed his gloved hands on either side of the top of the barrel, and hoisted himself up, planting both feet where his hands had just been.

He grabbed the rifle and straightened.

The roof was so low Ty could see over the cabin to where Matt was hunkered atop the ridge beyond the station yard. He thought he could see Matt gazing down at him through a gap in the rocks at the top of the ridge, but the sun was nearly behind the ridge—a vibrant painter's palette of a sunset—and Ty couldn't be sure.

Ty lay his Henry atop the roof, placed his hands on the roof edge and, grunting, hoisted himself up . . . up . . . up off the rain barrel, grimacing with the effort and against the pain in his elbows, shoulders, and forearms. He cursed his age. Back in his day, such a maneuver would have been no harder than climbing onto a horse—which wasn't so easy anymore, either!

The realization of his age was always a slap in the face.

Finally, when he was on the roof and down on both knees, he pricked his ears to listen, hoping against hope no one in the cabin had heard the straining in the rafters above their heads. Ty weighted a good two hundred pounds, and the roof of the cabin was no spring chicken, either. It had some give in it.

Relieved not to hear any voices raised in concern, he rose and made his way very slowly, setting each foot down at a time, toward the chimney pipe angling up from the middle of the shake-shingled roof. He glowered against the crunching of the old, moss-caked shakes beneath his boots. They crackled and broke beneath his weight.

Walking so slowly and carefully, it took him nearly two minutes to gain the smoke-spewing chimney pipe and wave the Henry at Matt, glad when Matt didn't wave back. The sunburst of a sunset behind him might have flashed off his rifle, giving away his position.

Ty hadn't told Matt not to return the gesture. Matt had come up with that one on his own.

Yeah, he was a man now, a pleasing notion despite its reminding Ty once again of his age and reminding him however vaguely that Matt had not yet decided whether he was going to remain at the Powderhorn or drift into a new and different life for himself.

Ty removed his hat, dropped to a knee, and placed the hat crown over the pipe. He pressed the top of the brown Stetson down taut against the pipe. Instantly, smoke stopped issuing.

Ty waited, holding the hat down against the pipe.

Seconds passed.

Then a minute.

A few more seconds.

Beneath Ty, a man coughed.

"Hey, that damn stove ain't drawin'!"

"Damn!" said another man in a pinched voice. "Who closed the damper?"

Ty winced, wishing they'd get out of there with Caroline. He hated doing this to his baby, but it was the easiest way to get her out of the cabin alive. He grew more and more surprised when he didn't hear either a woman's or a girl's cough or exclamation. The lawmen and MacKenna had both mentioned the flaxen-haired woman named Zenobia Sparrow.

More men's coughing and cursing rose from inside the cabin below Ty . . . but not a girl's nor a woman's.

Beneath Ty, the ceiling creaked.

It lurched downward, making Ty lose his balance so that he had to remove his hand from his hat and place it on the ceiling to keep from falling.

"Wait," he said. "*What . . . ?*"

He got a very sick feeling.

And then a falling feeling.

A *genuine* falling feeling because right after another,

louder crack had sounded beneath him, the ceiling had opened up like a gap in the earth during a quake.

"Ah, *hell!*" Ty yelled as the inside of the cabin opened beneath him, and he dropped with the roof dropping beneath him.

Time seemed to speed up and slow down at the same time. As he shot through the air and into the smoky cabin, broken roofing and splintering beams joining him on his fall, he saw through the smoke wafting around him a square table littered with pasteboards, coins, greenbacks, shot glasses, and a whiskey bottle. One of the four chairs around the table was overturned. Two others were vacant. In one sat a man with his forearm over his nose and mouth, blinking against the smoke.

As Ty tumbled toward him, the man snapped his black-hatted head up and gaped up at the ceiling and the man tumbling toward him. He was a black-bearded, thick-set man in a checked shirt. He pulled his thick forearm away from his mouth, and Ty recognized him as a long-looper who worked for a local cattle rustling syndicate—Blackie Darthmoor.

Realizing he and Matt had tracked the wrong four owl-hoots, Ty fell butt-first into the table in front of Blackie, breaking it down the middle in much the same way he'd broken the rotten roof. He struck the floor butt-first and then on his back and legs. Both halves of the table tumbled onto him, raining its contents of pasteboards, money, glasses, a bottle, liquor from the bottle, two ashtrays full of butts, ashes, and a lit cigar.

He lay amidst the debris, staring dazedly through the smoke wafting around him. Then he saw Blackie Darthmoor standing in front of the chair he'd been sitting in.

Pointing in shock down at Ty, he yelled, "It's *Ty Brannigan!*"

Ty glanced around quickly to see three other men standing around him, shrouded in the wafting stove smoke. One was in front of the front door, another in front of the range from which smoke still issued since the chimney lay amongst the other debris on the floor. Another stood to the right of the man in front of the range.

That man, whom Ty recognized as another known long-looper named String Lewis—tall and lanky, with an elongated head and bulbous forehead—shouted, *"Shoot him!"* He already had his pistol in his right hand and whipped it up, extending it at Ty.

Ty kicked the table toward his would-be executioner, fouling the man's aim. The bullet whipped a whisker's width off Ty's right ear to plunk into the floor dangerously close to Ty's head.

Ty shucked his own .44 and shot Blackie Darthmoor just as the man's own revolver cleared the soft brown leather of his low-hung pistol belt. Blackie wailed as he fired his pistol into the floor and stumbled backward, looking down in horror at the blood issuing from his belly through the .44-caliber-sized hole in his checked shirt.

Hearing the yells of the other two men, Ty rolled behind one of the two halves of the broken table just as both men's guns' roared. One bullet blew a chunk of wood from the edge of the table while the other bullet punched into it, making it lurch but not blasting all the way through the heavy oak. Ty shouldered the table aside, extended his cocked .44 around the side, saw in the wafting smoke the outline of the bare-headed man in front of the still-smoking stove, and tripped the Colt's trigger, adding another ear-rattling blast to the echoes of the previous shots.

The man, Ralph Hayes, former shotgun-rancher turned rustler who'd had an eye carved out by an Arapaho prostitute years ago in Somerset, yelped and flew backward over the stove, screeching as his flesh made contact with the stove's hot iron.

The fourth man wailed curses and blasted away at Ty.

From Ty's left, one bullet merely nudged the heavy table while the other round punched so far into it he could see the head of the slug bulging through the wood.

Ty yelled a curse of his own, twirled around on his butt, raised his knees, and thrust both feet against the table, kicking it across the room and into the fourth man.

The man yelled, "We wasn't rustlin' none of *your* cattle *this* time, Brannigan!" and extended his revolver though the revolver was the only thing Ty could see clearly in the wafting powder smoke.

Half-sitting up on his butt, Ty extended his Colt straight out over his right knee and—*bam-bam*—evoked a yelp from the fourth rustler just before the man flew backward and out the cabin's back door, knocking it off its leather hinges.

Ty sat up straighter. The fourth man lay just beyond the door in the fading light on his back, his arms and legs spread wide. He flopped like a dying bird trying desperately to take wing then stopped shivering and lay still.

"Pa!" Matt yelled from beyond the front door.

A loud crashing sounded behind Ty, and Matt yelled again, louder. "*Pa!*"

Ty glanced over his shoulder to see Matt standing just inside the open door, crouched over his extended Winchester carbine.

Ty blinked against the smoke stinging his eyes, spat grit from his lips. His voice low with disgust and grave disappointment, he said, "Stand down, son. They're all dead."

Matt lowered his rifle and stepped farther into the cabin, looking around. "Where's Caroline?"

Ty wagged his head in defeat. "Not here." He wagged his head again. He felt wretched, desperate. "I'll be buzzard bait if I didn't get in a big hurry and track the wrong four owlhoots. These are just local long-loopers. Must have been on the run from bounty hunters likely hired by the ranchers in these parts." Slamming the end of his fist down against his knee, he barked a curse that thundered loudly around the smoky cabin littered with debris.

While he'd been wasting time here, Caroline and the four killers who had her had gained several more hours' lead time.

CHAPTER 27

The horses, Caroline thought.

If she could climb onto one of the kidnappers' horses, she'd be able to get away from them much faster than if she remained on foot.

But if she was honest with herself—and this was something about herself she didn't like very much because it was yet another way she did not measure up to MacKenna—she was afraid of horses. She'd ridden a small one from time to time, when Pa, MacKenna, or Matt had been near in case she fell or the horse bolted on her, but she'd never ridden long. Being that high up off the ground and on so large a beast as even the smaller mounts she'd ridden, had made her a little sick to her stomach.

What was that Pa had told her?

You have to face your fears, Princess. That makes them go away.

That decided it.

Hearing the men and the crazy woman calling for her somewhere beyond the ridge she'd just descended, she strode in the direction of the kidnappers' horses. Three were tied to the tree near which Caroline had sat with Doc and Zee. The fourth one, Bear's pinto, was tied to another tree near where the Indian and the big white man called

Hungry Jack—he certainly *did* look hungry all the time, hungry and owly as all get out—had been putting its shoe back on.

Caroline chose the woman's cream horse mainly because it was the one she'd been riding before and it was probably more used to her, as she was to it. Quickly glancing back over her shoulder to make sure her captors were not returning, she untied the horse's reins from the tree then considered the left stirrup.

It was up too high off the ground. She'd never be able to put her foot through it.

Looking around, she saw a large rock several yards away in the brush. At first the horse merely eyed her skeptically, warily, as if wondering what trickery this little person was up to, but after coaxing the horse and tugging on the reins she led the reluctant horse over to the rock. Holding the reins in one hand, she climbed the rock then turned to the horse.

Her heart quickened as she looked the horse up and down. It was an awfully big horse. She'd had a sick feeling riding on it even with the woman steering it. She considered having the big beast beneath her alone—just her. She who had had very little experience with horses and never any with one as big as the woman's cream.

Caroline gave a shiver of dread; her hands grew sweaty.

Come on, Caroline. You're a Brannigan. Face your fears!

"All right, all right—I'm gonna face my damn fears," Caroline said, vaguely reflecting that had been one of the few times she'd sworn aloud in her life. Ma had said using barn talk wasn't worthy of a lady of Caroline's station. Ma had told her that with the shimmer of humor in her dark eyes, after Caroline had uttered an oath when a freshly washed sheet had blown off the clothesline, but the remonstration had stuck with her just the same.

Ma. Caroline sure missed her . . .

She shook off the thoughts. If this wasn't a curse-worthy

time, she didn't know what would be unless it was the times
Pa and Matt had returned to the Powderhorn headquarters
with lead in their hides. Caroline had been nearly as afraid
then as she was now.

Swallow it. Face your fears.

Taking a deep breath to calm her fast-beating heart,
Caroline stuck her left foot in the stirrup. Incredulously, the
horse craned its neck to look at her as it had before, as
though wondering what this little person was up to.

Swallow it!

Grabbing the horn, Caroline fairly flung herself onto the
horse's back. Wishing she knew how to adjust the saddle's
stirrups, her feet hung a foot above them, giving her very
little purchase. Taking another deep breath, she took the
reins in both hands, remembering what Pa and her older
brother and sister had told her about neck-reining.

"Okay," she said, hearing a tremble in her voice and reining the horse out away from the rock.

The cream shook its head then reluctantly stepped away
from the rock.

Then it stopped.

"Go," Caroline said.

The horse just stood there.

She remembered what she'd been told about making a
horse go and clucked to it, squeezing the saddle with her
knees.

Still, the horse just stood there.

"All right, now, dang it," Caroline said, frustration building in her. "I told you to go, so you *go!*" She hammered her
moccasin-clad feet against the horse's loins.

The horse lurched with a start, gave its head another,
more violent shake than before then lifted its head and
loosed a shrill, angry whinny.

"Oh, *no!*"

The horse lunged violently forward. Caroline couldn't

help but venting a scream of her own then leaning forward and grabbing the horn with both hands, holding on for dear life as the horse stretched its long legs into a ground-churning gallop.

"Oh, God! Oh, God!" she yowled, clinging so tightly to the saddle horn she could not manipulate the reins. She knew if she lifted even one hand she'd fly off the horse and into the brush.

She lowered her head even closer to the horn and squeezed her eyes closed against the panic racing like a runaway stallion in her heart. She could hear shouting behind her, beneath the thunder of the cream's galloping hooves. One of the shouters was a squeaky-voiced woman. In her panic, Caroline must have screamed loudly enough her captors had heard her and realized she was trying to flee on horseback.

Oh, she was fleeing, all right. But where she was fleeing *to* and if she'd be alive when she got there was anyone's guess! She lifted her head and cracked one eye open only to see pines whipping past her in a blur.

She gave another terrified yowl then squeezed that eye closed again and lowered her chin to the saddle horn, her body bouncing like a rag doll on the violently pitching saddle.

I'm gonna die, she thought. *I'm gonna die. Not like a Brannigan, either. I'm gonna go out howling like a schoolgirl with her pigtails caught in the privy door!*

The thuds of another horse rose in Caroline's ears beneath the din of the galloping cream. Not just one horse, she realized, as more thuds sounded around her. Two or three or maybe four or five more horses.

Her captors were catching up to her!

She lifted her head and glanced to her right just as a big, bearded man slanted his horse up close to the cream and grabbed the cheek strap of the cream's bridle, roaring, "Whoa!

Whoa! Whoa, now, hoss!" He slowed his own horse, pulling back on the cream's bridle.

Caroline felt the cream slowing, her poor, battered body finally getting some relief from the pounding it had been taking, her legs flopping over the cream's hips like that rag doll's would.

She didn't even care that her captors had caught up to her.

At least, that awful ride was over!

But wait. As the man riding a brown and white pinto to her left checked his horse down to a slow walk, checking the cream down, as well, Caroline was able to get a better look at him. At first, she'd thought he was the big, bearded man her other captors called Hungry Jack. But, no, this was another big, bearded man. This one was wearing buckskins and a gray wolf fur coat. He had an enormous nose and wide-set, deep-set gray eyes beneath the brim of his bullet-crowned, black felt hat. Four other riders were checking their own mounts down as they converged on Caroline and the bearded man who'd stopped the cream.

Hope rose in Caroline as she looked around at the other four men reining up around her. None of them were her captors, either. She didn't recognize them. In fact, they looked like a rather hard-bitten lot, not unlike the market hunters who stopped at the Powderhorn headquarters from time to time to water their horses and to chin with Pa. Ma didn't want Caroline or MacKenna outside when they were around. She'd never said why but Caroline knew it was because they were a rather crude lot.

Still, these men were not her captors. More hope rose in Caroline.

"Oh, please!" Caroline cried, jerking her beseeching gaze at the bearded gent who'd stopped the cream and sat his pinto facing her, regarding her curiously beneath the long ridge of his furled brows. "You have to help me. My name is Caroline Brannigan and I've been kidnapped!"

"Kidnapped," the bearded man said, keeping his dull-eyed gaze on Caroline. He didn't say it like it was a question but as though he was just throwing it out there to take a look at it and ponder on it.

"By who, little girl?" asked a man sitting his gray horse beside the pinto of the bearded man. He was bearded, too, and big and round-faced with a big, bulging belly. His beard was copper red. Two big pistols jutted up from holsters on his broad hips, in front of both flaps of his dirty cream duster tucked behind them.

More hoof thuds rose behind Caroline.

She gasped as she whipped a look over her left shoulder then gasped again.

Galloping toward her were four people on three horses. The woman was riding behind Doc, her blond hair bouncing on her shoulders as she peered over Doc's left shoulder toward Caroline and the five strangers. Blood glistened on her left temple, running down in a six-inch line beside her left eye. She still wasn't wearing her hat, which Caroline had knocked off when she'd brained the woman with the branch.

Bear and Hungry Jack galloped to the left of Doc and the woman. Hungry Jack's mean, brown eyes wandered across the men surrounding Caroline as he slid the flaps of his duster back behind his pistols. Caroline saw Doc reach down and unsnap the leather thong from over the hammer of the silver-chased Colt holstered on his right thigh.

Bear was not as subtle as Doc and Hungry Jack. He reached forward and shucked his rifle from its saddle boot and rested it across his saddle horn.

Caroline whipped her gaze toward the bearded man who'd stopped her horse. "That's them! That's the four demons who kidnapped me! Please, don't let them take me back. They'll *kill* me!"

The two bearded men sitting their horses to Caroline's left and the three other men—one almost directly behind her, the two others on her right—reined their horses around to face Caroline's four kidnappers. They, too, slid coat flaps behind their own revolvers or unsnapped the leather thongs from over gun hammers.

"Be careful!" Caroline said. "They're awful mean an' nasty!" She couldn't help but loose a terrified sob. "Oh, please don't let them take me back!"

"Shut up, kid," said a thin, dark-eyed man sitting a black horse to Caroline's right. He hadn't looked at her when he'd given the order in a hard, quiet voice; he'd kept his gaze on the four newcomers drawing rein behind Caroline.

"There's my horse!" screeched the blonde, Zena. "Been lookin' all over for it!" She leaped backward over the tail of Doc's mount, hitting the ground flat-footed. Grimacing, she raised her hand to the bloody wound on her temple and sucked air sharply through her teeth in pain. She glared at Caroline and said in her screechy, whiny voice, "Miss Caroline, if you wanted to go for a ride, you might have *asked*!"

Caroline didn't know how to respond to the bizarre remark. But then, everything the woman said sounded bizarre to Caroline's ears. Why should it be any different?

The bearded man who'd stopped Caroline's horse put his mount forward three steps then canted his head toward Caroline. "You know this little gal, do ya?"

"They kidnapped me!" Caroline cried.

"Kidnapped you?" said Doc, regarding Caroline with false disbelief. "We did no such thing," he said to the bearded man who'd stopped Caroline's horse. "We found the child wandering lost and was merely taking her back to her family."

"He's lying!" Caroline cried.

"Shut up, kid," said the lean, dark-eyed man who'd told her to shut-up before.

Doc turned to the lean, dark-eyed man, studied him for a

moment, then gave a shrewd grin. "Well, well. If it ain't Jess Asper."

"Who's Jess Asper?" asked Zee, still probing her bloody temple with her fingers while looking up at Doc with one narrowed eye.

"Bounty hunter," said Doc and Hungry Jack at the same time, taking their dark, ominous gazes off Asper long enough to take in the others, eyes dropping to the prominently displayed weaponry.

"Doc, how long's it been?" asked Asper. His voice sounded funny in Caroline's ears—friendly and threatening at the same time.

Caroline saw his right hand move very slowly up his right thigh to the wooden-handled revolver holstered just above it and from over the hammer of which he'd already released the leather thong.

Oh, no, Caroline cried to herself, feeling as though, like Pa's old expression, she'd leaped out of the frying pan and into the fire. *There's going to be shooting and I'm going to be right in the middle of it!*

CHAPTER 28

"Been too long, Jess," Doc said, grinning the toothy grin of his that might make some think he had a heart of gold though Caroline knew much, much better. "Too darn long. Why, I haven't seen you since Nacogdoches. What a night to remember, eh? I'm still recovering from the hangover." The smile on his handsome mug tightened. "I heard you'd left the owlhoot trail in favor of bounty huntin'." The smile on his handsome mug grew even tighter.

So tight Caroline was beginning to think the expression might break his jaws. *Good!*

The man called Jess Asper chuckled though. Just as there was no kindness in Doc's smile, there was no humor in Asper's laugh. "Yessir, I sure did. Been huntin' outlaws for nigh on . . ." He glanced at the tall, blond man dressed all in black sitting a paint horse beside him. "How long's it been, brother Johnny?"

"I'd fathom it's goin' on eight years now, brother Jess." Johnny sat up straight in his saddle with a heavy sigh as though to distract from the fact he'd just placed his gloved right hand over the pistol holstered butt-forward on his left hip.

Doc caught it, though. He didn't miss much. Liked to act like he was a nice, carefree sort of fellow, but he was always looking and watching and listening, and had dark thoughts moving around behind those blue eyes of his.

Caroline didn't miss much, either. She'd quickly learned over the past two days she couldn't afford to miss much. She could tell the handsome devil had the very darkest of thoughts wriggling around like diamondback rattlers inside his handsome head.

Doc nudged his bowler hat down on his forehead as he scratched the back of his head. "Uh, Jess?" he said, keeping his eyes on Johnny. "Would you please have brother Johnny remove his hand from that Schofield .44 he's packin'?"

"What's that, Doc?" Jess said with a feigned innocent air.

Oh, boy, Caroline thought. *Oh, boy. Oh, boy. Oh, boy . . .* She wished there was some hole she could crawl into but she still sat the horse that had almost killed her. What would the horse do when the lead started to fly?

She knew very well what it would do.

She'd have jumped down but feared that, with the tension being as tight as it was, she might startle one of these brigands and get herself shot.

"You heard me," Doc said, still smiling with his eyes but no longer with his voice. "You see, I know *you* know that I an' my loyal pards here, the lovely Zenobia Sparrow included, have a good ten thousand dollars on our collective heads."

"Oh, we're not after you, Doc," Jess said, holding his left hand up, palm out. "No, we're after a passel of rustlers that's been winnowing the herd of a certain local rancher down to a dangerous degree. The rancher thinks they have a cabin out here somewhere. That's who we're trailin'. Not you. No, sir. We mistook your spoor for theirs. I'm frankly amazed to see you back in the old home country again. I remember you sayin' what a tough life it was for you."

"Haven't been back for years," Doc said. "Just turned out to be the best route from Laramie to Montana. The shortest."

His eyes acquired a cunning glint. "Hardest route to be tracked on, too."

"Ah," Jess said. "I see. You're on the run, are ya?"

Loudly, the Indian called Bear racked a cartridge into his Winchester's action and said, "Fish or cut bait!"

The bearded man who'd stopped Caroline's horse closed his hand over his pistol's grips and pointed an admonishing finger at the Indian. "Now that right there was not necessary. In fact, it was downright the *wrong* thing to do."

Caroline slid her gaze from man to man to woman around her in shock. *Oh, God. Oh, God . . .*

"I told you," Jess said to Doc, "this little reunion was merely a matter of coincidence. We're lookin' for *rustlers*."

"How much is that rancher paying you for those rustlers?" Zena wanted to know. She stood with her feet spread more than shoulder-width apart, the flaps of her leather duster drawn back behind her own twin revolvers, fists on her hips. She looked like she might have recovered a little from Caroline's braining though the blood was still on her forehead.

Johnny's lusty eyes crawled across the well-built blonde and whistled. "Doc, you sure do ride with some might purty ornamentation!"

"Answer the question?" Zena shot back at him, narrowing her own wicked blue eyes.

Johnny glanced guiltily at Jess and shrugged. "Around a thousand."

Doc said, "Like I said, I know you know how much we got on us. Because the man I once rode with in Texas knew everything. Don't tell me you're a bounty hunter who don't know everything—especially about how big a bounty's ridin' on me an' my loyal pards' heads. Don't tell me you're just gonna let that go and continue after some tinhorn long-loopers worth a couple of nights' of whiskey and women in Rawlins."

"With what we got us on," Hungry Jack said, grinning,

his little, deep-set pig eyes glinting shrewdly, "you boys could spend the winter in Old Mexico, lounging around the Sea of Cortez with the dusky-eyed señoritas."

"Can I say something?"

Caroline looked around to see who that strange voice belonged to then jerked with a start when she realized it belonged to *her*. She'd been the one who'd asked the question.

All eyes turned to her.

The world swirled around her. For a few seconds, she thought she was going to faint. Then she heard herself say, "I am an innocent party here. A mere bystander. If you all are going to shoot each other, could one of you please help me down from this horse and let me hide behind a rock?"

All eyes remained on her.

No one said anything.

Then, suddenly, Zee snorted a laugh and slapped a gloved hand over her mouth as though to stifle another one. Her eyes were wide and bright with humor as she stared at Caroline.

Most unexpectedly, the big Indian, Bear, snorted his own laugh.

Then, as though the laughter was as catching as the milk fever, all eight men and the woman were roaring with laughter. Doc leaned far back in his saddle, face twisted with uncontrolled amusement, pointing his finger at the source of his amusement and shaking his head.

The bearded man who'd stopped Caroline's horse roared loudest, slapping his denim-clad thigh.

The laughter continued for one minute, then another minute.

Then it began to dwindle until all eight men sat their saddles in red-faced exhaustion, still smiling. Zee's own laughter settled to a slow simmer before stopping altogether and the woman tossed her hair back behind her shoulders.

"Whew!" she said, heaving a ragged sigh.

They looked around at each other, still smiling.

Caroline grew hopeful the laughter had blown out the storm of the coming violence.

She gasped as Bear suddenly snapped his rifle up, pressed his cheek to the rear stock, and aimed past Caroline at either Jess or his brother, Johnny. Before the move had fully emblazoned itself on Caroline's brain, the rifle roared, flames lapping from the barrel.

A man bellowed and then all nine people around Caroline were bringing guns up so quickly they were all a blur. But then suddenly the world grew very dim, as though the sun had gone under a heavy cloud, and it grew quiet, as well. At least, Caroline heard the popping of the guns as though from a great distance and why this was to be she did not know until she opened her eyes and found herself lying on the ground.

She must have passed out and tumbled off the cream. Or maybe the cream had bolted and thrown her. Whatever had happened, she was on the ground.

Loud foot thuds rose to her ears, replacing the previous muffled cacophony of the lead swap. Caroline felt the reverberation in the ground beneath her back and then a gloved hand appeared before her, slanting down from an extended arm.

"Come on, Calamity Jane who wields a mean tree branch!" intoned the bizarrely high-pitched voice of Zena. "We got 'em on the run!"

She was on the back of the cream horse, leaning down toward Caroline. Caroline could hear the dwindling thuds of many horses as well as the jovial whooping and hollering of several men.

"Come on!" Zena said, scowling down at Caroline, closing then opening her gloved hand.

Caroline shook her head slowly. "You're gonna . . . you're gonna . . ." She was staring at the line of dried blood running down from the woman's left temple.

"Kill you?" Zena smiled. "Not a chance. Leastways, not yet. You, young lady I have a newfound respect for. You got sand. No, no. When it's your time, you're gonna die right an' proper!"

Caroline had no idea why she did what she did next. It was as though she were in a trance. Or maybe she just knew there was no way she was going to be able to *not* be recaptured by these savages.

Numbly, she raised her hand. Zee closed her hand around it and drew Caroline up onto the cream's back.

CHAPTER 29

A brusque hand tugged on MacKenna's arm, making her bed jounce like a rowboat on choppy seas. In her ear, her youngest brother said in his teenager's changing voice, "Mack! Mack, wake up!"

MacKenna groaned and rolled away from her tormentor.

"Mack!" Again, Gregory grabbed her arm and tugged. "Mack, get up! Ma says we're ridin'!"

That bit of information did what her brother's hand had not been able to do. MacKenna opened her eyes and sat up, sweeping her long, sleep-tangled black hair back from her face. "*What? Did you say ride?*"

MacKenna blinked up at her long-limbed, broad-shouldered brother gazing down at her in the semi-darkness of the early dawn. Gregory was in his longhandles and a ratty red robe he'd worn since he was twelve and had badly outgrown, the shoulder seams fraying. His longish sandy hair was also tangled from sleep. He held one of his manure-encrusted clodhopper boots in one thick, deeply calloused hand.

Gregory may have been only fifteen but he worked like a plow horse. Why he held that boot and not the other one was anyone's guess. He often seemed to belong to another, more mystical realm than the other Brannigans.

"His head cleaving the clouds like a ship's prow parting the ocean waves," their father often said with a smile.

"That's what Ma said. She said ride." Gregory turned his head to MacKenna's open door and yelled, "Ma, you said *ride*, didn't ya. Mack don't believe me!"

Footsteps sounded downstairs, growing louder until they stopped and Beatriz Brannigan's voice carried up the stairwell, *"¡Ustedes dos, niños, vístanse y estén listos para montar en cinco minutos!"*

Footsteps sounded again, dwindling.

"Ah, heck," Gregory said, running a hand through his mussed hair. "She's all excited an' speakin' Spanish. She knows I can't keep up with her English let alone Spanish."

"She means business!" MacKenna tossed her bedcovers aside and dropped her bare feet to the floor. "She said we have five minutes to get dressed and be ready to ride!" She rose and brushed past Gregory, who at fifteen was two inches taller than her own five-seven, on her way to the open door.

Behind her, Gregory said, "Do you think she's sleep-walkin' again?"

"I don't think so, little brother," Mack said, striding barefoot down the hall toward the still-dark stairwell. "Get dressed. She's speaking Spanish. When she speaks Spanish, she means business!"

"Ah, heck. It's still early and she knows I can't ride," Gregory complained as MacKenna, on the stairs, heard him shuffle across the hall and into his room.

"You're a better rider than you think!" MacKenna paused to call up to him from the bottom of the stairs.

She hurried into the kitchen to see her mother standing at the food preparation table, cutting into a loaf of crusty, brown, fresh-baked bread by the guttering light of a hurricane lamp. The coffee pot gurgled on the ticking range, filling the room with the rich aroma of fresh Arbuckles. What was left of a pot roast sat on the table as did a crock of pickles and pickled eggs and a half wheel of cheese.

MacKenna paused just inside the kitchen door, eyes widening in startlement. Her mother wore riding slacks and a cream work shirt, a wide, black, gold-buckled belt encircling her lean waist. A red bandanna was knotted around her neck, the long ends trailing down one side of her chest. Her mostly still-black hair was gathered into a large bun at the back of her head, making room for a hat.

MacKenna hadn't seen her mother dressed for riding in several years. Beatriz used to ride often. She'd grown up in town but her father, Mack's grandfather, Diego Salazar, had kept several blooded horses, and Beatriz had practically grown up in the saddle. But she had so much work to do in the Powderhorn lodge she rarely rode anymore, which MacKenna had always thought a shame. She remembered her mother was a beautiful rider who'd seemed one with her horse. MacKenna supposed it was from her mother she'd received her own natural riding abilities.

"Mama!" she exclaimed.

Beatriz looked up from her work with her cool, dark eyes glinting in the light from the hurricane lamp on the table before her. "You're not dressed."

"Where we riding to?"

"We're going after your father and Caroline."

"*What?*" MacKenna stepped forward, scowling her incredulity.

Beatriz was cutting into the roast now. "You heard me. *Vistete, por favor, MacKenna!*" Get dressed.

MacKenna took another dazed step forward. "Mama, Pa said . . . he didn't want me . . . I mean, his orders were really clear."

"MacKenna." Again, Beatriz looked up at her daughter,

her black brows raised. "You should know by now who is really in charge here at the Powderhorn!"

MacKenna closed her hand over her mouth to quell a cry of excited delight.

Slicing the roast and laying the slices on several pieces of bread laid out before her, Beatriz said, "Those people have your sister, my daughter. It's not that I don't have faith in your father and your brother. But I want to be part of getting her back." She glanced up at MacKenna. "And I know you do, too."

"I do! I do!—MacKenna started backing toward the kitchen door—"but Gregory—"

"It's his duty. We all must make an effort. They have taken one of ours. A Brannigan! We all must help to get Caroline back!" Those last few words came out as a sob. Beatriz slammed the butcher knife down on the table and closed her wrist over her quivering lips, tears streaming down her cheeks.

"Oh, Mama!" MacKenna hurried around the table and took her mother into her arms. "I'm so sorry, Mama," she said, breaking out in sobs now herself. "It's all my fault. I wish they would have taken me. I'm the one they—"

"No!" Beatriz pulled away from her daughter and placed two fingers over MacKenna's own quivering lips. "I will not hear any of that." She sniffed, quickly brushed her hands across her cheeks, swabbing away the tears. "What's done is done. They have Caroline. Now, you and I and Gregory are going to help your father and Matthew get her back."

Scowling, puzzled but eager, MacKenna said, "How are we going to be able to follow them?"

"We follow their sign," Beatriz said. "It hasn't rained since Caroline was taken. You can track. I know you can. And so can I. It's a matter of being observant."

MacKenna nodded quickly, swabbing tears from her own cheeks. "All right, Mama. All right."

"What about the horses and old Agnes?"

They turned to see Gregory standing in the kitchen doorway. He was dressed as he always dressed for work around the yard—bib-front overalls over a plaid work shirt. His leather-billed immigrant cap sat on his head, his uncombed hair spiking out from under it. He held a pair of saddlebags over his right shoulder. He did not have an eager look on his face. But then, the awkward child rarely did. Like his little sister, Caroline, he was skeptical of everything.

"Ralph Little is here," Beatriz said. "He rode over late last night, just before I was about to try to get a little sleep. He rode through the other day to water his horse, and I told him about Caroline. He came last night because he wanted to help. I told him the best way he could help would be to stay here in the bunkhouse and tend the horses and the milk cow while we are away. He agreed. He is out there now. Ralph's coming is why I made the decision that all three of us would ride out to help your father get Caroline back."

Ralph Little was an elderly ranch hand, mostly retired, who lived in an old mining shack on Powderhorn range and occasionally lent Ty a hand though he was getting so up in years forking a saddle was painful for him. He came by the headquarters frequently, however, always offering to help with this or that, with some repair or another or with branding. He saw it as his way of repaying the Brannigans for allowing him to live on the ranch.

"All right, then!" MacKenna nearly yelled at the rafters. "Let's ride!" She ran past Gregory and out the door to the foyer then stopped, turned around, and poked her head back into the kitchen. Wide-eyed, she regarded her mother who'd returned to making sandwiches for the trail. "As long as you make double sure Pa knows this was your idea and not mine." Mack shook her head slowly, awfully but with humor in her hazel eyes. "Or I'm likely to get the strappin' I haven't had since I was twelve and locked little Gregory in the root cellar!" She laughed then swung around and ran through the foyer and up the stairs.

"I still have nightmares about that!" Gregory's changing voice thundered behind her.

That night, camped in a ravine along a trail clearly showing several sets of hoof prints made over the past several days, MacKenna woke with a quiet gasp. She looked around the dark camp, seeing the silhouettes of her brother and mother lying in their soogans around the fire that had burned down to a few glowing coals. There was no moon. There were so many stars, however, MacKenna could see a good distance into the dark forest beyond the camp. On either side of the ravine it seemed to radiate its own soft blue light.

MacKenna swung her head first left, then right then left again, peering into the forest on the south side of the camp.

Something or some*one* was out there.

She didn't know how she knew it, but it had come to her in her sleep. It was like that sixth sense Pa always talked about—a cold witch's finger of caution poking him. Or maybe she'd heard something. She wasn't sure. But that cold witch's finger was poking the base of her spine, sending chills up her back and lifting chicken flesh on the back of her neck.

Gregory was curled on his side, head resting on a grain sack, muttering in his sleep.

Beatriz was breathing softly where she lay curled on her left side, both her black-gloved hands lying flat between her left cheek and the wooly underside of her saddle. Her own Winchester repeating rifle lay propped against a nearby rock at the base of which lay her saddlebags and canteen.

"Uh-uh," Gregory muttered, several feet to the right of their mother. "That was mine . . . It had my hook first then went for yours . . ." He was arguing with his friend, Glenn

Thomas, son of a neighboring rancher, about a fish. The two boys often got together on Sunday afternoons to fish a nearby creek. It was their only free time, as the rest of the week was filled to brimming with ranch chores.

Gregory's soft mutters were the only sounds.

Was his muttering what had awakened his sister?

MacKenna didn't think so. Gregory's muttering, which she was accustomed to hearing at night in the Powderhorn lodge, as his room was right across the hall from hers, did not give her chills.

MacKenna decided to investigate the southern forest. She'd do it quietly so as not to awaken the others. She'd let them sleep. There was a good chance any danger was only her imagination, which was understandable after her encounter with the four human demons who'd ogled her in the pool at the base of the falls along Lone Squaw Creek.

Beatriz, Gregory, and MacKenna all had ridden hard that day, and her mother and brother were not accustomed to all day rides in the mountains. They'd both been walking mighty stiffly after Beatriz had finally called a halt to their day's trek just as the sun was dipping behind the western ridges.

MacKenna tossed her covers back. Doing so, she noted a heaviness, a stiffness in her arms. That was fear.

She was not normally a fearful person.

Something was out there in the woods south of the camp. Maybe just a coyote or even a raccoon, though Mack doubted she'd react so powerfully to a coyote or a raccoon.

She'd check it out.

Heavily, feeling the stiffness of fear in her joints, she rose from her soogan, stepped into her boots, pulled on her wool coat against the high-country chill, and grabbed her rifle.

CHAPTER 30

"Glenn, that's my lure—I carved an' painted that frog myself!"

MacKenna gasped and jerked her head to her left. Gregory sat up, propped on his elbows, staring right at her. At least, he seemed to be staring right at her. She couldn't see his face clearly, for the starlight was blocked by the tall pine looming over him.

"Shh!" MacKenna said, placing two fingers to her lips. "You'll wake Momma!"

"Huh?" he grunted.

To Gregory's right, Beatriz stirred, groaned, lifted her head from the saddle to glance over her shoulder at her son. "Gregory, it's just a dream. Go to sleep, child." She lay her head back down against her hands.

Gregory grunted, shook his head as if to clear it, brushed his fist across his nose, then lay back down with a groan.

MacKenna released a held breath then stole away from the camp through the darkness. Holding her rifle, she climbed the ravine's northern bank, entered the woods, and continued north, weaving around the columnar pines, keeping her rifle up high across her chest, squeezing it nervously. She had the vague sense she'd imagined trouble and the feeling of deep anxiety. Maybe she was just afraid of the four killers who'd kidnapped her sister, and that fear was what had awakened her.

She moved slowly, stepped over a deadfall tree.

Ahead and to her right sounded a soft thud, the light snap of a twig beneath a foot . . . maybe.

Mack stopped, heart quickening, staring in the direction from which the sound had come. There was another footfall, then another, growing fainter.

Someone *was* out there . . .

"Who's there?" MacKenna called quietly but with an edge in her tone.

She had heard something, after all. Or her inherited sixth sense had alerted her to trouble even in her sleep. She considered going back to the camp and alerting her mother and Gregory, but maybe what she'd heard had only been the soft tread of a fleeing deer. She doubted it. But it was remote country. The nearest ranch was miles away. Who else would be out there?

She'd investigate further.

She continued ahead, angling to her right, holding the rifle out in front of her now.

She walked maybe another fifty yards and was climbing a slight rise when another crunching footstep sounded ahead of her. In the darkness beyond, a shadow moved, sliding from left to right then disappearing behind a tree.

"Hold it!" MacKenna yelled. "Stop or I'll shoot!"

Whoever was ahead of her broke into a run. There was a very slight pause and then a louder footfall as the running man—yes, it had to be a man (unless it was Zenobia Sparrow, MacKenna thought with a shudder)—possibly leaped a deadfall or blowdown. MacKenna thought she heard the rasp of a labored, excited breath.

MacKenna lowered the rifle. Her threat had been a hollow one. She wasn't going to shoot until she knew whom she was shooting at.

She quickened her own pace, suppressing her fear and moving ahead at a jog in the darkness. She had to find out who was lurking around. She'd like to just go back to camp and forget about it, but the lurker would likely only lurk again.

Could it be one of the four who'd taken Caroline? MacKenna couldn't help considering the possibility. Had they circled around behind Pa and Matt, maybe heading back to the Powderhorn to fetch her—MacKenna?

That seemed too crazy to be possible. But they'd backtracked, ridden back to the Powderhorn after they'd killed poor Adam and Deputy Calhoun. Those four crazy people were capable of anything.

MacKenna topped the rise and stopped. She stared down the decline before her, eyes widening in surprise when she saw the flickering glow of a campfire maybe fifty yards ahead and slightly to her right.

Someone was camped out there.

Who?

Punchers off some ranch maybe. Doing what MacKenna and her father and brother had been doing just a few days ago, before the current trouble had come calling—consolidating their herds for the coming fall gather.

The only other people MacKenna, her mother, and brother had run into on their ride today were three men filling canteens at a creek. MacKenna had thought they were probably prospectors. They'd had that bearded, half-wild, dirty, ragged look about them. Beatriz had bid the men good day with a cordial nod as she, Mack, and Gregory had ridden past them, but the three men had said nothing.

Mack had noted uncomfortably, however, that they'd stared at her too long. After she'd ridden a good distance beyond them, she'd cast a look over her shoulder to see them still staring at her, one nudging the other with his elbow and

moving his lips, saying something that Mack had been too
far away to hear.

Men's too-long stares often made her uncomfortable in
town, and those three men's too-long stares had done the
same thing—in spades.

Had they followed her?

Could they be that goatish and depraved?

She remembered the lusty stares in their cold, dark eyes.

"Hello, the camp!" MacKenna called, stepped slowly forward and down the slope.

As the fire grew before her and she could begin to hear it
snapping and crackling, she could better see the area around
it lit by the fire's guttering glow. Saddles had been laid out
and gear was piled around them, including saddlebags and
food sacks. That was all that seemed to be in the camp just
now—gear.

"Hello?" MacKenna called, taking another slow, cautious
step forward, then another, setting each booted foot down
carefully, holding the Winchester straight out before her.

Somewhere ahead, beyond the fire, a mule brayed.

That made MacKenna gasp with a start and stop dead in
her tracks.

The mule brayed again and then there was silence save
for the crackling of the fire, which also made a popping
sound and filed an extra edge on MacKenna's nerves. Glowing cinders rose in the darkness before guttering out, turning
dark.

"Who's out here?" MacKenna called, trying to suppress
the frantic beating of her heart as fear and anger grew in her.
"I know you were lurking around our camp. Who are you
and what do you want?"

A man's voice said behind MacKenna, "You, little lady!"

MacKenna had just started to whip around when a
man's thick, wool-clad arms wrapped around her waist from
behind, lifting her up off her feet and causing her to trigger

the Winchester straight up above her head with a ripping report.

"No!" Mack cried, dropping the Winchester and using both hands to pry the man's thick arms from around her. The man's sour sweat and alcohol stench was heavy in her nose as the man, giggling girlishly, spun Mack full around.

"Hold her, Rafe. Hold her!" came another man's jubilant shout.

As Mack clawed at the hands and arms of the man who had her in a bear hug from behind, and wildly kicked his legs with the heels of her boots, two more men materialized in the darkness around her—one tall and thin, the other short and with an enormous belly. She recognized them from earlier in the day, all right.

The men who'd been filling their canteens at the creek had followed her. To fulfill their own goatish needs.

"Let me go!" Mack screamed. "Damn you, let me—"

Her cry was cut off by the loud report of a rifle. Mack saw the orange blossom in the darkness to her left and maybe fifty feet away. The man with the huge belly grunted and dropped as though his legs had been kicked out from under him.

Instantly, the big man holding MacKenna released her. She hit the ground on her feet but awkwardly, losing her balance. As she fell, the rifle thundered again.

Another man grunted and groaned and in the corner of Mack's vision she saw the tall, thin man stagger backward, clutching his hands to his belly before falling back against a pine then straight down to the ground.

Standing near Mack, the big man who'd grabbed her from behind swung around and raised both hands high in the air. "No! Wait! Stop! Don't—"

His plea was cut short by another ripping report of the rifle, which flashed in the darkness straight out away from him. The big man screamed and stumbled backward, tripping over MacKenna's legs and then falling into the brush just beyond her, smacking his head on a large rock with a sickening, crunching thud.

Mack rolled onto her back and pushed up onto her elbows, staring in wide-eyed shock as a dark silhouette strode toward her. Mack couldn't see the figure clearly in the darkness but there was something vaguely female in the shape of the silhouette.

The figure, clad in a dark skirt and a black, hooded cape strode past MacKenna still staring up in mute shock. The figure stopped over the big man, who lay on his back, groaning and flopping his arms, futilely trying to gain his feet.

"No, lady—don't!" he cried in agony, lifting one hand, palm up, with beseeching. "Please, don't kill me!"

"Pig!" came the woman's brusque voice.

She angled the rifle down toward the man thrashing at her feet. It flashed and bucked. The thunder of its report caromed skyward.

The big man grunted and lay still in the brush.

The woman turned around, taking her smoking Winchester in one hand and using the other hand to shove the hood of her cape back behind her head.

"Mama . . . ?" MacKenna rasped, her chest rising and falling sharply as she breathed.

Beatriz Salazar shook her long, black hair back behind her head and strode over to gaze down at her daughter. "Let that be your lesson to never leave the camp alone, *mi hija*."

CHAPTER 31

Four days out from the Powderhorn, on the trail of their kidnapped daughter and sister, thunder drummed, echoing off granite ridges around Ty and Matt. Witches' fingers of lightning danced atop those ridges. It occasionally sizzled against a knob or a thumb of rock, kicking up a brief but sunset-bright glow, sometimes freeing rock and sending it roaring down the side of the ridge, felling pines and firs in its path, to pile up in the valley below.

The valley through which Ty and his son were riding, heading for shelter from the storm.

The rain hammered down at a forty-five-degree angle, causing both riders to tip their heads against it so the crowns of their hats received the brunt of the storm's assault. Wind and rain lashed at the yellow oilskins they had donned when the sky had started spitting and thunder had started rumbling roughly twenty minutes ago.

"So much for trail sign, Pa!" Matt yelled on the heels of an especially loud thunder peel that made both horses tense with starts.

Ty's chestnut lifted its head and gave a grieved whinny. It did not like storms.

"Yeah, so much for the sign of those we're after, but there's really only one way through the northwest end of the

Bear Paws, and that's the saddle below Bailey Peak. All we have to do is continue following the old stage road. It leads right over the saddle and out of the mountains. The problem is we lost damn near a day when I made that tinhorn blunder and went after the rustlers. This storm is gonna cause us to lose even more time!"

"These horses are spooked!" Matt yelled.

As wind gusted, blowing the rain even harder against him, Ty held his hat on his head with his left hand. "Yeah, and that creek at the other end of the canyon is gonna be flooded and there's no way around it, so we'll hole up at Indian Head Station until the weather clears!"

"Where's Indian Head Station?"

"If my memory serves—and it's been a while since I've been to this neck of the Bear Paws—it should be right around the next bend. Possibly the one after that. That's Indian Head Rock up there"—Ty gestured through the waving curtains of rain at a vast mound of pitted rock bulging up on the ridge, the largest, tallest formation in view in the valley—"and the station sits right below it."

The station was not around the next bend in the valley but when they rounded the one just beyond it, the three-story, adobe brick building with a brush-roofed pole ramada out front and with lamplight flickering in the windows, appeared in a large horseshoe formed by a V-shaped notch in the ridge wall.

A large log barn and corral flanked the place, barely visible through the rain.

Indian Head Station was no longer used by the stage line that had once run through the valley before most of the gold in the area had been plundered by jealous prospectors and miners. Indian Head Station became a somewhat notorious watering hole and brothel right after the stage line abandoned the building.

Ty hadn't stopped there in years, not since he'd once

bought a small herd of horses in the town of Big Sandy and trailed it through the valley on his way back to the Powderhorn. He'd heard through idle chatter in town and out on the range by other cattlemen that Indian Head Station was still open for business.

He was glad to see its flickering lamplight. The storm showed all the signs of continuing for at least another hour, and he and Matt and their horses needed a break from it. The devils that had Caroline were probably holed up somewhere, waiting out the gully washer, as well. At least, Ty hoped so for Caroline's sake. Like the chestnut, the frail child was afraid of storms.

As he and Matt booted their horses around the side of the road ranch to the rear, heading for the barn and corral, Ty winced and wagged his head dreadfully. His poor child.

He'd been trying to keep his mind off his youngest. It didn't do any good to worry or make up dark scenarios in his head. On the other hand, sometimes he just couldn't help it. Terror weighed heavy in his chest. It made his heart throb and race. He did not want to stop even for the storm, but he had no choice. He and Matt had been pushing hard. They and the horses were exhausted. They wouldn't be able to take on the killers who had Caroline if they were half-dead with trail weariness.

A hopeful thing, however, was Ty's belief that they were likely only about a half a day behind Smilin' Doc's bunch. That's how hard he and Matt had been pushing their four horses. Likely, they'd catch up to them tomorrow.

They reined up in front of the storm-lashed barn whose frame creaked against the wind.

Ty stepped down, opened the big, double doors, swinging them wide, the rain sluicing off the front crease in his hat brim. "Come on, boy. Let's get 'em settled!" he yelled to Matt.

They led the horses into the barn. Five other horses were

also in the barn, each in its own separate stall along both sides of the alley. The horses' large eyes regarded the newcomers suspiciously in the barn's near darkness, ears twitching. One of the horses whinnied and Matt's roan answered in kind.

Ty and Matt unsaddled their own mounts and set the saddles on saddle trees at the front of the barn, hanging the blankets from spikes driven into square-hewn ceiling support posts to dry. When they'd rubbed the horses down with scraps of burlap, squeezing the excess water from their hides, and had grained and watered them, they led them into one large stall at the rear of the barn.

The chore complete, they made their way up the barn's earthen-floored alley toward the open front doors. As they did, one of the other horses shoved its long snout over the door into the alley and gave a skeptical whicker.

"Oh, hush," Ty said, giving the horse's snout a reassuring pat.

Ahead of him, the rain was a gauzy curtain over the open double doors. Heavy streams of water dripped from the eaves to dig a long, silver-foaming channel in the ground at the base of the building.

"Hey, Pa."

Ty stopped and glanced back at his son. Matt stood a few feet behind him, regarding a saddle resting on the front door of one of the stalls. "What is it, son?"

"Look at this." Matt raised a wet, gloved hand to indicate a heavy brown stain covering the saddle horn as well as the pommel. The stain continued down the side of the saddle to about halfway down the tooled, chocolate-brown stirrup fender.

Matt scowled at his father. "Is that blood?"

Ty removed his right-hand glove, smeared his finger in the dry, brown substance, and looked at it, rubbed it with his thumb. "Sure looks like it."

"That's a lot of blood."

"Helluva lot of blood."

They shared a curious look then turned away from the saddle, made their way outside, back into the hammering storm, and closed the heavy barn doors and latched them with the locking bar. Crouching and holding their hats on their heads against the wind that seemed to be getting fiercer, they jogged back around to the front of the road ranch, climbed the steps of the gallery, and paused to scrape mud from their boots on the coarse hemp rug fronting the door.

Even above the storm's din, Ty heard a man shouting inside the place.

Shouting and bellowing.

Ty and Matt shared another curious look. Then Ty turned the knob and shoved open the rough-weather door that had been closed against the storm. Instinctively, out of long habit, he stepped to one side of the door as he entered and noticed that Matt stepped to the door's other side. Inwardly, Ty smiled at that. He hadn't coached his son on the move. Matt had simply picked up the maneuver from his old man.

No wonder he wanted a change of pace from the day-to-day ranch routine, Ty vaguely thought. He was a chip off the old block.

Seeing no immediate threat after a quick scan of the room before him, Ty kicked the door closed. He had to kick it twice. The gusting wind wanted to keep it open.

He turned again to face the room.

Only two other customers were in the place—a big man in his forties with a large, red walrus mustache and thick, wavy red hair in a three-piece black suit and another younger, slender blond gent in a fringed buckskin jacket and red string tie. Both men had turned to regard the newcomers sullenly. Ty noticed the blond young man had one brown and one very blue eye. His blond hair was gathered in a mare's tail that hung halfway down his back, secured with a beaded, rawhide thong.

He had two big pistols on his hips and another pistol shoved through his cartridge belt over his belly. A loosely rolled quirley smoldered between his lips. He was dragging on it, blowing the smoke out his nose.

Arching a brow, he looked from Ty and Matt to the big, redheaded man, whom he was playing two-handed poker with at a small, square table just ahead of the newcomers and to their left. The redheaded man, whose broad, craggy face was covered with large, brown freckles, returned his card partner's look of mute interest, maybe with a tad of incredulity, too. He wore little, round, steel-framed spectacles that flashed with the lightning flashing in the windows.

Ty had the uneasy feeling he should know the redheaded man, who was big and broad-shouldered with a heavy gut that hung down over his cartridge belt beneath the table. Why the feeling was uneasy, he wasn't sure. Was the man an old enemy?

Lord knew Ty had made enough of those.

"*Ohhh, God it hurts, brother Jess!*" came a howling wail down the stairway that rose on the far side of the room from Ty and Matt.

Another howling wail, rather. Several had caromed down the stairs from the second story since Ty and Matt had entered the place. The howls had been accompanied by the violent ratcheting of bedsprings. The wail was followed by sobbing.

Another man, likely brother Jess, said, "Oh Lord, Johnny—there's nothin' I can do! You're hit bad, brother!" He raised his voice sharply. "Give him more of that stuff! What're you doin'—hoardin' it all for yourself!"

A young woman's voice said, "If he has anymore, it's gonna kill him. That's dang near one-hundred percent opium! Miss Lucretia always cuts it!"

"*Give it to him!*"

"*All right!*" the girl returned. "*Quit yellin' at me!*"

Ty glanced at the ceiling around where the cacophony seemed to be originating then turned to the two card players who had not resumed their card game but kept their critical, pensive gazes on Ty and Matt.

Ty said, "Injured man, eh?"

Neither the older redheaded man or the younger blond with the mare's tail and one brown and one blue eye said anything for around fifteen seconds. Then they shared another silently conferring glance before the blond turned back to Ty and said, "Injured man."

"Saw the blood on the saddle out in the barn," Ty said.

Finally, the big, redheaded man said something. "You did, now, did ya?"

"We sure did," Matt said. "How'd he get hurt?"

The redhead and the blond just stared at Matt. They didn't say anything.

"Come on, son," Ty said, canting his head toward the bar, which ran along the wall to his left.

Behind it stood a short, fat, round-faced man with stringy dark-brown hair and long, mare's tail mustaches, leaning forward against the plank-board bar, looking grim. Each time a howl caromed down the stairs and echoed around the cavernous place, he winced and frowned up at the ceiling.

"Quite the din," Ty said, stepping up to the bar and tugging his wet left glove off his hand and setting it on the bar before him.

"That's been goin' on since yesterday," the apron said with a look of bald disapproval, keeping his voice down.

"Bullet?"

The apron nodded.

"Where'd he get it?" Ty asked.

The apron pointed at his bulging belly clad in a coarse, white shirt under a dirty green apron.

"Ouch," Ty said.

The apron nodded grimly. "He's been howlin' about it so long I feel like I took one, too."

"Give me a whiskey," Ty said. "Set the lad up with a beer, will you? We'd take food, if you got it. Ridin' in that storm, a feller works up a powerful hunger."

The apron studied Ty, frowning. "You're Ty Brannigan, ain't ya?"

Ty inwardly winced then glanced into the back bar mirror at the two cardplayers. Both looked at him with renewed interest before sliding their gazes to Matt then exchanging conferring glances once more and returning to their card game.

Heck . . . Ty had hoped he'd be anonymous. He hadn't liked that way the two card players had just looked at him.

Nor the way they'd looked at Matt.

"The whiskey and the beer," Ty said, returning his gaze to the bartender.

"I have chili in the back," the apron said. "Full pot. I usually have a booming lunch business with mule skinners passing on the old stage road, but this weather likely has 'em all holed up somewhere. There's a few more abandoned relay stations up and down the trail. The freighters make use of them in weather like this."

Ty glanced at Matt. "Chili, son?"

Matt smiled. He was as worried about Caroline as his father was but they'd both worked up a hunger, just the same. Which was good. They couldn't face Caroline's kidnappers on empty bellies.

When the apron set a shot glass in front of Ty and hauled a whiskey bottle down from a back bar shelf, Ty laid his hand flat against the bar and splayed his fingers. "You haven't seen four riders pass through here, have you?" He gave a heavy sigh, betraying his worry. "Three men, a blond woman, and a little girl?"

The apron opened his mouth to speak but stopped when the big, redheaded man hipped around in his chair to say, "We did, Brannigan. The same bunch as has your little girl gave brother Johnny upstairs that pill he couldn't digest."

CHAPTER 32

His pulse quickening, Ty glanced at Matt then strode over to the card players' table. He tried to keep his voice calm as he said, "Where'd you run into 'em?"

The redheaded man canted his head. "Back down the canyon about two miles."

"The girl—how was she?"

The blond man hooked a wry smile and said around the quirley bobbing between his lips, "When we saw her, she was trying to escape. Lit out on a horse—a cream that was too much for her. Ran away with her. We ran her down. That's when them four led by Smilin' Doc Ford came gallopin' in."

"You swapped lead with Ford's bunch?" This from Matt, who walked over, his own expression one of keen interest and anxiety over the fate of his little sister.

"We did."

"Why?" Ty asked, his voice urgent. "Caroline—was she . . . ?"

"They knew we were bounty hunters, the redhead said. "Doc knew one of the fellas upstairs who leads up our gang—Jess Asper—and knew Jess wasn't *not* gonna make a play on 'em, given the reward on their heads. Things got a might tense, and then the big Indian snapped his rifle up and drilled Jess's brother, Johnny, in the guts."

Ty leaned forward, placed his clenched fist atop the table between the two men and cast his hard, enervated gaze at the redhead. "The girl. How'd she fare in the lead swap?"

It was the blond who answered, shaking his head and exhaling smoke through his nostrils. "Don't know. There was a lot of close shootin'. Wild shootin' since we were all on horseback. I don't think we hit any of them, the horses were so spooked. They killed one of ours, shot Johnny. It was a crazy damn situation and as soon as Johnny was shot, Jess yelled for us to get the hell out of there."

"Caroline was there?" Matt asked, stepping up closer to the table, his voice insistent. "She could have been hit?"

"Hell, she was right in the middle of it." The redhead shrugged. "Might be better if she took a bullet. You know— faster that way."

"Why, you—!" Matt leaped forward, grabbed the man's shirt collar and cocked his right fist for a vicious blow.

"Matt!" Ty grabbed him by the back of his shirt collar and pulled him back just as he swung, making his fist connect only with the air in front of the redhead's face.

Ty swung Matt back and behind him with one hand but with so much force Matt lost his hat, hit the floor, and slid up against the closed front door. He sat up against the door, shaking his head as though to clear the cobwebs, his hair hung in his eyes.

The blond man laughed.

"That's not gonna do any of us any good, son!" Ty roared at his frustrating son.

Red-faced with fury, Matt shook his hair from his face, cast his enraged gaze at the redhead, thrust his arm, and angrily jutted his finger at the man. "That man is one of them who ambushed me the other day, Pa! I just now recognized him. Ambushed me and shot Frisky out from under me!"

Ty studied the man as the redhead frowned curiously at Matt.

Ty rubbed his jaw and said, "Now I remember you. Ed Tabor. Bounty hunter. Been awhile." Anger burned in Ty. "Why'd you bushwhack my son?"

Recognition donned in the redhead's eyes as he continued to study Matt. "Thought he looked familiar." He pointed a finger and narrowed an eye accusingly at Matt. "You shot Del Hardin in town."

"That why you bushwhacked my son, mister?" Ty said, louder, grinding his fist into the table and closing his other hand around the grips of his holstered .44.

The redhead switched his gaze to Ty. "That was you who shot Joe Walsh."

"Answer the question," Ty said. "Did you ambush my son because he shot Hardin? Hardin braced him and drew first."

"Don't get your neck in a hump, Brannigan," said the blond, whom Ty now recognized as yet another regulator who often worked for local cattle associations—Lyle Coffee. "We thought he was one of the rustlers we were looking for. Thought you were, too." He looked at Matt. "As for Hardin—we couldn't care less he's pushin' up daisies. He was all mouth and not real friendly when he drank. As for the kid here, though"—Coffee arched his brows in admiration at the young man before him—"he's gotta be fast for one so young. To kill Del Hardin, an' Hardin drew first. Watch your back, boy. Watch it good. Others are gonna want to test you now."

Ty glanced at Matt, who flushed and sucked his cheeks with chagrin.

"You were there, too," Ty said, turning to the blond.

Taking another drag off the quirley drooping from between his lips, the blond set his cards down on the table and raised his hands, palms out. "What can I tell ya? We made a mistake."

"I thought I recognized the kid's hat and the horse," Tabor

said. "String Lewis rode a cream and he wore a Stetson and a green neckerchief just like the kid's."

"Pull your horns in, Brannigan," Coffee said. "I reckon you evened the score by shooting Walsh." He glanced at Tabor. "Where in the hell do you suppose Lewis and Darthmoor and the other two are?"

"Long gone by now, most like," Tabor said, reaching for his own hide makings sack. "With this rain wiping out their sign . . ."

Ty straightened, hitched his gun and cartridge belt higher on his hips. "They're dead."

Tabor arched a skeptical brow. "Dead?"

Matt heaved himself up off his feet and brushed sawdust from his denims. "Pa shot 'em."

"By mistake, though I can't say I'm sorry. Those four have been a thorn in every Bear Paw rancher's side for the last ten years." Ty headed back toward the bar where the barman had set up his whiskey shot, two beers, and two steaming bowls of chili, then turned back to the bounty hunters. "I mistook their trail for the trail of the owlhoots who have my daughter." He picked his beer and whiskey shot off the bar and glanced back at Coffee and Tabor. "I reckon you mistook the trail of the owlhoots *we're* after for the rustlers *you* were after."

Sprinkling chopped tobacco onto the wheat paper troughed between the thumb and index finger of his right hand, Tabor winced and shook his head. "And Johnny Asper bought a bullet for our mistake."

They all glanced at the ceiling. Upstairs, the wailing had continued but with less volume than before.

"Smilin' Doc's a bad one. They all are. I'm sorry they have your girl, Brannigan," Tabor said.

The wailing picked up with another agonized cry caroming down from the second floor. It was followed by a man shouting, "I'm sorry, brother, but I can't take it anymore. I gotta end it!"

"Jess, no!"

The girl screamed.

The thunder of a revolver made Ty flinch with a start. He'd turned to the bar to retrieve his chili, but turned back to gaze in the direction of the stairs. Matt had just retrieved his hat from where it had fallen on the floor when Ty had thrown him across the room. He stopped brushing sawdust from the crown to cast a startled look at the ceiling before turning to his father, eyes wide in shock.

"Well, I'll be," he mouthed. His eyes looked genuinely stricken.

Ty thought his son had seen enough death . . . caused enough of it himself . . . to be jaded by it. But that gunshot had struck a nerve.

Brother killing brother . . .

Ty stood frozen at the bar, holding his steaming bowl in his hands, staring at the ceiling. Matt, Coffee, and Tabor also stood or sat frozen, staring at the ceiling, their eyes following the slow, ponderous thuds of heavy footsteps angling across the ceiling.

The thuds sounded on the stairs. Ty saw the banisters shake slightly before the booted feet and then the black-denim clad legs of a man appeared, shrouded in the jostling flaps of a long, yellow rainslicker.

Next, Ty saw the twin Remingtons holstered on the man's thighs, and twin cartridge belts encircling his waist. Then he saw the blanket-wrapped body slung over the man's right shoulder, a pair of scuffed brown boots dangling down beneath the blanket. Jess Asper was dark-haired, with almost Indian-dark features. He wore mostly black, including a black hat, except for a powder blue work shirt under a black broadcloth jacket and a brown leather vest. His face was grim, his brown eyes dark and staring into space as he continued down the stairs, his brother's body on his shoulder.

Ty didn't remember him from the four that had ambushed Matt. Maybe the gang had split up to look for the rustlers they'd been commissioned to hunt down and kill.

Asper stepped down onto the saloon floor, looked at Tabor and Coffee, who sat frozen in their chairs, studying their gang leader with a mix of grimness and incredulity in their gazes.

"Couldn't take it anymore," Asper said. He stood staring at Tabor and Coffee and then, as if sensing a new presence in the room, glanced at Matt and then at Ty and said, "Who're they?"

"Ty Brannigan," Ty said. "That's my son, Matt."

Asper gave a slow nod of understanding. "Ah." He continued across the room to the door, the continuing thunder of the storm occasionally drowning out the thuds of his heavy boot steps.

"Where you goin'?" Coffee asked, following the grim-faced man with his eyes.

"Gonna bury my brother," Asper said, continuing to the door.

"In *this* weather?" Tabor asked.

At the door, he swung around and cast a cold, hard, resolute gaze at his two cohorts. "Won't have time in the mornin'. First thing, we're gettin' after Smilin' Doc and those other killers. That big Injun took a sucker's shot at my brother, and here he is. He's gonna get the same, and I'm gonna dance while he bawls and wails and begs me for the bullet I gave Johnny but will *not* give him. When he finally dies, wailin' like Johnny did, I'm gonna make water on his body and leave him to the coyotes and crows." He turned his head forward, opened the door, stepped out onto the gallery, and left the door standing open behind him, lightning streaking the floor that was instantly wet from the rain lashing through the opening.

Matt set his hat on his head then walked to the door and stood there a minute, gazing out at the man about to bury his brother in the lightning, wind, and rain. He cast his father another wide-eyed, stricken look then closed the door. As Ty sat down at a table near the bar and set his chili down, Matt took his own chili and his glass of beer to the table, kicked out a chair across from his father, and slacked into it. He looked at Ty.

Keeping his voice down, Matt leaned forward, canted his head to Coffee and Tabor, who'd resumed their card game, and said, "They could be a problem, Pa."

Ty set his hat down on the table and ran a brusque hand through his hair in frustration. "You're tellin' me."

"Why don't you go upstairs and get some sleep, son," Ty said, nudging his son's shoulder.

It was eleven-thirty. The earlier storm had finally played itself out about an hour after Jess Asper had come in from burying his brother and sat down at a table all by himself at the back of the drinking hall. He drank whiskey straight from the bottle, staring moodily out through a front window at the stormy night closing down over his brother. Another storm rumbled in roughly an hour and a half later. That one, too, had rumbled on but not before whitening the ground with about an inch of marble-sized hail. For the moment, the rain had stopped but thunder continued to burp and belch in the distance, like the drumming of a distant war party, and lightning occasionally made the whole sky light up beyond the road ranch's windows.

Ty and Matt sat at the table near the bar where they'd sat most of the evening, drinking hot black coffee and playing two-handed poker to pass the time. Between storms they'd checked on the horses, but otherwise they sat at the table, both men wishing away time and trying to keep from worrying about Caroline. Trying to keep from wondering if she was dead.

An impossible task.

Matt had finally sunk back in his chair and crossed his arms on his chest, quickly nodding his head as sleep tried to claim him.

After Ty's nudge he yawned, lifted his head, and raked a work-calloused hand down his face. "I don't know if I could really sleep, Pa. Can't get her out of my head." He cast his worried gaze to a night-dark window right of the door. "Thinkin' about what might be happening to the squirrel even as we sit here. Wonderin' if she's—"

"Don't even say it, son." Ty placed a hand on Matt's shoulder. "Go up and try to sleep. A few winks couldn't hurt."

"What about you, Pa?"

"I'll try to catch a few winks here," he lied. He knew he wouldn't sleep. At least he had food in his belly.

Matt yawned again and slid his chair back. "All right. If you say so. I'll try."

When Matt's footsteps had dwindled up the stairs, Ty rose with a weary groan then walked over to where the barkeep, a man named Stockton who owned the place after buying it from a previous owner, had set a pot of coffee on the potbelly stove before he'd retreated to his living quarters at the rear of the building. Tabor and Coffee had gone upstairs to bed around ten. Asper had sat drinking and staring out at the night for another half-hour then rose drunkenly to his feet and made his way up the stairs.

Only one girl up there, Ty had overheard the other men saying. She and Asper had made some noise right after he'd gone upstairs, but the noise hadn't lasted long. The man had been too drunk for what passed for love in a brothel. Ty was glad. He didn't like exposing Matt to that kind of high jinks, which he supposed was ridiculous since the young man was nearly twenty and he'd been exposed to the killing of men.

It wasn't easy being a father. So much he felt the need to protect them from. One such thing he'd never thought would endanger them, though, were four misfits of the ilk of Smilin' Doc Ford, Zenobia Sparrow, the Indian called Bear, and Hungry Jack Mercer.

Ty poured himself a fresh cup of coffee then returned to his chair. He'd just sat down when a yell sounded in the second story, nearly directly above his head.

"*It's them!*"

The girl gave a startled cry. "*What?*" she asked, her voice shrill with incredulity.

"It's them! They're here! They backtracked for us!"

Above Ty's head, bed springs jostled violently. A pounding sounded—Asper stomping into his boots. Fast footsteps thundered in the ceiling, angling toward the stairs until the dark-haired, dark-complected bounty hunter was on the stairs, running down two steps at a time, his gun in one hand, steadying himself on the rail with his other hand. He wore only longhandles and boots, his hair spiked from sleep.

"*They're here!*" he shouted, his booming voice echoing around the drinking hall.

Ty's own hand closed over the Henry on the table before him, blood quickening. He watched Asper cross the room at a dead, resounding run inadvertently kicking chairs.

He was still drunk, his eyes glassy from the whiskey. He whipped open the door and ran out shouting, "You murderin' devil, Doc!" His gun thundered six times. Between reports were several shrill yips and the soft thuds of running, padded feet.

"Oh, for chrissakes," Ty said. Leaving the Henry on the table, he rose from his chair and walked to the door.

Asper stood before him, the man's Remington extended

straight out into the night. He smelled like a still. Beyond the smoking barrel of the gun, Ty could see the silhouettes of several jostling, doglike forms running off into the sage straight out beyond the road ranch.

"Coyotes." Ty placed his hand on the man's gun, shoved it down. "Just coyotes. Not even Smilin' Doc's devils would be out on a night like tonight."

"Maybe." Asper looked at Ty. His eyes glinted with the lunacy of the grieving and enraged. "Maybe not." He turned and walked back into the saloon.

Beyond him, Matt stood at the bottom of the stairs, his rifle in his hand, looking toward Ty incredulously. Tabor and Coffee stood on the stairs behind and above Matt, each with a pistol in his hand, also shuttling incredulous gazes between Ty and Asper.

The portly Stockton stood in a rear doorway, holding the curtain aside and scowling. He wore a blanket around his shoulders and a night sock on his head.

"False alarm," Ty said. He gazed at the back of the retreating Asper, scowling his dismay.

Since they were hunting the same group of thieving, kidnapping killers, he and Matt would likely end up riding with Asper, Tabor, and Coffee.

How was Ty going to make sure no harm came to Caroline with a kill-hungry, shoot-happy man like Asper dogging the heels of her captors? "Yep," he said to himself, dread burning in his loins. "He's gonna be a problem."

If he had to shoot him to save Caroline, he would.

CHAPTER 33

Ty sat at the table, drinking coffee and smoking cigarettes, nodding uneasily off for maybe fifteen minutes until the first gray wash of dawn streaked the sky beyond the eastern windows. He stubbed out his last cigarette and cocked an ear to the ceiling.

Several sets of snores issued through the rafters.

Hope rose in him.

Asper had been so drunk he'd likely sleep in. The other two men were in no hurry to get after Smilin' Doc's gang. It wasn't their brother the Indian had killed. They were just riding with Asper.

Maybe Ty and Matt could ride out well ahead of the three bounty hunters and run down the gang and extract Caroline from their clutches before Asper, Tabor, and Coffee could catch up to them.

Ty rose from his chair, crossed the saloon to the rear, and began slowly, quietly climbing the stairs, wincing every time a riser complained beneath his feet. When he'd gained the top of the stairs, he stopped and frowned down the dark hall before him.

Six closed doors faced the hall, three on each side.

Quite a bit of loud snoring was going on. Although he didn't know which room Matt was in Ty knew his son wasn't a loud snorer and should be able to find him by avoiding the doors behind which loud snoring sounded. He assumed Asper, Tabor, and Coffee each had a room to themselves, Asper maybe sharing a room with the girl.

Moving slowly down the hall, Ty passed a door on his right and on his left, and the next one on his right due to the log sawing behind each. No snores issued from behind the next door on his left. He was about to check it when the last door down the hall on his right opened suddenly. Ty jerked with a start and swung his head around.

Relief touched him. Matt stood in the doorway, his rifle in one hand as he set his hat on his head with his other hand.

"Oh . . . sorry, Pa. I didn't realize how—"

"Shh!" Ty said, pressing a finger to his lips. He cocked an ear and winced when the snores around him dwindled.

Behind one door, a man muttered incoherently. Bed springs sang and again Ty winced, imagining the man rising from the bed. The man muttered again and after another few seconds there was a sigh and then snoring resumed behind that door—the one directly to Ty's right.

And then snoring resumed sounding behind the other two doors, as well.

Ty turned to Matt and beckoned quickly. "Come on. *Quiet!*"

Matt moved on out of the room and they walked slowly on the balls of their feet down the hall toward the stairs, Ty rejoicing in the snores he heard behind three of the six doors. He had a feeling the three men—bounty hunters or regulators—would sleep at least another couple, possibly three hours.

Good.

When he and Matt reached the stairs, they moved slowly down the steps, both wincing when the risers complained beneath their boots. The snorers, however, kept snoring.

Near the bottom of the stairs, Matt turned to Ty and said quietly, "What's goin' on, Pa?"

"I want to get out of here well ahead of those three bounty hunters."

"Good thinkin'. That Asper's a loose cannon!"

"You can say that again."

They grabbed their oilskins and rifles and, walking nearly as carefully as they had upstairs—boot thuds on the wood floor seemed to echo around the entire cave-like building—made for the door. Ty quietly opened the door, they stepped out onto the porch, and Ty drew the door closed, quietly, carefully latching it. Then the two continued stepping carefully across the wooden-floored gallery and down the steps.

Once in the yard, Ty gave a heavy sigh of relief. "So far, so good," he whispered.

He and Matt headed around the saloon toward the barn, the ground soggy beneath their boots. They swung wide around large mud puddles. Ty glanced back over his shoulder at the road ranch's second story windows, hoping against hope the three so-called bounty hunters continued sawing logs. He did not want them tagging along and getting in too big of a rush to kill the man who'd killed Asper's brother. Getting Caroline killed in the bargain.

If she is still alive. Ty grimaced and shook his head. That thought stopped him cold and he could not afford to be stopped cold or in any way distracted. *No, don't even think that.*

Once in the barn, they led their mounts to the front and quickly saddled and bridled them. They gave both horses a handful of oats and some water from buckets they'd filled from an outdoor rain barrel. A better breakfast would have to wait until they were well up the trail. Ty wanted to put a good bit of distance between them and Asper.

He considered bridling the horses of Asper's men and leading them off into the tall and uncut and letting them go, buying him and Matt even more time. But there were five of them, one likely belonging to the member of the group who'd been killed during the shootout. It would take too much time to bridle them, and then leading them outside and up the trail would likely make too much noise and thus give away what Ty and Matt were doing.

Just getting a good head start would have to be enough.

He and Matt led their four horses outside. Ty mounted his coyote dun while Matt mounted his blue roan and, leading their second mounts, they headed on up the trail at a slow walk, not wanting to make too much noise and awaken Asper's men. Ty cast several anxious glances back at the Indian Head Station lodge. The windows were paling as the dawn grew, the pearl blush in the east widening, silhouetting the sawtooth ridges before it. Birds piped and flitted this way and that in the rookery searching for breakfast.

He didn't see any of the curtains move, and for that he was grateful.

Yeah, Asper's men would likely sleep another couple of hours.

A good seventy yards or so up the old stage trail, heading northwest, Ty glanced at Matt. "Let's go, boy!"

They booted their mounts into trots and held them there, not wanting to run them yet with the ground being as soft and wet as it was and with the sun not high enough to reveal trail hazards—some of which could be concealed by the pools of muddy water filling the chuckholes and short stretches of wheel ruts remaining from when the trail had still been used by the stage line.

As the sun rose higher above the eastern ridges, taking some of the fall chill out of the damp air and drying out the ground, Ty and Matt urged their horses faster up the trail. Slowing them down was a creek crossing made perilous by the previous day's storm, as the muddy water churned swiftly between high, muddy banks. They swam their horses across the creek but not before the water had carried them a good hundred yards to the south.

When they gained the opposite bank at last, they had to ride north to regain the old stage road.

Roughly three hours after they'd left Indian Head Station, they rode into the yard of the next relay station up the trail—Hell's Angel Station—named for the appropriately named creek Ty and Matt had just crossed. They were going to switch horses and continue on up the trail but a big, tarp-covered freight wagon was parked in front of the corral to the left of the low-slung, sod-roofed station building, wind-mill, and stone water tank. The old Pittsburg freighter's tongue drooped onto the ground.

Four mules milled in the corral beyond the wagon. One brayed and then another one brayed, all four of the animals moving up to the front of the corral to regard the newcomers uneasily.

"What is it, Pa?" Matt had mounted his second horse and stared down at his father, frowning curiously.

Ty had grabbed his pinto's reins and had started to toe a stirrup but stopped when he'd seen the mules. "What's a freight wagon doing, sitting here in the middle of the morning?"

Matt hiked a shoulder. "The skinners must be inside, sleepin' in. Probably waiting for Hell's Angel Creek to drop so they can cross it."

"Yeah, maybe." Ty turned to study the humble cabin.

The peaked roof dropped down to the right and the left. One shuttered window in the front wall, the wood badly sun-blistered. A rusted old washtub hung on the log wall to the left of the plankboard door that was missing a good six inches of the bottom of one of its planks. There was no stoop or gallery, just a badly worn spot in the ground beneath the door. Someone had set a rock on the ground to make the step into the cabin a little easier.

Ty studied the ground fronting the cabin. Seeing something, he dropped the pinto's reins and walked around the horse, absently trailing his gloved hand across the rump and over the tail. He strode toward the cabin. After only a few steps, he stopped and dropped to his haunches, lacing his hands together as he studied the ground.

"What is it, Pa?" Matt asked again, reining his black over to his father.

"Hoof prints," Ty said. "Fresh." He glanced around. "Several sets of them. Boot prints, too."

Again, Matt hiked a shoulder. "I don't get it, Pa. What's so special about that? You saw the wagons, the mules."

Ty looked at the cabin again. "Yeah, but where are the freighters?"

"Like I said"—Matt was growing impatient—"prob'ly inside waiting for the creek to drop. Look, Pa—don't you think we should get on up the trail? Like you always say, we're burnin' daylight."

"I got a feelin' . . ." Ty said, rising.

"What kind of feelin'?"

Ty strode toward the cabin, boots crunching softly in the still-damp sand and gravel. "A bad one."

"You'll only wake 'em up," Matt warned. "And make 'em mad."

"Maybe." Ty walked up to the cabin, stopped, and yelled, "Hello the cabin!"

The only response was the breeze and the sound of running water issuing from the windmill as the blades lazily turned, squawking softly.

Ty glanced back at Matt who'd ridden up to sit the black only a few feet behind him.

Ty turned to the door again, tripped the metal latch, and opened the creaky door, which sagged on its leather hinges.

He poked his head inside and immediately drew his head back, grimacing when he saw two glassy, brown eyes staring up at him from a round, sun-seasoned, bearded face on the floor only two feet from the threshold.

Thick, red blood had pooled broadly on the floor beneath the man's head and broad, denim-clad shoulders. The blood had come from a long gash arcing across the man's neck, from ear to ear.

"Oh, Lordy . . ." croaked a voice from deeper inside the cabin's murky shadows.

"Who's there?" Ty said, looking around.

"Here," came the weak voice again. "Back here . . . by the stove. Oh, Lordy . . ."

"What's goin' on, Pa?"

"Bloody damn murder!" Blood warming and quickening in his veins, closing his right hand over the grips of his .44, Ty stepped up into the cabin and made his way around a long, wooden eating table strewn with plates, tin cups, and food scraps. He stopped near the black, potbelly stove near the room's rear.

A man lay on the earthen floor beside the stove.

Like the dead man near the door, he was heavily bearded. He wore only longhandles and wool socks. Two light-blue eyes gazed up at Ty from beneath heavy, gray-blond, sun-bleached brows. "Mister," the man said, clutching his two bloody hands to his bloody left side, just up from his hip. He lifted his head up off the floor with a grimace, casting his beseeching gaze at Ty.

He groaned, stretched his lips back from his large, yellow teeth, and said, "Would you . . . kill me?"

CHAPTER 34

"Ah, hell, mister," Ty said. "Who did this to you?"

He knew. Who else? He just wanted to hear the man say it.

"Devils, sure enough," the man said. "Came for . . . came for water . . . robbed us . . . fella in a suit . . . handsome devil . . . cut Ernie's throat for no good reason. A woman . . . purty one at that . . . shot me in the guts. They robbed us . . . took two mules . . . left me here to bleed out . . . slow. The woman laughed about it." He stretched his lips back from his teeth in an agonized grimace. "Please end it . . . mister!"

"My God, Pa!"

Ty glanced over his shoulder to see Matt standing in the open doorway, gazing down in shock at the dead man. "Stay there, Matt."

Ty turned back to the gut-shot man before him. "Was there a little girl with them?"

The man shook his head. "None that I saw."

Ty winced at that, felt a rusty nail of dread stab his guts. "What's your name?"

"Gorder. Sh-Shank Gorder." He lifted his head a little to glance at the dead man on the other side of the table. "He's Ed Sleighbough. A good man!" Gorder sobbed, tears filling his eyes.

"Anyone I should contact for you?"

"We w-work for the Stratton Freighting out of Glendive."

"All right," Ty said, rising. "I'll let 'em know." Before he could overthink it, Ty slid his .44 from its holster, stepped back, and aimed down at the dying man's head.

Gorder gazed up at him, the glint of gratefulness in his otherwise pain-racked gaze. "Thanks, Mister, uh . . ."

"Brannigan."

"Ah, Ty Brannigan. You'll go after 'em?"

"I'll get them. Don't worry about it."

Another faint glint shown in the man's eyes. "Give 'em one for me an' Ernie?"

Ty nodded, forced himself to aim down the barrel of the .44 that shook slightly in his shaking hand. The gun roared. He turned away quickly, trying to blink the image of Gorder's pain-racked face from his eyes. It didn't work. He strode back across the cabin to where Matt stood staring at him, lower jaw hanging.

"I'm . . . I'm so sorry, Pa."

"Don't think I ever had to do anything I hated more than that," Ty said, an emotional quiver in his voice.

Matt stepped back out of the doorway, glancing once more at the dead man before him, then turned to stare off across the yard. Ty stepped out of the cabin and headed for his horses.

"Don't think about it, son. Just mount up. They're close. They're damn close!"

Matt strode over to his black, grabbed the reins, and swung up into the leather. "How could they be close? You thought they were still a day's ride ahead of us."

"They must've slowed down for us. They want us to catch up to 'em now. We're near the edge of the mountains." Ty grabbed the reins of his dun and his pinto and swung up onto the pinto. He glanced at the hoof prints scoring the ground still damp from the storm then slid his rifle from its scabbard, cocked it one-handed, and looked around, warily. "Keep your eyes skinned, Matt. They're close."

Ty felt his heart throbbing anxiously, eagerly. He dreaded catching up to Caroline's kidnappers and looked forward to it like nothing he'd ever looked forward to before.

Would Caroline be with them?

If not— Ty shook his head, grimacing away the bleak possibility, then touched spurs to his dun's flanks. "Come on, Matt!" He glanced over his shoulder as Matt spurred his black after him. "Keep your eyes skinned!"

Matt slid his Winchester from its scabbard and rested the barrel across his saddle bows. "I will, Pa." His eyes were dark, grave.

Wishing Matt hadn't seen what he'd had to do, Ty wished *he* hadn't seen it, either. He'd likely see it on his deathbed.

Keep your mind on the killers, he told himself. *They're close. So close you can smell them—the smell of brimstone and death and the sickly-sweet smell of the Devil himself.*

Ty held his horse to a trot, holding the rifle with one hand, his reins in his other, scrutinizing the terrain around him. Occasionally, he glanced down at the trail in which four sets of hoof prints shone clearly in the damp dirt, sand, and gravel. Smilin' Doc's bunch had made those tracks only a couple of hours ago.

They were close. Real close.

Ty had to make sure he and Matt didn't ride up on them unaware and get blown out of their saddles.

Fury burned in Ty, even hotter after he'd seen what Smilin' Doc's bunch had so casually and unnecessarily done at the relay station. Gorder had had it right and he'd had only a glimpse of them. They truly were devils.

Devils that needed to be sent back to the hell that had spawned them.

Once Ty had retrieved his daughter from their clutches . . .

He cleared his thoughts as they rode for another hour . . . then another . . . the clearly defined tracks in the trail urging them on. At the bottom of a steep rise, tall pines and firs on both sides of the trail, Ty checked down the dun, which he'd switched to an hour ago.

"What is it, Pa?" Matt asked, stopping his own two horses behind his father.

Ty gazed up at the rise. "We old fellas get a feelin' when trouble's afoot." He glanced at Matt. "You get that when you've been at it long enough."

"You think they're on the other side of that rise, waitin' for us?"

"I don't know. I'm gonna check it out. You wait here." Ty dropped the dun's reins and booted the pinto up the rise, holding the horse to a fast walk. Turning his head to his left and then to his right, Ty scanned the tall-stemmed conifers on both sides of the trail. The gang's tracks were still clear on the old stage road, but that didn't mean they hadn't stolen back to flank the two men they likely knew were behind them.

A few times along the trail from the station that had become a grave for Gorder and Sleighbough, Ty had the uneasy sensation he and Matt were being watched. He'd looked around carefully and had spied no telltale sun flashes off the lens of a spyglass or field glasses. But then Smilin' Doc was likely far too cagey to let himself be given away by the sun.

Ty was pretty sure Smilin' Doc and Zenobia Sparrow knew exactly where he and Matt were. They were waiting for them to ride into a bushwhack.

Ty halted the pinto a dozen yards below the crest of the ridge. He swung down, dropped the reins, and walked slowly toward the top, doffing his hat then dropping to his knees and casting a cautious look over to the other side.

He'd been hearing the sound of running water for the past several minutes, and saw its source.

A waterfall not unlike the one on Lone Squaw Creek—but faster, running on the heels of the storm—lay in the stone-walled canyon below on the left side of the old stage trail. Just beyond the falls, in a gouge in the canyon's southern wall, lay another stage relay station. Angled to face the ridge, it consisted of an age- and sun-silvered cabin similar to the one where Gorder and Sleighbough lay dead. Just beyond the cabin was a large corral and stable. The place appeared to be abandoned—no signs of life or movement of humans or animals.

But Ty wasn't going to take any chances. He rose to a knee and beckoned to Matt. Grabbing the reins of his and Ty's spare mounts, Matt rode up the rise before stopping beside the pinto.

Ty touched two fingers to his lips and said quietly, "Step down and cover me. There's another station below. I'm gonna check it out. It's a deep canyon, a good place to set up a whipsaw."

"You got it, Pa." Matt dismounted, dropped the reins of both spare horses, and quietly racked a round into his carbine's breech. Kneeling, hatless, beside his father, he took a look into the canyon, at the falls and the relay station, then turned to Ty. "That sense you old-timer's get," he said with an ironic half smile. "Is it tellin' you they're down there?"

"That's the trouble with us old-timers. We often develop a sense for trouble but that sense never tells us exactly where it's coming from." Ty donned his Stetson and rose and started down the ridge toward the canyon. "Keep an eye out."

"Pa?"

Ty paused, glanced behind him.

"If they're down there, you could be walking right smack dab into a bushwhack."

Ty smiled and gave his head a fateful wag. "Nothin' else I can do, son. They have your sister."

Matt glowered, lifting his sun- and wind-burned cheeks and narrowing his eyes.

For the second time that day, Ty saw fear in his son's eyes. He'd thought the young firebrand had lost his fear. In a way, Ty was glad to see it back. He had every right to be fearful.

As his father did . . . and was. Fearful mostly for the fate of his youngest daughter, but fearful, just the same.

Ty gave Matt what he hoped was a reassuring wink then continued down the ridge, holding his Henry up high across his chest, keeping an eye on the station ahead, on the steep crag rising on the left side of the trail, and on the boulder-strewn forest off the trail's right side.

It was a storybook kind of place, with the falls tumbling from a hundred-foot-high ledge into a pool that bled off into a creek rushing off into the forest on the trail's right side. An old wooden bridge, splintery and gray with age, spanned the creek that churned loudly with yesterday's rain. Every bit as storybook a place as MacKenna's once-secret falls and pool, but touched now with the seedy darkness of the killers who had at least passed there if were not holed up, intending to ambush the father of the little girl they'd stolen out of her own bed.

Crazy world that has men and a woman like them in it.

Ty had been a town-taming lawdog for many years, and he'd never seen anything even close to the evil of those four.

He crossed the bridge and noted the four riders whose tracks he'd been following had swung their horses off the trail on the other side of the bridge to water them—two on each side of the bridge. They'd swung back onto the trail. Judging by the tracks on the trail, it appeared the riders had passed right on by the falls and the cabin without stopping other than to water their horses.

But Ty wasn't taking any chances. They could have circled back.

He walked past the falls, feeling the chill and humidity of the tumbling water. He angled off the trail toward the shack—just a square pine box with a shake-shingled roof, a stone chimney running up the cabin's right wall. The remaining tatters of a wolf hide was nailed to the log wall right of the door.

As Ty approached the shack, which had no shutters over the windows—they'd tumbled into the brush at the building's base and were rotting—he thrust the Henry straight out from his right hip and clicked the hammer back to full cock. Ten feet from the front door, which hung by only one hinge in its frame, he stopped suddenly.

He'd heard something.

He cocked his head, frowning, listening.

A woman's laugh caromed around on the breeze.

Again, she laughed, jeeringly. Teasing. Mocking. She was somewhere in the distance beyond the cabin.

Caressing the Henry's trigger with his gloved right index finger, Ty strode to the right end of the cabin and stopped, peering around the cabin back toward the stable and the corral flanking it. The stable, too, was age silvered; brush and sage grew up around its base and along the base of its connecting corral.

Again, the woman laughed. It had a hollow ring to it. It was coming from inside the stable.

Something moved ahead of Ty. He tightened his finger against the trigger then eased the tension in it. A black cat slipped through a gap in the stable door and the frame and dashed off into the brush to Ty's left before swinging around the front corner of the stable and running, tail raised, down the side of the stable toward the rear.

Ty's heart had picked up an anxious rhythm in his chest.

Zenobia Sparrow was in the barn. Taunting him. Mocking him.

He remembered the terrified look in the eyes of young Deputy U.S. Marshal Adam Parker.

Fury seared the back of Ty's breastbone. Gritting his teeth, hardening his jaws, slitting his eyes, and squeezing the Henry in his hands, he strode forward, heading for the barn and likely a meeting with his maker. But he couldn't stop himself.

His feet kept moving, faster and faster.

CHAPTER 35

The cackling laughter sounded again.

Ty grabbed the iron handle of the stable's left door, jerked it open so quickly, so hard, he ripped it off one rusty hinge and a corner dropped to the ground with a crunching thud. He threw himself forward, striking the hard-packed ground on his chest and belly, and rolled to his right twice to avoid the lead he was certain would be caroming toward him.

As he rolled onto his belly, the cackling laughter sounded again.

The woman yelled, "Hi-yahh, girl. *Go*!"

Ty peered through the stable's shadows just as the double doors at the far end burst open, rammed wide by a blond woman in a black hat and black duster and riding a cream horse. Again came the laughter . . . amid the thunder of the cream's pounding hooves, the squawk of tack, and the jangling of bridle chains as horse and rider galloped wildly out of the barn.

Ty thrust the Henry straight out before him, pressed his cheek against the rear stock, lined up the sights on the back of the woman's neck, and squeezed the trigger. At the same time, the woman swung the cream to the right, and Ty's .44 round found only empty air before plunking into a fir bole fifty feet beyond.

He cursed, scrambled to his feet, knees and elbows aching from the fall, and shambled forward. Breathing hard, he crossed the stable, dropped to a knee in the rear doorway, racked another round into the Henry's breech, and fired at the woman and the cream just then swinging onto the old stage road.

The Henry roared.

The woman's jouncing, fast-moving figure was a hard target. Ty's bullet flew wild and clipped the branch of a sage shrub on the trail's far side, beyond the woman and the horse. She turned her head toward Ty and threw her head back, laughing loudly, shrilly, her flaxen hair bouncing on her shoulders.

Ty cursed, pumped another round into the Henry's breech, and fired three more rounds but the woman and the horse were out of sight behind the pines and firs. Ty's bullets only clipped branches, plumed dirt and pine needles, and blew bark from tree trunks.

He heaved himself to his feet, again wincing at the ache in his knees and ran out away from the stable, angling toward the trail over which the woman's dust was still sifting in the late-day, salmon sunlight angling through the forest. He ran into the middle of the trail, racked another round into the Henry's action, and dropped to a knee. He snugged the Henry's butt plate against his shoulder then pulled it back down when the woman turned a bend in the trail, swinging out of view. The thuds of the cream's hooves dwindled quickly beneath the chittering of an angry squirrel.

"Pa!"

Ty glanced over his shoulder to see Matt galloping hell-for-leather down the ridge, trailing both his and his father's two horses. As he thundered across the bridge, Ty rose. Matt galloped up to him, stopping and curveting his black, the other two horses stopping behind him, the thick cloud of their dust catching up to them.

Red-faced with worry, his eyes were bright beneath the brim of his cream Stetson. "You all right, Pa?"

Ty turned to stare after Zenobia Sparrow. "I'm all right, boy," he grunted out in deep frustration.

"What happened?"

"Funnin' with us," Ty said, jaws hard. He spat angrily to one side. "Taunting us."

"We gonna go after her?"

Ty shook his head. "That's what she wants. Likely lead us into a bushwhack."

"What're we gonna do?"

Ty turned to his son still staring down at him, flushed with excitement. "We're gonna sit tight. Let them come to us. Somehow, he added in deep frustration. "We have to get Caroline away from those crazy sons of—"

"Pa?"

As if in response to the unfinished statement, a little girl's voice called from far away.

Ty looked around quickly, hope rising in him. "Caroline . . . ?"

"Pa?" came the little girl's voice again, muffled by distance.

"That's her!" Matt said, also looking around, eyes wide. "Where the hell is she?"

"Up there!" Ty stood facing the boulder-strewn forest carpeting the eastern ridge.

Sure enough, a very small figure stood atop a boulder at the very top of the ridge, staring down toward Matt and Ty. They could see Caroline's short hair blowing around her head in the wind. She appeared to wear a wool shirt and pants of some kind, both garments way too big for her..

"Caroline!" Ty yelled, stepping forward, heart racing hopefully but anxiously, as he wondered what in hell were they up to.

He sucked a slow breath through gritted teeth when a big nightmare specter of a man stepped up behind Caroline to tower over her, dwarfing her. Caroline's head came up to only the buckle of the man's cartridge belt. The big man—it had to be the Indian, Bear, as his features appeared dark—cupped his hands around his mouth and shouted in a booming monotone, "Come and get her, Brannigan! Your life for hers!"

The words echoed hollowly, ominously around the canyon.

Ty cupped his hands around his mouth. "I'm coming!"

Matt whipped a horrified look at his father. "Pa!"

Ty turned to him, placed a hand on his shoulder. "What choice do I have, boy? That's your sister up there."

"No." Matt shook his head slowly, resolutely. "You can't!" Tears glazed his eyes as he swung his head back toward his sister standing on the distant ridge, dwarfed by the granite-like spectre of the big Indian.

Ty walked over to his dun, grabbed the reins. "You stay here, Matt." He swung up into the saddle and gave his son a hard, commanding look. "You stay here," he repeated. "I'm gonna send Caroline back on my horse." He softened his voice. "Take her home, boy. Forget them. The fates will take care of them. They'll be judged one day."

Tears were streaming down Matt's cheeks. "Pa!"

"Do as I say, boy." Ty started to boot the dun ahead but stopped when the rataplan of galloping horses sounded behind him.

He turned to see three riders galloping down the hill, each pulling a tan dust cloud. Black-clad Jess Asper was in the lead. The big, bearded Ed Tabor galloped off Asper's left flank. The tall, thin Lyle Coffee brought up the rear on a paint horse. Each man was holding a carbine and their faces were hard, eager.

"Heard the shootin'!" Asper yelled, reining his pinto to a skidding halt and looking around. "Where are they?"

"They're on the run!" Ty said. "Our horses are blown!"

"Well, ours ain't!" The wild-eyed Asper glanced at his two partners and bellowed, "Come on, boys! Hi-yahh!"

"Hi-yahh!"

"Hi-yahh!"

They galloped on up the trail, hooves thudding loudly until they'd disappeared around the same bend the woman had galloped around not fifteen minutes before.

"Pa," Matt said, regarding his father in exasperation, slowly shaking his head. "What—?"

"I don't know why it didn't occur to me before," Ty said. "But those three might just be the distraction we need. Besides"—he gave his head a shake—"there was no holding 'em back. Asper has the vengeance fever." He looked up at the rock atop which Caroline and the Indian had been standing moments ago.

They were gone. Only sky was up there, a fading one, at that. It was early evening.

"Mount up, son," Ty said. "Leave your second horse!" He swung his dun around and booted it down the trail, in the opposite direction Asper, Tabor, and Coffee had just gone. Atop the rise from which he and Matt had scouted the abandoned relay station, he'd spied what had appeared on quick survey an old two-track trail meandering off through the trees and rocks, generally angling east. His plan was to flank the kidnapping killers while they were dealing with Asper's men, and get Caroline away from them without being seen.

Once Caroline was safe, he'd go back and kill them.

Unless Asper's men got lucky, that was. He didn't think they would. They might have been right handy bounty hunters and regulators hired by some of the larger outfits in the Bear Paws and Wind Rivers, but they were no match for the diabolical Smilin' Doc Ford and Zenobia Sparrow. Especially the way they were going about it.

When Ty and Matt had gained the top of the southern ridge, Ty said, "This way, son!" and swung the dun off the trail's left side, following the old two-track trail he assumed had been carved by some old prospector's wagon likely pulled by a mule wearing a straw hat with cutouts for the ears. The rising trail, rocky and littered with blowdown, curved through the darkening pines. Ty and Matt had to pick their way carefully.

They'd followed the trail for about fifteen minutes, when angry shouting rose in the distance ahead and to the north, followed by the crackle of gunfire.

"That's them!" Ty said. At the top of the ridge, a little behind him and to his right, he could see the rock Caroline and the Indian had been standing on. He and Matt were dropping down the backside of that ridge, angling across the belly of the slope from south to north, angling around rocks and stunt pines and aspens. The shooting and continued shouting was coming from just ahead.

"Let's dismount!" Ty reined his dun to a halt and stepped down from the leather.

Matt did likewise, racking a round into his Winchester's breech and then following his father as Ty set out.

Jogging at a crouch and cradling his Henry in his arms, Ty moved toward the sound of the gunfire and intermittent, angry shouts. Ahead, the terrain dropped away to what appeared another canyon.

Crouching lower as he approached the lip of that canyon, he finally dropped to his knees behind a flat-topped rock. Matt knelt to Ty's right. Both removed their hats and cast a cautious look around the rock's sides.

Below, they could see where the trail wound up through the thick fir forest to enter the canyon. Asper's men were holed up in rocks a good hundred or so feet above and to each side of that trail. Ty could pick them out by the crowns of their hats and the smoke puffing from their rifles. Two of the three were holed up at various levels in the rocks left of the trail while the other one was holed up in the rocks to the right of the trail.

The four evil killers were hunkered down behind rocks spread out below, firing toward Asper's men. Ty could see none of the four but could pick out their locations by the puffs of their powder smoke.

No, he could pick out three of the four. He couldn't pick out the fourth.

Hard to say where Caroline was. They probably had her tucked away in the rocks of which there were plenty—of all shapes and sizes. Some wagon-sized, one or two nearly cabin-sized.

He waited then picked out the fourth shooter by his or her gunfire, shooting from farther below him and Matt and to their right.

Ty turned to his son. "Matt, you stay here. I'm gonna try to locate the fourth shooter and take him out."

"Want me to get a little closer to those other ones, and—"

"No. If they spot you, they'll kill Caroline. The fourth one's close. I'm hoping it's the Indian, and I'm hoping he still has your sister."

"Be careful, Pa."

"Keep your head down, Matt."

Ty donned his hat, crabbed several feet back from the lip of the ridge, rose, and strode off through the rocks, dropping across the sloping belly of the ridge again. He was low enough he couldn't be seen by the other three killers. With each step he took, the shooting of the fourth shooter grew louder before him.

Before him and below him.

He came to the curving ridge crest, removed his hat, dropped to hands and knees, and crawled forward. Crabbing between two large rocks, peered down the rocky slope.

His heart throbbed and blood drummed in his ears.

Only a few feet below and to his right, the Indian, clad in

buckskins and a straw sombrero, was shooting from a nest of rocks with a big pine growing up from the back of it. He knelt behind a rock at the front of the nest, shooting and pulling his head down when bullets fired from Asper's men slammed into the rocks around him.

Caroline sat back against the base of the pine, knees drawn up to her chest, hands over her ears. She wore denim jeans with the cuffs rolled up several times, and a wool shirt, the sleeves also rolled several times. She wore moccasins on her feet. Only about six feet behind the Indian, the bullets of Asper's men pocked the rocks around her.

Ty had to get to her fast, pull her up out of there before she caught a bullet.

He cocked and aimed the Henry straight out before him, pressed his cheek to the stock then pulled his head away from the gun, scowling. He didn't have a clear shot at the Indian. The charred skeleton of a lightning-topped cedar lay in his way, obstructing his view. He shifted his position, trying to get a clearer vantage. As he did, in the corner of his eye, he saw the Indian turn his head suddenly to his left, glancing back over his shoulder. If he lifted his eyes just a few inches, he'd be able to pick Ty out of the rocks above him!

Ty scrambled backward quickly, heart thudding.

The big Indian must have his own sixth sense for approaching trouble.

Ty crabbed to his right behind the low, broken wall of covering rocks. There wasn't a break for several feet. When he reached that break and peered through it, a cold snake flicked its tail in his belly.

The Indian was no longer in the nest of rocks below him!

Slowly, wincing dreadfully, Ty turned his head.

The big mountain of a man stood over him, grinning like the cat that ate the canary.

CHAPTER 36

Ty wheeled, bringing the Henry around quickly.

But not quickly enough.

The Indian stepped forward and kicked the rifle out of his hands. It flew back over Ty's head and into the rocks below with a sickening clatter. Before Ty could even start to haul himself to his feet, the Indian drew his right foot back and thrust it forward with an angry grunt, burying the toe of his boot in Ty's ribs.

The wind rushed out of Ty in a loud, raking groan.

Cocking the Winchester in his hands, the Indian raised the weapon to his shoulder, aiming it down at Ty's head. Thinking fast, Ty grabbed a rock and threw it as hard as he could from his compromised position. To his surprise, the rock struck the Indian with a dull *thunk* right where he'd aimed it—in the bridge of the man's broad nose!

The man dropped the rifle and staggered backward, blinking his eyes and shaking his head as if to clear it. Ty reached for his Colt, but the Indian recovered from the braining too fast, lunged forward with an enraged wail and, before Ty could get the Colt's hammer clicked back, kicked the Colt out of Ty's hand. The revolver went the way of Ty's rifle only seconds ago, clattering onto the rocks behind and below him.

The Indian reached for his own Colt jutting from the holster on his right hip. Ty rolled onto his side and scissored his left leg wildly, cutting the big Indian's feet out from under him. The man dropped the Colt and hit the ground with another enraged wail, dust wafting around him.

Ty heaved himself to his feet and for a split second considered grabbing the Indian's rifle but already the man nearly had it in his hands. Ty gave his own bellowing wail of fury and hurled himself onto the Indian, knocking him back against the ground, wrapping his hands around the man's stout neck, and pressing his thumbs against his throat. The man started to gag, his dark eyes bulging in their sockets.

Ty thought he had him whipped.

But stretching his lips back from his big, horselike teeth, the man raged and thrust both his arms straight up from the ground, breaking Ty's grip on his neck. Then he clenched his fists and smashed his left against Ty's right cheek and then the right fist against Ty's left cheek. Each was a savage, ear-ringing, eye-blurring blow.

Enraged even more, the Indian thrust his left fist up again. Ty turned his head away just enough that the blow merely glanced across the edge of his right jaw. If the fist had connected, it would have cost him some teeth.

Desperate and furious, Ty head-butted his opponent, making the man's eyes roll back in their sockets and for a moment the Indian's head fell back against the ground, stunning him. Ty took the opportunity to slam his own fists against the man's face—two resolute blows to the jaw and two more straight jabs to the mouth, laying open his lips.

Taking advantage of the Indian's momentary stupor, Ty lunged for the man's rifle. He got both hands on it and started to bring it up, sliding his left hand toward the cocking lever, but again, the Indian recovered too quickly. He gave another furious cry, spitting blood from his lips that looked like chopped beef. He rose onto his butt and, placing both hands flat against the ground, drew both his legs back to his chest then thrust them forward, ramming the soles of his boots against Ty's right shoulder and arm.

Ty dropped the rifle and flew sideways, landing a good ten feet from where he'd been kicked, feeling as though his shoulder had been hammered from its socket. He rolled in the gravel, wincing as rocks ground against him, tearing his flesh through his clothes. He rolled onto his back and looked up, his vision slightly blurred, and was not happy to see the Indian on his feet and striding toward him, jaws hard. That jeering grin was on the man's face again though it didn't make it to his cold, dark, bruin-like eyes.

"*Hah!*" The Indian threw both big arms up and savagely kicked Ty in the ribs with his left foot.

Ty groaned and rolled, clutching his ribs with his arms.

"*Hah!*" the Indian said once again, throwing his big arms up and savagely kicking Ty in the ribs with his right foot.

Ty groaned, grimacing against the agonizing blows, feeling he had some broken ribs to go along with that displaced shoulder.

"*Hah!*" the Indian repeated, kicking Ty in the ribs again and again and again. "*Hah! Hah! Hah!*"

Ty tried to crawl away, but he'd rolled into a nest of rocks and had nowhere to go.

Finally, mercifully, the man stopped delivering the vicious blows. Ty lay writhing and cursing, holding both arms against his battered sides. In the periphery of his vision, he saw the Indian walk over and pick up his Winchester. He dusted it off and turned to Ty. He'd lost his hat and his long, stringy, dark-brown hair hung in his eyes. His eyes blazed in a mask of animal-like fury, mouth bloody. He was breathing hard through gritted teeth as he loudly racked a fresh round into the rifle's action.

Ty rested his head against a rock, staring helplessly at the man who was about to kill him.

The Indian took two long strides forward then raised the rifle to his shoulder. "Good-bye, old man! You're gonna die hard but your daughter's gonna die harder!"

"You are!" came a girl's raking scream.

The Indian pulled his cheek away from his Winchester's rear stock and looked into the rocks beyond Ty, frowning incredulously. His eyes widened suddenly, shock glazing them. A rifle roared somewhere over Ty's left shoulder. Dust wafted from the Indian's buckskin tunic and he stumbled backward, fear showing in his eyes as he lowered the Winchester and stared down at the blood staining his tunic around a .44-caliber-sized hole in his chest. Befuddled, he looked up and stared into the rocks beyond Ty.

A girl's shrill scream accompanied the rasp of a rifle's cocking lever.

The Indian thrust out one hand up, palm out and shook his head. "No . . . *no*!"

Again, the girl screamed, and the rifle thundered once more.

That bullet took the Indian in the chest a little above the first one. He staggered backward then dropped without even trying to break his fall. As dust wafted around him, he groaned, sighed, and died.

Dazed from the braining and ribbing he'd just taken, Ty looked around. In the fading light behind him he saw movement in the rocks until a small, thin shape took form.

Caroline stepped out of the rocks, holding Ty's Henry repeater in her small, pale hands. The rifle was nearly as long as she was. Her short, light-brown hair jostled in the breeze. She looked down at Ty, her own eyes glazed with shock but also with—what?

Toughness.

The old, unflagging Brannigan spirit.

"Hello, Pa." She dropped to her knees beside him, resting the Henry across her thighs. "Did he hurt you so badly?"

"Oh, child!" No longer feeling any of the numerous and profound aches and pains penetrating every inch of him, Ty reached up, wrapped his arms around his youngest child's slender shoulders, and drew her to his chest, squeezing her hard.

She sobbed against him, placing her little hands against his face, pressing them into the unshaven flesh.

Suddenly realizing the gunfire had died, he eased Caroline away from him. "I need to get you out of here, child," he said quietly. Wincing and groaning, he tried to heave himself to his feet and gave up. His sore ribs felt like razor-edged pitchfork tines tearing into his flesh.

"Oh, Pa!" Caroline said, seeing him struggling. "What a worry you are!"

Ty had a good chuckle at that and placed a kiss on the girl's right cheek. "What a worry I am. Right." He took the Henry from her. "This'll help." He planted the butt on the ground and used the rifle as a crutch to help hoist himself to his feet.

Caroline wrapped an arm around his waist, grunting under the strain of helping lift her battered father to his feet.

"Thanks, baby girl," Ty said, keeping his voice down and turning to gaze back in the direction the other three killers had been shooting from. He didn't like how quiet it was beyond the brow of the ridge. He had to assume the other three killers knew they'd been flanked. They'd likely heard the commotion and were coming to investigate.

"Pa!" Matt's voice rose behind them, making Ty jerk with a start.

Ty whipped around. Matt stood between two cabin-sized boulders twenty feet away. "Matt!"

Matt placed two fingers to his lips then canted his head over his left shoulder, indicating the upslope. "They're heading this way—slow but sure," he whispered just loudly enough for Ty to hear. "They must've finished off the bounty hunters."

"All right." Ty grabbed Caroline's hand and, holding the Henry in his free hand, began moving forward, wincing with each step. A good many of his battered ribs were bruised but something told him one or two were cracked, as well. He'd had cracked ribs before, and they were no picnic.

He stepped up to Matt, again keeping his voice down. "Let's go back the way we came. I want to get Caroline good and out of here." He didn't add his intention was for Matt to start back to the Powderhorn with her.

Ty's plan for himself was to finish off the three scurvy devils who'd taken his daughter.

Matt looked at him gravely. "I'll hang back, Pa." He glanced down at his sister and reached out to squeeze her shoulder. "I'll take down those savages!"

"I got one of them," Caroline whispered proudly, narrowing her eyes angrily then glancing at Ty. "Didn't I, Pa?"

"I saw from up yonder!" Matt said, staring in wonder at his little sister.

"As for hanging back," Ty said to Matt, "forget it. We're *both* gonna get Caroline out of here."

"All right, all right," Matt whispered, taking Caroline's other hand. "Let's go, Annie Oakley."

She glanced up at her big brother and offered a proud smile.

With Caroline between them, they began walking through the strewn rubble some volcano had probably thrown up from the Earth's guts many eons ago. They climbed toward where they'd left their horses.

As they wove around the rocks, boulders, and the skeletons of fallen trees, Matt and Ty cast cautious glances around them. Ty wanted those three devils dead in the worst way but first they had to get Caroline out of harm's way, and he had to get his ribs wrapped.

Sticking to the shadows of the boulder-strewn slope, they moved slowly, keeping Caroline between them. With darkness coming on fast, it was going to be hard for Matt and Ty to get back to the main trail, but it would also be hard for the three remaining killers to track them.

The thought had no sooner passed over Ty's brain than a woman's laughter rose behind them. A coyote yammered. An owl hooted. The woman's laughter came again, louder, edged with lunacy.

"Faster!" Ty said, squeezing Caroline's hand harder and moving more quickly up the slope, passing between two more cabin-sized boulders.

A bullet whined loudly off the face of the boulder on Ty's left. The angry *spang* was followed by the belch of the rifle that had fired it. Running footsteps sounded behind them.

"Up and over this ridge!" Ty yelled. "You and Caroline keep goin', Matt!"

"What're you gonna do, Pa?"

"Finish it!"

They started up the ridge, half dragging the exhausted Caroline.

The footsteps behind them were louder; Ty could hear the rasping of strained breaths. The wolves were literally slathering over the blood scent.

More gunfire, bullets barking off rocks to either side of Ty, Matt, and Caroline.

When they gained the top of the ridge, Ty pushed Caroline into Matt's arms and said, "Keep goin', Matt!"

"We'll help you finish those jackals, mi amore!" yelled a startlingly familiar voice to Ty's right.

"Ma?" Matt cried, whipping around, eyes wide with incredulity.

Another familiar voice to Ty's left said, "We're here to help, Pa!"

MacKenna? Ty could make out three familiar silhouettes in the rocks of the ridge crest around him. He didn't have time to wrap his mind around what the rest of his family, including Gregory, were doing in the high-and-rocky area. The wolves were getting close.

Ty spun around, saw figures running up from the base of the ridge—the woman's flaxen hair glistening in the late light to the left, the handsome devil, Smilin' Doc Ford, in the middle of the three, and the big, shaggy-headed man known as Hungry Jack.

All were wielding rifles. As they stopped halfway up the slope and raised the long guns to their shoulders, the entire Brannigan family except Caroline—she'd already done her part—rose from the rocks, rifles raised, and began throwing lead at them. Five rifles spoke loudly, shrilly, lapping flames down toward three jackals who did not get a single shot off before the Brannigan bullets tore into them, shredding them, evoking startled cries and curses and agonized wails as each of the three curly wolves tossed away his or her rifle and went flying straight back down the slope.

They struck the decline and rolled, loosing rocks and gravel in their wakes.

Zenobia Sparrow's flaxen hair still glistened in the last light as it danced wildly around her hatless head, her black leather duster flapping like the wings of an enormous bat.

The rifles kept crackling until Ty yelled, "All right—that's enough, Brannigans. I think they're all accounted for!"

He cast his incredulous gaze around to Gregory, standing with his old-model Spencer repeater cradled in his thick arms, smoke still curling from the barrel. He looked at MacKenna standing beside her father, smiling up at him, her own Winchester still smoking. Finally, he turned to Beatriz, who'd dropped her own rifle, grabbed Caroline, and hugged her close, running her hand down the back of the girl's head.

"Are you all right, mi hija?" Clad in a long fur coat against the high-country chill, Beatriz rocked her youngest from side to side.

"Mama?" Caroline pulled away from her mother and gazed up at her. "After they first took me out of my room, I never thought I'd say this, but I *am* all right." She paused then crossed her slender arms on her chest. "Just fine, in fact!" she added proudly.

"Way better than the big bruin she took out!" Matt beamed down at his little sister then glanced at Ty. "I saw her shoot that big Indian when I was climbin' down from my perch in the rocks. Couldn't believe it was Caroline till I got closer and saw it was her with my own two eyes!"

"You shot the Indian?" MacKenna asked her sister, lower jaw hanging.

"Sure did or he woulda shot Pa!"

"I didn't know you could even shoot!" Matt said.

Caroline turned to her big brother. "I learned by watching"—she canted her head toward the downslope where the three devils had become carrion—"them. Believe me, they did a lot of shooting!"

MacKenna smiled up at her father. "That's both Brannigan daughters who've pulled your fat out of the fire, Pa!" She reached up and pulled his hat down over his eyes.

Chuckling, Ty poked his hat back up onto his forehead, stepped forward, and wrapped an arm around MacKenna's shoulders, wincing a little at the strain in his ribs, which he'd have Beatriz wrap later. "Don't rub it in!" He looked at his wife standing beside Gregory, who was standing behind Caroline, one hand on his little sister's shoulder. Those two fought like cats and dogs sometimes, but Gregory, too, was very glad to have his little squirrel back.

Or his little badger. Ty amended his thought with an admiring smile at his youngest. He turned back to Beatriz and shook his head in befuddlement. "How in the world did you ever track us?"

"Especially after that storm?" Matt added.

"With the help of your two trail-tough *niños* here"— Beatriz glanced at MacKenna then pecked Gregory's cheek and draped an arm around his neck—"I was able to track you far enough I knew where you were headed. The saddle under Bailey Peak is the only way out of the mountains in this direction, and I figured those devils were heading for open country. I know about Bailey Peak. *Mi padre* took me elk hunting several autumns in a row to this part of the Bear Paws."

"Well, I'll be!" Matt said.

Ty turned a mock cross look on MacKenna, whom he still had his arm around. "As for you, young lady, what did I tell you about—"

"Ma said I could!" MacKenna laughed.

Ty kissed her cheek then held out his free arm, repressing the pain in his ribs which no longer seemed to ache all that much—not with his entire family there and safe. "Come on, family! Get in here!"

"All right," Gregory said, grouchy as always. "But then can we break out the liniment, Ma?" He rubbed his backside. "I've never been on a horse for as long as I've been on one the past few days. Chasin' you an' MacKenna around these mountains, I think I done rubbed all the skin off my behind!"

They all laughed.

When they'd finally turned each other loose and headed off to retrieve their horses with the intention of setting up a quick camp, as it was too dark to ride down off the ridge until morning, Ty strode up beside Matt. "So, what do you think, son? Did you get your fill of this kind of life? Or do you still have some bullets left to cap?"

"You mean trackin' an' shootin' an' just generally stompin' with my tail up, like you did at my age?"

"Yeah, somethin' like that."

"I can honestly say I sure have, Pa. I'm done. In fact, I can't wait to get back to the Powderhorn!"

"That's good to hear, son. Very good to hear."

"You know what else?" Matt said as he and Ty approached their horses.

"What?"

"Remember Arlis Jessup?"

"The mercantile man's daughter who pesters you every time we go to town? How could I forget?"

"I think I'm gonna ask her to that dance they have out at Vott's barn every Saturday night."

"You don't say!"

"Yeah," Matt said, a thoughtful expression shaping itself on his face. "She's kind of a rather special girl, I've come around to believin'."

Ty hooked his arm around Matt's neck, drew him close, and pulled his hat down over his eyes. "You'll do, my boy. You'll do!"

Keep reading for a special bonus!

**William W. Johnstone
and J. A. Johnstone**

RIDING THE NIGHTMARE
A DUFF MacCALLISTER WESTERN

**Duff MacCallister left Scotland to forge a new life
in America, raising cattle on the western plains
of the growing nation.
But keeping his dream alive means facing off
against the country's most violent, bloodthirsty men . . .**

The Spencer family is part of a wagon train passing
through Chugwater, Wyoming, bound for the valley
of Longshot Basin. Unfortunately, the trail that leads there
has been buried under an avalanche.
The only route the homesteaders can take is the infamous
Nightmare Trail—a treacherous, terrifying steep
and narrow path along a mountainside
that has claimed many lives of those who dared travel it.

If that wasn't dangerous enough, the trail
is also a killing ground for the outlaw Hardcastle gang.
The disreputable Arkansas Ozark clan doesn't take kindly
to anyone trespassing on their road
without paying—in blood.

Duff MacCallister is not about to let the Spencers ride
the Nightmare Trail without his guidance.
He knows the terrain. He knows how to defend himself.
And he knows that when it comes to badmen like the
Hardcastles, the best defense is killing first—and fast.

Look for RIDING THE NIGHTMARE, *on sale now!*

CHAPTER 1

"There's hell in Thunder Canyon!"

The excited shout made everyone in Fiddler's Green turn their head toward the entrance, where a man had just slapped the batwings aside and rushed into the saloon.

"What the devil is that rannihan going on about?" asked Biff Johnson, the former cavalryman who owned Fiddler's Green. Biff had named the place after an old cavalry legend that said every man who had answered the call of "Boots and Saddles" would journey after death to an idyllic meadow with a tree-lined creek on one side, where he would be able to sit in the shade and visit with all his former comrades. Biff had made his Fiddler's Green into something of an idyllic spot, itself, seeing as it was the finest saloon in the town of Chugwater, Wyoming.

"Why dinnae ye ask him what he's on about?" suggested Duff MacCallister, who was sitting at a table with Biff, Elmer Gleason, and Wang Chow. The latter two worked for Duff on his vast ranch, Sky Meadow, at least technically speaking. In reality, Elmer and Wang were more like members of the family.

Biff nodded. "I'll do that." He pushed to his feet and started toward the agitated newcomer. Several men had gathered around to ask him questions.

Biff's powerful voice cut through the hubbub. "Pinky Jenkins, what do you mean by bursting in here and yelling like that? Can't folks enjoy a peaceful drink in the middle of the day without having their ears assaulted by your cater-wauling?"

Jenkins stared wide-eyed at him. "But Biff, there's hell in Thunder Canyon!"

"Yes, you said that. But what are you talking about?"

"Avalanche!"

That raised even more of a ruckus in the saloon. Duff stood up, went over to join Biff, and asked, "Was anyone hurt in this rockslide, d' ye ken?"

Jenkins turned his bug-eyed expression toward Duff. "It was more 'n a rockslide, Mr. MacCallister. The whole derned mountainside came down on the canyon! Closed it up, clear from one side to the other!"

"How do you know that?" asked Biff.

"I seen it with my own eyes!"

Biff grunted. "Then you can give us more details, or at least you should be able to."

"I reckon I can," Jenkins said. His tongue came out and swiped across his lips. "But the ride into town sure made me dry, Biff. I could prob'ly talk a whole heap better if my speakin' apparatus was lubricated some."

Biff glared, but it was all Duff could do not to laugh. Pinky was a decent wrangler and ranch hand, when he rattled his hocks long enough to actually work any. He had an inordinate fondness for Who-Hit-John, too, which meant that he had worked for most of the spreads around Chugwater at one time or another, sticking for a spell before he got drunk and did something to get himself fired. He was a colorful but amiable local character. Duff wasn't surprised Pinky would try to cadge a drink or two before he spilled whatever news he happened to have.

"Come on over to the bar," Duff told him. "'Tis happy I'll be to buy you a drink."

"I'm much obliged to you, Mr. MacCallister."

Duff put a hand on Jenkins' shoulder and steered him over to the hardwood. He nodded for the bartender to pour a drink. As the men pressed around him, Jenkins picked up the glass, threw back the whiskey, and licked his lips again.

"That helped a mite," he said, "but—"

"Tell the story first," Duff interrupted in a firm voice. "Perhaps then 'twill be time for another drink."

Jenkins nodded. "Yeah, sure, I reckon that makes sense. I was ridin' close to Thunder Canyon, thinkin' I might mosey up to Longshot Basin and take a look around. But thank goodness I wasn't in any hurry, because if I'd been in the canyon when that avalanche came down, I'd be dead now, sure as hell! I'd be on the bottom of thousands and thousands o' tons of rock."

Longshot Basin was an isolated valley some twenty miles northwest of Chugwater, Duff recalled. Although it was a large stretch of range with decent but not outstanding graze, no ranches were located there. The land was still open to be claimed because the basin was surrounded by sheer cliffs and there was only one way in or out: the trail through Thunder Canyon, a narrow slash in the rugged landscape.

Now, according to Pinky Jenkins, that trail was closed, meaning Longshot Basin was cut off completely from the rest of the world.

Elmer and Wang had joined the crowd gathered around Jenkins.

Elmer asked, "What started the avalanche? Rocks don't usually go to slidin' for no reason."

"That is not necessarily correct," said Wang. "A stone can be in perilous equilibrium and on the verge of falling for a lengthy period of time before it finally does so under the impetus of some force too miniscule for human senses to perceive."

Elmer squinted at him. "If you're sayin' what I think you're sayin', there still has to be somethin' that starts the ball rollin' . . . or the rock, in this case . . . even if it's too puny for us to feel it."

"Oh, I felt it, all right," Jenkins declared. "It was an earthquake, boys! Are you tellin' me you didn't feel it here in town?"

"I didn't feel any earthquake," Biff insisted. "In fact, I'm starting to wonder if maybe you were drunk and imagined the whole thing, Pinky."

"No, sir!" Jenkins looked and sounded offended at the very idea. "I was sober as a judge. More sober than some judges I've seen. Until the one Mr. MacCallister just bought me, I hadn't had a drink in three days." He looked a little shame-faced as he added, "Couldn't afford one. I'm stone-cold broke. That's the reason I was headin' up to Longshot Basin. I thought I might comb through those breaks and maybe turn up a few strays I could drive back to their home ranches. Figured I might get me a little, what do you call it, finder's fee that way."

What Jenkins said made sense. Even though no ranches— not even any little greasy-sack outfits—were located in the basin, from time to time a few cows wandered up through Thunder Canyon and got lost in the rugged breaks that filled the basin. Rumor had it a sizable number of wild critters lived there, descendants of stock that had gone in but never came back out.

"I still don't think there was any earthquake," said Biff, shaking his head. "They have them up in the northwest part of the state, around what they've started calling Yellowstone Park, but there aren't any around here."

"Dinnae be so fast to think that, Biff," spoke up Duff. "Now that Pinky mentions it, earlier this morning when we were loading supplies onto the wagon, I thought I felt the earth shiver just a wee bit under me boots." Duff's broad shoulders rose and fell in a shrug. "I said nothing about it because I was nae sure I felt it or not."

"You did," declared Wang. "I felt the same faint motion of the earth."

Elmer frowned at them. "Well, I sure didn't. How come you never mentioned it, Wang?"

"It seemed of little importance at the time. Simply an inconsequential geological . . . hiccup."

"Not so inconsequential, to hear Pinky tell it," Duff said. "An avalanche big enough to close off Thunder Canyon is pretty major."

One of the townsmen said, "Aw, nobody lives up there. What does it matter whether anybody can get in or out of Longshot Basin? Nobody gives a damn about that place."

Duff shrugged again. "Perhaps not. Go on with your story, Pinky."

Jenkins licked his lips again, but when Duff didn't offer him another drink and neither did anyone else, he continued. "The ground shook and scared the bejabbers outta me, and then I heard this big ol' roar. Thunder Canyon sure lived up to its name! It was like the biggest, loudest peal of thunder anybody ever heard. When I glanced up at Buzzard's Roost, it looked like half the mountain was comin' down. I never seen anything quite as . . . as awe-inspirin' as all that rock tumblin' down into the canyon and throwin' up a cloud of dust higher than I could even see! I tell you what, the ground shook some more when all that rock landed in the canyon. It sure as blazes did! And then . . ."

Jenkins' voice trailed off as he licked his lips again.

Elmer exclaimed, "Oh, hell, give him another shot o' whiskey!" He dug a coin out of his pocket and tossed it on the bar. "I'll pay for it this time." He waited until Jenkins had downed the whiskey, then growled, "Now get on with the story."

"Sure, Elmer. Don't rush me. As I was sayin', that avalanche made a terrible racket and kicked up the biggest cloud of dust you'd ever hope to lay eyes on, and the whole thing spooked my horse so bad, it was all I could do to keep it from runnin' away with me. But I was far enough off that I knew I was safe, and I wanted to see what things looked like when the dust cleared.

"Well, sir, what I saw was a wall of rock a good twenty feet high, stretchin' all the way from one side of the canyon to the other! Ain't no tellin' how far up the canyon it runs, neither. But it plugged that canyon up just like a cork in the neck of a bottle, ain't no doubt about that!"

Duff, in his explorations of the countryside after he had come to Wyoming and started his ranch, had ridden through Thunder Canyon and into Longshot Basin a couple of times. He recalled that the canyon was approximately forty yards wide. It would take an enormous amount of rock to close off the passage, but from the way Pinky Jenkins described the avalanche, he supposed it was possible.

"Anyway," Jenkins went on, "once I'd seen what had happened, I lit a shuck for town. Figured folks here would want to know about it."

"And you figured the story was worth a few drinks," said Biff. He shook his head and chuckled. "I suppose you were right about that."

"I'd just as soon never see anything like that again," Jenkins intoned solemnly. "For a minute there, it was like the world was comin' to an end." He closed his eyes and shuddered. When he opened them again, he continued. "And witnessin' somethin' like that . . . it sure does leave a man with a powerful thirst!"

Pinky Jenkins continued repeating the story as long as the men standing at the bar with him kept buying drinks.

Duff, Elmer, and Wang went back to the table where they had been sitting with Biff when Jenkins came bursting in to Fiddler's Green. Biff remained at the bar, keeping an eye on Jenkins.

Duff and his two companions had come to Chugwater earlier in the day to stock up on supplies. Their loaded wagon was parked down the street in front of the general store, ready to be driven back to the ranch. Because most folks around there knew the vehicle belonged to Duff, it was unlikely anybody would bother the wagon or the goods in the back of it.

And Duff MacCallister, for all of his mild, pleasant demeanor, was not a man anyone who knew him set out to get crossways with.

Tragic circumstances in his Scottish homeland had prompted him to immigrate to America. After spending some time in New York, he had headed west, eventually winding up in Chugwater and buying a ranch not far from the town. He had named the spread Sky Meadow, after Skye McGregor, the beautiful young woman he had loved and planned to marry, before she met her death at the brutal hands of Duff's enemies. Duff had avenged that murder, but vengeance didn't return Skye to him, so he had put that part of his life behind him and established a new life on the American frontier.

A tall, brawny, powerful man with a shock of tawny hair, Duff was a formidable opponent in any hand-to-hand battle, whether with fists or knives. He was a crack shot with pistol or rifle. But the quality that really made him deadly was an icy-nerved calmness in the face of danger. He never panicked, never lost his head and acted rashly. And if forced into a fight, he never quit until his opponent was vanquished, one way or another.

Because of all that, Duff had a reputation as a man not to tangle with. But he was also known as the staunchest, most loyal friend anyone could ever have. In times of trouble, he never turned his back on someone who needed his help.

As it turned out, after leaving Scotland under those heart-breaking circumstances, he had made quite a success of his new life in America. The newly acquired ranch had a gold mine on it, a mine no one had known about except Elmer Gleason, the colorful old-timer who had been hiding in the mine and working it in secret when Duff bought the place. Duff had befriended Elmer, and even though legally the mine belonged to him since it was on his range, he had made Elmer an equal partner in it. Elmer also worked for him as the foreman of his crew of ranch hands.

That crew had grown as Duff expanded the operation into raising Black Angus cattle, the first stockman in the area to do so. The effort had been successful and quite lucrative. Duff shipped Black Angus not only back east to market but also to other ranchers who wanted to try raising them.

The other man sitting with Duff in Fiddler's Green was Wang Chow, a former Shaolin priest in China who had been forced to flee his homeland, much like Duff. In Wang's case, the Chinese emperor had put a bounty on his head after he killed the men responsible for murdering his family. Duff had "rescued" him from a potential lynching, although it was likely that Wang, with his almost supernatural martial arts skills, could have fought his way free from the would-be lynchers. Just as in Elmer's case, that encounter had led to a fast friendship with Duff. They were a nigh-inseparable trio.

When they had finished their beers, they left Fiddler's Green, with Duff giving Biff a casual wave as they headed out. Biff just nodded, looked at the crowd still surrounding Pinky Jenkins, and sighed.

"Biff's a mite aggravated," commented Elmer, who had noticed the same thing.

"Aye, but as long as those fellows are buying drinks, I think he has little to complain about," Duff said. "Still on the same subject, I thought I might take a ride up to Thunder Canyon so I can have a look at this natural disaster with me own eyes." He had ridden his horse Sky into Chugwater today, so there was no reason he had to return to the ranch with Elmer and Wang.

"You reckon it's as bad as ol' Pinky made out it is?" asked Elmer.

"I dinnae ken. That's why I wish to have a look for meself."

"Thunder Canyon and Longshot Basin are a considerable distance from Sky Meadow," Wang pointed out. "Even if Mr. Jenkins' claims are correct, they have no bearing on our lives."

"Nae, 'tis true they do not," agreed Duff. "Just mark it up to curiosity."

"Sure, I don't blame you for that," Elmer said. "We'll see you later, Duff."

As Elmer and Wang climbed onto the wagon seat, Duff untied the team from the hitch rack in front of the store. Skillfully, Elmer took up the reins, turned the team and the wagon, and headed for home.

Duff was about to untie his horse so he could swing up into the saddle, when a voice said from behind him, "Not so fast there, Duff MacCallister."

CHAPTER 2

Duff turned his head and looked over his shoulder. A very pretty young woman with blond hair tumbling around her head and shoulders stood on the boardwalk and regarded him with a stern expression on her face.

Duff saw the good humor lurking in her blue eyes, though, so he wasn't surprised when a smile suddenly appeared on her lips.

"Did you really think you could come into Chugwater and then leave again without even saying hello to me?" she asked. The smile took any sting out of the question, which could have been taken as a reprimand.

"Sure, and I planned on stopping at the dress shop on me way out of town," Duff told her.

"Well, we'll never know, will we," said Meagan Parker, "since I spotted your wagon earlier and knew you were in town."

"Been keeping an eye out for me, have ye?"

She laughed. "Don't get a swelled head. Yes, I looked out the shop's front window every now and then to see if the wagon was still here, but I had other things to do, too, you know. My world wouldn't have come to an end if I'd missed a chance to see the great Duff MacCallister."

"But ye are glad to see me?"

"Of course, I am," she said, her voice softening. "You know that."

"Aye, 'n 'tis pleased I am to lay eyes on ye, too. Were we not in the middle of town, in broad daylight, I might lay a kiss on ye, as well."

Meagan sighed dramatically. "I suppose we should maintain some sort of decorum."

"I suppose," Duff said, "but 'tis not easy."

The romance between Duff and Meagan had begun pretty much at first sight, even though that moment had been in the middle of a gunfight and Meagan had been warning him of some lurking killers about to open fire on him. Since then, they had gotten to know each other very well, developing a relationship built on passion, trust, and genuine affection.

Meagan operated a successful dress shop in Chugwater, sewing dresses of such beauty and elegance that ladies from all over the territory hired her to add to their wardrobes.

She was also a partner in Duff's ranch, Sky Meadow, having loaned him some money when he was in financial straits. He could have paid back the amount many times over since then, but Meagan preferred to leave things the way they were, with her having a percentage interest in the herd of Black Angus.

Duff suspected that was because the arrangement gave her an excuse to visit the ranch from time to time, and also to accompany him when he delivered stock elsewhere. She was a partner, after all, so why not go along on those trips?

Most folks who knew them figured they would get married someday, but for now, they were both happy with the way things were and saw no reason to change the easy-going relationship.

An idea occurred to Duff. "Did ye finish those other things ye were working on at your shop?"

"As a matter of fact, I did."

"Then ye have no pressing business at the moment?"

Meagan shook her head. "No, I suppose not. I mean, there are always things that need to be done . . ."

"I'm taking a ride up to Thunder Canyon. Why dinnae ye come with me?"

"Thunder Canyon?" Meagan repeated. "Why are you going all the way up there?"

"Dinnae ye hear the commotion earlier when Pinky Jenkins came riding into town?"

"No, I didn't. Pinky Jenkins is a pretty disreputable character, isn't he?"

"He's known to be, at times," admitted Duff. "But he brought a very interesting tale with him today." He filled her in on the story Jenkins had told about the avalanche closing off Thunder Canyon.

"My goodness, it sounds like quite a catastrophe," Meagan said. "Do you think he was telling the truth?"

"He seemed mighty sincere, and he insisted he was nae drunk when it happened." Duff shrugged. "So I thought I would go and take a look for meself, and now I'm for inviting you to come along."

"Could we ride up there and be back before nightfall?"

"Oh, I think 'tis likely."

"Would I have time to pack a little food? I've been busy today and didn't stop for lunch, but I have a loaf of bread and some roast beef I could bring along, as well as a bottle of wine."

"'A jug of wine, a loaf of bread, and thou'," Duff quoted. "To my way of thinking, Omar Khayyam had it right, but I'll not pass up a chance to put that old saying to the test!"

Meagan wanted to change into more suitable clothes for riding, so while she was doing that, Duff rode to the livery stable and had the hostler bring out the horse she kept there. Duff saddled the mount himself to make sure everything was the way it should be. Where Meagan's safety was concerned, he took no chances.

He mounted up and rode to the dress shop, leading her horse. Carrying a small wicker basket with a clean white cloth draped over its contents, she was just coming outside when he got there. Even her denim trousers and a man's shirt made the clothes look good on her. Her blond hair was tucked up under the brown hat she wore.

They rode for about an hour and then stopped on a grassy, tree-shaded hill to enjoy the simple but delicious picnic lunch Meagan had packed. Duff enjoyed the wine, too, although he preferred coffee, tea, beer, or a good Scotch whiskey, for the most part. But not surprisingly, the company made everything better, as when they stretched out on the grass and lingered in each other's arms for a while, sharing kisses.

Then they rode on, following a faint trail Duff knew led to Thunder Canyon and beyond that to Longshot Basin.

Buzzard's Roost, the mountain that reared its ugly peak just southwest of the canyon, was visible for quite a few miles before they got there. Even though they rode steadily, it didn't seem as if they got any closer to the mountain. It still loomed ahead of them, tantalizingly out of reach.

To the northeast lay a vast, high tableland bordered by sheer cliffs that formed the other side of the canyon. Those cliffs curved around to merge with the lower slopes of Buzzard's Roost and completely enclose Longshot Basin. It was an impressive geographical barrier. A man might be able to climb the cliffs in a few spots, but a horse couldn't, and getting a wagon over them was downright impossible. Duff had never been atop that sprawling mesa and didn't know anyone who had.

Finally drawing close enough to see they were approaching Buzzard's Roost and an even more obscure trail veering off to the left, they reined in at that spot to allow the horses to rest for a few minutes.

As they dismounted, Meagan pointed to the path, which would have been easy to overlook, and asked, "Where does that go?"

"I could nae tell ye, lass," Duff replied with a shake of his head. "I remember it from the last time I rode up this way, but I did nae follow it. From the looks of it, it either leads up onto Buzzard's Roost or, more likely, peters out somewhere betwixt here 'n there."

"It must go somewhere," said Meagan, "or else no one would have come along here to make such a trail."

"Aye, what ye say is reasonable. I'll ask Elmer about it. He'll ken the answer if anyone in these parts does."

They rode on, their route curving around the base of Buzzard's Roost until they came in sight of Thunder Canyon.

Or rather, where Thunder Canyon had been. Duff pulled back on Sky's reins as he saw that the excitable wrangler had been right. The mouth of Thunder Canyon was completely blocked by a jumbled mass of rock—a pile of boulders that ranged in size from a few feet in diameter to huge slabs of stone the size of a house. Meagan came to a stop beside him, and they both sat there, staring at the impassable barrier.

"That's incredible," she said in a hushed, awed tone. "I'm not sure how far it goes up the canyon, but it would take weeks to dig through that."

Duff shook his head. "Ye could nae dig through it. Ye would have to blast a path with dynamite, which might cause even more rockslides. 'Twould be a job requiring months of hard labor. Maybe even years."

"And what's on the other side? Just an empty basin?"

"Aye. And you're looking at the reason why 'tis empty. Everyone in these parts knew that if such a thing ever happened as has occurred today, Longshot Basin would be cut off from the rest of the world."

A little shiver went through Meagan. "I'm glad I'm not on the other side of that."

"That goes for me as well, lass."

"What do you think caused it?"

Duff tilted his head back and stared up at the rugged slopes of Buzzard's Roost rising above them. He could see the long, fresh scar in the mountainside where hundreds of tons of rock had pulled loose and roared down into the canyon.

"Pinky Jenkins claimed 'twas an earthquake, and Wang and I felt it, too, although in Chugwater the effect was small enough that I was nae sure I hadn't but imagined it. Wang agreed with Pinky, though, and I trust his senses."

Meagan gazed intently at the devastation and said, "It's magnificent, in a way, isn't it? And yet, at the same time, I hate to think about how small it makes me feel. Humanity is really insignificant in the face of nature, isn't it?"

"Nae," Duff answered without hesitation. "If 'twere no humans to appreciate and be impressed by nature, what good would it be, I ask ye? The tallest, most majestic mountain . . . more majestic than ol' Buzzard's Roost here . . . would be nothing without human eyes to gaze upon it. Does anything truly even exist without someone to take note of it?"

Meagan laughed. "Why, Duff, you're becoming quite the philosopher. You must have been sitting out there at the ranch thinking deep thoughts."

"Nae, not really. But a man's mind does take strange turns now 'n then, when he's out riding the range alone."

They sat in their saddles for a few more minutes, drinking in the awe-inspiring sight in front of them, then turned their mounts and headed away from Thunder Canyon. The aftermath of the huge avalanche was impressive, but once you'd seen it, you'd seen it, Duff mused.

"You don't have to ride all the way back to town with me," Meagan said. "It would be out of your way. You should just cut back across country to the ranch."

"I would nae do that, leave ye to ride all the way back to Chugwater unaccompanied."

"Really, Duff, I'm not a helpless little child." Meagan patted the smooth wooden stock of a Winchester carbine that stuck up from a saddle sheath strapped under the right stirrup fender. "I'm not unarmed, either, and you know I'm a good shot."

"'Tis true," Duff admitted. "But ye would nae rob me of the chance to spend more time with ye, would ye?"

Meagan smiled. "Well, when you put it that way . . ."

Duff would have continued the enjoyable banter, but at that moment, from the corner of his eye, he spied movement off to their right. Turning his head to take a better look, he saw two riders angling toward them. After a moment, he realized the horsebackers were following the trail he and Meagan had seen earlier.

Meagan was to his right, between him and the pair of riders. Quietly, he said, "Move around here on the other side of me, lass."

"What? Is something wrong, Duff?"

"Nae, not that I ken, but yonder are a couple of strangers, and I'd be more comfortable if 'twas between you and them I was."

"Oh." For a second Meagan looked as if she might argue the matter, but then she slowed her mount, let Duff pull ahead of her, and swung around to his left.

"'Tis glad I am now that I dinnae let ye go on to Chugwater by yourself," he commented.

"You don't know those men mean us any harm."

"I dinnae ken they don't."

It was entirely possible those riders were as wary of Duff

and Meagan as Duff and Meagan were of them. As they drew closer, Duff got the impression the men hadn't been stalking them since the strangers were making no effort to conceal their presence. They had been following the other trail, and it could well be coincidence their route was going to intercept that of Duff and Meagan.

However, he could also tell the men had noticed them. One of them drew a rifle from its sheath and rested the weapon across the saddle in front of him. Duff did likewise, his movements casual and unhurried to show that he wasn't afraid, merely cautious.

Neither party slowed until they were about thirty feet apart. Then all four riders reined in.

Now that he could get a good look at them, Duff confirmed the two men were strangers to him, but at the same time, something about them seemed vaguely familiar. Since they were riding in the direction of Chugwater, the same as Duff and Meagan, he thought maybe he had seen them in town before. He had a good memory for faces.

And these two faces were memorable, in their way. The man who edged his mount slightly ahead of the other horse and rider was lean, with dark beard stubble covering the cheeks and chin of his lantern-jawed face. His eyes had what seemed to be a perpetual squint so pronounced Duff wondered how he could see through those narrow slits.

Duff knew the man could see him, though. He could feel the cold regard of that stare, almost like a snake was watching him, ready to coil and strike.

The man wore black trousers and a black coat over a white, collarless shirt buttoned up to the throat. His black hat had a flat brim and a slightly rounded crown. Duff spotted the walnut grips of a revolver under the man's coat, worn on the left side in a cross-draw rig with the butt forward. He was the member of the duo who had pulled his rifle out and had it balanced across the saddle in front of him.

The other man was much larger, with ax-handle shoulders, a barrel chest, and a head like a block of wood that seemed to sit directly on his shoulders with no neck. Dark, shaggy hair hung out from under a shapeless hat with a ragged brim. His bulk stretched the fabric of a patched, homespun shirt. His whipcord trousers were stuffed down in the tops of well-worn boots. He didn't have a rifle, but what looked like an old cap-and-ball revolver was holstered on his right hip.

Duff moved his horse a little to put himself more squarely between them and Meagan then nodded and said, "Good afternoon to ye, gents."

Neither returned the greeting. The man in black said in a flat voice, "What are you doing out here?"

Before Duff could say anything, the other man asked in a rather high-pitched voice, "Hey, Cole, is that little fella a woman? Look at the way his shirt sticks out in the front."

"Shut up, Benjy," the man in black snapped without looking around at his companion. He kept his reptilian gaze fixed on Duff and went on. "I asked you a question, mister. What are you doing out here?"

"'Tis open range hereabout, is it not?" Duff responded. "My friend and I are in the habit of riding where we please, as long as we're not trespassing."

The big man called Benjy got even louder as he said, "Damn it, Cole, that's a woman ridin' that other horse, I tell you. She's wearin' pants like a man, but she ain't no man."

"Benjy—"

"I'm gonna get her and take her home with me!" Benjy dug his boot heels into the flanks of the big horse on which he was mounted. The animal sprang forward. Meagan let out an involuntary cry of alarm and pulled her horse to the side.

Duff jerked his horse to the right as Benjy started around him, trying to get in the big man's way.

The man in black whipped his rifle to his shoulder and fired, the sharp crack of the shot echoing over the rolling landscape.

Visit our website at
KensingtonBooks.com
to sign up for our newsletters, read
more from your favorite authors, see
books by series, view reading group
guides, and more!

BOOK CLUB
BETWEEN THE CHAPTERS

Become a Part of Our
Between the Chapters Book Club
Community and Join the Conversation

Betweenthechapters.net